Edward Kennard

Wedded to Sport

A novel

Edward Kennard

Wedded to Sport
A novel

ISBN/EAN: 9783337393731

Printed in Europe, USA, Canada, Australia, Japan

Cover: Foto ©Andreas Hilbeck / pixelio.de

More available books at **www.hansebooks.com**

WEDDED TO SPORT.

A Novel.

BY

MRS. EDWARD KENNARD,

AUTHOR OF

"A HOMBURG BEAUTY," "THE GIRL IN THE BROWN HABIT,"
"MATRON OR MAID," "THAT PRETTY LITTLE HORSEBREAKER,"
&c., &c.

IN ONE VOLUME.

LONDON :
F. V. WHITE & CO.,
14, BEDFORD STREET, STRAND, W.C.
1894.

CONTENTS.

CONTENTS.

WEDDED TO SPORT.

WEDDED TO SPORT.

CHAPTER I.

BORN WITH A GOLDEN SPOON.

BEECHLANDS was a magnificent place. It stood in an extensive, undulating park, and the pleasure grounds gave employment to fifteen gardeners. Everything was on a similar scale and indicated great wealth, if not the most refined taste. Perhaps the wealth preponderated over the taste just a little too conspicuously for critical eyes. In addition to its many other advantages, Beechlands was situated in one of the finest hunting counties in England, whilst the shooting, if not exactly firstrate, was nevertheless very fair. But it possessed a grave drawback.

It was too new. The red bricks of which the immense house was built had not yet lost the fiery tint stamped upon them by the kiln. The trees in the park were mostly saplings, surrounded by iron palings to protect their tender shoots from greedily-nibbling deer; whilst the flower garden, in spite of its size and the money spent upon it, was stiff and conventional. It lacked the sweet, old-fashioned luxuriance, the tangled growth of creeper and tendril which Time alone confers. With all its splendour, Beechlands was deficient in the harmony and mellowness of colouring belonging to a long established structure.

This was not to be wondered at considering that only twelve years ago the ground on which the house now stood had been a famous grazing pasture for cattle, prior to sending them to the London market.

Good Thomas Verschoyle had originally hailed from the Midlands. When a boy he walked barefoot to the great Metropolis, beginning life with only a few shillings in his pocket. But he was an energetic, industrious lad, as honest as the day, and gifted with quick wits. Step by step he rose, until in process of time he became one of the wealthiest merchants in the United

Kingdom. His house did an enormous trade. The profits were steady and increasing. At this period of his career he was installed Lord Mayor of London. During Mr. Verschoyle's tenure of office one of the largest strikes between Labour and Capital took place that had ever been known. The masters were determined to fight, and so were the men. Both parties considered themselves in the right, and declined to make any concession. Things assumed a serious complexion. Meartime, the trade of London was almost completely paralysed. The strike affected nearly every branch, and many of the common necessaries of life rose to a ruinous price. The men refused to work unless their demands for increased pay and shorter hours of labour were satisfied. The dock directors declared that they neither could nor would yield to such extortion. For four whole weeks this state of affairs continued, and much as the country desired it, there appeared no prospect of a settlement. The government were not in a position to interfere. Strange as it may appear, a small band of directors on the one side, and of several thousand workmen on the other, had power to endanger and bring to a standstill the whole commerce of the Metropolis.

All the newspapers filled their columns with gloomy articles. They predicted that if once diverted England would inevitably lose her trade, and discover, when too late, the impossibility of redirecting it into its accustomed channels. They pointed out the dangers to which the strike exposed the kingdom, and urged an immediate termination to the dispute, no matter how great the sacrifices involved. Public opinion to a great extent sided with the men. Subscriptions in support of their wives and families kept pouring in from America and the Colonies. An agreement seemed as far off as ever. Neither party was inclined to budge from its position, and matters were entirely at a deadlock. At this juncture it was proposed that an Arbitration Committee should be formed in order to inquire into the differences existing between masters and men. Mr. Verschoyle, in his capacity of Lord Mayor, was appealed to. After much parleying, owing chiefly to his exertions, sound common sense, and excellent advice, a settlement was arrived at, in which the demands of the men were practically granted. Great rejoicings followed, and Thomas Verschoyle gained golden opinions. His name was in everybody's mouth, and when he quitted office it pleased her Most Gracious Majesty the Queen to bestow upon her late Lord Mayor the rank of Baronet.

Henceforth the plain, honest merchant began to conceive schemes of ambition apart from the City and money-making. He set himself to found a family, and was determined to make of his only son and heir a great county gentleman. He was getting old. Business had lost its charm, and instead of stimulating his faculties as formerly, now only irritated and fatigued them. For over fifty years he had toiled almost incessantly. It seemed to him that he had earned a right to enjoy the evening of his days. Sir Thomas Verschoyle retired from Lombard-street with an untarnished reputation, and an income variously estimated at twenty to fifty thousand a year. His first step was to buy a vast quantity of land in his native county and build Beechlands. It is not easy to describe the pleasure which he and his wife derived from the purchase and gradual development of their new estate. For years their dream had been to settle down peacefully in the country, for Lady Verschoyle was also Midland born. Their delight was unbounded, and when one by one the great county families began to call, and finding Sir Thomas a shrewd, straightforward man, and his wife a perfect lady, received them with the enthusiasm generally accorded to the possessors of unlimited wealth, the worthy Baronet's satisfaction was complete. He felt he had achieved the rare position of having nothing left to wish for. Alas! that precisely when such a climax of real happiness had been reached, it was ordained that he should merely touch with his lips the golden cup of human contentment.

A slight cold neglected—a chill, followed by an acute attack of laryngitis, and in a week the tender husband and indulgent father lay dead upon his bed. Death swooped down upon him with as little ceremony as if he had been some starving hawker in the streets, for the great Reaper with his " sickle keen " is no respecter of persons. He folds rich and poor alike in his icy embrace, and carries them off to Heaven, to Hell, to Oblivion—who knows whither ?

" *Le roi est mort, vive le roi.*" Sir Thomas's son reigned in his stead, leaving the disconsolate widow to bewail the loss of the truest, bravest, stoutest partner ever given to woman. Lady Verschoyle mourned for her husband with passionate grief. Hers was a gentle and tenacious nature, which could not live without love. Henceforth she concentrated all her affection on Philip, who, at the time of his father's death, had just gone to Oxford, having previously failed for the army. The fond mother's hopes were centred in her boy. She expected great things of him, and resolutely shut her eyes to certain faults in his character, which had become manifest since the days of his childhood. She trusted that time would cure them, but her expectations had scarcely been fulfilled. Young Philip's career at Oxford proved far from creditable. He drank, betted, gambled, got himself into a very awkward scrape, wherein a tradesman's daughter figured as heroine, and left College just soon enough to avoid the disgrace of being expelled. It was a terrible blow to Lady Verschoyle, but nevertheless she was firmly convinced that everything and everybody had entered into a combination against her Philip, and he was simply the victim of circumstances. So she welcomed the black sheep home with a serious countenance and open arms, and Sir Philip had not been five minutes in the house before he persuaded her that Oxford was an unholy and unrighteous place, to whose contaminating influences he ought never to have been exposed. As for his little flirtation with Miss Sarah Jane Jackson, of the High-street, he pooh-poohed that altogether, and said such trifles were not worth talking about. And no doubt he was right, for to a man with a handle to his name and forty thousand a year much may be forgiven. Before the world condemns him he must be a regular reprobate. In Sir Philip Verschoyle's case, dear old Mrs. Grundy was very lenient. She shook her sage head with a smile, and said, "Ah! well; young men must all sow their wild oats. He may have been just a little imprudent, but nothing more." Oh! dear no; nothing more, even although poor Sarah Jane was left with a blasted character, and henceforth every uncharitable woman might point the finger of scorn at her. She was a bad, wicked girl, turned out of house and home by unmerciful parents, crushed, ruined and degraded at the very onset of life. He was a fine gentleman, with plenty of money, and had only been "a little imprudent." Ho! ho! It is a nice world, a just and excellent world we live in, and the social codes of our vaunted civilisation are admirable. They protect the strong and destroy the weak.

Lady Verschoyle never knew the rights of the affair, and implicitly believed the scanty explanations which Philip vouchsafed to give concerning his College scrapes. She, poor soul! was only too thankful to have him at home again; but he had not been there long before a torturing suspicion began to creep into her mind that the present master of Beechlands was very unlike his father. Sir Thomas had always been courteous and considerate; Philip was rough and loud. Sir Thomas treated all women with chivalry in virtue of their sex; his son regarded them as inferior beings. The elder man's notions of honour were strict, not to say severe; the young baronet's seemed to his mother alarmingly loose. When she remonstrated with him on this subject he laughed, and told her she was delightfully innocent and charmingly old-fashioned. He assured her quite seriously that all her ideas of right and wrong were out of date, and took great pains to demonstrate that these terms were merely relative. She was not clever enough to prove the contrary; but in the depths of her simple soul she felt that a flaw existed in her boy's logic. How or where he had learnt it she could not conceive. She could only fall back on the conviction that the new generation was different from the old, and tried to put everything down to her own ignorance. But the attempt did not prove successful; for, in spite of her devotion to Philip, and the excuses which she was ever ready to make for him, in her secret heart, a terrible truth abided. She knew that she was deeply, grievously disappointed in him, and every day the feeling increased instead of becoming obliterated. A dull pain had fastened upon her brain. Every now and then she would rouse herself with an effort, and say, "What is amiss? Why do I suffer from this constant ache?" She did not dare formulate the answer in words. Had she done so the reply would have been, "It is Philip."

By the terms of her late husband's will, Beechlands belonged to the young baronet. Lady Verschoyle had been liberally provided for; but the place where she had been raised, as it were, from the soil—the place whose every stone and tree and shrub were dear to her as familiar friends—was his. This was as it should be. She would not have had it otherwise. So long as Philip remained unmarried she had his permission to look on Beechlands as her home. She made him an admirable unpaid housekeeper, and studied his interests far better than any ordinary dependent. He was well aware of this fact. When he took himself a wife, why then his mother would have to turn out and find a new abode in her old age. But, up to the time when our story commences, although he had thought of matrimony, he had never thought of it seriously. So many beautiful flowers offered themselves to his choice that he could not make up his mind which to cull. The whole race of mammas filled him with distrust. Whenever he met a pretty girl he was always harassed by the belief that she, or her relatives, wanted to catch him. He was perfectly conscious of his own value in the matrimonial market, and Belgravian mothers courted him in vain. Lady Verschoyle was most anxious to see her son settled, and constantly urged the desirability of finding a nice wife. But at nine-and-twenty Sir Philip had not yet seen fit to offer to any young woman the priceless treasures of his hand and heart. As a bachelor, with plenty of money to spend, any number of invitations, and everybody running after and making much of him, he found life very pleasant. It might not be quite so enjoyable were he to change his state.

During the winter months he resided principally at Beechlands, hunting six days a week, running up to town on the seventh. When the end of March came, he invariably took his departure, and often Lady Verschoyle would not see him again until he returned in September for the partridge shooting, accompanied by a party of gay friends, male and female. The latter were nearly all strangers to her, and she did not appreciate their manners, but she was assured that they belonged to a smart set, and, as usual, attributed her disapproval to ignorance of the world's ways.

During Sir Philip's absence she led a pleasant, tranquil, if somewhat monotonous, existence : but she had arrived at a time of life when monotony is not without charm. The garden proved a never-ending source of delight. She would spend hours bending over her rose-buds, snipping off the dead leaves and faded buds with a large pair of scissors, which she kept for the purpose ; or else trotting round the village intent on charitable deeds.

Everybody about the place, from the humblest kitchen wench to the stiffest and proudest county dame, loved Lady Verschoyle. She was the gentlest, kindest-hearted, and most unassuming creature imaginable ; hospitable to a degree when left to follow her own inclinations, and entirely free from all petty backbiting or taste for gossip. It was an exception to hear her speak an ill-natured word. When she did, the censure was invariably deserved.

Her chief pleasure consisted in entertaining the neighbours. On her afternoons " At Home " the big oaken hall was frequently crowded with visitors, who thought nothing of driving ten or twelve miles in order to enjoy a chat with the popular mistress of the mansion. Lady Verschoyle had many friends, but Beechlands was a large house to be occupied by one solitary woman, and often when her son was away she would have felt very lonely had it not been for the clergyman's widowed sister, Mrs. Fortescue, who kept house for her brother, and lived just outside the park gates. This lady seldom allowed a day to pass without seeing Lady Verschoyle. In fact, they were on terms of the closest intimacy, a fast friendship having subsisted between them for years. Mrs. Fortescue was strong, energetic, impulsive, and kind-hearted. She was one of those women— no doubt excellent in their way—who manage, or seek to manage, everybody with whom they come in contact. She ruled her brother, his household, and his parish with a rod of iron. Nothing ever went on without her cognisance. The interest she took in other people's affairs was both genuine and intense. She knew the history of all the old men and women about the place, doctored their bodies, and cared for their souls with untiring zeal. It was useless for them to shirk such kindly offices. They only laid themselves open to the charge of ingratitude, especially as there was no denying that, in cases of emergency, Mrs. Fortescue proved herself invaluable. She never lost her head, and knew exactly what ought, and what ought not, to be done. If people only followed her advice all went well, as a rule. This excellent lady possessed many virtues, but her enemies were wont to declare that her good qualities were marred by one grave defect. Mrs. Fortescue prided herself on her habit of plain-speaking. She looked upon it as a positive crime to say what you did not mean or to soften the truth simply because it was unpalatable. Had she confined herself to this the ill-natured might not have had so much cause for complaint ; but it must be confessed that she often went out of the way to make remarks which a very little tact and diplomacy would certainly have deprived of their sting. No one meant better than Mrs. Fortescue, but she laboured under a mistake in fancying that because she queened it over her brother and the parish, she could do so over all the rest of the world. Like attracts unlike. Lady Verschoyle's sweet nature and gentle disposition had inspired in Mrs. Fortescue an ardent affection, whilst the weaker will of her friend unconsciously derived moral support from leaning on one stronger than itself.

CHAPTER II.

A PLAIN-SPOKEN FRIEND.

ONE evening towards the end of August, the two ladies were sitting together in Lady Verschoyle's boudoir. It was the smallest, and consequently the cosiest room in the whole house, and its mistress much preferred it to the state apartments, which were only thrown open on grand occasions. The weather was unusually cold for the time of year. A gale of wind raged out of doors, and between the squalls the rain poured down in torrents, striking the window panes like countless small pebbles. The trees creaked and groaned with quite a wintry sound, and great tumbled masses of purple cloud had heaped themselves up in the heavens. As the blast impelled them onwards, their solid edges parted occasionally, and displayed a pale gleam of light. For a summer night it was about as bad as bad could be. Inside the room all was bright and cheerful. Two softly shaded lamps illuminated the apartments, and threw up the glowing tints of its rich Persian carpet, and crimson velvet curtains. Flowers were scattered about everywhere—in pots, in vases, in dishes. The atmosphere was heavy with the hothouse fragrance of clematis and tuberose. The slender green fronds of a large palm occupying a corner near the door glistened, as the wavering flames from a wood fire burning on the hearth rested capriciously upon them. The two friends sat on either side of the fire-place enjoying the generous warmth it threw out, their dresses turned up, after the fashion of ladies when alone. In appearance, as in everything else, they presented a marked contrast.

Mrs. Forteseue was small, plump, dark, and alert. Her round black eyes were as lively as a squirrel's, and her glance as penetrating as a gimlet. She had a straight, well-cut nose, a good colour, and a square, determined chin which bespoke character. For the rest, briskness and energy were written on every feature of her vivacious face. She might have been forty, judging from her looks. As a matter of fact, she had passed her fiftieth year.

Lady Verschoyle was fair and feminine. Her soft brown hair, which she wore plainly parted on either side of her somewhat high and narrow brow, had scarcely begun to turn grey, although she was not far off sixty. Her eyes must have been lovely in her youth, for they were very large and beautifully shaped. But age had dimmed their blue, and care had brought into their clear depths a timid, anxious expression which was strangely pathetic. Lady Verschoyle's eyes gave one the impression that their owner was never free from apprehension, and continually dreaded some misfortune. Of her face it need only be said that it was charming, and its sole defect consisted in a certain want of firmness about the lines of the delicate mouth. Naturally tall, her height was diminished by a slight stoop, and she was so thin that her clothes seemed to hang quite loosely. As a rule, she dressed very plainly, but no matter how homely and inexpensive the garment, she always looked a thorough lady. Hers was essentially a refined and sensitive nature. It would have been impossible to Lady Verschoyle at any period of her life to commit a vulgarity. Sweet, gentle, yielding, she seemed almost too fine-fibred to endure the buffets of this rough world without a strong and loving protector. Her sleek brown head, covered by a dainty lace cap, lay languidly against the cushions of her chair. She looked very worn and fragile. In her hand she held an open letter, which had arrived by the afternoon's post. Its contents proved so unusually exciting that she had requested Mrs. Forteseue to come to dinner, in order to discuss them with her friend. The subject was one of great interest, and which affected her very nearly. Certain fears were now at rest which had long proved a source of secret worry.

"I can't tell you, Anne," she said to Mrs. Fortescue, "what a relief this news is to me. You know, better than anyone else, how very, very anxious I am for Philip to marry and settle down; but if there was one woman on the whole face of the earth, whom I hoped and prayed he would never wish to make his wife, that woman was Blanche Sylvester."

"I am not surprised," rejoined Mrs. Fortescue. "You objected, I suppose, to their being first cousins?"

"No, my dear Anne, it was not so much the relationship, though of course that alone rendered their union undesirable. What I feared and dreaded beyond words can tell, was the girl's character. I don't wish to say anything against my poor Thomas's sister's child. I have tried my very best to get on with her, and to think lightly of her faults, but," and Lady Verschoyle sighed, "do what I will, I can't bring myself to like Blanche. She is plausible and pleasant enough to one's face, but all the time she is endeavouring to make herself agreeable, she leaves a painful impression of insincerity on the mind. I never could make out why Philip was so fond of her."

"Oh! he would like any girl who flattered him up, and allowed him to carry on pretty much as he chose."

"I'm by no means sure, Anne. I should be sorry to think so badly either of Philip or Blanche. But for some reason or other, there is no denying that ever since he grew up, she has possessed an unaccountable fascination for him."

"H'm!" snorted Mrs. Fortescue. "The sort of fascination that most free and easily conducted women have for fast young bachelors."

"Anne," said Lady Verschoyle, with the nearest approach to severity of which she was capable, "you are uncharitable."

"Perhaps I am. I quite acknowledge my faults. All the same, I am far from certain whether every now and then it is not almost one's duty to be uncharitable. This sounds an awful sentiment for a clergyman's sister to propound, I know, but experience has taught me that universal charity is a failure. As for Miss Sylvester, I detest her." And Mrs. Fortescue brought her mouth together with a snap.

"It is strange that poor Blanche should have so many enemies," responded Lady Verschoyle.

"Strange! Not at all. If she wants to make friends, she should behave herself. I haven't forgiven her yet for the way she ordered the servants about last winter when she was here, or for treating you like a nobody in your own house."

"It is not my own house, Anne. You never will remember that."

"Tut, it's yours as long as Philip remains unmarried. Certainly it is not the thing for any young woman of twenty-five to come here, and do all she can to put your nose out of joint. I wonder how ever you stood it. I said at the time that you were far too meek, and did not assert yourself sufficiently. The idea of a forward miss like that wanting to have everything her own way! If Philip hadn't been such a fool, he would soon have brought her to her bearings; but really, Blanche Sylvester quite seemed to turn his head for a while."

" I feared last winter that he was going to propose to his cousin," said Lady Verschoyle, a faint flush rising to her pale cheek.

" I didn't. Philip knows much too well how to take care of himself. He's uncommonly wary about making the fatal plunge, although somewhat given to fluttering moth-like round a centre of attraction."

" One never quite knows, though, when the attraction may prove too strong for the moth," responded Lady Verschoyle, with one of her quiet smiles. " People take odd fancies, and Blanche is very handsome, remember."

" Yes," admitted Mrs. Fortescue, " I suppose she is, although she's not my style. Personally, I see no beauty in her, but no doubt some men admire those bold, black-browed, big-busted, small-waisted girls. I don't. I call them horrid."

" My dear Anne, are you not just a little prejudiced against Blanche ? If her character were only equal to her looks, she would do well enough."

" Now don't go making excuses for her. How could I possibly stand by and see a saint like you insulted—yes, positively insulted — by a rude, ill-mannered young woman, without resenting it ? You mark my words, if Philip had married Blanche Sylvester, they would have fought like a cat and dog by the end of three months. They have far too many points in common to agree. They are both selfish, both passionate, both vain."

Lady Verschoyle gave a little nervous laugh. This enumeration of her son's faults was not altogether agreeable. Mrs. Fortescue's outspokenness was apt every now and again to touch some tender spot. She sought to change the subject.

" Well !" she said, with an attempt at cheerfulness. " We need not distress ourselves as to what might have happened had Philip and Blanche become man and wife. She is going to be married almost immediately to Colonel Vansittart of the —— Dragoon Guards, as she informs me in this letter. Next month he has to rejoin his regiment, and directly after the marriage the happy couple are to sail for India. Henceforth we shall **see** very little of Blanche."

"And a good thing too. The less the better. You are so innocent and unsuspicious, my dear Lady Verschoyle, that you don't half see what goes on, even under your very eyes. I look upon Miss Sylvester's engagement as quite providential, for I feel perfectly convinced in my own mind, that had it not taken place, before long she would have entangled Philip into marrying her." So saying, Mrs. Fortescue clasped her hands together with a most decided air, which seemed to intimate that when she formed an opinion it must necessarily be final.

"There was a strong flirtation going on, certainly," admitted Lady Verschoyle. "It made me very uneasy, for I began to fear the existence of some secret understanding between Philip and Blanche."

"They were on extremely intimate terms, even for cousins," responded Mrs. Fortescue, compressing her thin lips in a disapproving fashion. "And Blanche, for one, was getting herself very much talked about. I never shall forget the answer she made when I tried to give her some good advice, and told her no woman could afford to run counter to public opinion. 'Pray don't trouble yourself about my morals, Mrs. Fortescue. I like men, and always mean to have men friends, no matter how much ill-natured people may gossip.' There was a pretty speech for you."

"My dear Anne, we need not discuss Blanche's faults. No doubt she will turn over a new leaf now that she is engaged to Colonel Vansittart, and may surprise us all by developing into an excellent wife and mother. I don't believe she means half what she says, anyhow I feel far too grateful to her at present to care about dwelling on her shortcomings. I never liked to mention my fears before, but this projected marriage is quite a load off my mind."

"So I should think," rejoined Mrs. Fortescue. "And I hope when you get a daughter-in-law, you'll get somebody whom you like, and who will treat you with proper deference and respect."

Lady Verschoyle made no immediate reply. A shadow passed over her gentle face.

"I wonder what Philip will say when the news is broken to him," she said presently, in a voice that betrayed considerable anxiety. "You may think me very foolish, Anne, but somehow or other, I have a strong presentiment that he won't be at all pleased."

"It won't much matter whether he is or not," said Mrs. Fortescue. "Miss Sylvester's engagement is not likely to be broken off, simply because Sir Philip Verschoyle, Bart., does not approve of it. By-the-bye, he is coming to-night, is he not? I must be off." And Mrs. Fortescue rose from her seat. Between her and her friend's son there was no love lost. They had had one or two passages of arms on different occasions, and she did not care to meet him oftener than she could help. She resented his cavalier treatment of his mother, and he was a person who neither appreciated nor profited by plain speaking. A kind of tacit warfare existed between them, which continually threatened to break out into hostilities. When Sir Philip was at home, Mrs. Fortescue's visits to Beechlands became comparatively rare. It had been reported to her ears that the young man had once spoken indignantly of her as "a meddlesome old woman." She never forgave him. The wound inflicted on her self-esteem remained unhealed.

"Yes," said Lady Verschoyle, in answer to her companion's inquiry. "I expect Philip every minute, indeed he ought to be here by now. Unfortunately, I ordered the dogcart to meet him, and am afraid he will be vexed, but as a rule he dislikes a close carriage this time of year, and it was quite fine when John started."

"You can't help the weather, dear Lady Verschoyle. Surely Sir Philip cannot hold you responsible for it."

"No, but it has come on so wet in the last hour. The poor boy will be soaked."

"Well, and if he is, it won't hurt him. A strong, healthy young man of nine and twenty, surely need not mind a few drops of rain. You mothers are dreadful people. You spoil your sons to such an extent that half of them turn molly-coddles."

"You are very severe in your judgments, Anne; besides you don't know how apt Philip is to get put out by trifles."

"Oh! yes," retorted Mrs. Fortescue, with ruthless candour, for she considered this an occasion on which plain speaking was not only a virtue, but her bounden duty. "I know perfectly well that his temper is abominable, and that, although you love him dearly—ever so much more than he deserves—you are nevertheless afraid of him. The fact is, my dear, you are too meek, too unselfish and retiring. If it were me, I should pay him back in his own coin. He is a young gentleman who wants a strong hand over him——"

"I never could rule by force, neither would I wish to," interposed Lady Verschoyle.

"But you should. That's exactly where you make a mistake. You should let him realise that as long as you reside in this house, you're its mistress, and won't be put upon. I always say that it is a thousand pities Sir Philip was born with a golden spoon in his mouth, and has had his life made too easy. Very few people can stand prosperity. Now if he had been a poor fellow without one sixpence to rub against another, and obliged to earn his livelihood, he might have had a chance of turning out a decent member of society. At all events he would have got some of the nonsense knocked out of him, whereas now——"

" Anne," interrupted poor Lady Verschoyle piteously, with the tears starting to her faded eyes, " have you not said enough ? Philip is my only son. He is all I have in the world. You do not realise what exquisite pain it causes me to hear him abused. We are none of us so faultless as to condemn others."

Little Mrs. Fortescue ran to her friend's side, and kissed her effusively. She was conscious of having committed an indiscretion, and of having spoken out more forcibly than was altogether warrantable.

" Forgive me, darling," she said, penitently. " I would rather cut off my right hand than grieve you intentionally. In future I promise to be more careful, and not say anything that may hurt your feelings."

" Philip is not perfect," went on Lady Verschoyle, tremulously. " There are many things in him which I should like to see changed; but I have no other child. Surely it is not unnatural for a mother, situated as I am, to try to think well rather than ill of her only son. I cannot help loving him. If he were a criminal—if he had committed the most horrible sin, he would always be to me—my boy. I should think of him as he was in his childish days. I should recall the touch of his little warm hands straying against my bosom, remember his innocent smiles and ejaculations. No, no, Anne, if you value my friendship, never again run Philip down, for I—I cannot bear it." Her voice broke. There was something beautiful in this woman's passionate adoration of an unworthy idol. Mrs. Fortescue seemed to feel that opposed to such pure maternal affection, words were as sacrilege. She turned away, sorry for and ashamed of the part she had played. Henceforth, where Sir Philip was concerned, she determined to keep a guard over her tongue. At this moment wheels were heard coming up the gravel drive, shortly followed by the sound of a horse's feet trampling beneath the stone portico that guarded the front door. The colour rushed to Lady Verschoyle's face, tinting it a delicate crimson. Three months had elapsed since she had last seen her son. She rose to her feet with a little glad cry.

" I am so thankful Philip is alone," she said, " and that his friends don't arrive until to-morrow. I never could have broken this news about Blanche to him before a whole roomful of strangers. Now, at least, we shall have time for a nice quiet talk."

Mrs. Fortescue gathered her belongings together.

"Good-bye, dear," she said. "I don't suppose I shall see you again for some little while, unless you care to look in at the Rectory to-morrow afternoon, and drink a cup of tea. Mrs. Burton is coming, and Bligh—that is to say, if Mrs. Burton is able, but Bligh wrote saying her mother had been terribly unwell of late, and she might not find herself strong enough to travel when the day arrived. They have to take the train from Morthorpe, and I promised to meet them at the station. I am always sorry they live so far away that practically one sees next to nothing of them, for I like them both so much."

"I met Mrs. Burton and her daughter once, some years ago at a garden party," said Lady Verschoyle. "If I remember right, the girl was a very nice, quiet little thing, who pleased me by her evident affection for her mother."

"Yes," said Mrs. Fortescue. "Bligh is a pattern child. She devoted all the best years of her youth to nursing her father, and now she is doing the same thing by the old lady. You'll come if you can, won't you, dear?"

"Yes, provided Philip does not require my presence."

The two ladies kissed cordially—perhaps all the more cordially for their little fracas—and Mrs. Fortescue, hearing a loud voice in the hall which was scarcely indicative of good temper, took leave without any more of those last farewells which among women appear indispensable. "When my wife gets up, I sit down," once said a distinguished cavalry officer to the writer of this story. He was wise in his generation, and evidently had studied the idiosyncrasies of the female character. However, as Mrs. Fortescue did not want to meet Sir Philip, she made haste to go. A few moments after her departure, the young man, damp from the night air, and with rain-drops still glistening in his auburn beard, entered his mother's room.

CHAPTER III.

MOTHER AND SON.

WITH arms outstretched Lady Verschoyle went to meet him, her face turned upward. Sir Philip stooped, and just lightly brushed his moustache against her polished white brow. The salute was careless, and totally lacking in warmth. A close observer might have noticed that she shrank back, as if inwardly hurt, whilst the warm blood rushed to the surface of her transparent skin. For weeks past she had looked forward to this meeting, and now, before her son had opened his mouth, a vague sense of disappointment crept over her spirit, and robbed her of the joy which she had expected to derive from the mere sight of him. Of late it had always been thus. Whose fault was it, hers or his? Every year he slipped farther and farther away from her. Each fresh absence served to build up a subtle and indefinable barrier, which she felt herself unable to break down. The wall that divided them grew, and so did her mental despondency. But no sign of what passed through the mother's mind was apparent as once more she lifted a loving face towards him, and said:

"Well, Philip dear, so you have come at last? It seems a regular age since we met."

"Does it?" he answered indifferently. "I was here not so very long ago. Let me see, when was I here, May or June?"

"You ran down from town for a night in the beginning of May, and left again the next morning."

"This place is so beastly slow in the summer," he observed "There is nothing on earth to do."

"When one is the master of ten thousand acres of land one would think that there was always a certain amount to do," she rejoined.

"Oh! very likely; but I hate being bothered except on rent day. It's always pretty welcome."

Lady Verschoyle, suppressed a sigh, and changed the subject.

"How have you been, Philip?" she inquired, with fond, maternal solicitude.

"Oh! much as usual. My health doesn't trouble me, thank goodness. I hear fellows talking about their lungs and their liver, but for my part I never can understand it. By-the-bye," he added, giving himself a resentful shake, "what on earth induced you to send the dogcart for me on such a night as this? I'm chilled to the bone."

"Are you? I'm so sorry. Come near the fire, dear, and warm yourself. It was my fault. I've been miserable all the evening, thinking what a cold, comfortless drive home you would have; but when the trap started the weather was fine, and we never thought it was going to turn out so badly as this."

"Anybody in their senses would have consulted the barometer, and sent the brougham," growled Sir Philip, applying a white silk handkerchief with a bird's-eye border to his damp beard.

His mother overheard the remark, and again that nervous flush mantled her cheek.

"Have you had dinner?" she asked.

" Rather. I got a very tidy meal in the Pullman coming down. Nothing passes the time so quickly and agreeably when one is travelling as eating. The Americans thoroughly understand that."

" I presume you came from Yorkshire then to-day, Philip ? "

" Yes ; I left Baggerton this afternoon, and ought to have been here long ago, only there are so many changes *en route.*"

" What sort of sport have you had ? "

" Only fair. The grouse are not so plentiful on the moors this year as usual. A great many young birds were killed just after the hatching season by the severe weather and those that were left are uncommonly wild. By the way, how are we off for partridges here ? "

" Very well, I believe," answered Lady Verschoyle. " Turner was talking to me the day before yesterday——"

" Why the deuce doesn't he talk to me on these subjects, instead of you ? "

" But, Philip, how can he, when you are not even here ? "

" He might write. I told him to do so."

" Turner belongs to the old school, and is no great hand with his pen. When he was young education was not so universal as it is now, and people had not the same chance of learning to read and write."

" Well, well, never mind. What did he say about the birds ? "

" He told me that the coveys were not only more numerous this season than he ever remembered them, but also that the young partridges were exceedingly fine and well-grown. He thinks you ought to get over a hundred brace a day for the first week, and this without touching the outlying beats, where the birds run somewhat smaller."

" Come, that's good news," exclaimed Sir Philip, in a more amiable tone, leaning his broad back against the mantelpiece, and apparently enjoying the genial warmth thrown out by the fire. " You received my letter, I suppose, telling you I expected a houseful of friends to-morrow for the 1st of September ? "

" Yes ; the rooms are all ready, and everything is in order. Who have you got coming ? " Lady Verschoyle inquired timidly, as if fearful the interrogation might displease, and be attributed to undue curiosity.

" Nobody you know. Only five or six pals, a couple of lively married women, and an amusing girl. You needn't bother about them. They'll take care of themselves, no doubt. It is not the fashion nowadays for ladies to pay much attention to their hostess. As long as they please the host, that's considered enough."

" I don't pretend to know much about the fashionable world

since your poor father died," rejoined Lady Verschoyle, with a gentle dignity that became her well; "but as long as I remain here I consider it incumbent on me to do the honours of Beechlands properly. If others fail in their duty, that is no reason why I should."

"Oh! of course not. There is not the least occasion to take so serious a view of the question. All I meant was that I didn't suppose any of the people who are coming were exactly your sort."

"Nothing pleases me more, Philip, than to see you entertaining *nice* friends." And she emphasised the adjective. "I like to think that you have plenty of pleasant acquaintances."

"Unfortunately, my dear mother, your notions on these subjects are a little out of date, and what you call ' nice friends ' I don't. For instance, you are perfectly satisfied with the humdrum, slow-going old county folk about here. I find them tremendous bores."

"You very seldom have anything to do with them, Philip. Indeed, you are barely civil to your neighbours."

"Because I like people who amuse me, not ones who make me yawn the whole evening. Now you are so constituted that you don't mind being bored. I do. Life's too short to waste three or four hours at a time in the company of mumbling old women, who can talk of nothing but their servants and their parishes." This was meant for a cut at Mrs. Fortescue, but Lady Verschoyle wisely took no notice of the remark. She only looked sadly at her handsome son. As far as outward appearance went, Sir Philip was a splendid specimen of an English gentleman. He stood over six feet in his stockings, and his spare, muscular figure was admirably proportioned. He had a clear, healthy complexion, fair hair, an auburn beard and moustache, a straight, well-cut nose, and blue eyes, like his mother's. But their expression was very different; for whereas hers was sweet and soft and true, his was cold and uncertain. Sir Philip never looked you straight in the face, and in spite of the undeniable beauty of his features, the impression conferred on the mind was one of shiftiness and cunning. There was something feline and stealthy about him, which involuntarily inspired a certain feeling of mistrust. When he chose, his manners were singularly caressing, with the velvety softness of a cat, who puts out its paw gently before striking. The languid and drawling intonation of his voice produced a deceitfully soothing effect upon the nerves, until something happened to provoke him to anger. Then it became loud and harsh, and all the dulcet tones disappeared directly he was off his guard. At such times one felt there were unknown depths to Sir Philip's character—that the outward grace and fascination, which he certainly possessed in no small degree, were not real, but merely a thin veneer acquired by mixing in good society. Instinctively, one watched and waited for the man s true nature to reveal itself.

Sir Philip had heaps of acquaintances, but very few friends. Strip him of his title and his wealth, his fine house and his position, and he would not have found many people to stick to him. On the other hand, he might not have been singular in such an experience, so that perhaps the fact ought hardly to weigh against him. He took no pains to ingratiate himself with his neighbours, and looked down upon them as a set of old fogies, quite forgetting that old fogies have tongues, which they wag very energetically on occasions. He elected to fill his house with fast London folk, and asked them to shoot his game, rather than the sedate and steady squires who inhabited the county. It need scarcely be said that such conduct gave great offence, and the young baronet was by no means popular.

Although Sir Philip professed to despise country bumpkins— as he rudely called them—he, nevertheless, felt secretly irritated whenever he happened to appear amongst them that they did not receive him with more warmth. He was incensed and annoyed to find how devoted they all were to his mother, and how coldly and indifferently, in comparison, they treated him. When he got home he would shower abuse upon the worthy people, never once condescending to acknowledge that wounded vanity was mainly responsible for the very far from pretty epithets which he freely hurled against them. He was not candid enough to say to himself, "Their sin is that they do not sufficiently admire Sir Philip Verschoyle, Bart., even although they receive absolutely nothing from him in the way of game, civility, or hospitality." A few kindly words, one or two invitations to dinner, and how easy would it have been to convert enemies into friends ! But the young man did not choose to take the trouble, and failed to see how closely Politeness is allied to Self-interest.

Meantime, Lady Verschoyle cogitated anxiously over the best manner of breaking the news. Her son was not apparently in the most amiable of moods, and ever since his arrival she had gradually been feeling more and more nervous. Nevertheless, she realised that if she let the present opportunity pass of speaking to him in private, there was no knowing when she might get another. To-morrow he would have accounts to settle, and be busy probably the whole morning with affairs connected with the estate. He did not like her to interfere in such matters, and after his long absence no doubt many small things would require seeing to ; whilst later in the day the guests were expected to arrive. Then the prospects of a *tête-à-tête* were practically *nil*. When the house was full of visitors she saw nothing, or next to nothing, of her boy. Lady Verschoyle felt that she could not go to sleep with such an important piece of intelligence weighing on her mind. Moreover, she was curious to know how Philip would take it. If he heard the news calmly, and without displaying much emotion, her fears would be forever set at rest. She cleared her throat once or twice, and was just plucking up courage to commence when he stretched out his hand and rang the bell.

"What do you want, Philip? Anything that I can get you ? " she inquired, with maternal readiness to wait on her offspring.

"No," he said, curtly. "Nothing."

" Bring me a brandy and soda," he said to the footman when that functionary appeared. "And mix it pretty stiff ; I'm cold."

Lady Verschoyle was quite glad that this order put off her confession for a few minutes. Somehow, she was more than usually nervous to-night. "What a coward I am," she said to herself. "The thing has to be done ; therefore why delay? There is nothing to be afraid of. It is all my own imagining." Nevertheless, she waited and waited, until Sir Philip had almost finished his brandy and soda, and began to yawn and stretch himself as if he contemplated very shortly retiring to rest. Then, all at once she blurted out, without any preliminary—

" Philip, I had a letter from Blanche to-day. A letter whose contents you, as the head of the family, ought to be acquainted with."

He altered his position, and a look of interest stole over his face.

" Well," he said, with an assumption of indifference, " what does she say ? "

" A great deal. I have the letter in my pocket. I think it would be better for you to read it."

" Oh ! by all means. I always like Blanche's letters. They are almost as amusing and flippant as she is herself, which is saying a great deal. When one reads them one could almost fancy she was in the room, chattering away at her usual rate."

" There is nothing flippant about this note," said Lady Verschoyle, gravely. " I expect Blanche must have written it in a hurry, since she vouchsafes no details, but contents herself with the bare announcement of an important impending event."

" What the deuce do you mean ? " said Sir Philip, impatiently holding out his hand for the letter. " You talk as if some extraordinary mystery were about to happen. I hate people who make mysteries over every trifling occurrence, but you women are always doing it. It's a bad habit, of which apparently there's no curing you."

" Read the letter for yourself, Philip; then there will not be any ground for accusing either Blanche or me of wishing to be mysterious. I am sure nothing was farther from my thoughts."

Sir Philip took the note, and turned it over before proceeding to make himself master of its contents. A well-known perfume assailed his nostrils, recalling many a recollection of the past and of his handsome cousin.

" How fond Blanche is of that 'Wood Violet,' " he exclaimed, with more sentiment than he had yet displayed. " Whenever I smell it it always reminds me of her." So saying, he settled down to the perusal of Miss Sylvester's letter.

Lady Verschoyle watched him narrowly, and she was conscious that the beats of her heart became both faster and louder. Without exactly knowing why, some subtle maternal intuition told her that a crisis in his life was at hand.

Suddenly, Sir Philip's brows contracted, his face grew dark, and with an oath he threw the letter across the room.

" Blanche engaged ! Blanche going to be married," he cried, excitedly. " I can't believe it."

" But why not, Philip? " his mother asked in alarm.

" Why not ? For a hundred reasons. To begin with, she's not the girl to throw herself away on some sticky old colonel, and spend ten of the best years of her life in India."

" I don't suppose Colonel Vansittart can be much over forty," remarked Lady Verschoyle.

" Well, and Blanche is only twenty-five. She ought to marry a man nearer her own age."

" Surely that is her affair, Philip, not ours. She must care for this Colonel Vansittart, else she would hardly have accepted him ; and for anything we know to the contrary, they may be very much in love."

" Blanche isn't. I'll take my oath of that. Anyhow, I shan't allow the match to take place."

" I don't see how you can possibly prevent it. Blanche is her own mistress. Her stepmother does not exercise the slightest influence over her, and she is not a person who, having once made up her mind, will submit to being dictated to, either by you or by anybody else."

" She'll listen to me," Sir Philip said, confidently. " Blanche knows very well on which side her bread is buttered. I can make her throw over this damned old fool to-morrow."

The muscles round Lady Verschoyle's mouth twitched. She

sought hard to remain calm, and not to betray the excitement which was fast gaining possession of her.

" Really, Philip," she exclaimed, in a voice which, despite all efforts at self-control, revealed much inward agitation, "your language is most strange. What reason can you possibly have for making so extraordinary a statement."

" What reason! I have an excellent reason, an undeniable reason."

" For goodness' sake explain yourself."

" It is very simple. Blanche is head over ears in love with me, and has been so any time these last seven years."

" Oh! Philip," ejaculated Lady Verschoyle, faintly. " Are you—are you certain of this? "

" Quite certain."

" But how do you know? Girls do not generally confess to hopeless attachments."

" It may not be as hopeless as you conclude. That's my affair. Anyhow, the marriage must be prevented. The man has probably talked Blanche into giving her consent, and the chances are a thousand to one that she is wretched at the present moment."

" You have bewildered me," said Lady Verschoyle, who had turned ghastly pale. " Nevertheless, I don't quite see how you can interfere in so delicate a matter. If what you say about Blanche is true, your disapproval would only render her position the more difficult, without improving it materially."

" That remains to be seen. I flatter myself I might improve it very much indeed, let alone the pleasure of putting that ass Vansittart's nose out of joint."

Lady Verschoyle trembled. Her worst fears were verified. There was even more between Philip and Blanche than she had suspected.

" May I ask what you propose doing ? " she said, despairingly.

" I intend going to call on Blanche to-morrow." he answered, in tones of fierce decision. " She is staying in town for a few days, I perceive, so I shall leave by the first train in the morning."

" But, Philip, your friends arrive at four o'clock."

" Bother my friends ! Put them off."

" I can't well do that, seeing I neither know who they are nor where they live."

" Keep them going then till my return. Say I have been called away on business, but shall most likely turn up during the evening. Give them the run of the house, and plenty to eat and drink," he added cynically, " and they'll not miss me very much, I'll be bound."

" Philip," said Lady Verschoyle, making one last effort to divert him from his purpose, " I think you are very unwise, and had far better stay at home. What good can it do, unsettling Blanche's mind ? "

" What good ! " he exclaimed, and he turned upon her with his face ablaze, and his metallic eyes glittering like points of steel. " Great good. I shall propose to Blanche myself. We shall soon find out then," and he laughed a mirthless laugh, " whether she really prefers this Colonel Vansittart to me. I will believe it from her own lips, but from no one else's."

Lady Verschoyle stared at him in horror-struck incredulity.

" Are—you—in—earnest ? " she gasped, rather than said.

" Yes, very much so. Blanche Sylvester is the only woman I have ever seen whom I care about. We have the same tastes. She likes hunting and everything connected with sport, and rides like an Amazon——"

" I don't approve of hunting for young women," interposed Lady Verschoyle.

" It doesn't much matter, my dear mother, whether you do or you don't. As I have already had occasion to point out, your views in many ways are absurdly old-fashioned. Let this be understood. For several years I have always intended to make Blanche my wife, some day or other."

" But it is incredible," said Lady Verschoyle, pushing her smooth hair back from her brow, with a bewildered gesture. " Do you mean to tell me seriously, that having loved your cousin for so long, you have refrained from speaking out, and this without any special reason for keeping silent ? Why was it necessary to wait until you arrived at the age of twenty-nine, and she reached twenty-five ? To me such conduct appears quite unaccountable."

Sir Philip reddened.

"Well! " he said. "I was in no particular hurry to settle down. I wanted to sow my wild oats first, before encumbering myself with a wife and family ; and to tell the truth, mother, I always felt pretty sure of Blanche."

" You infer that she only waited to be asked ? "

He smiled consciously.

" Yes. In vulgar language, I suppose that was about it."

" And did it never occur to you that she might get weary of letting her youth and chances pass, awaiting your pleasure ? "

" No, it did not. She flirted about with other men, of course ; and always had a lot of fellows dangling after her, but I knew I could cut them all out whenever things came to a point."

" Perhaps Blanche's admirers possessed some of your caution, and never went the length of actually asking her to marry them," said Lady Verschoyle, with a touch of bitterness which she could not suppress.

"No. I fancy she had one or two decent offers, but," and Sir Philip smiled complacently, "she flew at higher game."

"You, in short."

"Exactly."

"And you really mean to marry this girl—this girl of whom you speak without one particle of deference and respect?"

"Yes, why not?"

Lady Verschoyle rose from her seat, a prey to the most extreme agitation.

"Oh! Philip," she said, earnestly, "I do not often interfere with you nowadays. I very seldom presume to censure your actions. Since you grew up, our paths have diverged, but perhaps that is more Nature's fault than yours. Nevertheless, I am your mother, and as a mother, knowing the female character better than you, and having had more experience of it, I feel it my duty, solemnly and seriously, to warn you against Blanche. Believe me, she is not a good girl—not a pure, modest, ladylike girl, gifted with refined tastes and domestic virtues, such as I should wish to see your wife and welcome as my daughter-in-law. Blanche is a product of the age. She is restless and without resources, and has an unhealthy craving for perpetual excitement and amusement. She cannot settle down for five minutes at a time, to a book, or to any quiet pursuit. God knows I don't wish to decry her, but what sort of a companion would such a woman make? How would one get through one's life with her? She will never render you happy, my boy, never —never. Oh! Philip, dear," she went on urgently, putting her long white hand upon his sleeve, "do listen to advice for once. Be warned in time. Leave Blanche alone. She is engaged to Colonel Vansittart of her own free will. In common decency she cannot throw over an honourable gentleman simply because at the eleventh hour she receives a better proposal. It would be downright wicked of you to put such a temptation in Blanche's way. Philip, dear Philip," and the white hand stole from his sleeve to his shoulder, from his shoulder to his neck, "if you have the smallest respect for my opinion, the least affection for me, do not, ah! do not go to town to-morrow."

The colour flew to his blonde face in an angry wave.

"Nonsense," he said roughly, shaking her off. "Let's have no more of this. You always were so infernally prejudiced against poor Blanche, that you refused to see any good in her whatever. I'm too old to be lectured like a schoolboy, and in-tend to please myself. Pray do not refer to the subject again, for it only makes me cross."

Lady Verschoyle sank back into the nearest chair. Dismay paralysed her faculties. She was hardly conscious of the rudeness and irritability of her son's tone. Once more Sir Philip rang the bell.

"William," he said to his valet, "order the brougham to be round to-morrow morning at eight o'clock. I am going up to town by the early train, and let breakfast be on the table at half-past seven, sharp."

Then he stalked out of the room, without bestowing a glance on the pale, sorrowful woman who had looked forward with so much pleasure to his arrival. She, on her part, did not dare to say another word. A great and exceeding bitterness flooded her heart.

CHAPTER IV.

A GIRL OF THE DAY.

THE West End of London was completely deserted. It might have been a City of the Dead. Blinds were drawn down, houses everywhere shut up. Colonel Vansittart's favourite sister and her husband, Mr. and Mrs. Normanby, were detained in the Metropolis by the illness of their youngest daughter. Wishing to make the acquaintance of Miss Sylvester, they had invited her to spend a few days with them in Cadogan-place. Womanlike, Mrs. Normanby was very curious to see her brother's *fiancée*, and to judge for herself of her perfections.

Blanche's last new habit wanted nipping in quite half an inch at the waist; moreover, she deemed it a good opportunity to have a personal interview with her dressmaker, and by informing her of her future prospects, pacify the excellent Madame Clementine, who for some time past had taken to giving trouble, and sending in her bills with impertinent regularity. Miss Sylvester foresaw that sooner or later she would have to go through the ordeal of all engaged young ladies, namely, run the gauntlet of her intended's family; consequently she accepted Mr. and Mrs. Normanby's invitation.

They proved to be strict, rigid, church-going people, and Miss Blanche had not been half a dozen hours under their roof before she inwardly determined to have as little as possible to do with them after her marriage. The Colonel should be weaned of his fraternal affection by all those arts which women have at their disposal. The process is simple enough. It begins with hints and innuendoes, and ends in ridicule. He would soon discover that, although no doubt the Normanbys might be good, worthy people in their way, they were not exactly his sort. A wife can so easily estrange a man from his family when she disapproves of its members, even without having recourse to the vulgar expedient of an open quarrel. Colonel Vansittart was in love—very much in love, and as a natural consequence he had stripped himself for the time being of all arms of defence. He had been introduced to Blanche at a Woolwich ball, lost his great, soft heart on the spot, and proposed three days after making her acquaintance. Since then, it could not be said that his passion had cooled, but every now and again in his innermost mind a suspicion would arise as to the wisdom of his choice. Wrestle with the doubt as he might, he could not banish it altogether. Blanche's rich, voluptuous style of beauty enslaved his senses, but he soon discovered that she was wilful and headstrong to a degree even greater than that exhibited by the ordinary run of beautiful women. In conversation many of her ideas clashed cruelly with his own. He kept these vague alarms to himself, however, for he would have considered it treason to the object of his affections to confide them to a soul. He hoped and believed that a fuller knowledge of each other's character would in the end smooth away any little disparities existing between them, and if Blanche had not cared for him, why—she would not have accepted him. So the good man reasoned, being, in spite of his forty-four years, in some things as simple as a child.

But just because of certain misgivings which occasionally impaired his felicity, he was the more anxious for Miss Sylvester to produce a favourable impression on his relatives, for whose opinion he had the highest regard. Very delicately and tenderly he hinted as much to Blanche, but he little knew the girl with whom he had to deal. She was one of those high-handed women, who set Mrs. Grundy at defiance openly and contemptuously. The censures of her own sex, even their avoidance, produced no effect on her whatever. She was impervious to female criticism. To please and be admired by men—to have them dangling about, professing devotion and rendering her conspicuous by their attentions, constituted her chief delight, and the object of her existence. She chafed at restraint, and would not brook the slightest authority, no matter how wise and legitimate. In short, she was vain, selfish, and frivolous to the very core. Her father had died many years ago, leaving her to the care of a stepmother, whose life she had rendered miserable. When she accepted Colonel Vansittart's proposal, everybody connected with her pitied him from the bottom of their hearts, and as far as she was concerned, regarded the engagement as quite providential.

"Blanche is getting on," they whispered among themselves.

" She is not so young as she was, and it is high time she should settle down. The match is respectable, if not brilliant, and really she is so exceedingly fast and independent, that it is a great relief to get her safely disposed of, before any terrible scandal takes place."

They were inclined to be very civil to Blanche, now that a prospect presented itself of the black sheep being turned into a white one, and made various amicable overtures when offering their congratulations ; but the young lady, who possessed a thorough knowledge of the world, laughed at them in her sleeve, and refused to make friends all round just because she had accepted a man with a fortune of three thousand five hundred pounds a year.

As for the Normanbys, she treated their house like an hotel, marching in and out without the smallest ceremony, keeping her hostess waiting for meals, and, worse still, flirting with that lady's husband whenever she got the chance. Now for twenty years Mr. Normanby had borne the marital yoke meekly and submissively. He was naturally of an easy-going disposition, and prepared to sacrifice most of his prerogatives for the sake of a quiet life. But amiable, sedate, pious as he might be, he had one grievous fault of which Mrs. Normanby had never wholly succeeded in curing him. Very much married, and father of half a dozen big boys and girls, he nevertheless was not entirely impervious to a pretty woman. Now, he did not approve of Blanche. Indeed, he took particular pains to assure his better half that had he been a bachelor, nothing—no, nothing on the face of this earth would have induced him to marry her, but a man's chivalry always prompts him to talk in a similar fashion, when he is carrying on a flirtation which his conscience tells him is not agreeable to the wife of his bosom. It is his talented way of throwing dust in her eyes, although it never by any chance blinds that sharp-seeing lady. In spite of Mr. Normanby's oft-declared compassion for Colonel Vansittart, the fact remained that he admired his *fiancée*, and found her an agreeable plaything with whom to trifle away a few spare hours. Under these circumstances, it is almost superfluous to state that the impression made by Miss Sylvester on Mrs. Normanby was distinctly unfavourable. She found fault with Blanche's dress, with her manner, with her appearance ; for if men are men, wives are wives, and the majority, in spite of many excellent qualities, fall victims to the " green-eyed monster," often on very slight provocation. Women of civilised countries are instinctively jealous of each other. The struggle to secure the favour of the males is too great for it to be otherwise.

The day after Sir Philip Verschoyle's conversation with his

mother, related in our last chapter, Blanche was sitting by herself in the drawing-room of the house in Cadogan-place. Colonel Vansittart had come up from Woolwich that morning, and the two lovers had spent the forenoon together. The society of her future husband did not tend to raise Blanche's spirits. It was an effort to act up to the ideal which he foolishly chose to form of her, and to be treated like a saint, knowing oneself a sinner, produced a sense of constraint, irksome to a degree. For three whole hours Blanche had been on her very best behaviour. She had an intuitive feeling that if he knew her as she was he would be inclined to back out of his engagement, and she meant to hold him fast until they were married. After that event, the sooner his eyes were opened the better. It would be impossible for her to go on playing at goody-goody for long; she was deadly tired of it already, and nothing but self-interest prevented her from breaking down in the part which she had chosen temporarily to assume. Colonel Vansittart appeared a desirable enough husband when at Woolwich, but when his ardour induced him to come to town, and pour forth strings of little commonplace, amorous sentences, then he bored her. It was useless trying to deny the fact. After ten minutes of his company she became conscious of a feeling of *ennui* and of an almost irresistible impulse to say something that would make his hair stand on end. Blanche lay on the big cretonne-covered Chesterfield sofa, and idly turned over the leaves of a novel written by a young girl, which had lately made some sensation in the fashionable world on account of its prurient character. But she did not get on very fast with her book, and it was evident her thoughts were elsewhere. In truth, she was thinking what a relief it was that her *fiancé* and his sister had gone out driving together, and that the fictitious plea of a headache had induced them to leave her alone.

"I wish he wasn't so ridiculously proper," she soliloquised. "He's not a bad old Thing in many ways. He's generous, confiding, and high-minded—too high-minded." And she heaved a sigh. "I quite see his good points, and yet he oppresses me. There's something narrow and ponderous about his virtue which irritates my nerves. I wonder if he has ever been tempted and yielded to temptation? I should like him all the better if he weren't so faultily faultless. He would certainly seem more human, and be more comfortable to get on with. Heigh ho! What an ill-assorted couple we shall make to be sure! Even now I have quite hard work not to shock him every time I open my mouth, and little things will slip out when one is off one's guard. I do my very best not to offend the poor dear's susceptibilities, but it is boring. Ah! boring "—yawning three or four times consecutively. "If we are not married very soon I never shall be able to keep it up. The strain is positively fearful." So saying, she lay back, and, recognising the uselessness of attempting to read, let the book fall slowly from her hands to her lap.

The hot summer sun poured in upon her. There was no one by to watch every tint of her complexion, and she had pulled the blinds up after Colonel Vansittart's departure, feeling a longing for light and air. The brilliant rays illumined her magnificent black hair and large, heavy-lidded dark eyes with shafts of tawny orange. They lingered lovingly on her clear olive face, with its full, red-lipped mouth, and saucy up-turned nose.

The physical congeniality of the sunshine, the warmth, the reposeful attitude, and—must it be added?—a heavy luncheon (for this splendidly-grown young woman possessed an excellent appetite), all tended to produce somnolence. She settled the soft cushions round the nape of her white neck, leant back her head, and slept.

Very beautiful she looked thus, with her crimson lips slightly parted, showing two rows of exquisitely white and even teeth. Even a man as upright and honourable as Colonel Vansittart might have been excused for jumping at the conclusion on first acquaintance that beneath so fair a form there must necessarily live as fair a spirit.

Alas! that it was not so; that in her case beauty of the flesh was not allied to beauty of the soul.

Whether she slept a minute or an hour Blanche never knew. She had not returned from the Land of Nod when her slumbers were disturbed by the door being thrown open, and a stentorian voice proclaiming, "Sir Philip Verschoyle." She started to her feet with a glad cry, and held out both her hands. Then, as if remembering that they no longer met on the same terms as formerly, she drew them back, and said, with an assumption of indifference, palpably more feigned than real—

"Hulloa! Philip. You are the last person in the world whom I expected to see. What brings you to town? I had a letter from your mother a day or two ago, and she told me you were going to Beechlands for the partridge shooting."

"I reached it last night at nine, and left this morning at eight," he replied.

"What a short visit!" she exclaimed, ironically. "Did not filial duty suggest a longer stay?"

"I wanted to see you," he rejoined, taking no notice of the interrogation.

"Indeed! I ought to feel very much flattered. Your desire must be extremely great when it induces you to leave your house and home in order to seek my poor society. It is a long time since I was so honoured." And she swept him a mocking curtsey.

"Blanche, do be serious, and drop that horrid sarcastic tone. I detest it."

"You have no reason to detest it, *mon ami*, seeing that you have brought it upon yourself."

"Are you alone?" he asked, impatiently. "I mean, is there no fear of our being interrupted?"

"None. My beloved and his charming sister have gone out for a drive together, and no doubt at the present moment are amusing themselves by talking over my imperfections. I fancy I can hear Mrs. Normandy saying, 'My poor Weldon, it grieves me to say so, but I don't approve of Miss Sylvester. I don't approve of her at all.'"

"Thank goodness! they are not at home," exclaimed her companion. "I want to have a chat with you, Blanche."

"What about, Philip?" So saying she reseated herself on the sofa, and made room for him to sit by her side.

"About this engagement of yours, of course. You could have knocked me down with a feather when I heard of it."

"Really! It is very good of you to interest yourself so much in my affairs." And, putting out one slippered foot, she looked down at it with pensive approval.

The calmness and composure of her manner provoked him. He had expected to be received with considerably more effusion. His fancy had pictured tears, reproaches, even embraces. This cold, self-possessed Blanche, so different from the volcanic creature of his recollections and anticipations, rather took him aback. What had come to the girl? He had not seen her since the spring. She was a changed being. He looked at her dissatisfiedly, and she returned the glance with a contemptuous defiance, which made his blood turn hot.

"You look cross, cousin mine," she observed, in a tone that irritated him still more.

"I look what I am, then," he responded, tearing savagely at the ends of his moustache, and catching them between his teeth, as he spoke.

"You'll spoil your moustache, Philip, if you nibble at it in that senseless way."

"Damn my moustache. What do I care about it?"

"You should; since it forms a very decided addition to your appearance. Must I remind you that your mouth is not exactly your strong point?"

"I wish you'd give over this confounded nonsense, and speak like yourself."

"Thank you. I am myself. I never was more myself than at the present moment."

"Upon my word, Blanche, you are enough to drive a fellow out of his mind."

"I should say that depended entirely upon the fellow's original stock of brains. May I ask what has put it out of temper?" And she screwed up her handsome face into a comical grimace.

"You know without asking," he responded, in a surly tone.

"I know! Oh! dear no. How should I?" she retorted, arching her level brows with an air of affected innocence.

"Blanche, tell me one thing. Is it true that you are engaged to Colonel Vansittart?"

"Yes, quite true. I wrote and informed your mother of the fact the day before yesterday."

"I saw the letter. She showed it to me."

"Well! And aren't you delighted? My relations have done nothing but congratulate me ever since. 'My dear Blanche,' they say, coming purring about me like so many cats, 'we are charmed. Such a nice, sensible match. So suitable and satisfactory in every way.' You don't mean to tell me you disagree?" she concluded, affecting surprise.

"Yes, I do, most emphatically. I have come here to-day on purpose to protest."

A warm flush rose to her dark face.

"I am infinitely grateful. Really, it is quite refreshing to meet a person whose opinion is so unlike the majority."

"If you marry Colonel Vansittart you will simply be throwing yourself away," he said.

"Thank you, Philip. I feel more and more obliged. My only regret is that you did not state your views before the gentleman proposed. No doubt, had you done so, my fate might have been different, and I might have been persuaded to throw myself away in another quarter. As matters stand, however, I don't quite see why you should object to my fulfilling the destiny of my sex. Are we not," she went on in a deep, vibrating voice, "all brought up from our childhood to look upon matrimony as the goal of a woman's aspirations and ambition——"

"Not one man in a thousand would suit you," interrupted Sir Philip.

"You are scarcely in a position to judge whether they would or would not," she returned. "At any rate, I am tired of playing the fool. I have tried that game," looking her cousin straight in the face, "for a good many years, and nothing very advantageous has come of it. Gradually and painfully I have grown to perceive the necessity of adopting a fresh tack, for the person who might have proposed to me, and who had led me over and over again to suppose that he intended doing so, did not declare himself. He proved a broken reed on which to rely. The years passed away, and little by little I realised that my youth might fade, my opportunities slip by, and one fine day I should wake up to find he was only indulging in an unprofitable flirtation at my expense. Well, Philip," she went on, her words coming faster and more vehemently. " it was not good enough, and I determined not to rot any longer on my stalk. Only after much reflection and bitterness of spirit did I come to this decision ; but having once arrived at it, nothing remained but to avail myself of the first good offer of marriage that should be made me. I wanted a home and a sufficient competence, combined with a man not actively objectionable, and a gentleman whom I should not feel ashamed to present as my husband. Colonel Vansittart possessed the requisite qualifications, added to the advantage of being madly in love with your humble servant. He is susceptible to female influence, and capable of being governed. With all due deference to you, once he gets broken in I believe he will suit me very well. Now," and rising to her feet, she confronted Sir Philip with the frankest impertinence, " have you anything to say ? If so, say it."

He made one or two hasty strides up and down the room. She followed him with mocking eyes, that goaded him almost to madness.

CHAPTER V

SIR PHILIP PROPOSES.

" YES," he cried, in accents of such triumphant possession that they produced a sense of repulsion in the woman with whom he had trifled so long; " I have a great deal to say. It is as I thought. You care no more for Colonel Vansittart than you do for the man in the moon. If you did you would talk of him very differently."

" Care ! " she said, pettishly. " No, of course I don't. I never pretended to ; but that has nothing to do with the matter."

" I should have thought it had a great deal to do with it."

" Then you thought wrong, Philip."

" But, Blanche, why on earth have you promised to marry him then ? "

She drummed with her strong white fingers on the top of the mantel-board.

" Dear me ! how stupid you are, or are you so sentimentally

constituted that you can't conceive of a marriage being arranged on any other basis than the worn-out one of true love? Really, Philip. I never thought much of your heart ; but it is more to be admired than your head."

"Abuse does not require a vast amount of talent either." he retorted: "nevertheless. it fails to explain your reasons."

"And why should people be expected to give their reasons for every simple action ? To hear you talk. one would think that no woman had ever married from motives of expediency before."

"You admit then that your marriage is purely one of expediency ?"

"I admit nothing : besides. I refuse to recognise your right to catechise me. I have already told you that the time has come when I perceive the necessity of being whitewashed. and, therefore. I desire a home and position of my own."

"You might have found them elsewhere."

"I quite agree with you there." she rejoined. vivaciously. "I might : only. unhappily for me, I didn't. Some women are fortunate from the beginning : others have no luck. I belong to the latter class."

"I don't see why you should say that. In many ways you have had an excellent time of it."

"To which. doubtless, you contributed." she answered. with a sneer. "For the first few years after she comes out a girl who is bold enough to free herself from the espionage of a chaperon may enjoy life very fairly well. But when she reaches the age of twenty-five there is another side to the picture. People begin to fight shy of her. Men don't propose with freedom, and she must either make up her mind to settle down with some individual as unlike her ideal as can well be conceived of. or else endure the supreme mortification of being left in the lurch, and laughed at, and pitied as a spinster. As I don't intend to degenerate into an old maid, forsaken by the male sex. and compassionated by the female. I propose to marry a good. worthy gentleman, full of negative qualities. who. unless I make a mistake in his character, will give me my own way. and let me do pretty much as I like. At any rate, I shall have his name, which is something. I am tired of Sylvester."

"Blanche." said Sir Philip. passionately. "you have acted like a fool. Did it never strike you that somebody else was willing to fill Colonel Vansittart's place ?"

"Somebody else should have spoken in time." she answered. coldly. "Somebody else had every opportunity had he chosen."

"He chooses now." said Sir Philip. "I came here to-day for the express purpose of asking you to be my wife." And he tried to insinuate his arm round her waist, with an air of confident proprietorship.

To his surprise she drew back, and laughed a scornful laugh.

" Does not your proposal come just a trifle late ? " she asked, sarcastically.

" Yes, perhaps it does; but to be quite candid, Blanche, until this news reached me, I always looked upon you as a sensible girl, above the common feminine folly of getting married at all hazards."

This speech, uttered coarsely and rudely, roused her to anger. Fire flashed from her dark eyes as, turning with a superb gesture, she fixed them full upon him. Insensibly his lids drooped before the withering indignation of her glance. He knew that she had just cause for wrath, and the consciousness did not add to his moral well-being.

" And you dare to tell me this—you dare ? " she said, in a voice ringing with passion. " You, who, for years past, have systematically trifled with my affections, kept me in perpetual suspense, and prevented me from accepting the few good offers that came my way? Had it not been for you I might have been well and safely married long ago. You have done me more harm than any man in creation, and now, after I have waited until I am tired of waiting, for you to declare your intentions, you actually are audacious enough to twit me for being in a hurry to change my state. It is monstrous—quite monstrous."

" Blanche, do be reasonable, and don't fly off into a fury about nothing."

" Nothing ! Do you call it nothing to deliberately win a girl's heart, promise her marriage in every way but words, and then shilly-shally for an indefinite period, until at last she loses all faith in you, and is bewildered as to her position? Ever since my seventeenth birthday, when I stayed at Beechlands for the Christmas holidays, if you had proposed to me you know what my answer would have been. You made love to me—you kept me from caring for anyone else, and—and—you taught me to be false and tricky and underhand like yourself. I was not so always. I have to thank you for the greater portion of my moral backslidings. For eight or nine years I waited patiently, hoping for the declaration which it has only pleased you to-day to make. Even now, although you seem quite sure of me, you are not sure of your own feelings."

" By Heaven ! Blanche," he interrupted, " you are wrong."

She smiled contemptuously.

" No, I think not. Had it not been for the appearance of Colonel Vansittart on the scene, you would have been content to drift on, on, on, in the same old groove. It is all very well to wake up now, and talk of your love. 'Your' love indeed! It is nothing but the meanest, lowest form of jealousy—the sort of jealousy which prompts a cur to snatch away its bone from another dog."

No need now to accuse Blanche of coldness. Her beautiful face was ablaze with passion. Her rounded bosom rose and fell like the waves of the sea, and with the same strong, undulating motion. By sheer force of feeling, all the skilful web built up by social conventionality was swept away. She stood before him like a tigress baulked of her prey, instinct with animal rage. Every word that she uttered struck home, for Sir Philip could not deny the truth of the accusations which she hurled so freely and furiously against him.

"Blanche," he said, "let bygones be bygones. I may have acted foolishly."

"Foolishly!" she interposed. "Cruelly, wickedly."

"But," he went on more firmly, "I am here to make amends for past mistakes. It seems to me that we have both made them, for I swear to you I always thought we understood each other, without there being any need for explanation."

"In short," she said, fiercely, "you deliberately intended to let me become an old, ugly woman, while you continued to amuse yourself."

"You never could be ugly under any circumstances, Blanche."

"Oh! don't pay me compliments. Why should I escape the common fate of most women. Once they cease to be good-looking they cease to be attractive."

"Hush, Blanche. All this is neither here nor there. I want you to listen to what I have to say. You don't care for Colonel Vansittart, and whatever you may pretend to the contrary you do care for me. You have accepted him out of pique. Why commit the supreme folly of making your whole life miserable?"

"It is miserable enough already. God knows," she said, wearily.

"Exactly: because you are giving yourself over to a man who, in thought, temperament, and feeling is utterly uncongenial to you. Take my advice, whilst there is yet time. Stand proof against a certain amount of gossip, and chuck the colonel over."

"And if I did," she said, slowly, "what would become of me then?"

"I offer to make you my wife. Surely you will not hesitate for a moment. All you have got to do is to choose between Vansittart and me. Blanche, dear," taking her hand in his, "show a little moral courage, and answer me according to your heart."

A dead silence ensued. A look of perplexity stole over the girl's face. Once or twice her lips moved as if she were making some rapid mental calculation. Sir Philip grew impatient, and also a little puzzled, for he had imagined that she would jump at his offer. He drew her nearer to him, and touched her cheek with his lips. She shivered, but said nothing. He never doubted what her reply would be. This beautiful creature was his, and the triumph of gaining her was all the greater from the fact of snatching her from another suitor. He laughed out loud.

"What are you laughing at?" she asked, suspiciously.

"At that old fool of a colonel. Blanche, darling, how awfully sold he will be."

Suddenly, she plucked away the hand which he still held in his, and retreated beyond reach.

"Philip Verschoyle," she said, "your merriment is as premature as your proposal is tardy, and out of place. You should have asked me sooner." Then her face softened, and she added. "If I could believe you—if I could trust you, but," returning to her former firm attitude, "I can't. You are too slippery, and, moreover, are quite capable of leaving me in the lurch even after I had complied with your demand. Then in what sort of a position should I find myself? I should fall between two stools, and the last case of that man—or, rather, woman—would be worse than the first. No, no," and she began pacing the room in extreme agitation "I dare not risk it. A fortnight—only one short fortnight—ago, and I should have said yes with pleasure. I was free and unfettered. Now, I am so no longer, and, for good or for evil, must abide by my choice."

"This is perfectly preposterous," said Sir Philip incredulously. "Surely you are not in earnest?"

"Yes, you appear to consider my decision strange, but I think that I am quite in earnest. With all my faults weighing heavily upon me I have not yet reached the pitch of baseness when I would deliberately and consciously commit a dastardly action, such as you propose."

"But why sacrifice yourself in this quixotic manner? I can see no object in it."

"You may not. I do."

"But, Blanche, by your own confession, you are not the least in love with Colonel Vansittart, and you are in love——" breaking off abruptly.

"With you. Pray don't spare my feelings." And her short, upper lip curled disdainfully. "What would you say if I told you I was cured of my folly?"

"I shouldn't believe you."

A flickering smile passed over her face, and died away, leaving it cold and stern.

" You are right," she said, in an artificial tone intended to hide all emotion. " I do love you, and I have always loved you, unworthy as you are. But you fail to understand how pride alters the views of a woman who has been badly treated. You ask me to be your wife, expecting me to jump straight away into your arms. I shan't do any such thing. I whom you have despised and played with, whose heart you have wrung till it feels as if it never could ache again, reject your offer of marriage, and, despite the glories of the position, decline to become Lady Verschoyle." And she tossed her head back defiantly.

" Blanche," he ejaculated. " Are you mad ? "

" No. I am restored to my senses after a long period of lunacy."

" What do you mean by this extraordinary obstinacy, for I can call it by no other name ? "

" The explanation is easy enough. During the various stages of infatuation through which I was fated to pass, I never ceased studying your character, and the result of my observations amounts to this. You are false, fickle, and incapable of a real passion. Self is the god at whose shrine you worship, and any woman giving herself into your keeping would run but a small chance of happiness. Seeing your faults as clearly as I do, I have often wondered lately why I ever lavished my affection on so unworthy an object. I knew that you were a bad son, and would also make a bad husband. Since the spring I have tried with all my might to forget you, and—and," tearing nervously at the corner of her pocket-handkerchief, " I have succeeded— partially. No, don't interrupt," as Philip tried to speak. " After all these years and years, it is a relief to have my say out. Colonel Vansittart is a good man—far too good for me. In my better moments I recognise his worth, and it is horrid of me to talk of him as I do. If I marry him, he may perhaps save me from myself. He loves me, his influence is salutary, and appeals to my higher nature. In course of time, I might grow to be more like him, and adopt his ideas about morality, religion, duty, and all that sort of thing. I think I should like to try. I am getting rather tired of flying about the world by myself, doing stupid things, and having nobody to protect or help me. A woman has to be very strong to stand alone. I begin to see that. When I go to India I shall break off with all my old lot, and start a new life altogether. Of course it is an experiment. You need not impress that fact upon me. I may not prove a success as the virtuous matron, but, as I said before, I mean to try. If I do not love Colonel Vansittart, I respect him. I loved you dearly once, Philip, but by degrees my love has given way to a profound distrust."

" You are demented, Blanche. Such a jolly girl as you were, too, before this confounded Colonel put all these starchy notions into your head."

" I have to thank you for the majority of them, Philip. They do not come naturally to me. They are the result of much bitterness of spirit, and of many a heartache. You forgot that whilst you trifled at my expense, I was gaining experience. God knows," she went on sorrowfully, " I would rather be without it—rather go back to the time when I was young and foolish, and unversed in the ways of the world, but I can't; and seeing things with eyes which you have opened, I refuse to dishonourably jilt a good man for the sake of a bad one."

Sir Philip's blue eyes glittered with an evil radiance. His handsome features were distorted by passion. Could he have foretold her answer, he would have cut off his right hand sooner than let her avenge herself in this signal manner. Henceforth Blanche would always have the satisfaction of telling her friends and relatives that she had refused Sir Philip Verschoyle, Bart. The mere thought was as gall and wormwood. Never had his vanity received such a blow. He felt a sudden inclination to wind his fingers round Blanche's throat, and silence for ever the sharp tongue which stung him with so many venomous truths. For the moment his affection was turned to hatred, and yielded to a murderous instinct. By a strong effort he controlled himself. He felt there was nothing to be gained by flying into a temper. Even now, he could scarcely believe that she was in earnest. To-morrow, or the next day no doubt, she would repent of her idiocy, and come grovelling to him for forgiveness. It would be his turn then, to pay her back in her own coin. Such ungenerous thoughts as these passed through his mind as he stood and glowered at the girl. A hostile pause succeeded her last plain-spoken speech.

At length he said in a cold, hard voice, " I am not the man to give a woman the chance of refusing me twice. Is this your final answer, Blanche ? "

She looked at him, and for a moment hesitated. He seemed aware of her indecision, and smiled in a lofty, patronising way. There was something about that smile, which, to use a vulgar expression, put her back up. It roused her spirit to find that he counted so surely on her accepting him.

" I have nothing more to say," she rejoined. " I have lost all faith in your word, and feel that I cannot trust you."

Then, all at once, the anger blazed forth which hitherto he had restrained with so much difficulty.

" So be it," he cried. " I shall not stoop to entreaty. But, mark my words, you will live to repent of your folly. As for forgetting the old associations, and striking out an entirely new path, the thing's impossible You never could settle down to respectable, humdrum boredom. You have too high a spirit. As regards Colonel Vansittart—I predict you will soon tire of him. The eagle and the jackass can't mate together. It is impossible that their union should last. You are not the woman to brook being dictated to, lectured, and ordered about. All your life you have been impatient of authority. You want some-body who knows your character well. At present, both you and the Colonel are full of illusions. They won't take long to dis-appear, and then you will regret this day's work, and come back penitent and submissive to me——"

" Never," she interrupted indignantly. " I would sooner starve first."

" Yes, you will. I know you better than you know yourself. But don't for a moment imagine that I shall grieve for a girl who has ventured to spurn me. No, no, my haughty Blanche. If you are proud, so also am I. Two can play at that game, and the very day you go to the altar, I intend to marry——"

" Who ? " she demanded eagerly.

He shrugged his shoulders.

" How do I know? Anybody. The first girl I come across." And he walked towards the door.

On a green velvet table in a corner stood the photograph of a young woman, with a small, grave face, and no particular pre-tensions either to beauty or fashion. Sir Philip came to a full stop before it, and gazed at it with an air of recognition.

" Who is that? " he inquired, abruptly.

Blanche lifted her eyebrows superciliously.

" Oh ! that's poor little Bligh Burton," she said. " It appears her father was at school with Mr. Normanby, and every now and then he asks Bligh up to town for a day or two out of charity. She's a harmless, insignificant little thing."

" I thought I knew the features," said Sir Philip. " I danced with Miss Burton once at a ball, and I rather liked her if I remember. I'll marry her. She'll do as well as anybody else, and will serve," he added nastily, " to show the world how little I take your marriage to heart."

" No sane man could propose in such an unheard-of fashion ! " cried Blanche aghast. " You must be stark, staring mad, Philip."

" Very much the reverse. Surely you did not fancy I was go-ing to wear the willow for you. Good morning. I hope the Colonel may make an obedient husband. and answer your expectations." Before his cousin could make any reply, he had stalked out of the room.

When he was gone past recall, she burst into a passion of tears. "I wonder if I have done right!" she cried. "Oh! how I wonder if I have done right!" Deep sobs shook her from head to foot. "If Philip were only like other men," she mused—"if only one could believe in him. He says I might be his wife—his wife"—and she heaved a sigh. "Ah! why is it that all the good things of this life come too late. Heigh ho! it's a very hard, perplexing world for an unfortunate young woman to find the right husband in. The one she likes, she can't get; and the one she can have, she doesn't care for. Philip, Philip, why did you not speak sooner—why did you not speak sooner? It is you who have driven me to this extremity." The hot sun, heedless of her grief, poured in upon her, and heated the salt tears as they rolled down her cheeks, until they burnt like sparks of fire.

CHAPTER VI.

BLIGH'S FIRST LOVE AFFAIR.

BLIGH BURTON was an only child, and a better daughter never existed. Her life for many years past had been one long sacrifice to filial duty, performed so quietly, so cheerfully, and unobtrusively, that nobody seemed to realise the fact of its being hardly natural for a girl, from the age of eighteen to eight and twenty, to devote all her days to nursing a pair of invalid parents. The springtime of youth had passed away, and with one notable exception, Bligh had enjoyed but few of the pleasures which form part of a happy girlhood. She seldom went from home, and in the little country village where she lived, there were not many attractions to be found. But Bligh did not crave for amusement. She had other things to occupy her, and her days, if monotonous, were busy. In great measure they were taken up with petty household cares, small worries—often so much harder to bear than big ones—and a continual anxiety as to the state of the exchequer. For they were very poor. Captain Burton was a man of good family, but thirty years ago, he had hopelessly offended his relatives by running away with a penniless governess, whose charming face and brilliant accomplishments counted for nothing in their estimation, in comparison with the almighty dollar. His father cut him out of his will—an act of injustice which for ever embittered the old man's memory, and so long as Captain Burton remained in the army, he had only his pay to live on.   As the future looked hopeless, after a while he left the service, and settled down in the country.

Here, for a few years, owing chiefly to the kindness of some friends who interested themselves on his behalf, he did fairly well as an army coach.   They were palmy days for the Burtons, when from eight to ten young fellows, paying about a hundred and fifty pounds a year each, resided under their roof.   The Captain, assisted by a couple of first-rate masters, was so successful in passing his lads for the different examinations, that he seldom had a vacancy.   If his health had but held good, he might have died a rich man ; but always delicate, the long hours of teaching, combined with the responsibility, put too great a strain upon his constitution.   A slight stroke of paralysis warned him that he must not over-tax his brain.   By degrees, the management of the establishment devolved upon subordinates.

This was the period of Bligh's great happiness and subsequent disappointment, which converted her from a bright, high-spirited girl into a sad and sober woman.

She was eighteen—joyous eighteen, when there came to her father's house for the purpose of cramming for the army, a youth named Duncan Cameron, the eldest son of a Scotch peer. Duncan soon showed that he had no taste for books.   Although a shrewd, clever enough fellow in many ways, he displayed a marked aversion for mathematics, or anything requiring much study.   It was impossible to make him work.   As a candidate for military honours, his teachers gave him up in despair.   The consequence was, the young gentleman had a good deal of idle time on his hands, which, after the first few days had gone by, he spent very agreeably in making love to his tutor's daughter, then a fresh, pretty girl who looked upon him as the greatest hero ever born into the world.   Bligh returned her admirer's attentions by the total surrender of her innocent heart.   It had never yet been assailed by any masculine creature, and perhaps its conquest was easier than might have been the case with a young lady accustomed to society and flirtation.

Anyhow, Master Duncan was not long in discovering that love-making presented infinitely more points of attraction than cramming.   He took to the one naturally ; whilst for the other he displayed a profound distaste.   He had not the slightest objection to being adored by a nice-looking girl.   Indeed, he found it so agreeable, that one fine day he proposed to Bligh, by way of testifying his appreciation of her devotion.

" I daresay the governor will kick up no end of a row at first," he observed, consolingly, to the object of his affections.   " Parents always do where their sons' happiness is concerned.   Mine will fly into a rage, no doubt, and vow I'm too young to think ot marrying, and all that sort of thing. I fancy I can hear them saying it. But a man of nineteen," and he made a fruitless endeavour to twiddle the white down on his upper lip, "must know his own mind better than his father and mother ; and if we stick to each other, Bligh, matters are bound to come right sooner or later."

In reply to this speech, Bligh of course declared that she could never, never care for anyone else but her dear, self-sacrificing Duncan. She deplored her own inferiority in the most sweetly humble manner, and was rewarded for such perfectly natural humility by a lordly kiss which set her tender heart a fluttering for the rest of the day.

The amorous lover retired to the sanctity of his own apart-ment, there to compose a letter addressed to his father, in which he intimated his firm intention of getting married imme-diately.

Unfortunately, the course of true love did not run smoothly. It seldom does when people are happy and foolish, and have yet to be imbued with worldly knowledge gained at the expense of youthful sentiment. Yet no love ever approaches the first, when on the maiden's side all is belief and innocent credulity, and on the man's there is at least freshness of feeling. A woman then is to him a goddess, a saint, a divine mystery, whom he approaches with awe, instead of with the familiarity of his later days. By return of post came a letter from Lord Kirk-wall, in which he roundly told his son that he was a damned young fool ! Captain Burton also received a communication from the irate father, containing some very severe strictures, and announcing his lordship's intention to remove the Honour-able Duncan at the end of the term.

Here was a pretty state of affairs ! Bligh wept her eyes out, and with generous self-accusation declared that it was all her fault, and that she ought to have known better. "Lord Kirk-wall was quite right to think she was not half good enough for Duncan. No one realised the fact more keenly than she did herself, etc., etc."

Offended by the sight of her grief, and incensed at finding his wishes thwarted by a father who hitherto had never denied him anything, Duncan displayed great spirit, and far from giving up his inamorata, swore undying and eternal constancy.

"After all, Bligh," he said, "it don't much signify. We are young, and can afford to wait. If the worst comes to the worst, I come in for a couple of thousands a year when I am of age, over which the seniors have no control, and I can snap my fingers at them then. Our marriage is only a question of time, so cheer up little woman."

Was there ever such a lover?　Bligh thought herself the most fortunate girl in the world.

"Oh! but Duncan," she said smiling through her tears, "you must not offend your people.　I can't think of allowing you to injure your prospects for my sake.　It would not be right."

"Tut, tut," he responded.　"What do I care about my prospects so long as I have you."

"Duncan," said Bligh.　"You are too good, too noble.　But why not go and see Lord Kirkwall, and hear what he has to say. A personal interview is always so much more satisfactory than writing."

"By Jove!" he exclaimed, struck by the force of her reasoning.　"I think I will.　That is a happy thought of yours, Bligh."

A few days later a meeting was effected in town between father and son.

The young man came back in a much more hopeful frame of mind.　His impassioned appeals had not been in vain.

"Things are not so bad, Bligh, after all," he said to the girl on his return.　"I'm to leave at the end of the term.　The governor thinks I'm too young to know my own mind, and insists on my going.　But of course all that's bosh.　We shall never forget one another.　The only hard part of it is, he has made me promise not to write to you, or hold any communication with your family for a year."

"A year!　Oh! Duncan, that seems a long time."

"Awful.　But now comes the good news.　At the end of our period of probation, if we still remain true to each other, which, as far as I am concerned, is an absolute certainty, the governor says we may meet, and has so far unbent as to declare that he will consider the question seriously.　So you see, I've done a lot of good by running up to town."

"That you certainly have," said Bligh, her face all rosy from her lover's kisses.　Then she sighed, and added wistfully—

"You will forget me sooner than I shall forget you, Duncan."

"Nonsense," he rejoined.　"I shall do no such thing.　A year will soon go by."

"It's a very long time to which to look forward," she returned.

"Never mind, Bligh, darling.　We shall laugh at it once it's over.　My father has arranged for me to leave here on the 26th of July, and I am to meet him in town, when we go to Scotland together for the grouse season——"

"So soon!" ejaculated Bligh, clasping her hands together with a gesture of despair.

"Yes, it can't be helped.　I had to agree.　But never mind,

Bligh dear. On the 26th of July, next year, you shall come to the station, and await the three o'clock train. You know the one I mean. It leaves London somewhere about half-past twelve. I will be there without fail. Come now, promise to greet me on my arrival."

They kissed and parted under the weeping willow that adorned a secluded corner of Captain Burton's small garden, and the roses and carnations nodded their heads, and filled the sunlit air with their fragrance. The world looked very bright on the summer afternoon when Duncan Cameron bid good-bye to Bligh Burton. The birds seemed actuated by a perfect rage of song, flowers bloomed everywhere around, fields lay yellowing in the sunshine, leaves stirred with gentle melody, shivering under the influence of the balmy breeze. All the earth was fair and full of promise. Only in the maiden's heart dwelt a vague, unconquerable sadness. It ached, almost without her knowing the reason. For Duncan was right. A year was nothing—a year would soon pass. It was downright wicked to be so depressed, and to cast a cloud over his spirits. He looked forward to the future with such confidence. Why could not she do the same ? Was it because a man's portion is easier than a woman's ? Because it is so much less hard to go out into the world and act than it is to sit at home doing nothing, fading and waiting, waiting and fading, and brooding over the same thought. Bligh determined not to give way selfishly to her sorrow, and once Duncan had fairly gone, she adhered bravely to her resolution.

She kept her regrets, her anxieties to herself, and instead of moping, tried the effect of increased occupation.

At last the cold, dreary winter came to an end. Then when the tender buds burst their sheaths, when the buttercups and daisies starred the fields, and the vernal spring sent a glad thrill of youth and health through her veins, she said softly to herself, " Duncan is coming, Duncan is coming. On the 26th of July I shall see him." And every day the voice grew louder and louder, which whispered the good news in her heart, until at last it rang out clear and strong, like the nightingale's song at evening. In those days she went about the house with a quick, springy step, and eyes brightened by hope. On her round young face lived a perpetual smile. " He is coming. He is coming," she warbled in triumphant accents, the joyous words often penetrating to the ears of her father and mother. At such times, they would look at each other with quiet satisfaction, for much as they loved their daughter, and greatly as they should feel her loss, it was a relief to both their minds to know that she would soon be happily married. For they had no fortune to give her, and whenever death claimed the father of the home, she would be left almost penniless.

At length the long-expected and anxiously-awaited day arrived.

It came in heralded with lowering clouds, a blustering wind, and driving rain. But what did Bligh care? After a year's separation she was going to see Duncan once more. Everything else was insignificant in comparison with the one important fact. She dressed herself very carefully, trying on her hats and jackets one by one, to ascertain which was the most becoming. Then she put on a waterproof—for the rain was coming down steadily—and taking an umbrella in her hand sallied forth bravely to the station.

Her parents saw her go.

"Ought we not to send somebody with her?" said Captain Burton to his wife. During the last twelve months, he had taken to confirmed invalid ways, and now seldom ventured out of doors.

"Bligh would sooner be alone," replied Mrs. Burton, with a fuller comprehension of the feminine mind than that possessed by her husband. "When people are very happy, or stricken by a great grief, they invariably prefer their own society. Thank God, our darling child has no cause for sorrow. It does one's heart good to see her so blythe and gay."

The walk to the station was long, the distance being nearly two miles and a half, but Bligh's little feet pattered over the wet mud at railroad speed. Not a first-rate pedestrian, as a rule, to-day she knew no fatigue. With bright, unseeing eyes she looked on the familiar objects by which she was surrounded. Borne on the wings of love, her spirit flew onward, engrossed by one absorbing thought. The boisterous wind sought to oppose her progress, but she defied its angry buffets. Did it think it could keep her from Duncan. Ah! no. Ah! no.

When she reached the station her cloak was dripping wet. It dawned upon her mind vaguely that Duncan would not clasp her to his arms in this moist state. So she went to the cloak-room, and divested herself of her damp garment. Then she sat down on a bench in the centre of the platform, and waited impatiently for the train to arrive. She had come to the trysting place too soon—ten whole minutes too soon, but what were they when compared with a long and cruel year? How tedious it had been, how slowly the time had gone; but now, thank God! thank God! the period of probation was at an end, and she and Duncan would be together again, as in the dear old days.

Bligh's face was flushed with excitement. The wind and the rain had lent it a fresh pink colour which made it very pleasing to behold. In her clear eyes there beamed the light of a great and innocent love. And as she sat there on the wooden bench, she offered up a prayer to the Almighty thanking him for her exceeding happiness. It scarcely seemed right that so much joy should fall to her lot, when others went through their whole lives destitute of affection. She had once heard a woman in the village say that she looked upon man as her natural enemy. To Bligh, such a state of mind appeared inconceivable, and sad to a degree.

She did not judge the woman, but she thought that there must be something radically wrong about her composition. At length the train was signalled, and she rose to her feet, all joy and expectation.

Nearer and nearer came the dull, ponderous roar of the engine. A red light pierced through the mist and the rain, and grew steadily larger and brighter. Then the smoke became apparent, hanging heavy on the damp air, as it issued from the funnel in soft, curling clouds that resembled grey fur. Bligh's heart beat so fast that for a moment it seemed to suffocate her. A dancing haze obscured her vision. It cleared away just in time to let her see the train pull up, and the passengers leap out on to the platform. She scanned their faces narrowly, eagerly. Was this Duncan in the grey-checked suit and the brown pot hat ? A little way off she made sure it was he, but on drawing nearer the illusion vanished. Further on, perhaps, she might find him, and she walked the full length of the platform. Then she pushed her way back to the luggage van, and stared with hungry eyes at the young men clustering round. Where was Duncan ? She looked in vain for his sandy head with its homely Scotch features. A sickening sensation of terror stole over her. A flood of despair swept sharply through her whole being. The reaction was great, and totally unexpected, for she had trusted him too implicitly to dream of his proving fickle. Even now she thrust the idea from her in horror. She, who was incapable of change, could not credit any alteration of feeling in him. Yet such things were. She had read of them in books. Other women had trusted and been deceived, loved and been forsaken.

Scarce knowing what she did, she leant against an iron column for support, whilst the rain dripped down upon her from a hole in the glass dome overhead. Her limbs trembled ; a sudden mental paralysis benumbed her brain. She no longer felt capable of thought or action. The blow had fallen with such stunning force that it prostrated every faculty. Like a person recovering from the effects of chloroform, she asked herself, " Is this reality, or only a bad—bad dream ? " And yet, all the time she knew that it was no dream, but the hideous truth. Duncan had failed to keep his word. Nothing could soften that fact. As long as she lived she should never forget the pang occasioned by this bitter disappointment. No subsequent joy would ever altogether atone for the total overthrow of her hopes. One by one the passengers bustled off, leaving her alone in her misery. A porter passed, who, struck by the suffering expression of her white face, stopped, eyed her curiously, and said, with gruff sympathy, "Anything I can do for you, miss?" The sound of his voice restored her to a sense of her surroundings. Reason began to reassert itself. What a fool she had been, to be sure! When she came to think the matter over there were so many things which might account for Duncan's non-arrival. He might have missed his train; his father or mother might have fallen ill; he might even—for he was always careless—have made a mistake in the day. Perhaps he fancied the "rendezvous" was the 27th instead of the 26th. That could easily be. Whilst she was going through tortures here, a telegram with some explanation was very likely awaiting her at home. It was quite possible that Duncan had not sent it off soon enough. She laughed hysterically.

"Anything the matter, miss?" inquired the porter, who did not like her manner.

"Nothing, thanks," she faltered in return. "I—I was expecting a—a friend. Perhaps you can—tell me when the next train is due from town."

The man walked to a wall where the time-tables were posted up, and returned with the desired information.

"There ain't another fast train from London, miss, till 7.30," he said.

Bligh gave a groan. It was now only a little past three, and she could not loiter about the station for four hours and a half. There was nothing for it but to accept the common lot of women, and wait.

Mechanically she went back into the cloak-room, and took up her waterproof and umbrella. How dark and dismal everything seemed to have turned all of a sudden. The pattering rain descended to the earth with a steady, monotonous sound. As she toiled dejectedly homewards the wet mud splashed about her ankles, and the weight of her draggled petticoats grew more and more insupportable. All the way back she kept trying to think of reasons which might have prevented Duncan from keeping his promise. Suddenly a thought occurred to her which sent an icy chill travelling through her veins. Could it be that he was dead? Ah! no, not dead—not dead. She felt then that she could bear silence, injury, desertion—anything, rather than death. She trudged on and on, dimly conscious of an overpowering fatigue to which her whole frame succumbed. Mrs. Burton sat at her bedroom window. It commanded a view of the road.

Far off she spied the solitary little figure, battling wearily with the wind and the rain. There was an unspeakable wretchedness about Bligh's aspect which revealed all to the fond mother. With dismay and compassion she ran downstairs, and opened the front door. No need to ask any questions. One look at the girl's poor, quivering face was enough. It made the mother's heart bleed to see its woe-begone expression. The responsibility of having brought a living child into the world only to suffer almost overwhelmed her.

"Is—is there a telegram for me?" Bligh asked drearily, and in a dull, strange voice.

Mrs. Burton shook her head, and tried to smile; but it was useless attempting to appear cheerful.

"Oh! Bligh," she said, "what is the matter?"

"D—Duncan has not—come."

"Not come, darling?"

"No. I waited until all the passengers had left the train, and—and he was not there." Then, unable any longer to control her grief, Bligh burst into a passion of tears and rushed upstairs, feeling she could not stand being cross-examined, no matter how kindly or gently. Her wound was yet too new to bear probing.

The wise mother did not seek to follow her. She knew that there are some sorrows which can only be borne alone, and whose first poignancy even sympathy cannot soften. The tears stood in her sweet eyes as she watched the girl disappear. She, too, was possessed by a presentiment of evil. The sight of Bligh's pathetic little face, the tone of her voice, when she sadly said "Duncan has not come," were exquisitely painful. She would willingly have given her life to secure the happiness of this dear only daughter. And now, instinct told her it was all shattered at a blow, for the lover who proves faithless once can never be trusted again with the same trust as before.

The hours went by. Day faded into twilight, twilight turned to night, and the anxious parents sat together almost in silence, not daring to disturb the seclusion of their child. At last, Mrs. Burton could endure the tension no longer.

"I must go and see what has become of Bligh," she said to her husband.

"Aye, do," he responded. "The foolish girl takes it too much to heart. Duncan always was a free and easy, forgetful sort of fellow. As likely as not he'll turn up to-morrow, just as if he had never been expected to-day."

"Let us hope so, for Bligh's sake," answered Mrs. Burton, not very sanguinely.

She stole upstairs, and tapped softly at her daughter's door, which was locked.

"Bligh," she called out. "Bligh, my dear child, let me come in."

Silence followed this request; then, slowly, the key creaked in the keyhole, and the door was opened.

Bligh stood on the threshold, still clad in her wet walking garments, with her hat pushed back, and her soft brown hair hanging in damp wisps about her face. Her eyes were red with weeping. She averted them quickly, so that the light from her mother's candle should not reveal the full extent of her sufferings.

"My darling," said Mrs. Burton, tenderly, "do not grieve so. Very likely it is all a mistake."

Bligh shook her head despondently.

"No, mother," she said. "My heart tells me differently. If I had been in Duncan's place I could not have acted as he has done. He has got tired of me, and repents of our engagement. That is why he has not kept his promise."

"Nonsense, child. We shall get a letter by to-morrow's post, and then you will have to apologise to Duncan for all the foolish things you have said and thought about him. Come, cheer up."

The kind tone, the gentle voice, the compassionate look which accompanied these words, went straight to Bligh's heart. She flung her arms round her mother's neck.

"Mother," she cried. "Mother, darling, how selfish I am to think so much of myself when I have got you. There!" and she dried her eyes and tried to smile. "Whatever happens I must not worry you with my troubles."

"Who is so fit to share them?" murmured Mrs. Burton, kissing Bligh's tear-stained face.

And then these two fond, foolish women began to cry again in each other's arms, although they had just made up their minds that there was nothing to cry about, and matters would no doubt come right if only they exercised a little patience, and forced themselves to look at the bright, rather than the gloomy side of things. They kissed and wept, feeling that whatever ill the future might contain they were very dear to one another, and could not be wholly unhappy so long as they were together.

And the sullen clouds lifted, the angry wind dropped, the rain ceased, and after the dismal day the silvery moon shone out clear and bright. Her rays falling on the wet earth made it gleam as a mirror, in which the stars were reflected like points of steel.

Oh! weak tears and brave hearts, let no one scoff at thee, least of all those who cause the former to flow, the latter to hide their wounds behind the grey and Quaker garb of duty.

***

CHAPTER VII.

FIGHTING THE FIGHT.

Two days of torturing suspense followed. Every sound, every ring at the door, brought the colour rushing in a hot wave to Bligh's cheek. She was restless and nervous. The little commonplace round of daily duty seemed suddenly to have become almost insupportable. It was terrible work going into the kitchen, arranging meals with the cook, and minutely inspecting the mutton bone left from yesterday's dinner, when her mind was preoccupied with Duncan. It required a stupendous effort to talk of Irish stews and rice puddings whilst every thought was given to him. Nothing but long habit enabled her to get through the ordeal without a total collapse. For in her present state the sordid details of housekeeping on nothing a year were simply loathsome. The young person who reigned over the culinary department appeared more full of wants and complaints than usual, and less capable of relying on the somewhat limited stock of brains with which Nature had endowed her. Every morning when Bligh descended to the lower regions she began, " Please, Miss, we're out of coals. Please, Miss, the b'iler's gone wrong. Please, Miss, the But-cher 'as not called. What am I to do ? " etc., etc. Bligh had to soothe and pacify and devise. In an ordinary way she was accustomed to an undercurrent of grumbling running through the establishment. When people are poor it is an experience they have to put up with ; but just now it irritated her nervous system and taxed her patience well-nigh beyond endurance.

She had a longing to get away from home cares for a time, and to go to fresh scenes and surroundings, where she should not be constantly reminded of her love. But this she knew was impossible. The household could not dispense with her services. Her father was rapidly becoming a confirmed invalid, and her mother's health had also shown symptoms of giving way latterly. Luckily, or unluckily, for herself she was essential to both parents, and could not afford to indulge in any selfish whims. So she went about as usual, conscientiously striving to perform her accustomed duties, in spite of the dull, heavy pain that incessantly weighted her heart. But the strain was too great, and on the evening of the second day she broke down. She was hot and feverish, and complained of shooting fires in her head which made it throb with an unendurable violence. After a restless night, when the morning came Mrs. Burton insisted on her breakfasting upstairs.

" Give way a little, Bligh dear," she said. " It will be better for you in the end, and your father and I quite understand."

Bligh looked at her mother with piteous eyes.

" Don't you think it very strange that he has not written ? " she asked.

" Yes, darling, very ; but the post is late. Perhaps we may hear to-day."

" Only bad news," said Bligh, with an uncontrollable burst of sorrow. " It can only be bad news. Good would never have been so long in coming. Oh ! mother, are all men false ? "

" Not all, but many. It often seems that where they are concerned change is the law of Nature. One wonders why women pin their faith to such unstable creatures. And now I must go down to your father. He will be waiting for his breakfast, and I will send you up yours."

" I don't want any," said the girl, who, in the last four and twenty hours, had begun to experience a strange distaste for food.

" Bligh, dear, do eat something if you can, if only to please me."

" Very well, then," resignedly. " I'll try, but I'm not hungry."

Whilst Captain and Mrs. Burton were sitting at breakfast the postman came. Shortly afterwards a maid-servant entered the room bearing a letter addressed to Bligh in a strange handwriting. On inspection a Scottish postmark revealed itself.

" It is from Lord Kirkwall," exclaimed Mrs. Burton. " I feel sure that it is. Oh ! what can he have to say to Bligh ? " And in her excitement she allowed the water from the urn to run over the teapot.

Captain Burton put down the cup which he was in the act of raising to his mouth.

" Nothing very pleasant, I am afraid," he said. " I have always distrusted his lordship ever since that impertinent letter he wrote me when Duncan proposed to Bligh ; just as if you and I had been setting a regular trap to catch him. I wish to goodness that young cub of his had never come near the place, for my belief is he has pretty well broken the child's heart. I never saw anyone so changed in the last few days."

" Bligh will have heard the postman's ring, and she is very anxious for news," said Mrs. Burton. " If you don't mind,

William, I'll just run upstairs and give her her letter. I'll be back in a minute."

" Don't trouble about me," responded the captain, in spite of paternal anxiety, applying himself to his breakfast with an undiminished appetite. " If you push the toast and the butter this way I shall be all right."

Mrs. Burton at once carried off the letter, and placed it in her daughter's hands without a word. Indeed, she did not know what to say. She dared not raise her hopes by giving vent to any favourable prognostications.

Bligh glanced eagerly at the superscription, and the light that had momentarily illumined her face died out of it.

" A letter," she said, listlessly. " Who is it from ? "

" I fancy it is from Lord Kirkwall," rejoined Mrs. Burton, trying to suppress her growing excitement.

The colour flew to Bligh's cheeks, dying neck, ears, and brow crimson.

" Lord Kirkwall ! " she exclaimed, tremulously. " Oh ! mother, read it. I have not the courage."

Thus bidden, Mrs. Burton tore open the envelope, and in a voice almost as unsteady as her daughter's, read the following :—

" DEAR MISS BURTON,—In my son's name I owe you a thousand apologies. I only discovered yesterday that in an unguarded moment he had foolishly made an appointment to meet you on the 26th of this month, which promise he was not in a position to keep, owing to altered circumstances. A year ago both you and he were very young—too young to know your own minds, as is evident from the change which has taken place in Duncan's. He now sees, as clearly as I do, the folly of committing an early and imprudent marriage. Pray forgive my plain speaking ; but in cases such as these the truth often saves much subsequent unpleasantness. It is for this reason that I am writing to you instead of my son, who, however, is quite aware of the step I have taken. If, like him, you have learnt wisdom in the last few months there remains but little to be said. On the other hand, should this unfortunately not be so, and you still cling to memories of the past, I can only repeat my profound regrets and apologies for the pain which, in his thoughtlessness, my son may have caused you.—Believe me to remain, dear Miss Burton.   Sincerely yours,

" KIRKWALL."

The letter dropped from Mrs. Burton's hands. Its cold, heartless tone made her tingle with indignation. It confirmed her worst fears. Nothing could be more deplorable than this, or more galling to a high-spirited girl's pride.   For a few seconds she positively dared not look at Bligh.   Duncan's treachery, and his cowardly, contemptible way of getting out of the engagement, scarcely troubled her thoughts in comparison with her daughter's unhappiness.   The slight, the insult, these were what she felt most keenly.

From under the bedclothes there came the sound of smothered sobs.   Lord Kirkwall's letter contained no news to Bligh. From the first her heart had foretold its contents.   Forsaken— jilted, it seemed to her as if never again could she hold up her head.

"Mother," she faltered, after a long and painful silence, "I —knew how it was.   D—don't pity me please.   I c—can't bear pity even from you."

"Oh! my darling, my darling," cried Mrs. Burton, distracted at seeing her child's anguish, "is there nothing I can do for you?"

"Nothing," answered Bligh, drearily, "except to leave me to myself."

"We needn't talk, dear, if you would rather keep quiet, only just let me sit in the room with you, so that you may feel there is someone near."

"Mother," said Bligh, with a pathetic quivering of the lips, "don't think me ungrateful or insensible to your kindness, but I want to be alone—quite alone for a while."   Then she gave a wan smile, and added, "I understand now the longing of dumb creatures for solitude when they are mortally wounded."   These words stabbed Mrs. Burton to the heart.

"As you will," she said, in subdued tones, stealing towards the door like a culprit.   Then she paused, and taking courage, added, "Bligh, dearest, listen to my advice and don't shut yourself up too long.   A grief is always worse when unshared, and I"—breaking down—"I do so feel for you and love you."

How Bligh spent the long, weary hours that followed must for ever remain a secret between the girl and her Maker. Towards evening, when the glaring sun had sunk to rest, and the garish day faded into twilight, she dressed herself, and crept downstairs.   Her eyes shone with a feverish radiance, whilst on her cheeks burnt a fierce, unnatural colour.   When she entered their sitting-room, her parents watched her movements with a kind of morbid dread, as if they feared what she was about to do or say.   They need not have been afraid.   Bligh was fashioned of the stuff of which heroines are made.

"Father, mother," she began in a trembling voice, which grew stronger as she went on.   "I want to say something to you

—I have been thinking this matter over. It will be better not to discuss it more than is absolutely necessary, for the simple reason that there is nothing to be done. Only don't blame Duncan. After all, it was not so very wonderful that his feelings should have changed. I am not pretty—I have no fortune, in short, nothing particular to recommend me. I ought to have seen this before, only my eyes were blinded by happiness. And now I see something else. I see that you want me more than ever Duncan could, and so, instead of bemoaning my fate, I am going to try to be brave—not to bother you with my troubles, or make your home gloomy. Dear father, dear mother," she continued, holding out a hand to each, "it is not always easy to stick to one's good resolutions. You will bear with me sometimes, won't you, and help me on?"

Before either Captain or Mrs. Burton could make any answer to this affecting speech, a violent shudder ran through Bligh's frame, she uttered an inarticulate cry, and fell fainting to the ground. The strain which she imposed on her overwrought nervous system was greater than it could bear, and for the moment the shock she had received triumphed over the girl's gallant spirit. The next day she was tossing about in bed with brain fever, and for weeks her life was despaired of. Her cheeks grew thin and hollow, the blue veins showed with startling transparency on her temples, and the pretty brown hair which constituted her chief beauty had all to be shorn off. She looked a ghost of her former self.

But she did not die. She was too strong to sink beneath the first stroke of misfortune, and gradually a changed, quiet, sober Bligh was given back to life. One by one, she took up her former occupations, with feeble health but indomitable courage. The delirium of fever gone, Duncan's name did not once pass her lips. She never complained, never indulged in weak self-pity; only her smile grew rarer, her manner staider and more sedate.

This affair seemed entirely to have crushed out all the aspirations natural to her age. She only wanted to be left quiet, and allowed to get over her hurt in her own way. As for men and marriage, she no longer cared for either, or thought of them in connection with herself. In the years that ensued, she had several fairly good proposals, for her reputation as a daughter enhanced her value as a wife, but she declined them firmly. It was as if the one great disappointment of her youth had forever destroyed her belief in the male sex. She treated them with politeness, but indifference, and never made the smallest effort to attract their attention. Perhaps that was why the better class of men cherished a peculiar regard for

Miss Bligh Burton. which their female belongings could not understand, and secretly resented.

"Such a dowdy, insignificant little girl," they would say. "What on earth do you see in her to admire?"

In these days the hours which Bligh did not devote to her parents, and the management of the household. were given to study. She read a great deal: principally works of philosophy. science, and theology. and set to work systematically to improve her mind, rather with a view to banish thought than from any ulterior motive. Music proved a consolation and delight. Mrs. Burton. who had been a fine vocalist. derived much pleasure from the training of her daughter's voice—a powerful mezzo soprano. very pure in quality. By the time she had attained her twenty-fifth year. Bligh had developed into a thoroughly accomplished woman. capable of playing a sonata. or of cooking a dinner. discussing the most vital questions of the day with almost a man's breadth of comprehension, or of cutting out and tacking a gown.

Every now and then. when some emergency arose which rendered her vaguely conscious of the power and ability slowly strengthening within her. and which were the natural outcome of energy and brains. added to sorrow well borne, she would give a melancholy smile. and say to herself, "This is better than being a coward—better than making my grief a source of misery to others. especially those who are nearest and dearest to me. If people honestly endeavour to help themselves. in course of time God grants compensation." But then again there were other moments. when in the secret agony of her soul. she would exclaim—

"Ah! what is it all worth? What does it amount to in comparison with being loved? Knowledge is a magnificent possession. but it can never equal happiness. The latter contents. but the other only creates a perpetual craving to unravel the mysteries of the universe. It is a striving and striving. and an ending in nothing. Ah! Duncan, why did you forsake me. or having forsaken. why cannot I forget you?" Then the hot tears came gushing to her eyes. and the fight had to be fought all over again.

But in spite of bad quarters of an hour, and many a sleepless night, Bligh struggled on. ever on, steadily keeping the same goal in view. In her darkest moments she never lost sight of it. From the first she had laid down two fixed rules. She would try to do her duty, and to improve. She would not sink in the slough of despondency, but battle her way inch by inch to the shore. For cowardice in any shape or form she entertained a supreme contempt. When she read works of fiction, all her sympathies were with the brave, strong women who did not give in. She never could bring herself to admire the weak, plastic type. But the tension was great—too great to be altogether natural. Her mother, looking at her with a kind of reverential awe, often wondered how long Bligh would go on without breaking down. As for Captain Burton, he believed that Duncan was totally forgotten.

So Bligh fought for victory. Wherein she succeeded, and wherein she failed, it will be for the reader to judge.

CHAPTER VIII.

A LITERARY ASPIRANT.

As the years passed they brought trouble to the Burton establishment. The head master obtained a better appointment and left; his assistant married and set up for himself. Pupils became scarce, and Captain Burton no longer found it as easy as formerly to obtain recruits. It had got about that he was in bad health, and incapable of personally attending to business. The loss of his connection was, however, softened by the zest with which he entered into a fresh pursuit. It was one which for some time past had held out a captivating vista of success to his exuberant fancy.

To be brief, he commenced a book on military tactics. In it he pointed out a method which, by a very small additional expenditure, would materially increase the defences of the country, rendering London in particular quite safe from an enemy's attack. His brain had long been full of this interesting scheme, to the detriment—it must be confessed—of his youthful scholars. He was tired of teaching, and turned to literature as a relief, believing that up till now he had missed his vocation, and only just discovered where his real talent lay.

Bligh helped her father in his labours, and indeed may be said to have written the greater portion of the work. When finished, it was placed in the hands of a London publisher, and then followed a period of consuming anxiety, during which the author could neither eat, rest, nor sleep, and spent the majority of his time at the post-office. Would or would not the book be accepted? That was the burning question of the hour. Every other paled before it.

Fortunately for Captain Burton, the times were favourable to the introduction of military subjects, for the national mind was just beginning to wake up to the importance of the national safety.

After a whole month had elapsed, there at length came a letter from Messrs. Fiddler and Flumm, stating that they were prepared to undertake the publication of "How to Defend Ourselves at an Insignificant Cost" on the following conditions, which they assured Captain Burton was their usual way of doing business with authors whose names were not known to the world, and which he would find most advantageous. He was to pay a sum down of one hundred pounds towards the expenses. These would ultimately be defrayed from the proceeds, and the deposit was merely a formal arrangement against contracting bad debts. They further agreed to bring out an edition of one thousand copies to be sold at five shillings and sixpence each, less trade discounts, the profits to be divided in equal moieties between the author and the publisher, and an account to be rendered at the end of six months, on the 1st of January and on the 1st of July.

When Captain Burton received this communication he was in ecstacy. Everything seemed fair sailing now. The road to fame lay before him, and he had only to gallop along it. On more mature consideration, however, his joy became slightly damped at being requested to furnish a hundred pounds in advance. It was all very well to console himself with the thought, " Oh I shall get it all back again out of my book," but he did not happen to have so large a sum of ready money on which he could lay his hands at a moment's notice. It was only to be obtained in one way—namely, by borrowing at a high rate of interest. The family were taken into council, and the trio talked matters over in all their bearings. They were unanimous in deciding that the book must be published at any cost. Bligh perhaps was less enthusiastic than her father and mother, but then she was younger, and therefore naturally not so good a judge of high class literature as the elders. Nevertheless she was of the opinion that the money should be found, and the publishers' terms complied with.

" We think a great deal of this hundred pounds," said Captain Burton, whose nature was exceedingly sanguine, " but after all, it's only lending it to oneself. When the book comes out, I'm bound to get it paid back. There's not the least risk. Of that I feel sure."

Then Bligh came forward, and to the surprise of both parents, stated that out of the very small sum allowed her weekly for housekeeping expenses, she had managed to put by fifty pounds in the last five years, which now were entirely at the author's service. She produced her hoard triumphantly, being more than rewarded for its loss by her father's gratitude and delight. Mrs. Burton would not be outdone in generosity. She sold the few jewels she possessed, and contributed twenty pounds to the fund. There only remained thirty to raise, and through the kindness of private friends this was accomplished without having recourse to gentlemen of the Israelitish persuasion. The agreement between Captain Burton and Messrs. Fiddler and Flumm was duly signed, and after a while the first proofs were despatched.

Who shall describe the author's rapture at seeing his name in print. Even the vanity of the most modest man is tickled by the spectacle of his cherished periods set up in type. They possess an indescribable fascination, which induces the writer to gaze at them with almost paternal tenderness. In public he may pretend to be indifferent, but in private he never wearies of staring at his proofs, and reading his pet passages over and over again. Captain Burton pored over them until he must have known every word by heart. He could not bear those long, inconvenient strips of paper out of his sight. He ate with them, he slept with them. If anybody happened to call he alluded with pride to his occupation. All the neighbourhood knew that he was bringing out the smartest, cleverest, most invaluable book on national defence that had ever been produced. He opened a private subscription list, and cunningly induced his acquaintances to put their names down for copies almost before they knew what they were about. In short, if he had worked half as hard at cramming as he did to ensure the success of the great work, his fortune must have been made. As for the proofs—they were corrected and recorrected until the poor man's head felt quite in a muddle. He kept inserting fine, long-sounding words instead of short ones, whilst impressing upon Bligh all the time that the great thing for every young author to aim at was terseness and simplicity of style. Yet he continued to add so many flourishes to his sentences that they stood in danger of becoming all flourish and no sense. Luckily Bligh kept her head, and after arguments which often lasted several days, pruned down the fertile aftergrowth of her father's imagination, in spite of much indignant opposition on his part. She always would stick to the meaning, and ruthlessly sacrificed ornamentation.

" People like to understand what they read," she said. " It is always safer to assume that one's public is stupid rather than clever."

There was no getting her to budge from this standpoint, and Captain Burton had to submit to seeing many of his very choicest, and grandest adjectives struck out. It was a great blow, and doubtless authors will sympathise with him.

For instance, Bligh would take up the proofs and read, " The enemy began scaling the heights——"

“Don’t you think,” interrupted Captain Burton, “that scaling is rather a common word ? ”

“No, father, it does not strike me as being so.”

“What would you say to ascending the heights, Bligh, or encompassing the heights. Encompassing sounds well, and to my mind lends importance to the action.”

“We will stick to scaling,” Bligh answered, in her quiet, determined way. “It’s better English. Why,” she continued, “what have you here ? An officer’s enfolding panoply ! What does that mean ? ”

“A tent, Bligh, a tent,” he exclaimed, half proudly, half apologetically.

“Then we had better call it by its right name,” she replied, running her pen through the enfolding panoply.

However, at last the proofs were all finished, though never had the father and daughter come so near to quarrelling as during the process of correction. The book made its appearance, and the moment proved propitious. A Conservative Government had just asked for a large grant of money towards the army and navy, and the Liberals—as customary, when any question of expenditure is under discussion—had placed themselves in active opposition. Public opinion, however, supported the Tories, and “How to Defend Ourselves at an Insignificant Cost,” partly owing to a taking title, and partly owing to some intrinsic merit, went off well. The reviews did it good service. By the virulence of their criticisms they aroused the popular curiosity. They created a demand for the book, and the first edition was quickly sold out. A second and a third were called for. When Captain Burton ran up to town, and looked in at Messrs. Fiddler and Flumm’s office, he was received with a politeness and an urbanity that were simply delightful. Nothing could exceed Mr. Fiddler’s courtesy. He treated the captain as if he were his bosom friend, and then proceeded to sound him gently as to whether he were writing another book.

On the strength of his success our author decided to give up coaching altogether, more especially as coaching had long shown symptoms of giving him up. He determined to devote the remainder of his days to the engrossing and, he confidently hoped, the lucrative profession of literature, for which, as before stated, he felt himself specially adapted. Bligh prudently hinted that it might be as well to await the accounts before taking so decisive a step; but her advice was summarily pooh-poohed. “So many thousand copies at five and sixpence were bound to realise a handsome sum. ‘How to Defend Ourselves at an Insignificant Cost’ was certain to go on selling. It would prove as good as an annuity, and hi- ‘... :s, so startling, so original, that when they appeared in print they would bring in a considerable income." Thus Captain Burton reasoned, buoyed up by hope and the small measure of fame to which he had attained through one successful publication. He believed that his name and his fortune were both made.

To cut a long story short, " How to Defend Ourselves " was responsible for most of the misfortunes which subsequently befell the Burtons. It reduced them from a state of comparative security to one of poverty and hazard. To begin with, the accounts, when rendered after repeated requests, proved a bitter disappointment. In spite of three editions sold, Messrs. Fiddler and Flumm had so contrived to add up costs, advertisements, gift books, trade discounts, 225 copies sold as 208, 104 as 96, publishers' commission, and one thing and another, that there remained next to nothing to divide. The profits melted—positively melted away, and the only satisfaction the author had was a melancholy conviction that there was something wrong somewhere. But what that something was precisely, or where, he was powerless to point out, and had, therefore, to content himself with the glory and none of the remuneration. He might have his suspicions as to whether Messrs. Fiddler and Flumm were not more fortunate than the writer, but he possessed no means of verifying them. By this time Captain Burton was deep in his great novel, entitled " The Pharisee and the Sadducee," and it prevented him from dwelling too much on the pecuniary fiasco. His mind seethed with incident, and refused any longer to dwell on commonplace objects.

Henceforth, Mrs. Burton and Bligh were doomed all day and every day to hear " The Pharisee " talked of. It became the one topic of conversation, for his absorption rendered him egotistical, and to a great extent blunted his perceptions. When he was at work nobody was allowed to make the least sound throughout the house, for fear of checking his inspiration. Bligh could no longer play or sing as formerly. " The Pharisee " did not progress very fast. " The Pharisee " was made an excuse that shielded Captain Burton from everything he didn't like. If any stupid visitor called he could not possibly see him, he was engaged on " The Pharisee ; " if a creditor appeared inconveniently he retired to his room with " The Pharisee," and left his wife and daughter to bear the brunt of the battle. This important work of fiction upset all the household. It rendered meals unpunctual, destroyed order and regularity. Its author grew more and more erratic, preoccupied, and cantankerous. When his ideas did not flow readily—and, poor man, they often seemed defective —he got cross, or else uncomfortably depressed. His moods became painfully uncertain, and his female belongings bitterly regretted the day when he had abandoned coaching for literature.

The two women were admirably patient. They discussed "The Pharisee" with unflagging vivacity, and admired the various developments of its plot and characters. Mrs. Burton believed implicitly in her husband's genius and it seemed perfectly natural to her that all things in the household should be made subservient to it. She waited assiduously upon the accomplished man of letters, whom she was proud to call her better half. She shielded him with almost motherly care from every worldly element likely to exercise a pernicious effect on his pen, and avoided any allusion to the unsatisfactory state of their finances, which invariably cast a shadow over his talent. He accepted all her wifely sacrifices calmly, and as if they were his due. In fact, as time went on, he made larger and larger calls on them.

At length, heralded by a great flourish of trumpets, "The Pharisee" was given to the world. Alas! the world proved singularly unappreciative. It declined to buy "The Pharisee," would not be coaxed into a good-humour by the Sadducee, and refused to have anything to do with either.

The book proved a dead failure in every sense of the word. Captain Burton sank beneath the disappointment. He had talked himself into the belief that his novel was quite equal to one of George Eliot's or Thackeray's. It is pleasant enough to pose as a genius before one's wife and daughter. To have the pedestal ruthlessly hewn away from one's feet, and suddenly to be brought in contact with the barren earth, no doubt is not an agreeable process.

About this period the unfortunate author was seized by a second attack of paralysis, which deprived his lower extremities of all motion and sensation. He lingered on for six months, and when the spirit moved him wrote now and again in a desultory fashion. He always kept up the illusion with his family that he was a great writer, and hinted in a variety of delicate ways that it was the common fate of all great writers not to be appreciated in their lifetime.

Bligh nursed her father devotedly. Everything that loving care and filial attention could do to relieve his condition she did. But each day Captain Burton grew feebler and feebler, more and more helpless. The paralysis was creeping up slowly, but surely. His legs began to swell, and he realised that the end was not far off. One evening Mrs. Burton retired early to rest, worn out by grief and anxiety. Bligh was left alone with the sick man, whom she believed to be dozing. Suddenly, he put out his hand, and beckoned for her to draw near.

"Bligh," he said faintly, "I feel as if I were dying. There is such a cold, dead weight at my heart."

"You want raising up in bed," she answered, trying to conceal her tears. "Put your arms round my neck and I will lift you. There!" arranging the pillows deftly. "Do you feel easier now?"

"Yes, a little; only it is so cold—so cold." He was silent for a few moments. Then a flickering colour rose to his cheek, and he added: "Bligh, before I go, I—I should like to tell you something."

"What is it, dear father?" she inquired, looking down at him with humid eyes.

"It is not easy for me to say it, but—but—the fact is, I never could have been a great author. It was not in me."

"Oh! never mind about that now," said Bligh, soothingly. "What does it matter?"

"Since I have been so ill," he went on, unheeding her words, "it has seemed to me that I must often have tried your patience sorely. My books absorbed me to the exclusion of everything else. I pretended to be a genius, and—I was a hypocrite," turning his head to the wall.

A pause ensued. The girl was too taken aback to make an immediate reply.

"Bligh," said the invalid, the flush on his cheek deepening, "I think you knew it. I am almost positive that you knew it."

"Well!" she said, seeing that he hung feverishly on her answer. "And if I did, what then? It never made any difference between us."

"You knew that I was an impostor, and yet you never said a word. You turned yourself into a slave, who, without a murmur, obeyed my every whim. I was often a hard taskmaster, Bligh. I took advantage of your goodness and unselfishness. I did not see this at the time—that's my only excuse; but I see it now quite clearly. Can you forgive?"

"Forgive!" she cried, flinging herself down by his bedside. "Oh! father, I have nothing to forgive. We all of us have our weaknesses. Yours was a very harmless one. It hurt nobody, and I was glad to be of service to you."

"You knew that I was a humbug all along," he repeated, with bitter self-condemnation, "and yet you never breathed the secret to a soul."

"Why should I?" she responded, bending forward and kissing his damp brow.

For a long time he lay quite quiet. His breathing was getting more and more difficult. Twice, thrice, she propped him up with extra pillows.

About midnight he raised himself on one elbow, and fixing his dim, sunken eyes on his daughter, said :—

"Bligh, you are a—wonderful girl. There are not—many—like you. Dear child!—don't ever tell—your mother. Let her b—believe in me to—to—the last."

And with these words still lingering on his lips he fell back into the cold arms of death, which for months past had been stretched out ready to receive him. They folded him in their chill embrace, and for ever quieted the unrest of existence.

Bligh never alluded to what had passed between them. She looked upon her father's dying confession as sacred. Because she had long since taken the measure of his literary pretensions that was no reason why she should not love him. Our dear ones are seldom faultless : perhaps they would not be so dear if they were. Nevertheless, she was glad that he had spoken, for, strive to disguise the truth as she might, there had been times when the thought would intrude. "You are a hypocrite, and a selfish one into the bargain." Now she could cherish his memory without a shadow rising up to dim the tenderness of her recollections. His humility had disarmed every unpleasant reminiscence.

She took a pair of scissors and reverently cut off a lock of the dead man's hair, which she pressed to her lips with filial fervour.

Ah ! how sad life was, how hard, even, when one tried to be brave. She was not the only person to find it so. He had suffered also, and his last words were words of excuse to his own daughter. His end struck her as very pathetic. It made a vivid impression.

She did not wish him back. He had suffered too much, and she had long ago realised that his continued existence was but a burden to himself and a pain to those who loved him best and most truly. She believed he was better dead than struggling, ever struggling, against the sharp pinch of poverty and disappointment. Then, all at once, her fortitude gave way, the weariness of living flooded her spirit with a great wave of anguish, and she cried aloud, " Ah ! why didn't you take me with you ? Father, father, why did you not take me with you ? "

CHAPTER IX.

THE PINCH OF POVERTY.

WHEN the widow and daughter came to look into the affairs of the deceased, they found them in a most deplorable condition. A few hundred pounds laid by during comparatively prosperous years represented his entire fortune. Although Captain Burton had often talked of "insuring his life," it now appeared that he had failed to do so. Consequently, a difficult problem stared Mrs. Burton and Bligh in the face. How were they to live? The elder lady, as soon as she had recovered from the shock of being parted from one with whom she had dwelt on terms of close companionship for over thirty years, discussed the matter continually, but without being able to arrive at any practical solution. Her health was so bad that she felt herself unfit for active employment, and her inability to earn a livelihood fretted her sorely, in spite of Bligh's assurances that she was quite capable of working for both. Indeed, the girl was but too sadly aware that she must depend on her own exertions, since her mother's delicacy increased daily, and with alarming rapidity. An immediate change was necessary. They could not afford to remain where they were.

They left the comfortable home which they had inhabited for so many years, and rented a tiny cottage in the village, formerly occupied by a sporting pupil's groom. It was a mite of a place, but large enough for their present requirements. The servants were all dismissed save one, a devoted creature who had been Bligh's nurse, and who vowed that she would rather receive no wages than be parted from her beloved young mistress. The faithful soul, whose name was Deborah, undertook to cook, wash, scrub, and superintend the entire establishment, so as to leave Bligh free to pursue the difficult profession of money-making. The girl now reaped the reward of her studies and of having cultivated those natural abilities with which Providence had endowed her. Long ago she had acquired a considerable reputation in the neighbourhood as an accomplished vocalist and musician. It was acknowledged that she possessed two great merits. When asked to perform she never made a fuss, but complied cheerfully and readily with the request, and, unlike a certain proportion of amateurs, who are so charmed with their own music that once they begin they go on *ad infinitum*, she always knew when to leave off. The consequence was she rendered herself very popular at small parties, and, when trouble came, several ladies with whom she was on friendly terms at once stepped forward and promised to assist her by sending their daughters for lessons.

By degrees Bligh got quite a connection, and was so busy that she scarcely had a minute's leisure during the day. If only Mrs. Burton had been strong they could have managed very fairly well, but her continued ill-health proved a source of great expense. As time went on Bligh became convinced that her mother ought to have better medical advice than was obtainable in the village. But how to get it ? They could not afford the journey up to town or to hang about the anterooms of celebrated physicians. Their means were too limited to allow of the smallest additional expenditure.

One day Bligh happened to mention her growing anxiety respecting Mrs. Burton to Mrs. Lomer, a lady whose little girls she taught, and who was one of her kindest friends. " I do not know what to do," she said, sadly. " Mother gets worse every day before my eyes, and I feel myself powerless to obtain a thoroughly good opinion on which I can rely. Yet something ought to be done. She should not be allowed to go on as she is doing. Doctor Jones is very kind ; nobody could be kinder. He constantly sends round medicines and refuses to make any charge for them ; but, all the same, I am positive he does not understand the case, and that, owing to some cause or other, it is beyond him."

" Oh ! " exclaimed Mrs. Lomer. " I am so glad you mentioned the matter to me, for I really do believe I can help you. My brother is one of the first surgeons in town. Perhaps you may have heard his name—Neal Donnington, and as good luck will have it he is coming to spend a few days with me next week. I'll tell you what I'll do. I'll bring him over in a friendly way, and get him to see your mother professionally. He is an extraordinarily kind-hearted man. I think the knowledge of what suffering goes on in the world renders him more than commonly sympathetic, and I know he will tell you honestly what ails Mrs. Burton, and without putting you to any expense."

Bligh was profuse in her thanks, and looked forward eagerly to the eminent surgeon's arrival. He came, on the very day that Sir Philip Verschoyle proposed to Miss Blanche Sylvester, who, in spite of her love, distrusted him too much to surrender herself into his keeping.

Mr. Neal Donnington was a tall, spare man, with quick eyes, straight-cut features, and hair just beginning to grizzle. He might have been between forty and fifty years of age. The expression of his face was both intelligent and kindly. Bligh liked him at first sight, and felt a sense of confidence in him, such as not many members of the male sex had hitherto inspired.

" It is so good of you to come in this sort of way," she said, after Mrs. Lomer had introduced them to each other. " I scarcely know how to thank you enough."

" My sister has been telling me something of your history," he responded, with a grave respect, which sent a little thrill of pleasure through Bligh's veins. " I am truly pleased to be of service to you, Miss Burton. Is your mother too ill to leave her room ? "

" She happens to be particularly unwell to-day, and I persuaded her to stay upstairs."

" I will visit her there then," said Mr. Donnington.

Bligh accompanied him to Mrs. Burton's apartment, and returned in order to keep Mrs. Lomer company. They chatted away for a considerable time, though the girl was evidently pre-occupied. At length, as her brother remained with the sick woman longer than Mrs. Lomer had anticipated, that lady rose to go, saying, " My husband has run up to London for the day, and I promised to meet him at the station. Will you tell Neal that I have walked on ? "

Scarcely had she gone when Mr. Donnington re-entered the sitting-room, in which Bligh had given many a weary lesson to dull, unintelligent pupils. She ran towards him. The expression of his face had changed. It was kindly still, but very grave. Instinctively her heart sank as their eyes met. There was a pitying look in his, which brought a lump to her throat and made her white linen collar feel like an iron band.

" Where is my sister ? " he inquired.

" Mrs. Lomer has just left in order to meet her husband at the station," she responded faintly, feeling as if some terrible blow were about to strike her.

" Ah ! well," he said, sinking into an arm-chair. " I should like to have a little talk with you alone." Then he glanced at his companion, as if taking her measure, and added, " I fear, my dear Miss Burton, that your mother is in a very serious condition."

Bligh clasped her hands tightly together, and she was conscious of a nervous quivering in the eyelids which refused to be suppressed.

" I—I—was afraid you would think so," she faltered in return.

" It would not be right of me," he continued, " to conceal from you the gravity of her state. Fortunately, she herself has not the least idea how grave it really is, and I would strongly recommend you to keep the knowledge from her."

"Oh! Mr. Donnington!" cried Bligh, turning pale. "You confirm my worst fears. Surely, surely, she is not in danger."

He remained silent, his eyes seeking the carpet.

"Can nothing be done to relieve her?" went on the girl, with growing agitation. "Is there no remedy which will restore her to health?"

He sighed and shook his head. Bligh's distress evidently touched him.

"An immediate operation might perhaps sa——" Then he checked himself suddenly, as if he had said more than he intended.

"Her life?" she broke in, in an agonised voice. "Oh! Mr. Donnington, tell me the truth. In Heaven's name conceal nothing from me. She is all I have—all that is left me in this wide, cruel world to love. I am strong—see," and she brushed the tears away and made a gallant effort to compose her twitching features. "I will be strong for my mother's sake. Don't treat me like an inexperienced girl. I am eight and twenty, and I might be a hundred from my feelings, for I have known what trouble is. But this suspense is more dreadful to bear than anything I have ever endured. In mercy end it, and tell me the name of the malady from which my poor darling is suffering. After all it is only a name. It cannot affect the fact or render me more miserable than I have been for weeks—months—past, seeing her fading and wasting beneath my eyes. Most girls have many people whom they love, but she is my all—my all."

"My dear young lady," said Mr. Donnington slowly, and with infinite compassion, "I hardly know whether to tell or withhold the truth. You say you are strong, but you do not look so."

"Oh! my appearance counts for nothing. Pray—pray tell me everything. I must—I will know the worst."

"Then," he said, in a curiously subdued tone, "it is a case of—cancer."

Bligh covered her face with her hands.

"Cancer!" she groaned. "Oh! good God, this surpasses my gravest fears. Can nothing—nothing save her?"

"An operation performed at once is the only hope I can hold out to you. No doubt it would prolong her life for a year or two. If the disease did not spread she might even recover; but cancer is generally in the blood, and absolute cures are, comparatively speaking, rare."

Bligh struggled hard to avoid breaking down.

"How much would an operation cost?" she asked hoarsely.

" A hundred pounds," he answered.   " That is the customary fee.   Will you excuse my putting a question ? "

" Certainly, Mr. Donnington."

" You are very poor, are you not ? "

" Yes," she said, without the smallest attempt at concealment. " We are about as poor as it is possible to be in our class of life."

" I understand.   My sister led me to infer as much.   Well, if you wished me to perform the operation I would accept a much smaller sum.   In fact, you should pay me at your leisure. Or, if you did not object to the idea, we might get Mrs. Burton into the Cancer Hospital, where I would attend her entirely free of charge.   By paying two guineas a week she can have a separate room, and not mix with the other patients."

Bligh rose to her feet, a prey to emotion which she no longer was able to conceal.

" Ah ! " she cried.   " I wish I could manage it.   I wish to goodness I could manage it."

" Are there still difficulties in the way ? " he inquired gently.

She remained silent for a moment, as if hesitating to bare her heart.   Then, taking courage from his evident sympathy, she said :—" Mr. Donnington, I will be quite frank with you.   You are very kind.   Don't think that I am insensible to your kindness ; but when my father died, rather more than a year ago, he left exactly three hundred pounds of ready money.   Out of this I had the doctor's bill and funeral expenses to pay, besides various long-standing debts.   After all claims were settled very little remained.   I have endeavoured to support myself and my mother by giving music lessons, but often it has been a desperate struggle to make two ends meet.   Since her illness, rightly or wrongly, I have pretended we are better off than is actually the case, so as to free her mind from worry.   Otherwise she would have deprived herself of sustenance.   The consequence is," she went on, blushing a guilty red, "instead of our having fifty pounds at the bank, as mother believes, at this moment we have not a farthing.   When the doctor here has ordered her to take little delicacies I could not let her go without them."   Bligh did not mention how she had trained herself to subsist on the smallest possible amount of food, and often went for days and never tasted meat.   All that was too natural to be talked of.

" Are you in debt ? " queried Mr. Donnington.

" No, not yet ; but—it is better to conceal nothing—at the present time I positively have not got money enough to take my mother up to London and place her in a hospital.   Latterly, I have kept all financial troubles from her, and have sought to make light of them, but—but—" and Bligh's voice trembled, "it has not been possible to do so without practising some deception. Do you blame me very much for it?"

There was something infinitely touching and pathetic in the way Bligh made the inquiry. Mr. Donnington felt strangely affected by the small, white, womanly face turned so humbly and piteously towards him.

"Blame you?" he exclaimed. "My poor, brave child, I honour and respect you, and in proof of it beg you as a favour to let me help you. I can very well afford a temporary loan," and he reddened in his turn, "even if your pride refuses a gift."

"The latter is out of the question," she said decidedly. "And, as for a loan, what means have I of repaying it?"

"Miss Burton, you are too proud. How should we ever get on in this world if we refused the assistance of our fellow-creatures?"

Mr. Donnington said this; nevertheless, in his heart he admired her for her independence.

"You don't understand!" rejoined Bligh. "If I saw the slightest chance of being able to pay back the debt it would be different; but there is none—absolutely none. I am paid three shillings and sixpence an hour for my lessons. Out of the proceeds we have to live, feed, dress, keep ourselves respectable, and pay one servant. If I lived to be a hundred I should never succeed in saving the necessary sum for the operation at this slow, monotonous drudgery."

It was the first complaint that had passed her lips. The first hint she had given as to how intolerable was her life.

Mr. Donnington looked at her. This little, pale girl, with the worn face, clear eyes, and soft brown hair, interested him. He vaguely realised that beneath her quiet exterior she possessed unusual force of character.

"I am going to be in this part of the world for another three or four days," he said. "I will think the matter over, and consider what is best to be done. Before I go you shall either see or hear from me. Meanwhile, don't lose heart, and, above everything, refrain from arousing your mother's suspicions as to her condition. It would only have an injurious effect upon her spirits."

Bligh bore his steady gaze unflinchingly.

"You can trust me," she answered, with a little catch in her voice.

"I feel sure that I can." So saying Mr. Donnington held out his hand, and pressing Bligh's warmly, wished her good-bye.

"Poor child!" he said to himself, as he walked homewards.

"She is not one of the common sort. She does not say much, or fall into hysterics. A body might fancy she was cold and reserved, unless he were a pretty good judge of human nature, but in reality she feels everything most desperately. Words go quivering right into her, and yet she hides their effect. How light she made of her own trials and privations, and how proudly she refused help from a stranger. These brave, independent women, who would rather work themselves into the grave than become objects of charity, make a man think well of their sex, in spite of its faults. I wonder what that girl's history will be in the future. According to my reading she will suffer through the heart and conquer by the head."

For some time after Mr. Donnington's departure, Bligh paced the room in mortal anguish. This fresh blow well nigh crushed her. She could not bring herself to contemplate the possibility of losing her mother, whom she loved with an absorbing love. But after a while the strength of mind which she had acquired during long years of inward struggle and control came to her aid. It would not do to give in selfishly to her grief, or allow the dear sufferer upstairs to imagine that Mr. Donnington's report had been unfavourable. He had specially enjoined caution, and whatever her anxieties she must keep them to herself. When the night came—when she was alone in her own room, then she would think over ways and means. At present her first duty was to prevent her mother from guessing that anything unusual had taken place.

Bligh resolutely forced a smile to her face, and, before it could fade, ran upstairs and entered the invalid's room.

Mrs. Burton was sitting in a large arm-chair, propped up by pillows. Her shoulders were covered by a woollen shawl which Bligh's nimble fingers had knitted during their rare hours of leisure. Her countenance wore an unhealthy, waxen hue. The skin was stretched tightly over the nose, and the cheeks were hollow. One could see, however, that in her youth she must have been a very beautiful woman. On perceiving Bligh she brightened up, as if the mere sight of the girl did her good.

"Well!" she said. "Has Mr. Donnington gone?"

"Yes, mother dear," answered Bligh, stooping down and kissing her on the forehead. "He has just left."

"He seemed a nice sort of man," observed Mrs. Burton, "and I should think very clever, for he appeared to understand my case perfectly. The only thing was he would not open up very much about it. His reticence rather disappointed me. Did he enter into particulars with you, Bligh?"

"Yes, more or less."

"Ah! I thought that he very likely would. These doctors

are all so afraid of frightening one, just as if I were nervous, and could not bear the truth. I hate secrecy where one's health is concerned. Come, child, tell me, what did Mr. Donnington say?"

Bligh averted her face, so that its expression should not tell any tales.

"He did not think you were very well, dear mother," she said, in quiet, constrained tones.

"No, of course not. I know that myself."

"He said I was to take great care of you, and that he would either write or call in the course of a few days."

"Really! How excessively kind! Does he think he can make me quite right again?"

Bligh's voice shook a little.

"He hopes so, darling; though perhaps a slight operation may be necessary."

"I shouldn't mind an operation," said the sick woman eagerly. "I shouldn't mind it a bit, if only I could get strong. It fidgets me to death to have to sit idly at home doing nothing, whilst you wear yourself out in the way you are doing."

"I am well, and it does not hurt me to work," answered Bligh.

"Perhaps not—in moderation. But you are often quite knocked up, though you never complain or make any fuss. And since we came here all your dresses have got too large for you, and your colour has almost completely gone."

"You forget that I am getting old," rejoined Bligh, with an attempt at playfulness, which contained a strong element of sadness. "When one is eight-and-twenty one can't expect to look as young as one did at eighteen. That is an ugly fact which most women have the pleasure of facing."

"Nonsense, child; I can't bear to hear you talking like that, just as if everything were over and done with. You are worn and fagged, owing to overwork, and then your thoughts take a morbid turn. Introduce a little sunshine and amusement into your life, and you would soon be a different creature."

Bligh stifled a sigh. Her mother was right. She knew it in her innermost consciousness, but she could not help asking herself where sunshine and amusement were likely to come from. The horizon presented a very lowering aspect. No light pierced through the clouds. Ten years ago the sun had set for Bligh. It had never shone since with the same generous warmth. There had always been a chill at her heart. The pain was gone. It had died out little by little, as also the hardness and the bitterness; but a feeling of numbness remained, which she was unable to conquer. Life no longer seemed a good gift of God, but a burden to be borne as patiently as might be.

"Now," resumed Mrs. Burton cheerfully, "if I could only get back my health sufficiently, so as to cease being a dead weight on you and contribute something towards my maintenance, I should be a thousand times easier in my mind."

"Mother, dearest," cried Bligh, kneeling down by her side, "don't ever talk of being a dead weight on me. To work for you is the one pleasure I have. It makes me so proud, so happy, to think that we can live comfortably on my earnings. All I want is to get you strong, for," and the moisture sprang to her eyes, "what should I do without you—what should I do without you?"

Mrs. Burton tremblingly put out her thin hand, and fondly rested it on the girl's head.

"Oh! Bligh," she said, with much emotion, "what a good daughter you are! I wonder if ever woman had so good a one before. When I think of what a life of devotion and sacrifice yours has been for the last ten years I sometimes feel as if I could fall down and kiss the hem of your garment."

"Hush, mother, hush," cried Bligh, deeply moved. "You must not talk like that. Who else have I to love but you?"

Mrs. Burton looked at her wistfully.

"Ah! my darling," she said, "I wish I could find you a husband worthy of you. It is terrible to me to watch your youth slipping by, and to feel that I am in a measure instrumental in defrauding you of those treasures which are a good woman's due —children and a happy home."

"Don't ever fret about my being an old maid," said Bligh. "Spinsterhood suits me best, and I accept my fate cheerfully. Once, perhaps," and a faint colour suffused her cheek, "I might not have been so resigned; but now I no longer allow men and matrimony to occupy my thoughts. Besides," she added, with a fond caress, "no home would ever seem happy to me where you were not."

"The parting would indeed be terrible; nevertheless I must not selfishly stand in the way of your prospects," said Mrs. Burton.

"As I have none," rejoined the girl, "at any rate of the kind you mean, we need scarcely discuss the point. And now, mother dear, you have talked enough. Don't you think if I were to draw down the blinds that you might get a little nap before tea-time?"

"Yes, perhaps I might. I had a very bad night, and begin to feel rather sleepy."

"Then I will leave you for a while." So saying Bligh darkened the room, arranged her mother's pillows, and retired to her own apartment, there to think over the events of the day. But they were not yet at an end. She had hardly closed the door before old Deborah opened it excitedly and cried out :—

" Miss Bligh, dear, there's a gentleman downstairs as wants to see you very particular."

" A gentleman ! " exclaimed Bligh, in surprise. " Who can he be ? "

" Sir Philip Verschoyle. He gave me his card. See, there it is," thrusting it into her young mistress's hand.

" There must be some mistake. Anyhow I cannot see him. I am not in a mood to receive strangers. Go, Deborah, there's a good soul, and make some excuse."

Deborah did as she was bidden, but returned almost immediately.

" It's no use," she said. " He won't stir. He begs, as a particular favour, that you will grant him five minutes' conversation."

" It is very strange," said Bligh. " I hardly know Sir Philip. What can have brought him here ? "

" If I might make so bold as to speak my thoughts," returned Deborah, with a kind of suppressed triumph, " I should say you had."

Bligh blushed and laughed.

" Nonsense, Deborah. You are such a dear, fond, foolish old thing that you quite forget other people don't think me as attractive as yourself."

" And the more fools they," muttered the old woman, looking after Bligh's retreating form. " I've no patience with the men. They're regular idiots, that's what they are. They'll go and run after some fast, flighty creature without a single good quality to recommend her, and never take the least notice of a girl like our Miss Bligh, who would make any decent man a perfect treasure of a wife. But there ! I often think these angels of women are wasted on the male sex. They are not good enough to appreciate them, and feel uncomfortable in their society."

Whereupon Deborah descended to the kitchen, where she went about her work devoured by a burning curiosity to know what Sir Philip Verschoyle, Bart., of whom she had frequently heard as one of the greatest gentlemen in the county, could be saying to her dear Miss Bligh.

She longed to peep through the keyhole, but being the soul of honour, she resisted the temptation, and contented herself with smoking Mrs. Burton's arrowroot and letting the kettle boil over.

CHAPTER X.

KING COPHETUA AND THE BEGGAR MAID.

SIR PHILIP was in the white heat of passion when he left his cousin. Without giving himself time to consider, he took the first train back to the country, hired a fly, and drove straight to the village of Elmsley, where an obliging rustic informed him Miss Burton now resided. He knew Elmsley of old, for once or twice during the winter the hounds met in its vicinity.

Had he paused to reflect no doubt the absurdity of his conduct would have appeared in its true light; but he yielded to the impulse of the hour, and thought was precisely what he most wished to avoid. Anger and disappointment combined had for the nonce completely upset his mental equilibrium, and many a lunatic shut up in Bedlam was less mad than he. His one fixed idea was to pay Blanche out at all hazards. He had a notion it would annoy her beyond measure if he could write to her on the morrow and announce the fact that he also was going to be married. At any rate, it would prove conclusively that he didn't care twopence about her engagement to Colonel Vansittart.

His motive in seeking Bligh Burton was both selfish and ignoble. He knew she was poor, and consequently he made sure of gaining her consent. In his present mood one girl was much the same as another to him. All he sought was to gratify certain feelings of vanity which Blanche happened to have wounded. He had so long been accustomed to have his own way in everything that he could not bear the slightest opposition, and in spite of his age he was nothing more nor less than a big, overgrown, spoilt child, with a fine fortune and position which concealed many defects from the world.

When Deborah opened the hall door and showed him into the family sitting-room, he looked around with a comprehensive glance. The furniture was plain and homely. The threadbare hearthrug and shabby carpet told a tale of scanty means. There were no luxuries or superfluities. The brightest ornament consisted of a pot of sweet-smelling musk placed on the window-sill. The chairs were covered with a common chintz. The curtains were made of the same material. Everything, from the old-fashioned cottage piano in one corner to the tiny grate with its bright fire-irons and paper lining, betokened limited resources.

A satisfied smile passed over Sir Philip's face.   He foresaw but little difficulty.

"Hum!" he soliloquised.   "They are poor—poor as rats. Anybody can see that with half an eye.   Well! so much the better.   The girl won't give herself any airs, and will jump at my offer.   She'll be a fool if she don't, for it's a precious good one for a young woman in her position.   If I weren't in such a confounded hurry of course I might pick and choose, but that's just where it is.   I'm driven into a corner, and out of all the women of my acquaintance there's scarcely one to whom I could propose without a little preliminary trouble and delay.   Now this poor little thing won't stand on ceremony, and I shall be able to revenge myself upon Blanche.   She may say what she likes, but I know she'll go wild when she hears that I am about to commit matrimony.   Ha, ha!   I fancy I can see her face of disgust on learning the news."

Whilst thus cogitating the door opened, and Bligh entered the room with a quiet grace which apparently was inborn, since it never forsook her.   They had not met for several years, and his first impression was one of disappointment.   He said to himself, "Why, you are ugly, downright ugly!"   Then he looked again, and modified his opinion.   "No, you're not," he thought.   "I made a mistake.   If you filled out and lost those dark marks under your eyes, and got a little colour in your cheeks, you'd be rather nice-looking than otherwise.   Not a beauty, of course ; but still passable when you came to have dress and additions. The expression of your face is pleasing, not to say intelligent, and I shouldn't be surprised if you had more in you than most girls."

Unconscious of her visitor's reflections, Bligh advanced towards him with an air of inquiry, which mutely, but politely, demanded the purport of his visit.   Sir Philip had thought there would be no difficulty in explaining the reason why he sought Miss Burton's society.   He had taken it for granted that her poverty would render her an easy prey.   But when Bligh stood there, looking at him with her clear, questioning eyes, and waiting for him to speak, he began to experience a certain sense of embarrassment.   It required a considerable effort to break the ice.

" I daresay you hardly remember me, Miss Burton," he blurted out at last, seeing that she did not attempt to begin the conversation.   "Of late years we have not met very often, and nowadays we never see you at the meets."

"No," she said, quietly.   " My father is dead, as perhaps you may have heard, and we can no longer afford to keep a pony. I think I should have recognised you," she added, " though it is a good many years now since we danced together at the Midland Hunt Ball."

"By Jove, yes. It must be nine, ten years ago. Do you know, Miss Burton, that you made an indelible impression upon me on that occasion. Although you may not believe what I say, I have never forgotten you." And he drew his chair an inch or two nearer Bligh's side, and tried to look sentimental. She retreated in exact proportion as he advanced. He struck her as being insincere, and slightly familiar.

"You are very kind, Sir Philip," she answered composedly. "Either your memory must be a remarkably tenacious one or else I ought to feel extremely flattered. At any rate, you appear to have learnt the art of making pretty speeches, whether they contain much element of truth or not. Truth is immaterial, I suppose, in polite society, but I beg to remind you that I am not accustomed to fine compliments."

Bligh's tongue could be incisive enough on occasion, and she was peculiarly sensitive to ridicule. She imagined that Sir Philip was making game of her, and resented his conduct accordingly.

"You are frightfully sceptical," he said. "Have you forgotten how we sat out in the supper-room together after our dance was over?"

"No, indeed. I retain a distinct recollection of what an exceedingly excellent meal you made. Please forgive my putting the question, Sir Philip, but I happen to be much occupied this afternoon. Did you come here to-day for the purpose of discussing the reminiscences of ten years ago?"

He reddened. It began to be clear to him that however humble and lowly this girl's position might be she was nevertheless a lady, and one who would not brook the slightest insolence or familiarity. Consequently, he changed his tactics.

"Don't you find it awfully dull in this little place?" he inquired abruptly.

"No," she said. "I have not time to feel dull. I am too much occupied."

"How do you amuse yourself, Miss Burton?"

She smiled faintly.

"I can hardly be said to amuse myself. From morning till night I give music lessons as a means of earning a livelihood. My few spare moments are devoted to nursing my mother, who, alas! is a great invalid."

"Hum. It don't sound very lively."

"When people have to work for their bread, Sir Philip, I hardly think the majority do extract much liveliness out of life. They keep their bodies going, and that's about all. The survival of the fittest entails a desperate struggle upon those who have nothing to rely on but their own merits. I speak feelingly, and from experience."

" I wonder you don't marry, and put an end to the difficulty in that way," he said bluntly.

She coloured and made no answer.

"Supposing, now," he continued, "that some good fellow with plenty of money were to propose to you, would you take him ? "

" As such a supposition is quite beyond my mental grasp it would be sheer waste of time to speculate upon it."

" Come, confess. You thought it awfully strange my appearing here to-day, didn't you ? "

" I was certainly astonished when our maid brought up your card."

" The fact is, Miss Burton, I have come on business."

" So I concluded, though I could not imagine for whom you required my services as teacher. I may as well tell you at once, though, that my time is fully occupied, and I am unable to take more pupils at present."

" Will you listen to me for a few minutes? I have something very important to say, and of a nature different from what you anticipate."

She bowed in response. The gravity of his manner excited her curiosity and made her wonder what the communication could be which he desired to make.

" I told you just now that I had never forgotten you," he resumed, with a clever combination of truth and untruth, which he knew well how to employ on occasions. " My mother is most anxious for me to marry and settle down. She belongs to the past generation, and has a particular dislike to the fast, slangy girls of the period. I believe it would break her heart were I to choose one of them, and for a long time she has been endeavouring to find me a wife to her mind. But we never can quite agree in our taste, although I don't want a London girl, or a regular society girl. They are too empty-headed and frivolous, and care for nothing but dress and admiration. A quiet, domestic woman, somewhere between twenty-five and thirty, would suit me ever so much better, yet she must not be a mere country bumpkin. Of late, I have thought the matter over a good deal, and, curiously enough, whenever I have done so my thoughts have always reverted to you. No," as Bligh made a gesture of disbelief, " please hear me out. On all sides I heard your praises sung. You are lauded throughout the county as a pattern daughter. My interest became awakened, and I said to myself, ' A good daughter always makes a good wife.' To

cut a long story short, I am here to-day for the purpose of offering you my hand and my heart."

He spoke in a clear, precise voice, much as if he were repeating a lesson laboriously acquired and mechanically delivered.

A flush of indignation rose to Bligh's cheek.

" Are you doing this for a wager, or what ? " she said. " If
so, indeed it is a sorry joke."

" Please don't be angry, Miss Burton," he returned, with more
vivacity than he had hitherto displayed. " I assure you that I
am in earnest, and mean every word."

" But I don't understand. How can you possibly wish to
make me your wife when to all intents and purposes I am practically a complete stranger to you ? "

" I know you well enough by repute, as I stated just now."

" That is not sufficient. Marriage is a very solemn affair, Sir
Philip, not to be lightly entered upon. To a woman it is the
great event of her life, which means either the highest happiness
or the greatest misery. She cannot back out of it, if she finds
she has made a mistake, without injury to her good name ; therefore, it is of paramount importance that she should choose wisely.
In a man's case, matrimony is perhaps not the be-all and end-all
of existence. He has a wider sphere of activity, and more loop-
holes of escape. Nevertheless, an unsuitable alliance can render
him very wretched. You know nothing of me or I of you. We
have not the least idea whether we are suited to each other, and
on neither side can there exist any affection. Surely—surely—
you have not considered all this."

" Your arguments are not new to me," he returned. " They
are, in fact, what I expected : but they do not make the slightest
alteration in my feelings."

" Your feelings, Sir Philip ! How can you possibly have
any ? "

" Do you suppose that I am not capable of appreciating virtue,
and goodness, and talent ? Believe me, Miss Burton, you under-
rate yourself."

His words were very subtle. Every woman, no matter how
sensible she may be, has a certain leaven of vanity in her composition. Bligh began to think that it might perhaps be true
that Sir Philip had entertained a sneaking liking for her all these
years. So many strange things happen in this world. She
lifted her eyes, and took a long, steady look at him. His
clear-cut features and fair beard were sharply defined against
the window-panes. She saw that he was handsome, and possessed the outward appearance of a gentleman. Save for the
uncertain expression of the face, the head might have been that
of a Christ. His good looks made a favourable impression on

her artistic sensibilities. And as she continued to gaze at him critically, thought after thought flooded her brain in quick succession. Like a flash of lightning it suddenly occurred to her that here was a way of escape from the difficulties which threatened to surround her, a sure and easy method of saving her mother's life. Once Lady Verschoyle and she could secure comfort and affluence for the beloved being who was dearer to her than anyone else on earth. The luxuries so indispensable to an invalid would then be within her reach.

And for herself, what did it matter, since she had no love left to give to any man? Her heart was dead, like a withered tree bereft of sap, which stretches gaunt arms to the sky, and never can put forth fresh blossoms, even though spring after spring comes round, and all things else are rich and green with renewed life. From a worldly point of view, Sir Philip possessed advantages which were beyond the wildest expectations of a person occupying her humble position. It was a regular case of King Cophetua and the beggar maid. When one had known what it was to have no money, and to toil hard for every morsel of food one put into one's mouth, a comfortable home represented the goal of almost every desire. Two lone women had so much to contend with, and where livelihood depended upon health, it was impossible to be ever wholly free from anxiety. Moreover, of late, Bligh had had sundry warnings that she was no longer as strong as in her youth. She lived in morbid dread of some illness overtaking her, which might incapacitate her from work. If this were to happen, starvation stared them in the face. It was only staved off by her own slender life. On the other hand, if she accepted Sir Philip's offer, all her anxieties would be at an end. She did not care for him. She must tell him so plainly, in order that there might be no deception; but in course of time she would perhaps get more fond, and even if the worst came to the worse, she could always do her duty. Thus she reasoned, whilst Sir Philip sat and watched the various shades of expression which swept over her face. He saw that some mental conflict was going on within her brain, and that this should be the case, taking all the circumstances into consideration, excited his curiosity.

"What are you thinking of?" he asked, when he found that the silence threatened to become prolonged.

She stretched herself like one just awakening from a dream.

"I was thinking that I don't suppose you quite realise how great a temptation you are putting in my way."

"How do you mean?" he inquired, surprised by the extreme candour of her words, which seemed at variance with her reserved and guarded manner.

"Don't you understand? I am poor; report says you are a Crœsus. It is my fate to be a social nobody. You occupy the proud position of being a somebody. From the world's standpoint, the advantages are entirely on your side. You might marry almost anyone you chose, whereas I"—looking down at her shabby black frock, "am no longer very young, have not even beauty to recommend me, and am accustomed to a much humbler sphere. I want to put all this plainly before you, as I cannot believe that the proposal you have made me emanates from any personal affection. To say that I do not feel flattered by it would not be true. To deny that such a marriage would free me from many anxieties is also useless, but, at the same time, I wish clearly to point out my shortcomings and deficiencies. You ought to marry someone younger, brighter, more calculated to adorn your home than I."

"It's no use persuading me against you, Miss Burton. As far as I am concerned, my mind is quite made up, and I beg you to give me an answer one way or the other. I think I have a right to demand a reply."

"Sir Philip," said Bligh, twisting her fingers together in perplexity. "You must forgive me for saying so, but there is something about this matter which I don't understand. I cannot believe that you care for me. It is impossible; neither for my own part can I pretend to any affection. We are almost strangers. As far as I make out, you have some hidden motive for this proposal which I am unable to fathom. Either you are acting from delusion, or else you entertain some totally unfounded and imaginary ideal. You appear to have invested me with so many qualities that you do not see the real Bligh Burton as she is. In no other way is it possible to account for your infatuation. But, when the profit is all on my side, I should scorn to take advantage of it."

"By Jove!" he exclaimed, bringing his right hand down on his knee. "You are a good, honest girl, whatever else you may be, and sharp into the bargain. So you think I have a reason for proposing, do you? Well, well, it won't hurt you, my dear—it won't hurt you, and that ought to be enough. The proverb says, 'It's an ill wind that blows nobody any good.' The person who profits by the breeze ought never to want to know from which quarter it blows."

"I am glad you admit the truth of my suspicion," she said, "because it will simplify matters very considerably if we are perfectly frank with each other. Granted, then, that you have a motive for wishing to marry me. I may be a tool, an instrument of spite—anything for aught I know. But if I told you that I too had a motive," and she cast a scrutinising glance at him, "for desiring to change my state—a motive on which all my future happiness depends, what would you say?" The words came low and deep, breathed as it were from the innermost founts of her being.

"I shouldn't say anything," he responded, somewhat impatiently. "All the same, I should like to know what your motive was."

"I will tell you, Sir Philip. Perhaps, after all, you have been sent here by Providence. My mother is desperately ill—dying," and the moisture sprang to Bligh's eyes. "This very afternoon a London surgeon told me that an immediate operation might prolong—if not save her life. I want money," she went on excitedly. "I want money, oh! so badly. A month—a week hence it may be too late. Ever since Mr. Donnington was here I have been in a frenzy. There is nothing so awful as to feel yourself powerless in an emergency of this kind. Don't you understand now why I said you were tempting me?"

"How much do you require?" he asked.

"A hundred pounds for the operation, and fifty for the expenses. God knows where I can find such a sum."

"You shall have it to-morrow."

"Nobody ever gives anything for nothing in this world," said Bligh, who had had cause to realise the truth of the axiom. "Your conditions?"

"My conditions are that you should become my wife. And yours? Since we are making a formal contract, it is better to define them beforehand."

"Will you promise faithfully not to part me from my mother, but to let her live under the same roof?"

"Agreed." Inwardly he said to himself, "I daresay the old woman won't live long."

Bligh put out her hand. A sense of responsibility weighed heavy upon her, caused by the singular compact into which she had entered.

"Sir Philip," she said, "this is a strange engagement, is it not? and I should hate myself if I practised any deception in the matter. You must not expect too much from me all at once. I do not profess to love you now, but I hope to do so in the future, and whatever happens I shall honestly try to make you happy, and perform my duty as a wife. You know the reason why I want a home, the necessity that forces me to marry without affection. Yesterday I should have said no, unhesitatingly, to your proposition, because," blushing deeply, "I believe in the sanctity of love; but to-day the conditions have changed. If I am wronging you—if selfishly I think more of my own interests than yours, go away, and all this shall be forgotten. There is still time to retract."

Sir Philip's pride was hurt. He had imagined that this poor, half-starved little drudge, as he mentally apostrophised her, would have knelt at his knees in joy and thankfulness. The high moral tone which Bligh chose to assume irritated him. If she could have divined his motive, conscience suggested that she need not have made so many excuses for her own. He had only to look round the room to see the straits to which she was driven. A frail girl, an invalid mother, a scanty purse, it did not require much imagination to realise the state of affairs.

" You don't seem over and above pleased with your bargain," he observed surlily.

She took him up short.

" It is not a question of pleasure. I thought I had made that clear. I don't want to marry you under false pretences, and if you think I personally covet your riches and title, you are greatly mistaken. I cannot close my eyes to the fact that our union will be a very grave experiment on both sides. It may or it may not turn out well. We are running an immense risk, and such being the case, one can hardly look forward to the future without some anxiety. Therefore, Sir Philip, I am unable to regard this business in any but a serious light."

" Well! perhaps you are right," he said, feeling impressed by the solemnity of her manner. " And now the next question is, when will you marry me. If we have to make acquaintance with each other, we may as well do it after the ceremony as before."

" There are a great many things to be arranged first. There is no immediate hurry, is there ? "

" On my part, yes," he returned. " I want the affair settled quickly. The sooner the better."

" But my mother——" began Bligh.

" Is not likely to offer any objections to our speedy marriage. You say that she is ill, well, consider how it will benefit her. You shall have a cheque to-morrow, and you can take the old lady up to town at once. You yourself declared that delay might prove fatal. Get the operation over, and there is no reason why we should not be married in a fortnight or three weeks from now. I am sure it would be to your mother's advantage. We shall have to spend our honeymoon abroad, I suppose, and for my own part I should like to get back to Beechlands for the finish of the cub-hunting season."

Bligh thought a moment or two. It was impossible to gainsay the truth of Sir Philip's words. Mr. Donnington had laid particular stress on the operation taking place without loss of time.   Every day, every hour, might prove of consequence in the critical condition of the invalid.   And since she had quite made up her mind to sacrifice herself, it really signified little whether she took the plunge with a trifle more or less premeditation.   Her reluctance was to a great extent unaccountable, for here was a brilliant match—a match such as would have delighted nearly every noble maid in the land, and yet it did not occasion her the slightest thrill of elation.   She looked forward to it soberly and apprehensively.   Somehow Sir Philip's manner did not inspire confidence, and she scented a mystery.

But since Mr. Donnington's visit all question of personal feeling had become extinguished.   Her individual welfare and happiness were narrowed into this : What were the best means of saving her mother's life ?   The answer was, by marrying Sir Philip.

So she said gravely and quietly, and without any of the hot blushes usual to a young lady when asked to fix the day, " Settle it as you please."

He rose from his seat, apparently very much relieved by her reply.

" I presume you have no objection to my announcing our engagement to my mother directly I return home.   There is my cousin too—Miss Sylvester, I should like to write to her by to-morrow's post."

Something in his tone made Bligh look up.

" You are at liberty to do as you think best," she said.

" It's a real pleasure to deal with such a sensible girl," he exclaimed, in high good-humour.   " By-the-bye, Miss Burton—Bligh, I mean—I must get into the way of calling you Bligh now—are you fond of sport ? "

She shook her head and smiled.

" I am afraid I don't know very much about it."

" Ah ! well, never mind.   You'll soon get accustomed to horses and dogs when you are Lady Verschoyle.   I wonder how you would look in a habit."

" Not very ornamental, I fear," she answered.

" I'm not so sure of that, if you went to a good tailor, and got binged up."

" What does ' binged up ' mean ? " she inquired, with an attempt at playfulness.

" Binged up means smartened up," he rejoined graciously, glancing at his watch.   " By Jove ! I must be going, or I shall lose my train back to Beechlands.   I should like to have spent the evening with you, Bligh, but they are expecting me at home."

He took up his hat and cane, and then as if struck by a happy thought said, " I say, little woman, will you give me a kiss ? "

The colour flew to her face in a burning crimson wave. Save her father's no man's lips had touched hers since she had said good-bye to Duncan Cameron. The past came rushing back, filling her mind with a host of painful memories. She shrank away from him.

"I—I would rather not, Sir Philip, if you—d—don't mind."

"But I do mind, very much."

"Not just yet," she mumbled confusedly. "Oh! not just yet. Give me a little time to get used to it all."

He laughed carelessly and coarsely.

"Pshaw! What a prude you are, to be sure. I shall have to cure you of this extraordinary modesty. Why! most of the young ladies of my acquaintance have not the smallest objection to being kissed."

"They must be funny girls, then," said Bligh indignantly.

"They are very nice ones, and belong to the smartest set in London."

So saying he caught her in his arms, and before she could offer any resistance, embraced her with the mischief of an insolent schoolboy rather than with the passion of a lover.

The iron entered into her soul. She realised then the extent of her degradation. She had sold herself for gold. A deadly shame ran quivering through her veins. In her despair and self-loathing, she could have knocked him down. Strange! that she did not like him better. He was young, handsome, muscular. Why were his caresses so unendurable? Was it because she was not used to being made love to. Ah! no, her heart told her otherwise. She remembered Duncan, and the delight his mere presence had occasioned.

Sir Philip held her tight. She felt a veritable weakling in his grasp. Another laugh, another kiss, and then he let her go free.

"There!" he said. "I must not frighten you too much. Good-bye, Bligh. You shall hear from me to-morrow."

"Not a bad little innocent thing," he soliloquised as he drove off, highly satisfied with the success of his visit. "I daresay I shall lick her into shape after a bit. Ha, ha! What a joke it will be writing to Blanche. I wonder what my fine lady will say when she hears the news."

When Sir Philip was fairly out of the house, Bligh covered her face with her hands, and burst into agonised tears.

"Oh! mother," she sobbed, "I did it for you—only for you. It went against my conscience, and I am being punished already. How shall I bear it—how shall I bear it. I have sinned for your sake, and with my eyes open. May God forgive me."

She was shaken to the depths of her being. That rude caress filled her with a sense of abasement. She had lost her independence, and this was the natural consequence. But by degrees she began to see a reverse side to the picture. If she had bartered away her freedom and peace of mind, she had at least secured her mother's welfare. They would live in the same house, and never be parted save by death. And if the grim reaper could only be thrust back into the shadowy future, then she would not grudge the price paid.

Bligh dried her eyes. Her sobs ceased. She walked up and down the room endeavouring to compose her countenance, and to regain her customary calm. Henceforth she had a part to play.

"Mother," she said, softly to herself, "whatever happens, you must never know what this has cost me—never—never. No matter how great the suffering it entails, I must bear it alone."

And there, in the little shabby, homely room she registered a vow not to let any word of regret or self-pity pass her lips.

CHAPTER XI.

MATERNAL SOLICITUDE.

WHEN Sir Philip reached Beechlands it was quite late. The various guests had retired to rest, and he was informed that Lady Verschoyle, after sitting up for some time awaiting his arrival, had also gone to her room.

He was in that state of excitation when he felt an imperative need of confiding the events of the day to someone, and, naturally enough, he turned to his mother. It did not occur to him, however, that by imparting his news at so advanced an hour he would probably give her a bad night and banish sleep. Where his immediate wishes were concerned he was but little accustomed to consider other people.

So he marched straight upstairs and knocked loudly at the door of Lady Verschoyle's room. Receiving no response he knocked again, more imperiously than before.

"Who's there?" at length cried a startled voice from the inside.

"Only me," he called out. "May I come in? I want to speak to you."

"Oh! it's you, Philip. How you frightened me," she said, as he turned the handle and entered.

She was in bed, and had evidently been woken up from her

slumbers. At first she seemed a little bewildered by this nocturnal visitation ; but as her faculties returned, and she remembered the mission on which her son had gone forth in the morning, she looked at him anxiously, and said, " Is anything the matter ? "

" No," he answered. " But I thought I should like to see you and tell you the news."

Lady Verschoyle clasped her thin hands nervously together.

" You—you are really engaged then, Philip? "

He chuckled.

"Oh ! yes, I'm engaged right enough."

A faint colour flickered to her cheek, and for a few moments she lay quite quiet.

" Well ! " he said with a lame attempt at jocularity. " Why don't you congratulate me ? "

" I wish I could. I wish from my heart that I could. But since everything now seems settled between you there is something I must say. It is possible my judgments may have been too severe. Henceforth I will endeavour to entertain no harsh or uncharitable thoughts, and strive all I can to like your wife.

"Oh ! " he rejoined. " You two will get on like a house on fire. I have not the least fear of that."

She shook her head and sighed.

" I doubt it ; but, at any rate, it shan't be my fault if there is any breach of the peace. I suppose I had better write a line to Blanche to-morrow morning, and ask her to come and stay here. Under existing circumstances she cannot find it very pleasant remaining with Colonel Vansittart's relations."

" Don't ever mention Blanche's name to me," he cried excitedly. " From to-day I wash my hands of her, and never wish to have anything to do with her again. She has insulted me most grossly."

Perplexity clouded Lady Verschoyle's dovelike eyes.

" Philip, what do you mean by talking in this extraordinary way. Are you not going to marry Blanche ? "

" No, I'm not. After what has passed between us I would not have her at a gift. She's a nasty, cold, heartless girl, who thinks of nothing but her own interests, and who is willing to sacrifice every feeling of affection to expediency."

" How long have you held those views ? They surprise me, although to a great extent I confess that I share them. Nevertheless, only this morning, when you left for town, you distinctly stated your intention of proposing to your cousin."

" And I acted up to my intention," he said, gloomily. " It appears she prefers her colonel to me. At any rate she pretends that she does, although I don't believe she cares two straws for him in reality."

" I always thought Blanche was in love with you, Philip."

" So did I, else I should not have exposed myself to the humiliation of being refused."

" Did she actually refuse you ? "

" Yes ; she said I ought to have proposed sooner ; that she was quite tired of waiting for me to speak my mind, and, therefore, had decided on feathering her nest before it was too late."

" Well ! she was right there.   She is getting on in years you must remember."

" My belief is," he said, " she wanted to play fast and loose with me, but I wasn't going to stand any nonsense of that sort ; so when she said no once I gave up pressing her, and told her she should see I could soon find somebody else."

" Philip, I can hardly follow all this.   Did my ears deceive me just now when I understood you to say you were engaged to be married ? "

" No, it's quite true, only the young lady does not happen to be the one I originally fancied.   It seems funny, doesn't it ; but after all, I'm not sure that in the long run she won't suit me a great deal better than Mademoiselle Blanche, with her airs and graces. This one is a good, quiet, meek little thing, without an atom of humbug in her composition, and, as I said before, you'll like her even if I don't."

Lady Verschoyle's heart thumped so loudly against the fine white calico of her nightdress that its pulsations were quite painful.

" Philip," she said, in tones of extreme agitation, " who is the girl?   You forget you have not yet told me her name."

" She is Miss Burton—Bligh Burton, who lives at Elmsley, on the other side of the county."

Lady Verschoyle's astonishment was so great that for a few seconds she felt incapable of giving expression to it in words.

Sir Philip stood by, enjoying the amazement depicted on his mother's countenance.   He had a good deal of the accomplished actor in him, and derived genuine pleasure from a situation.   It was a favourite amusement of his when at home to play on her feelings.   They were so innocent and childlike that they never failed to inspire him with a sense of superiority.

" Miss Burton," she gasped at last.   " But this is simply incredulous.   You are scarcely acquainted."

" At any rate, we know each other well enough to have settled the matter between us."

" Have you been meeting her lately, Philip, by any chance ? "

"No," he answered, evasively. "Not quite lately. I went over there to-day after I had seen Blanche, and found Miss Burton in great distress about her mother, who is seriously ill. It seems the doctor advised an expensive operation, and Bligh had no money. I offered to lend it. One thing led to another, and we ended by coming to an understanding satisfactory to both parties."

"And you actually mean to tell me, Philip, that it is your intention to marry in this offhand sort of way?"

"Yes," he said, irritably, annoyed by the reproof expressed in her tone. "Why not? After all, marriage is a lottery, and whether one ponders over drawing a number or takes the first that happens to turn up makes very little difference. The great Napoleon was a sensible man. He said that 'Matrimony was against Nature, and merely a product of civilisation.' I agree with him."

"It is monstrous, perfectly monstrous, to marry in the way you are doing," exclaimed Lady Verschoyle, with the nearest approach to indignation of which her gentle nature was capable. "How can people expect to be happy when they enter into such a solemn compact with so little forethought?"

"I don't know that I do expect to be happy," he responded. "Most of the husbands and wives of one's acquaintance don't seem to live together in a state of beatitude. Fortune is hardly likely to favour me more than my neighbours."

"I can't understand Miss Burton's conduct," observed Lady Verschoyle. "I have always heard her well spoken of, and it completely destroys my good opinion to find her jumping so indelicately at a man whom she scarcely knows."

"Look here, mother," said Sir Philip, "you need not blame Bligh for what has happened. She's as good and as straight a little girl as ever stepped, I'll take my oath of that. She didn't jump at me. On the contrary, she did all she could to dissuade me from carrying out my intention. She even went the length of running herself down, and calling my attention to her shortcomings, which is a long sight more than most women would have done in her place. I liked her for it, and stood my ground firmly. At last, when she saw I really was in earnest, and took no heed of her objections, she confessed that she was in desperate straits, and would make any sacrifice in order to save her mother's life."

"As far as I can gather," said Lady Verschoyle, with profound sadness, "this strange affair of yours may be thus summed up : On one side it is a marriage of pique, on the other of necessity. That is the plain fact shorn of wrappings."

"Exactly," he admitted, nibbling at his nails. "You have hit it off to a T   I was determined not to let Blanche crow over me."

"Blanche, Blanche, always Blanche.   Why should her opinions be of so much importance ? "

" Look here, mother, you may as well understand this matter thoroughly, and then, as it is not a very pleasant one, especially to me, we need never allude to it again.   Blanche is the only woman I ever cared two straws for, and when she refused my proposal, and declined to throw over Colonel Vansittart on my account, it made me regularly mad.   I didn't know what I was about, and I swore to marry the first girl I came across, just to spite her.   For, mark you, she loves me—she did not attempt to deny that ; only I have played the fool too long, and she got tired of waiting.   There! now you know the whole truth.   It's not a bit of good lecturing me or telling me I'm a born jackass. I know it, but I vowed I'd be equal with Blanche, and I will. For God's sake, don't give me advice."

The tears dropped fast from Lady Verschoyle's eyes, falling in little wet rounds upon the sheet.

" My poor boy," she said.   " My poor, foolish, wrong-headed boy !   What advice can I give you that you are likely to take ? For years past you have elected to walk alone, and I have looked mutely on, sorrowing very often, but never venturing to remonstrate.   You are your own master, and must do as you choose ; but I hardly know which to pity most—you or Miss Burton."

" I think she has the best of it," he remarked glumly.

" One thing is clear," said Lady Verschoyle, with unusual decision.   " Miss Burton should be told the real state of the case, and the reasons which drove you to propose."

"If you say one single word to Bligh, mother, I shall never forgive you.   She'll find it out soon enough for herself.   Interference won't help either of us.   We are quite capable of managing our own affairs.   As for Bligh, she's a clear-headed, sensible sort of girl, who thoroughly understands that the engagement on both sides is not one of sentiment, but expediency."

" Marriage without love is to me a profanation, Philip."

He gave a short laugh.

"Love !   There is a great deal said and written about it, but it's a fraud.   The fiercer the passion the sooner it dies out.   At best the state is a very disagreeable one.   It turns women into Delilahs, and shears men of their strength.   With any luck, no doubt little Bligh Burton and I will rub along as well as the great majority of respectable married couples.   We shall squabble and fall out until we ascertain by experience who is the master.   The weaker vessel, perhaps, may grumble, but she will accept her position after a time.   Or if the husband is a donkey, he accepts his. That is the law of marriages. One rules, the other suffers. One commands, the other obeys. Hooray! I know who'll be ruler in my case."

"Oh! Philip, it grieves me beyond measure to hear you talk in that odious, cynical fashion."

"Can you deny its truth?"

"It is just because your words contain a germ of truth that they strike such a chill to my heart. But all marriages do not resolve themselves into a question of brute force. Some are happy."

"Precious few."

"Mine was. Your father and I lived together for five-and-twenty years and never had a difference. But then we were engaged for a long time before we were married, and were quite sure of our own minds."

"Ah! well, mother, people either glide tranquilly or else fall headlong into the fatal noose, according to circumstances and their different dispositions. I have made my plunge, and so far don't experience any very terrible consequences. Therefore cheer up. If I am satisfied, surely you ought to be so also."

"I can't be—I can't be," she sobbed. "The whole thing seems so wrong and unnatural."

He stooped and kissed her. Her grief moved him more than he chose to own. Warmed by this kindly action, her heart swelled almost to bursting. She put her arms round his neck and clung to him in a passion of maternal tenderness.

"Oh! Philip," she said. "My boy, my boy. I would give my life to secure your happiness. However bravely you may attempt to carry off matters I know that at this moment you are miserable. Ah! my poor boy—my poor boy."

"Miserable!" he echoed scoffingly. "What? because one silly girl has refused me? No, not I. There are plenty more to fall back upon, as Blanche will soon perceive. Confound these women!" he went on, in an altered tone. "A good horse and a good hound are worth the whole lot of them put together. Henceforth Sport shall be my bride, and none other. And now, mother, I'm off to bed. Good-night, old lady. Hope I haven't disturbed you."

So saying Sir Philip took up his candlestick, whistled a comic air out of pure bravado, and departed.

Lady Verschoyle sighed heavily. She felt that she did not understand him. His character was beyond her comprehension, and there were times, as to-night, when it was a mystery how to such parents as herself and Sir Thomas such a son had been born. The boy had nothing of his father in him. He lacked the equable temper, the strong principle, the sound, shrewd common-sense of his progenitor.

Disturbed indeed ! How could any mother sleep after such a conversation. She lay awake, quiet and unhappy, pondering over Sir Philip's words. To her it seemed sinful to marry in such a reckless fashion : but, being a woman, she blamed Bligh more than she blamed him. She could not believe that the girl had not spread some snare into which the foolish and impetuous young man had blundered with his eyes shut. Like a ball on the rebound, Miss Burton had caught him, taking advantage of his weakness to suit her own purposes. Even the gentlest and kindest of women are hard occasionally upon their own sex. They may not mean to be so, but their sympathies insensibly side with the masculine rather than with the feminine portion of creation. They can forgive a man a fault more easily than they can a woman, and thus it was in Lady Verschoyle's case. As she lay there in the darkness she thought hard thoughts of Bligh Burton. She was an unscrupulous, designing adventuress, ready to snap up the first rich husband who presented himself. If she had talked sensibly to Sir Philip, no doubt he would never have proposed. He would have looked about him and chosen some-one more suitable and in his own position. But she had egged him on—she must have egged him on. In her own mind Lady Verschoyle felt no doubt whatever on that point. Good and charitable as she was, she did poor Bligh considerable injustice. But no doubt most mothers will forgive her. The maternal instinct, in spite of its strength, is often blind.

CHAPTER XII.

THE OLD SCHOOL VERSUS THE NEW.

WITHOUT being worldly, Lady Verschoyle nevertheless felt disappointed at Sir Philip seeking a wife in a rank of life lower than his own. County people are notoriously exclusive. Living in a narrow world they require to know the genealogy of persons desiring to enter into what they call " their set." It may be ever so stupid, ever so dull ; but they themselves are convinced of its superiority. Now the Burtons had never been received on equal terms by the leading families of Midlandshire. There was nothing against them, only folks who have to work for their bread sink back in the social struggle for pre-eminence, and cannot be expected to associate with the fortunate owners of ten or twenty thousand a year. Nowadays money is at the bottom of most differences and distinctions. Those who have none go to the wall, and lose caste in the estimation of their neighbours. Mr. Snooks soon ceases to be " a good fellow" when there are no more dinners to be got out of him, and when she leaves off entertaining poor Mrs. Snooks forfeits her reputation of being " a really charming little woman."

Having in process of time earned for herself an honourable place amongst the county magnates, Lady Verschoyle was quite aware that when her son's engagement to Miss Burton became known the general verdict of her friends would be that he ought to have done a great deal better. The daughter of a humble crammer, supporting herself by teaching music, was scarcely a fitting partner for a man of Sir Philip's standing and position. Lady Verschoyle felt keenly alive to this fact, and already, in anticipation, dreaded the comments which were certain to circulate round her large circle of acquaintances. " People will talk so," she mused disconsolately. " Every tongue in the county will be set a-wagging at Philip's expense." But after the first shock had passed away, little by little her mind familiarised itself to the idea of his making a comparatively bad match from a worldly point of view. She consoled herself by thinking that things might have been worse. Miss Burton was respectable and a lady—two great points in her favour. Her poverty was really all that could be urged against her. Moreover, it was an immense relief to know that Blanche would not be the future mistress of Beechlands. She should not have to resign her home, her son, her poor people in the village to a successor whom she both disliked and distrusted. Blanche's influence over Philip had always been bad, and she could have gone down on her knees and thanked her niece for having refused him. Yes, of the two Bligh Burton was distinctly preferable.

The next day happened to be Sunday. The house was full of fashionable gentlemen and ladies, friends of the young baronet.

On the previous evening they had been uncommonly lively, playing at battle-door and shuttlecock in the long corridor which led from the central hall to the drawing-room, frequenting the billiard-room, and amusing themselves extremely well despite their host's absence. But when the Sabbath came all their energy and vivacity seemed to have departed in the most extraordinary manner. One lady felt so indisposed that she requested her breakfast might be sent up to her in bed. A second did just manage to straggle down, but complained of a racking headache, which quite incapacitated her from setting foot out of doors ; whilst a third, who cherished agnostic tendencies, openly stated that she looked upon going to church as a work of supererogation.

As for the men, they withdrew in a body to the smoking-room, where, by the aid of much strong tobacco and numerous brandies and sodas, they contrived to while away the hours of Divine service. Poor Lady Verschoyle felt that there was something radically wrong with the morals of the rising generation, but she was too timid and retiring by nature to protest. She could only show her disapprobation by example. Consequently, she put on her bonnet and cloak, armed herself with an umbrella—for the day was drizzly, and she made a point of never taking the carriage out on Sunday—and walked off alone to church. It was a small, but very beautiful, old building, which Sir Thomas had restored a short time previous to his death.

As Lady Verschoyle entered, the rich notes of the organ were rising and falling in harmonious waves of sound. She glided noiselessly into the big family pew, now, alas ! so seldom occupied by anyone save herself. To the sad, lonely woman it was a relief to come to this sacred spot and pray away on her knees the many worries by which she frequently was beset. The atmosphere seemed purer than at home, and it soothed and rested her to look at the cool, marble columns, the carved oaken pulpit, the school children's little, unequal heads, and to hear the rector's mellow voice enunciating stereotyped platitudes, nicely suited to the simple minds of his rustic listeners. There was a sense of repose about it all, not to be found at the Hall.

But to-day Lady Verschoyle's attention wandered somewhat, despite her efforts to keep it concentrated on the service. She caught herself devoutly hoping that Bligh Burton did not belong to the new school, who scoffed at religious beliefs, and desired nothing better than to see them swept away altogether, although incapable of suggesting any substitute in their place. She had a perfect horror of the loose atheistical talk in which so many of her son's friends indulged. It made her flesh creep to listen to the wild, vague, and irreverent notions which they propounded. It seemed to her an awful thing to live without faith—to run down all that was holy and pure, and deny the existence of an immortal soul. She shuddered when she heard such language, and the conviction that Philip, in his heart of hearts did not disapprove of it, caused her poignant sorrow.

She prayed fervently that Bligh might be a well-principled, properly-conducted, young woman, who went respectably to church of a Sunday, and believed in the higher teachings of Christianity as implicitly as she did herself. Her anxiety on this point was so great that she longed impatiently for the sermon to come to an end, in order that she could cross-question her friend, Mrs. Fortescue, as to what kind of a girl Bligh Burton really was. Everything, she felt, would depend upon that. But the excellent rector had got on one of his pet hobbies—foreign missions, and he could not tear himself away from the blacks in Africa, whom he referred to repeatedly as heathens. His account of their condition was so appalling that it made it very hard to believe these degraded savages could have been created by the same merciful Deity who permitted Christians to be born into the world. The worthy man's discourse was embellished by no less than three "in conclusions," the two first being productive of extreme disappointment among the more youthful portion of the audience, who, on each occasion, assumed a cheerful and expectant attitude at the prospect of a speedy emancipation. After their hopes had been falsely raised they began to cough, whisper, fidget and drop their prayer-books until called to order by the bell-ringer, who took a peculiar delight in pouncing upon the offenders and tweaking their ears.

At length, however, Mr. Roden bade a pathetic farewell to the blacks, called down a blessing upon the congregation, and allowed them to depart in peace. Almost immediately a great shuffling and pattering of little feet was heard, and out rushed the school children into the fresh air, followed more soberly by their seniors. Lady Verschoyle waited for Mrs. Fortescue, who was almost the last to leave the sacred edifice.

"Good-morning, Anne," she said, as soon as they were clear of its precincts. "Are you busy? If not, I wish you would walk home part of the way with me. I have something most astonishing to tell you."

"Indeed!" exclaimed Mrs. Fortescue, pricking up her ears. "What is it?"

"Just fancy! Philip is engaged, and who do you think to?"

"Miss Sylvester, I suppose."

"Nothing of the sort. Blanche has refused him."

"Well! I am surprised. I suppose she was bound hard and fast to Colonel Vansittart."

"Yes, I expect so. But that's not all my news. What do you think that foolish boy Philip has done?"

"I haven't an idea."

"He has gone and asked your friend Miss Burton to marry him."

"Nonsense!"

"He has though. He did it out of pique—pure pique. He had some absurd notion in his head that it would vex Blanche, if he went straight off and proposed to somebody else, and so he fell back upon Miss Burton, though my belief is he has only seen her two or three times in his life."

"Well! I declare. Wonders will never cease. And did Bligh take him?"

"Oh! dear yes. Philip pretends that she didn't show any indecent eagerness, but in reality she seems to have jumped at the chance, though it appears they are so poor, one can hardly blame her for doing so. The mother too was ill, and Philip offered to help her. Altogether I am so upset that, I am ashamed to say, I hardly heard a word of your brother's most excellent sermon."

"It was an old one," rejoined Mrs. Fortescue, with a sisterly contempt born of familiarity. "Charles is getting rather hard up for ideas, and has delivered it three times before. He thought it would do again, however, if he transferred the scene from India to Africa, which, I am bound to say, he did very cleverly—but about Bligh Burton. I really am dumfounded. She is the last girl in the world to marry for money. Why! only the year before last she refused young Hornblower, of Stonyholm, because she said she did not care for him. He was quite desperate about her for a time, until he consoled himself with Lady Hilda Berry. I know that for a fact."

"You can imagine my feelings," said Lady Verschoyle, "when Philip burst into my room last night, and told me this astounding piece of news. It quite took me by storm."

"So I should think. In one sense the match is but a poor one for your son."

"Yes, that's exactly my opinion. He ought to have looked higher."

"On the other hand," resumed Mrs. Fortescue, with her usual bluntness of speech, "Bligh is ever so much too good for him."

"Anne!" exclaimed Lady Verschoyle, indignantly, "what do you mean by such a speech?"

"I mean what I say, as is my invariable habit. Bligh Burton is a most accomplished and intellectual young woman, and I do not think that even you can maintain the people by whom Sir Philip surrounds himself are either very cultivated or very intelligent. To be quite frank, I doubt his capacity to make Bligh happy. What her motive in accepting him is, I am not in a position to know, but I would stake my life that self has nothing to do with it, and that, to the best of her ability, she will perform the vows uttered at the matrimonial altar. I never came across a girl who possessed a stronger sense of duty. You need fear nothing on Sir Philip's account. He will be quite safe in her hands. It is of Bligh herself I am thinking. She requires a very superior man—a very superior man indeed."

Mrs. Fortescue's tone rendered it patent that her opinion of the baronet was by no means exalted. Lady Verschoyle winced.

"Anne," she said, plaintively. "I am so fond of you—I

always come to you in all my troubles for advice and support. But why—why do you invariably say things that hurt me? It is not kind."

Mrs. Fortescue's conscience smote her, as it very frequently did after the utterance of one of her plain speeches.

" I am a brute," she exclaimed. " My only excuse is that I don't mean to be one."

" Let us leave Philip out of the conversation," said poor Lady Verschoyle, with tears standing in her eyes. " We are none of us so perfect as to judge the faults of others. He has had many temptations, and sometimes it occurs to me that with the best intentions in the world perhaps his father and I may have spoilt him. An only son is so precious, and parents are apt to err on the side of over-indulgence. Now tell me about Bligh. I am dying with curiosity to hear what my future daughter-in-law is like."

" She is the best and most conscientious girl in the world," responded Mrs. Fortescue, who was as good a friend as a hater.

" If I were a man I would marry her to-morrow, and I am not easy to please, as you know. Bligh's life has been a very sad one. She has had to contend against disappointment, and sickness, and poverty. Many a woman in her place would have degenerated into a sour old maid. But hers is a noble nature, and suffering seems to have strengthened its finer qualities, instead of nipping them in the bud, as is often the case. She is as good as gold. Her only fault is that she happens to be a humble music teacher, who has had to live by her own exertions. If she had been my Lady Isabel or my Lady Jane all the county would have raved about her perfections long ago. For my own part, I both respect and admire her. Under exceedingly trying circumstances she has behaved like a heroine, and, without any wish to offend your feelings, I must repeat what I said before. I only hope Sir Philip may make her happy."

Lady Verschoyle's pale face brightened, as its owner listened to this eulogy, which made all the greater impression since it came from one not generally addicted to indiscriminate praise.

" Anne," she said, " I am so glad to hear what you say. It takes quite a weight from my mind." Then she hesitated, and added meekly, " After all, it was very wrong of me to be so ambitious for Philip, and to wish him to make a fine marriage of which the neighbours would approve. We are only humble people ourselves. When my dear husband first went to London he was nothing but a poor working lad. His fortune was entirely of his own making. We have no blue blood in our veins to give ourselves airs about. I ought never to have forgotten that."

Mrs. Fortescue was touched by her friend's humility.

"Dear Lady Verschoyle," she exclaimed. "I am sure no one could accuse you of being purse-proud."

"I hope not, but I have been to blame about Philip, and unconsciously have wronged Miss Burton. She is a lady by birth, and that ought to be enough, and henceforth shall be enough for me. Fancy if he had fallen in love with a barmaid, or an actress, or—or "—lowering her voice, "even worse. Some people's sons do terrible things. They disgrace themselves for life, and sink down into the very mire. My boy has not done that. My boy has done nothing to be ashamed of. I have indeed cause to be thankful."

"I think you will say so when you come to know Bligh better."

"Ten years hence," went on Lady Verschoyle, with a hopeful smile, "nobody will care in the least whether Philip chose a music teacher or a countess for his wife. It is far more important that he should marry some good, honest girl capable of recognising the manifold duties which wealth and position invariably bring in their train. These fashionable women seem to have no sense of responsibility, no deep side to their nature. They care for nothing but amusement, although the more they seek excitement the less it satisfies them. They are not women, according to the true meaning of the word, but merely a painful variety of the nineteenth century, the product of fast—if not vicious—surroundings. However, now," and she gathered her shawl more tightly together, " I shall go back to Philip's fine ladies feeling quite comforted."

"You do not care for them, then, any better than the last lot of visitors?" inquired Mrs. Fortescue.

Lady Verschoyle pinched her lips together in an endeavour not to say anything unkind.

"No, I scarcely expected to. I suppose I am getting prim and old-fashioned in my ideas, but I can't say that I approve either of the manners or the conversation of the rising generation. The whole tone is different from what it used to be in my time, and I often think that if I were a great lady—a really great lady, I mean, who was a star of importance in society, the first thing I should try to do would be to purify it. What a noble mission there is for some beautiful, high-born woman, who has courage enough to close her doors on all those of either sex, no matter what their rank or position, whose lives are not well conducted, and whose reputations will not bear investigation. She would incur a good deal of abuse in the beginning, but if she was impartial and sincere, the end would atone for many difficulties."·

" Society has certainly got to a shocking state," said Mrs. Fortescue.

" Shocking. Do you know, Anne, that these smart ladies say things which, old as I am, positively make me blush for shame. As for the men, they tear them to pieces behind their backs, and encourage them to their faces. Both laugh at what, in our youth, we were taught to regard as sacred. They have no reverence for age, no sympathy with misfortune. The one is ridiculous, the other a bore, unless it affects themselves. Their perceptions are narrow, and all their instincts selfish and material. The men care only for sport and food, the women live solely for dress and admiration. And this is the use they make of the lives which God has given them! Philip laughs at me whenever I speak to him on the subject. He tells me it is all right, and I do not know how fashionable people behave, but nevertheless, I cannot believe that it is all right." And a painful flush rose to her cheek.

" Of course it is not," responded Mrs. Fortescue, indignantly. " The fact is, Sir Philip of late years has got into a fast, slangy set, and I wish to goodness we could get him out of it."

" Perhaps Bligh will," said Lady Verschoyle, hopefully. " When he is married he will surely stay at home more. But to give you a specimen of the conversation that goes on at Beechlands. There is a girl staying there now—a Miss Violet Crisper, who, I believe, is a great success in society, and what do you think she said last night at dinner ? "

" I haven't an idea."

" They were talking about some play—not a very proper one I gathered, and somebody asked her how she liked it. ' Oh ! ' she answered, ' I thought it awfully good. It was not perhaps just the sort of piece I should take my mother to, but I enjoyed it tremendously.' Now, Anne, what do you think of that ? " demanded Lady Verschoyle.

" Terrible," answered Mrs. Fortescue, unable to repress a laugh, in spite of her condemnation. " It only shows what girls are coming to. It's the poor innocent mothers nowadays whose morals require looking after. Bligh Burton is not one of your Miss Violet Crispers, fortunately. She has been brought up in a totally different school, and you would never hear her say a thing like that."

" Thank goodness ! " exclaimed Lady Verschoyle, fervently. " I should sink into the ground if she did. You are sending me home almost happy, Anne, and I am longing to make

Bligh's acquaintance, for I feel sure now that I shall like her. I can forgive everything if only she is not fast."

" Poor Bligh ! " said Mrs. Fortescue. " You need not be afraid of her being fast. She has had too much trouble."

" We must try and make her life a little more cheerful for her, Anne. It is very hard at eight and twenty to look back upon a sad past. One feels as if one had been robbed of one's due. Good-bye, dear, come and see me soon, for somehow or other I always feel very lonely, and glad of the sight of a familiar face when all these fine visitors are about."

Mrs. Fortescue looked after the retreating figure of her friend. " Poor darling ! " she soliloquised. " I could thump that wretched son of yours. He ought to know better than to ask you to associate with such a lot. They are not fit to sit at the same table with you, but if Bligh can effect a reform, she will be even cleverer than I give her credit for being."

CHAPTER XIII.

A TERRIBLE ORDEAL.

HAVING once arrived at the momentous decision, which henceforth would entirely change her life, Bligh did not allow the grass to grow under her feet. By the first post on Monday morning Sir Philip received a letter from his *fiancée* stating that she had arranged to go to town with her mother on the Wednesday, and had been recommended some quiet, airy rooms in Baker Street, where Mr. Donnington was in the habit of sending his patients. Bligh gave him their number, and requested that if he had anything to communicate he would either write or else pay her a flying visit at the lodgings. It was a short, businesslike letter, very different from the epistles usually despatched by lovers, for, to tell the truth, there was not a single word of love in it, from beginning to end.

Fortunately Sir Philip did not notice the omission, or if he did he realised that it simplified matters very considerably, neither party pretending to any affection. Besides, it happened to be the 1st of September, and his thoughts were far more full of partridge shooting than of the movements of his affianced bride. Whether she went to London a few days sooner or later interested him but little. Having settled his affairs he experienced no burning desire to see her again immediately. He could exist quite well in her absence, for she was by no means essential to his happiness. After breakfast he took his mother aside and placed Bligh's note in her hands.

"She wants to be off at once," he said. "I suppose it does not matter, and she won't rest till she gets Mrs. Burton's operation over."

Lady Verschoyle read the letter carefully, noting with pleasure the neat handwriting and clear signature. They differed from the sprawly smudges which Blanche had been in the habit of sending, and which often were quite undecipherable.

"Oh! Philip," she said. "I should so like to see Miss Burton. Do you think I might send her a telegram in your name and ask her if she can manage to come over here to-morrow? It hardly seems right to let her go away without my making her acquaintance."

"You will have plenty of time for that afterwards," he said.

"Yes, no doubt; but even if she does not come it will be a way of showing her that I know, and approve, of the engagement. If I take no notice she may fancy that I am displeased about it, and I should not like her to imagine anything of the sort."

"She can't do the least good by coming," he objected. "Besides, we shall be out shooting. I arranged with Turner yesterday afternoon that we would shoot the Top Farm beats to-morrow. Very likely Bligh might think I ought to stop at home to receive her, and I certainly don't mean to spoil my fun on her account."

"There is no occasion to give up your day's shooting, Philip, especially as you have friends staying in the house. I am sure Bligh would not wish it."

"Having already made my plans I can't very well alter them at a moment's notice. I think you must see that, mother."

"If you are going to shoot the Top Farm," returned Lady Verschoyle, feeling hurt by the indifferent tone in which he talked of his future wife, "you will not be very far away from home, and if the day be fine I could drive Miss Burton and the other ladies out to lunch."

"Oh! they're coming with us, I believe. At least they said they were going to last night."

"Not Mrs. De Morbey surely! She told me she felt so ill yesterday that she could not walk a step—not even to church."

Sir Philip laughed.

"That was because it was Sunday. She has revived to-day. According to my experience these delicate ladies can always do everything they like, and make their health an excuse for everything they don't like."

"Philip," said Lady Verschoyle imploringly, "do let me ask

Bligh. I will take care that she does not interfere with your amusement, and this is the only chance I may have of seeing her for several weeks to come."

"All right," he said. "But if you bring her to lunch don't stay too long. The 'guns,' including Violet Crisper, are all tremendously keen, and we shall want to get to work again immediately. One comfort is Bligh does not care for the billing and cooing part of the business, and won't expect me to be very attentive."

"In all probability she will have to catch an afternoon train back to Elmsley," said Lady Verschoyle, pleased at having gained her point, though her son's indifference occasioned an increasing sense of pain. "Anyhow, she shall be made to understand that the visit is to me and not to you."

The gentlemen departed in high spirits, looking forward to doing great execution among the young coveys. The three ladies accompanied them, attired in smart shooting costumes "built" by first-rate London tailors. Directly Lady Verschoyle was alone she sent off a telegram to Bligh, begging her to come over for a few hours on the morrow. The receipt of this message occasioned quite a stir in the little household at Elmsley. Bligh was very busy packing, and had a variety of things to attend to before leaving home. She wanted all her time, and her first instinct was to send back a refusal. The mere thought of going to Beechlands all alone, to be inspected by Sir Philip's mother and Sir Philip's fine friends, frightened her almost to death. She would rather have faced any ordeal, for she felt terrified of Lady Verschoyle and of what she might say. It never occurred to her that she could entertain anything but disapprobation for the match.

But a very few minutes' reflection showed Bligh the impossibility of sending a reply in accordance with her inclinations. From the moment when she accepted Sir Philip she ceased to be her own mistress, and undertook obligations which she was bound not to ignore, simply because they entailed a disagreeable effort. No matter how repugnant it was to her feelings to go and be stared at and appraised, put in the scales and, most probably, found wanting, she had no alternative but to submit to the process. She saw that clearly, and braced herself to face the situation, with much the same desperate courage as she would have gone to the dentist and had a tooth out.

"What do you say, Bligh?" said Mrs. Burton. "Shall you go?"

"I must," she answered reluctantly. "I have no choice."

Mrs. Burton put out her hand and placed it caressingly on her daughter's shoulder.

"Don't be afraid, my darling," she said. "I can quite understand that it seems a little alarming at first, making acquaintance with one's new relations; but Lady Verschoyle is certain to like you when she comes to know you. Everybody does."

Bligh shook her head.

"You are too partial, mother dear. I suppose I am a sad coward, but I would give a ten-pound note—that is to say if I had it—to get off this visit. I never felt so nervous in my life. I quite dread meeting Lady Verschoyle, and yet report says she is charming."

"Mrs. Fortescue never can sing her praises enough," observed Mrs. Burton. "She talks of her as if she were a saint."

"Do you know, mother," said Bligh, gravely and quietly, "I feel as if I had committed a sin against Lady Verschoyle in accepting Sir Philip."

"Good gracious! child, what an extraordinary way to talk. Really, you carry modesty and self-depreciation to an extreme. For my part," and Mrs. Burton held up her head with motherly pride, "I consider my daughter a fit match for the finest lord in the land."

Bligh stifled a sigh and made no reply. It was impossible to explain what she felt. If she had loved Sir Philip ever so little her mind would not have been disturbed by half so many doubts and hesitations. She regarded her want of affection as a sin, but she could not speak of these things to her mother, although Mrs. Burton tried hard to break through the crust of her reticence, and made several attempts to learn how so astounding an engagement had been brought about. But Bligh kept her own counsel, and the elder lady could only arrive at the conclusion that she was glad to escape from the hardships of her life.

As for Bligh, having once decided that the visit to Beechlands must be paid, and an excuse was out of the question, she wired back to Lady Verschoyle, with characteristic promptness, "Will be at station to-morrow by train arriving 11.15." This done she set to work with redoubled energy to get through the business in hand. There were notes to write to her several pupils, wishing them good-bye, and informing them of her altered prospects; sundry small bills to pay, and a whole host of parting injunctions to give to Deborah, who, it was settled, should remain in charge during their absence. Whilst all this was going on, Mrs. Burton remained in complete ignorance as to her real condition. The bustle and excitement of leaving home at such short notice acted as a stimulant on her spirits, and she was more cheerful than she had been for a long time past. Indeed, she had every reason for being so, since she believed that she was about to undergo an operation which, in all human probability, would entirely restore her to health. Bligh, of course, knew differently, and was unable to share her mother's hopefulness: but she would not have destroyed it for the world, and placed a careful guard upon her tongue. A new sense of responsibility, accompanied by an indefinable oppression, weighed upon her spirit. She had staked all upon one die, and could not conceal from herself that if the issue proved unfavourable she should be a heavy loser. Her anxieties were the worse to bear because there was nobody to whom she could confide them. Old Deborah, in spite of her devotion, had never acquired the art of keeping a secret, and would soon have revealed to her mistress Mr. Donnington's ultimatum. So, while she strove hard to maintain a calm demeanour, Bligh shut her troubles up in her own breast. She knew by instinct that she could not share them with Sir Philip. Her swift perceptions had already told her that he was deficient in sympathy and cared nothing for the misfortunes of others, provided they did not affect himself.

She wondered if the mother resembled the son in this respect. If only Lady Verschoyle were nice and accepted her kindly what a difference it would make to her lot. Yet she had no right to expect a gracious reception. She was keenly conscious of the inferiority of her social position and of her own short-comings. Had she possessed more self-assurance she would have been far happier; but, as Mrs. Burton had truly said, she carried modesty to an extreme. That first great disappointment was responsible for much of her humility. From then until now she had always felt there must be something wanting in herself. A girl who could not keep a man's affection was surely lacking in charm. It might be weakness, but ever since Sir Philip's visit Bligh suffered from a longing for moral support. The truth was she did not feel satisfied either as to the wisdom or the propriety of her conduct. Look at it as she might she could not lose sight of the fact that she had solemnly promised to marry a man for whom she entertained no sentiments of affection whatever. In her heart she knew that she rather disliked him than otherwise, and vaguely realised they were antipathetic to each other. The magnetic current between individuals, which acts as the basis of all love and hatred, had, in her case, set sharply in the latter direction. Sir Philip's first embrace had made an indelible impression. Her whole woman's nature was offended by its coarseness and its levity.

Packing and thinking, thinking and packing, midnight found her still apprehensively looking forward to the future. Bodily she was thoroughly exhausted, but when she went to bed her active brain kept sleep at bay. Thought succeeded thought in wearying succession, and not until the grey rays of dawn stole softly into the room did an uneasy slumber close Bligh's eyes. She rose unrefreshed, and, remembering the visit in store, took out her Sunday frock and tacked a piece of clean frilling into the neck and sleeves. It was the only ornamentation within her power. She had worn the dress many times without ever caring whether it were becoming or not; but to-day the shabby black merino was responsible for a considerable loss of equanimity. She uneasily recalled how badly the village dressmaker had made it, and how often the seams had had to be altered and realtered to render the garment anything like wearable These reminiscences were not reassuring, particularly as she was conscious that even now the gown fitted horribly, and did grave injustice to her figure. On appealing to her hand-glass, it revealed a great wrinkle that lay right across her back, extending from one sleeve to the other. The waist, too, was absurdly short, and the tail went all off to one side, though she stuck a long pin right through it in a vain endeavour to keep it in its place. After a while she put down the glass with a sigh.

"It's no use," she mused despondently. "I must try not to think about my appearance People may say what they like, but there's an immense deal in dress, and I defy any civilised woman to feel comfortable or at her ease when she knows that her gown is a misfit. It doesn't signify for oneself. One doesn't care how dowdy one is when there is nobody to notice; but from the moment you have to run the gauntlet of other women's eyes, then, no matter how little vanity you may possess, it's awful – simply awful. Oh! dear, oh! dear, I wish I weren't such a fool as to mind."

Very dissatisfied both with herself and with her toilette, and feeling that she was old and ugly and unlike other people, poor Bligh gave her mother a farewell caress and walked disconsolately to the station. This girl, who had bravely looked poverty in the face, and who had probed her courage on many trying occasions, was now as frightened as the veriest coward. The prospect of going to a fine house, of which she was about to become the mistress, and making acquaintance with its inmates, tried her nerves to the utmost. Of late years she had lived such a solitary and secluded life that she seemed completely to have lost touch of the world. It required a supreme effort to talk and laugh and jest like the rest of mankind. She had grown silent and meditative, given to thought rather than words, to books than people. Talking for talking's sake was an art which she had not had the leisure to cultivate. She was accustomed to grave, rational conversation, and had no idea of the modern "chaff" which passes for wit in polite society. When she came across smart, fashionable women her feeling always was that an immense gulf divided them. She looked upon them with mingled awe and fear. They seemed like beings from a different world, with whom she could have nothing in common. Their gay chatter about dress, theatres, and mutual acquaintances, struck her dumb, and made her realise that she was indeed, what no doubt they mentally dubbed her, an " outsider." And then sometimes, on nearer acquaintance, her reserve would be fairly conquered, and she was agreeably surprised to find that after all these charming women were human like herself, and not nearly so formidable as she had imagined. She discovered that although she could not keep up a continuous flow of society nothings, in some ways she knew more than they did, and the stream of her conversation, if not so sparkling, was certainly deeper.

Balzac, than whom a more profound psychologist never existed, avers that solitude is apt to render a woman morose. In many instances it occasions a kind of savage distrust and defiance, both of herself and of others. This morbid condition has its birth almost entirely in insufficient intercourse with one's fellow-creatures. The softening influences of civilisation are swept away, and man regards man as his natural enemy, simply because he is not properly acquainted with him. Some such process had already begun to take place in Bligh's case, and her social qualities suffered from the hard, narrow life she had been forced to lead. Her natural modesty had given place to a perfectly painful shyness. She positively dreaded meeting strangers, or having to deviate from the straight groove of her accustomed duties. A fashionable girl, used to seeing new people continually, would have thought nothing of going to Beechlands and making her future mother-in-law's acquaintance. She would have entertained few misgivings, either as to her dress or the impression she was likely to make. In fact, no panic of depreciatory self-consciousness would have assailed her. But for Bligh the effort was enormous. She felt like a snail suddenly made to forsake its peaceful shell, and face the wide world naked and unprotected. The nearer the train bore her to her destination the more loudly did her heart beat. Her little hand grew quite hot and damp within its black kid glove, carefully mended at the finger-tips.

Always industrious and seeking after knowledge, even in idle moments, she had brought a book of science with her; but although she read most perseveringly the words left no impression on her mind. It was full of thought and refused to grasp theories of solar heat, missing links, and tertiary man. For her there were problems of the future which seemed of even greater importance than those contained in one of the most remarkable works of the age. By-and-bye, the train came to a standstill, and, in fear and trembling, she descended. On the platform her attention was arrested by a tall female figure clad in black. The owner glanced uncertainly around, and then advanced with both hands outstretched. If Bligh could have run away at that moment and hidden herself out of sight she would have done so. But before she had time to put such cowardly intentions into execution a soft cheek was pressed against her own, and a charmingly modulated voice said, "How do you do, my dear? You are Bligh Burton, I feel sure, and I am Lady Verschoyle. Let me thank you for coming so promptly in answer to my telegram. I fear it may have been inconvenient; but my anxiety to make your acquaintance must be my excuse."

Bligh looked at the sweet, worn face, with its kindly expression and tender eyes, and all at once she felt reassured. Her dread of Lady Verschoyle vanished, never to return. It proved, indeed, a case of mutual liking at first sight, for the anxious mother was delighted to find a quiet, pleasant-looking girl, whose appearance and demeanour at once betrayed no affinity whatever with the fast school she so detested.

"I could not do anything else but come," returned Bligh pleasantly. "It was sufficient for you to express a wish."

Lady Verschoyle was not accustomed to such courteous treatment from her nearest and dearest. She blushed with pleasure.

"Do you know," she confessed, "I was so impatient to see you that I felt as if I must come to the station."

"It was very kind of you to meet me," said Bligh gratefully.

"Not at all. Now, jump into the carriage, and we'll have a nice drive home together. I seem as if I had so many things to say to you that I hardly know how to begin. But, first and foremost, Bligh, I want you to regard me as a friend. Do you think you can?" And she turned appealingly to her young companion.

Bligh's favourable impressions were more than confirmed by this question. Her heart was quite won, and she began to wonder how she ever could have been afraid of meeting Lady Verschoyle. No wonder people always alluded to her as a charming woman. She seemed totally devoid of angles, and her gentle, deprecatory way of speaking possessed a peculiar fascination.

"A friend!" exclaimed Bligh impulsively. "Oh! how can I thank you enough for receiving me so kindly?"

Lady Verschoyle smiled.

"I hope we may grow to be very dear to each other," she said. "I will not deny that at first I was greatly surprised to hear of the engagement. I even fancied," here she hesitated, " well ! it is best not to have any concealments—I even fancied Philip ought to have made a more brilliant match——"

"Yes, I know that he ought," said Bligh, humbly. "No one feels it more than I do."

"But," continued Lady Verschoyle, " I despise myself already for my worldliness, and ask your pardon for having entertained such a thought. My friend, Mrs. Fortescue, has been telling me all about you, Bligh, and now I can truthfully say I am not only satisfied but deeply thankful that Philip has made so wise a choice."

The colour flew to Bligh's face. She felt like an impostor.

"Lady Verschoyle," she said, with much emotion, "I do not deserve your good opinion. You would not—could not—think well of me if you knew all. There is something very painful for me to say, and yet which it is my duty to tell you."

"I cannot believe anything bad of you, Bligh ; but if you wish to confide in me your confidence shall not go further."

"No doubt you think that—that I—love Sir Philip," said Bligh, turning from red to crimson, "but I don't. Perhaps I may learn to be fond of him in time. I hope so. I shall try very hard ; but it seems awful to marry in this sort of way. Had it not been for my mother's illness I could never have reconciled it to my conscience—never—never." And she looked away to hide the tears that sprang to her eyes.

"A great many things happen strangely in this world," said Lady Verschoyle gently. "Let us hope all will turn out well in the end. For my own part I cannot believe that so good a daughter will ever make a bad wife."

"I am glad I have told you the truth," said Bligh, in a curiously subdued voice. "I should have hated myself if I had concealed anything from you. Now, at least, you know the worst of me. My motive in marrying is intelligible, but Sir Philip's remains a mystery."

"He has been a bit of a spoilt boy all his life," said Lady Verschoyle. "His actions never were quite like other people's."

"That may be ; but why should he propose to a girl whom he does not care the least for, and insist on marrying her all in a hurry, just as if he were violently in love ? I have thought the matter over until I am tired of thinking about it, and admit to being fairly puzzled. And yet," she added, thoughtfully, "there must be some solution, if only I could get at it."

"Bligh, dear child," rejoined Lady Verschoyle gravely, "I quite understand your perplexity ; but if you are wise you will take Philip as he is. Even I, his mother, do not always know the reasons by which he is actuated."

"Surely you can guess what made him propose to me," said Bligh, fixing a pair of bright, inquiring eyes on her companion.

"Perhaps I can."

"Oh! then, do tell me."

"Will it be for your good?"

"Yes, it will help me more than anything else to shape my conduct. At present I have no clue. I grope about in the dark like the veriest mole."

"Well, then, Philip has had a disappointment."

"What sort of a disappointment? Did he want to marry some other woman?"

"Yes."

"Then why didn't he?"

"The lady was already engaged."

"And he cared for her?"

"He imagined so. In reality, what he felt was not love, but infatuation. It is better that you should know the truth. Just now he is sore and angry, but he will get over his indignation after a time."

"Ah!" exclaimed Bligh, with a look of comprehension. "That explains everything. Poor Sir Philip! I am sorry for him. We are quits. If I succeed in making your son happy, Lady Verschoyle, will you forgive me the sin I commit in marrying him?"

"My dear!" said the elder lady in a trembling voice. "You do not know what an escape Philip has had. This girl would have rendered him miserable. I could go down on my knees and thank God that he has got into good hands, for I have been very anxious about Philip. I am an old woman, and don't understand the art of managing him properly. But a wife will be quite different. She will be able to exercise a salutary influence over him. Not that he is bad or wicked," she went on, her maternal affection overpowering every other feeling, "but young men of his fortune and position have so many temptations put in their way, have they not?"

"Yes, no doubt," answered Bligh, feeling painfully impressed by the pathetic look in her companion's eyes.

"There are some people in this county," resumed Lady Verschoyle, "who don't get on well with Philip. It grieves me very much to know that this is the case. I do not think Philip is to blame, but they have never understood how to take him. He just wants a little humouring, and I am convinced that a clever, good-tempered girl, with a fair amount of tact, could manage him without any trouble."

Bligh put out her hand sympathetically. In spite of Lady Verschoyle's guarded words and evident affection for her son, she guessed at the disappointment he had caused his mother.

"I will do what I can," she said.

"Thank you, Bligh dear. Pray don't think I am complaining of Philip. Nothing was further from my intention, but everything will be new to you at first, and a few hints from a man's mother are sometimes not out of place."

Chatting confidentially, they arrived at Beechlands. Lady Verschoyle was charmed with her daughter-in-law that was to be. She listened so patiently and deferentially to all she had to say, and appeared so extremely sensible. Unconsciously, she unbosomed herself of many anxieties, little suspecting how quick Bligh was at forming conclusions. Her delight reached a culminating point when, on rounding the bend in the park, the church and distant village lay revealed.

"What a dear little church," exclaimed Bligh. "I shall like going there of a Sunday. It looks so peaceful."

"You do go to church, then?" asked Lady Verschoyle, a flush of pleasure mantling in her cheek.

"Why, of course. I generally conduct the choir at Elmsley."

"Oh! my dear," said Lady Verschoyle. "I have much to be thankful for. I can't tell you how glad I am that you are coming to live among us. People nowadays seem to have no respect for religion whatever. It is very dreadful, is it not? If you could only get Philip to observe the Sabbath I should die happy."

Bligh suppressed a sigh. She felt that more was expected of her than she would probably be able to perform. It is no easy task for a woman to reform a man close upon thirty years of age, and who does not pretend to care for her. Bligh knew enough of the world to be aware of this fact.

***

CHAPTER XIV

A SHOOTING WOMAN.

WHEN she set foot inside her future home, Bligh experienced a great relief on hearing that Sir Philip and his guests were out shooting. Lady Verschoyle conducted her all over the house, and showed off the different rooms with evident pride. Her visitor's admiration of their size and number afforded considerable gratification.

"I shall feel completely lost here," said Bligh, gaily, "and

scarcely know where to sit with such a choice of grand apartments."

"If you take my advice," responded Lady Verschoyle, " you
will turn my boudoir into your private sitting-room. It looks
south and east, and gets all the morning sun—a great advantage
in the winter time."

"Your boudoir!" exclaimed Bligh. "I should never dream
of appropriating anything that belongs to you."

Lady Verschoyle smiled sadly.

"My dear," she said, "you need have no scruples about me,
for when Philip marries I shall no longer be here."

"You don't mean to say that you are going away?"

"What else can I do? A mother-in-law's society is seldom
conducive to the happiness of a newly married pair."

"That depends on the mother-in-law," rejoined Bligh. "Nobody could possibly desire your absence."

"It is very kind of you to say so, but Philip and I settled it
long ago between us. There is a small dower-house just outside the park gates, which will suit me nicely in my old age. I
shall be near you, and able to see you every day without living
under the same roof." And she tried to look cheerful.

"And will Sir Philip actually let you go?" asked Bligh, indignantly, for she had already seen how deeply attached Lady
Verschoyle was to the home where she had lived so many years.

"Certainly; he is the master, and since he came of age, it
has always been an understood thing that I should only continue
to reside here as long as it suited his convenience. I don't complain—indeed, I have nothing to complain of, since when Sir
Thomas made his will, he consulted me on every point, and we
arranged it together. We both agreed that whenever our son
took a wife, we would turn out and leave the young couple in
possession of Beechlands."

"Won't you feel the change dreadfully, Lady Verschoyle?"

"Yes, perhaps I shall at first. When people get to my age,
it is wonderful how they become rooted to the same spot. Besides, it would be useless to deny that this place is associated in
my mind with a great many tender reminiscences. I can never
forget the happy days that Sir Thomas and I have spent here."
And she sighed, as she looked round, like a true and tender
woman bearing ever in her heart the image of him whom she
had loved and lost.

Bligh thought for a moment or two, then she said suddenly—

"Dear Lady Verschoyle, supposing Sir Philip and I both
begged of you to remain as a favour to ourselves, would you
stay?"

The elder woman changed colour. The mere suggestion sent

a thrill of joy travelling through her veins. She had never quite realised until now how painful it would be to her to leave Beechlands.

"I don't know," she said, hesitatingly. "If I could help either of you in any way—if I could be of the slightest use——"

"For my part, I feel convinced that I should never get on without you," returned Bligh. "Just think of poor little me transplanted to this great big house, and possessing no knowledge or experience whatever. Why, I should be lost, simply lost in it."

Lady Verschoyle gave a faint laugh.

"You've got a good head on your shoulders, Bligh. You'd soon find yourself quite competent to assume the reins of government."

"No, I shouldn't, and even if I did, it would not be for ages and ages. Imagine the change. I am not ashamed to confess our poverty. Almost ever since I can remember it has entailed the strictest economy. We have had to think twice about spending every sixpence. One's ideas of money grow narrowed like everything else, when one is honest and poor. It is the inevitable result of insufficient means to meet the daily wants. Picture to yourself a person brought up in a very small way suddenly placed at the head of a household like this. Of course she will commit errors—any amount of them at first starting, and few men are tolerant of mistakes which may have the disagreeable effect of interfering with their comfort. Literally, if I were left to myself, I should not know what to order for dinner. A couple of chops, a cutlet or two, or a little minced meat satisfy mamma and me. I ask you, would that satisfy Sir Philip?"

"Well! no, perhaps not," admitted Lady Verschoyle.

"Exactly. You see yourself that it will take me some time to master all the details connected with a large establishment; to know what the proper expenditure should be, and how much waste one must shut one's eyes to. No doubt I can learn. Given a certain amount of good-will and intelligence, and most things are to be acquired, but all the same I shall want help sadly to begin with, and that help you can give me better than any other person."

Lady Verschoyle listened, half persuaded. Bligh had a clear, forcible way of representing matters which struck home.

"I am so afraid of an old woman like myself being in the way," she said. "Philip likes young people about him, who mix in what he calls 'his set,' and even now I often feel as if my presence were a restraint. I belong to a past generation, and don't understand the modern jokes and allusions."

"In future you will have my mother to keep you company. Didn't Sir Philip tell you that he had promised to let her live with me?"

"No, he never mentioned the circumstance."

"He must have forgotten to do so, then, for it was strictly on this understanding that I accepted him. She would have died unless I had been able to pay for the operation. Surely Sir Philip will not wish you to leave Beechlands now?"

"I do not know," said Lady Verschoyle. "He may."

"He shan't," declared Bligh, energetically. "This very day I will speak to him and get the affair settled. It will be such a pleasure, such a support, to have you in the house. The thought of your going away makes me wretched. Dear Lady Verschoyle, I can't bear the idea of supplanting you, that's the truth. You are so kind and so good. Besides it is not fitting that Sir Philip's mother should leave her son's roof whilst mine remains beneath it."

Lady Verschoyle felt deeply moved by this speech. She had never expected to meet with such consideration from her son's bride. Blanche would have been impatient to get rid of her. She was quite prepared to resign the reins of government to a successor, but she was not prepared for the delicacy of feeling displayed by this little, humble girl, whom she herself in the first instance had looked down upon. Her heart grew big and soft. The tears rose to her dim eyes.

"If Philip wishes it—if—if Philip has not any objection——" she faltered.

"I will ask him to-day, before I return," said Bligh decidedly.

"Oh! my dear, aren't you rather venturesome? It may make him angry."

"I must run the risk of that."

"I am afraid he will think I have been putting you up to this," said Lady Verschoyle nervously.

Bligh laughed.

"Nothing venture, nothing have," she said cheerily. "It won't do for me to begin by showing the white feather, and I am sure Sir Philip is too much of a gentleman to refuse my first request."

Lady Verschoyle made no reply. She was not nearly so confident as Bligh, and feared that her audacity might lead to an unfortunate result, perhaps even a quarrel which might put an end to their present relationships, and this she dreaded beyond measure, for, little as she had seen of the girl, she liked her immensely.

The arrival of a pretty basket chaise, drawn by a small, broad-backed pony, here brought the conversation to a close. The two ladies seated themselves therein, the luncheon having already preceded them, and were soon jogging soberly along to the place of meeting. It was a clear, sunshiny day. Here and there the blue sky overhead was streaked by airy white clouds as fine as lawn, which sailed imperceptibly over its azure surface. The foliage of trees and hedges had not yet begun to drop, though green leaves were slowly taking on autumnal tints, whilst some few hung dead and shrivelled, ready to fall at the first touch of frost. The tops of the turnips, laden with raindrops from a recent shower, sparkled like diamonds. Their white roots gleamed above the rich earth. The level rays of the sun poured down upon the yellow stubble fields, and the sheaves of standing corn gathered up ready for carting. White roses clustered round cottage porches, and boldly climbed thatched roofs, scenting the air with their delicious fragrance. Hollyhocks and dahlias nodded their gay heads in the gardens, whilst the proud sun-flower shone like a golden disc against lichen-covered walls. Far off stretched a vast green vista of undulating pastures, which rolled away to the horizon in endless billows of grass. And on the sky line stood a celebrated fox covert, known far and wide by the name of Caryl's Clump.

Sir Philip was a strict preserver of foxes, and his shooting suffered somewhat in consequence. Fond as he was of the gun he preferred the saddle, and placed hunting at the head of all sports. Although Midlandshire could not be considered a good game county it nevertheless yielded fair, if not sensational, bags, and the proprietor of Beechlands owned some remarkably fine partridge ground. The present season promised well, and birds were reported more plentiful than usual. It had been arranged for the party to lunch at one end of an open common which adjoined the Top Farm, and which lay close to the last field of the morning beat. Towards this spot Lady Verschoyle guided the pony. As they advanced nearer to it they perceived a row of figures in the distance, marching towards them in a straight line. Suddenly a large covey, consisting of two old and ten young birds, rose with a whirr. Bang! bang! rang out the guns on the still air, and three fluttering victims fell beneath the shower of shot directed at them. The others escaped and flew away, pitching finally beneath a hedgerow some thirty or forty yards distant from where Lady Verschoyle had brought the pony chaise to a standstill. Looking through a gap she and Bligh could see the poor things quite plainly, crouching in terror under the turnip tops.

"How I wish we could save them," exclaimed Bligh. "I can't bear to see any creature killed that God has endowed with life."

But, alas! they were doomed to further destruction. On, on came the sportsmen and gamekeepers, pressing in from every side, until at last the goaded birds once more sought refuge in flight. This time four of their number fell, a handsome girl clad in a short tweed petticoat, leather gaiters, a Norfolk jacket and cap, being responsible for the death of one. Her face flushed with triumph as she threw away the end of her cartridge.

"Bravo! that was a capital shot of yours!" exclaimed Sir Philip, who happened to be next her, and who, having finished his forenoon's sport by a brilliant right and lefter, was in an unusually good humour. "I congratulate you, Miss Crisper. With very little more practice you'll take the shine out of half the men."

Delighted at this compliment, Miss Crisper grinned and showed her teeth, which were exceedingly fine. Women with bad ones always keep their mouths shut—that is to say when they are desirous of making a favourable impression.

"Yes," said the young lady complacently. "I flatter myself I potted that bird rather neatly. This makes five brace to my own gun. Not so bad for one belonging to the inferior sex, eh?"

"There's mighty little inferiority about you, Miss Vi," laughed Sir Philip in reply, with a familiarity which men frequently assume when in the presence of ladies who insist on sharing all their pastimes. "You're as smart as they make them, and can ride to hounds, bring down your bird, and toss off a brandy and soda in real good form."

"I should consider myself a hideous duffer if I couldn't," retorted Miss Crisper. "Women who sit at home and darn stockings have an awful time of it nowadays. I presume that in your opinion, Sir Philip, the last of my accomplishments is the greatest?"

The baronet reddened somewhat consciously.

"None of your chaff," he said. "A fellow's naturally thirsty when he has been walking in this blazing sun for two or three hours."

"And does that account for a fellow's natural thirst at ten o'clock in the morning? Oh! don't blush. I saw you having a quiet little nip in the smoking-room before we started, and, to tell the truth, I had a very good mind to follow your example. Hulloa! there's my bird fluttering about just under your heel. Pick the poor wretch up, there's a good soul, and put it out of its misery."

With which merciful request Miss Crisper vaulted lightly over a low stile which separated the turnip field from the common, and proceeded carefully to wipe the barrel of her gun with a silk bird's-eye pocket-handkerchief

Bligh stared at her in amazement. This was her first experience of the shooting woman, and the shortness of her skirt, the loudness of her voice, and the general mannishness of her demeanour, produced a startling impression upon her nerves. Miss Crisper seemed entirely at her ease, and after a general introduction had been effected, returned Bligh's stare with interest. By this time the guests had all heard of their host's engagement, and the ladies were extremely curious as to his choice.

"Humph!" murmured Miss Crisper, contemptuously, to Lady Rachel Rasper, "just fancy that being the bride. Well, I am astonished."

"A regular little country dowdy, who looks like a dug-up fossil," responded her ladyship, who was considered one of the most fashionable women about town. "Why, her hat is at least three seasons old. What in the name of wonder could Sir Philip have seen in her?"

"She has regularly got hold of him, depend upon it," said Miss Crisper. "I never trust these quiet, demure little persons. They're as artful as they can be, and always know uncommonly well on which side their bread is buttered."

She had come to Beechlands with the distinct intention of laying siege to its master's heart, so that her disapprobation was sufficiently intelligible. Even had Bligh been a professional beauty she would still have picked holes in her; but, as it was, Miss Crisper's indignation knew no bounds. True, it did not prevent her from eating a remarkably good lunch and casting her bright eyes in the direction of Captain Treherne, who also was regarded by society as a *parti*, but, while she quaffed her claret cup and made great inroads on an excellent pigeon pie, she kept thinking to herself all the time what a very much better, smarter, and sprightlier Lady Verschoyle she would have made than that poor, pale-faced little thing sitting opposite. When she summed up her own charms and compared them with Miss Burton's, she could not imagine where Sir Philip's eyes were.

CHAPTER XV.

LUNCH ON THE COMMON.

MEANWHILE Bligh was conscious of showing to the worst advantage. These smart ladies, with their audible comments, who stared at her through their eyeglasses as if she had been a perfectly unique specimen of the female race proved exceedingly overpowering to the timid girl, so long withdrawn from society. The shyness and sense of isolation from which she frequently suffered when in the presence of strangers returned in full force, whilst the thought of that great wrinkle across her back made her perfectly wretched. Whenever she was forced to move she tried hard to keep her face towards the ladies, and although her nature was by no means petty, and she was freer of small jealousies than the majority of her sex, she caught herself looking enviously at the admirably-fitting tailor-made gowns of Mrs. De Morbey and Lady Rachel Rasper. How beautifully straight their seams were, and how differently their bodies were cut from her clumsy, puckered affair, which was tight where it ought to be loose, and loose where it ought to be tight, squeezed her across the chest, and deprived her waist of all shape. She wished the day had not been so fine, then she might have put on a jacket to cover its defects. Never had they appeared more patent; for, as if out of pure malice, the searching sun poured down upon her rusty merino, making it look browner and shabbier than ever. Its bright rays illuminated her finger-tips, bringing into prominence every stitch with which she had striven to make her gloves presentable on the previous night. She buried them in the folds of her dress, but not before she was aware that Miss Crisper's sharp eyes had detected their existence.

Once she began to make comparisons between herself and her neighbours they seemed unceasing.

Even her boots were all wrong—great, square, ugly things; whereas the other ladies displayed the smartest of smart Russian leather, brown in colour, with polished pointed toes most becoming to the little feet they showed so liberally. Their hair, too, was curled and frizzed all over their heads, and of a lovely nut-brown shade, somewhat darker at the roots, that gleamed like burnished gold in the sunlight, whilst hers was plain and smooth, and plaited in old-fashioned braids on the nape of her neck. Even to the smallest detail there was a tremendous difference between her and them. They were so beautiful, aided by every adjunct which art and fashion could bestow: lovely, with powdered noses, gently touched cheeks, and pencilled eyebrows, whose adornment Bligh was both too generous and too innocent to suspect. But she felt that she could not compete with them. They outshone her as a star outshines a farthing rushlight.

No doubt Bligh was foolish. She ought to have risen superior to such trifles as a shabby frock and a pair of darned gloves; but she was only a woman, and a very sensitive one into the bargain, on whose impressionable nature everything took effect.

Whilst luncheon went on she sat by Lady Verschoyle's side, thankful for the protection afforded by her hostess, and only speaking when addressed. The three fashionable ladies might really have been forgiven for whispering to each other that she was as stupid as an owl ; nevertheless, if they could have looked into that shy, quiet girl's mind they would probably have been surprised at its powers of observation.

Bligh, on her part, was astonished at the frivolous talk, and wondered how any member of her own sex could permit such free and easy remarks from the men. Once or twice she was conscious that the colour mounted to her cheeks in a hot wave of shame. She dropped her eyes on the white tablecloth, and hardly dared to raise them, for, as the meal proceeded, the gentlemen grew more and more familiar, the ladies increasingly indulgent. " Chaff " summed up the conversation, and it appeared to Bligh that the coarser and riskier the better it was received. Real wit was conspicuous only by its absence. When Miss Crisper called for a brandy and soda, drank it off at one gulp, and was vociferously cheered by the men, she could perceive nothing very admirable in the proceeding. Neither did she think any better of Sir Philip because he finished a whole bottle of champagne almost at a draught, became very noisy and facetious, and played practical jokes on Lady Rachel Rasper, which consisted in dropping little bread pellets down her back, and taking flying shots at Miss Crisper's nose across the cloth. Bligh noticed that the effect of the numerous drinks he tossed off with such apparent relish was to deepen the flush on his handsome cheek, lend a glitter to his cold blue eyes, and deprive his manners of their finish.

From time to time Lady Verschoyle glanced anxiously at him.

" Philip has a great horror of getting fat," she confided to Bligh. " When you are married you must impress upon him that nothing adds so much to a person's weight as liquids."

" What's that you are saying about me, mother ? " he shouted out.

" I am telling Bligh you don't want to get fat."

" Quite right, quite right. Blazes ! how hot it is. Here, Spicer," calling to his valet, " mix me a brandy and soda. I can't be so ungallant," bowing to Miss Crisper, " as not to follow your lead."

The muscles round Lady Verschoyle's mouth contracted. Bligh wondered why the expression of her face was so very sorrowful. From under her soft eyelashes she watched mother and son in turn. Since she had heard of Sir Philip's disappointment he had become very much more interesting to her The light streamed full upon his yellow hair and auburn beard. It lay in a polished line along his straight nose, and deepened the blue of his well-opened eyes. The warmth of the day and the champagne had lent an unusual glow and animation to his countenance. Bligh was struck by his good looks, and took to wondering why she was not more elated at what Miss Crisper had already incidentally referred to as " her luck."

" He does not give one the idea of a man in love," she mused. " Who can the lady be ? I must find out later on."

Meanwhile the meal was drawing to a conclusion. Ample justice had been done to the good fare provided by Lady Verschoyle. The empty bottles were everywhere dotted about the tablecloth, whilst their corks strewed the ground. Miss Violet was the first to intimate that hunger and thirst were satisfied. She drew a neat leather case from her breast pocket, and calmly proceeded to light up a cigar, taking it so much as a matter of course that it never occurred to her apparently to ask Lady Verschoyle's permission. Fairly startled out of her shyness Bligh gasped—

" Do you—do you like smoking, Miss Crisper ? "

" Why, naturally I do," came the prompt reply, " else I shouldn't be such a fool as to smoke ! "

" I wonder it does not make you feel ill."

" Well ! " avowed Miss Crisper, frankly, " when I first began I was as sick as a cat ; but I hate being beaten, and so I stuck to it."

" But for what reason ? "

" I am vain enough to think that whatever a man does a woman can do very nearly, if not quite, as well. Personal experience goes far to confirm my opinion. A year ago I could not look at a cigar ; now,'' and inhaling a quantity of smoke, she puffed it out through her nostrils in airy rings, an operation which she watched with immeasurable pride, " I can consume as much tobacco as most fine gentlemen. That reminds me," she went on, addressing Sir Philip, " I had a match the other night with Tolly Greene, and beat him easily. He's a poor creature, and turned it up after the third cigar. I was proud of that achievement, if you like. It made one feel so superior when he began to choke and grow yellow in the face."

" And supposing the same mishap had befallen you ? " said Bligh, not knowing whether to be most amused or shocked.

" What ! turning yellow in the face ? I never should."

" Is Nature or art so kind ? " inquired Sir Philip, playfully.

" Nature, of course, you rude man. I shall owe you one for that. Did you ever see a lady yellow in your life, because if you have she was either a fool or else crossing the Channel ? "

Everybody laughed at this speech : not that it was particularly funny or clever, only Miss Violet had a way of saying things which her admirers called *chic*. Bligh laughed with the rest. She thought Miss Crisper the most extraordinary girl she had ever met, and listened to her much as she would have listened to a comic actress in a burlesque. It seemed hard to believe that she was not acting a part. This playing at being a man appeared a strange *rôle* for a good-looking young woman to assume, and if it were intended to secure a husband Bligh was quite sure that Miss Crisper made a mistake. Men might flirt with but they never married such girls.

Sir Philip now showed symptoms of impatience, and was anxious to recommence work. He rose to his feet, saying, " Come, we have wasted enough time. Let's be off, for there is a great deal of ground before us still, and it's a pity not to take advantage of this glorious day. A week hence and the birds won't lie anything like so well." This was the signal for a start, but during the delay inevitable to departure Bligh managed to take him aside.

" May I have a word with you ? " she said.

" Yes," he replied : " but don't be long about it, there's a good girl. We're in a hurry to be off. If it's of any importance you can write. You see how it is, Bligh. One's not one's own master when there are other fellows about. I can't even drive you back to the station and see you off comfortably."

" I quite understand," she said quietly. " Pray don't allow me to disturb your arrangements. It is about your mother I wished to speak. She has been talking to me to-day of leaving Beechlands."

" Well, of course, she'll have to go when we are married."

" I don't quite see the necessity The house is large enough for us and her."

" Oh ! it's large enough, certainly. For the matter of that, there are more rooms than one knows what to do with. But she would be awfully in the way. She's so infernally strict and Puritanical in her notions. It's impossible to tell a good story before her."

" She is your mother," said Bligh gravely, " and she is no longer as young or as strong as she was. I am sure you would not like to let her go away, and, for myself, I should feel quite distressed if she did, since, were she to leave Beechlands, I believe that it would pretty nearly break her heart. She is devoted to the place."

" Yes, you're quite right there. The old lady is never so happy as when she is pottering about the garden or the village."

" Then why not let her remain happy till the end? The best part of her life is gone. Is it not for us to embellish her remaining days? Your mother is not an ordinary woman. I admit that with some mothers difficulties might arise ; but she is so kind, so good, so unassuming, that I feel sure we should never clash. Her presence, too, would be of great assistance to me, for you must remember that I am not accustomed to a fine house and plenty of money, and in all probability will have much to learn."

Sir Philip was in a remarkably good temper. He had shot brilliantly, " wiped " Captain Treherne's eye twice, and altogether Bligh could not have chosen a more propitious moment. He looked at her not unkindly.

" Have you sufficiently thought over what you propose ? " he said. " It will be an experiment which, once made, is not easy to back out of."

" Nevertheless, I think we ought to try it."

" Well ! you're the rummest girl that ever I came across. I never heard of one before who wanted her mother-in-law to live in the same house with her. Generally they are all anxiety to bundle them out."

" There will be my mother too," said Bligh timidly, wishing to recall their compact to his mind.

" Damnation, yes. It strikes me you want to turn Beech-lands into an asylum for old women. What are we going to do with them when we have a dinner party, and fill the house with nice, cheery people ? They'll be awfully out of it."

" Mamma would greatly prefer remaining upstairs. She is not likely to trouble you much. Such small details are easily arranged, and neither the presence of your mother nor mine shall ever interfere with the duty I owe to you."

Her words pleased him. Like all rich and idle young men he had great ideas about the superiority of the male sex. In his opinion a man's actions were always pardonable, a woman's never. From a wife he expected complete submission, a total surrender of will, no matter whether he were right or wrong. He flattered himself that he was very strong, and above feminine influence. How weak he was in reality we have already seen.

" You have an answer for everything," he said, in reply to Bligh's last remark. " What do you want me to promise ? "

" Give me leave to tell Lady Verschoyle that she may stay, at all events for a while."

" Let it be a temporary arrangement then. I must have that distinctly understood. There's no saying what the future may bring forth, and I don't wish to bind myself to any solemn
pl

"Oh! Philip," cried Bligh gratefully, for the first time calling him by his Christian name, and dropping the prefix, "this is very kind of you. I won't forget it in a hurry, and if I can show my gratitude I will."

"Tut, tut," he said, pleased by the evident impression he had made, and feeling that he really was a very good boy indeed, which sensation proved agreeable from its novelty; "I haven't done anything so wonderful, and, mind you, I don't bind myself."

"No, I shall remember the reservation."

"Well, good-bye, Bligh, I must be off. There's Miss Violet making faces at me from behind her gun. I'm glad you like the old lady. She's a good soul in the main, though, of course, her way is not exactly mine."

"Good-bye, Philip," said Bligh, with a nearer approach to liking than she had yet entertained for him. "I don't think you will regret having made this concession. In my humble experience people never do repent of their kind actions; it's only the unkind ones which they look back upon with remorse."

They shook hands cordially and parted, Sir Philip beginning to feel a vague respect for the girl whom he had chosen to be his wife, Bligh with hope and gladness springing up in her heart like beautiful flowers. If she could only live in peace and amity, and render others happy, then she would ask for nothing more, and from the ashes of the old love a new might arise. Until to-day she had doubted herself; now she felt that their future rested with him.

Ah! if men only knew how easily they can win women through kindness, and how little they gain by brute force.

CHAPTER XVI.

MARRIED AND DONE FOR.

ALTHOUGH Sir Philip particularly desired to be married as soon as possible, and lost no time in announcing his engagement in the *Morning Post* and the principal Society papers, over a month elapsed before Mrs. Burton had sufficiently recovered from her operation to be moved from town. By Lady Verschoyle's wish, directly she was able to travel she and Bligh went straight to Beechlands, and on the 7th of October, 189—, the wedding was solemnised by Mr. Roden in the Parish Church.

Sir Philip had begun by insisting on its being a very grand affair; but, owing to the joint persuasions of his mother and bride, the ceremony was ultimately performed quite quietly, and in the presence of only a limited number of intimate friends. Mrs. Burton's recent illness formed a good excuse for dispensing with the pomp and the fuss which Bligh secretly dreaded. The deed once done she felt comparatively happy. It put an end to all the doubt and indecision by which she had been assailed during the period of her engagement. Now that her fate was decided her sense of responsibility weighed less heavily upon her. There was much to be thankful for, apart from any question of personal feeling. She realised this very forcibly.

It was a wonderful thing to wake up of a morning with a mind entirely free from anxiety as to how two ends could be contrived to meet, and to know that, well or ill, willing or unwilling, she need no longer tramp along the muddy roads going from house to house in search of a livelihood. Only those similarly situated can fully comprehend the relief which Bligh experienced in staying quietly at home whenever she had the wish, being worried by no financial cares, and once more becoming her own mistress. It was like a haven of rest after tossing about on the wide sea, in constant fear of sinking. Now all the planning and thinking, the miserable struggle to keep up appearances in a country where poverty is a crime, was at an end.

When Bligh returned from London, in spite of a hard bout of nursing, Lady Verschoyle was quite surprised at the improvement that had taken place in the girl's appearance. She was plumper and brighter. Her face had filled out and wore a delicate bloom, which made it look at least five years younger. Added to this Sir Philip had insisted on her profiting by her stay in the Metropolis to visit some of the best modistes, and he himself was startled at the results.

A good dressmaker and pretty frocks did wonders for Bligh, as they do for most women, and the consciousness of being properly equipped lent a certain confidence to her manner which it had hitherto lacked. She began to think society was not so very dreadful when one could enter it on equal terms. With one of her new gowns on she should not feel half as afraid of Lady Rachel and Miss Crisper when she met them again.

Sir Philip was so astonished at the metamorphosis effected by his generosity that, instead of mentally apostrophising her as "a plain little dowdy," as he had hitherto done, he began to admit that, if not exactly a beauty, she was quite nice-looking, and had an air of grace which proclaimed her unmistakably to be a lady. Bligh rose considerably in his estimation, and, despite the hastiness of his choice, he confessed to himself that although he had not succeeded in getting precisely what he wanted he might have done a very great deal worse.

Blanche's name never passed his lips. It was as if he had forgotten her existence.

Nevertheless, his mother noticed that every day the first thing he did on taking up the paper was to eagerly scan the matrimonial advertisements, as if he were looking out for some announcement. He had not to wait long. Just a week before his own marriage took place he found what he sought. Lady Verschoyle was made aware of the fact by hearing him breathe two or three deep breaths and seeing his face grow dark and stern.

"What is it, Philip?" she asked timorously "Is anything the matter?"

"Oh! no, nothing. Merely the announcement of Blanche's lovey-dovey match in the paper," he replied.

"She was married the day before yesterday," said Lady Verschoyle. "I sent her a set of pearls in a present."

"And I sent her nothing."

"Didn't you, Philip? Won't that look rather shabby?"

"I don't care if it does. She'll know the reason fast enough."

There was silence for a few minutes, then, breaking into a harsh laugh, he added :—

"When she has had a sickener of India I shall write and ask her to come and stay here, just to let her have an opportunity of realising the extent of her folly."

And with that he walked out of the room and did not say another word on the subject. Whatever were his thoughts he kept them to himself.

Lady Verschoyle shivered.

"Let us hope," she murmured fervently, "that Blanche never will come back from India—at least, not for a long, long time. I have a presentiment that if she does mischief will arise."

For two or three days afterwards Sir Philip was unusually taciturn and reserved, and Bligh racked her brains to think what she could have done to offend him. However, as he chose to withhold his confidence, and shortly regained his usual manner, she wisely did not question him regarding the cause of his ill-humour. No doubt if she had been deeply in love his moods would have proved more disturbing to her equanimity. She had already discovered that his temper was extremely variable, and that a very little sufficed to upset it: but she did not expect perfection, and, like a sensible woman, was prepared to put up with some few drawbacks in return for the many advantages which he had so strangely offered for her acceptance.

Whenever she thought matters over she always finished up by

saying to herself, " It is not reasonable to imagine that one is going to get so much good without some slight mixture of evil. Philip has been spoilt by an excess of prosperity and having everything made too easy for him. Consequently, if the least trifle happens to go wrong he feels aggrieved, and can't bear annoyances like people who are accustomed to being worried. It's purely the result of circumstances and of his education. I must be patient with him, and whenever he loses his temper try not to lose mine, for I hope—I believe—that his heart is in the right place. What faults he has are mostly on the surface."

Just at this period Bligh was in a singularly hopeful frame of mind and inclined to look at things from an optimistic point of view. The respite from toil, the freedom from monetary anxieties, lightened her brain much as if a great. dark cloud had been rolled away from it, and, in addition, her mother seemed stronger and better than had been the case for many months.

Although Mrs. Burton's malady remained unchanged, Mr. Donnington had assured Bligh, after the operation, that if the disease did not spread, the patient might live for years to come. At the same time he did not disguise the fact that cancer was generally in the blood, and therefore liable to break out afresh in spite of every human precaution. Bligh, however, could not help feeling sanguine, for the remarkable improvement which took place in the invalid's health seemed to justify her best hopes. It was a source of abiding thankfulness to see her mother well housed and cared for, able to drive out in a nice, easy carriage, and to command those luxuries which her state demanded, yet which hitherto had been totally beyond their means. Even if Sir Philip were sometimes rude and cross, spoke roughly and plainly showed his indifference, what did it signify in comparison with the all-important fact of this darling mother being raised above want?

Bligh felt that she could bear a great deal, and ought to bear a great deal, as a way of paying back what she had received. Her heart was full of gratitude. It made her very gentle to Sir Philip, very ready to make excuses for him, and to shut her eyes to his faults. In this spirit she approached the hymeneal altar, and from poor, struggling, brave little Bligh Burton was converted into Lady Verschoyle, the wife of one of the largest and richest landed proprietors in the county. Fortune's wheel had perched her up on high, and elevated her to a position which even in the dreams of her youth she had never contemplated. Many a fashionable girl envied her as she read the account of the wedding in the newspapers and ran over the list of presents, in which the name of the heir to the Throne figured, presenting the bridegroom with a handsome silver hunting flask. And Blanche

Vansittart, the bride of a week, pored over it also, and as she did so a vague feeling of regret and dissatisfaction sprang up within her breast, making her feel curiously discontented with her own lot.

" I might have had him," she sighed uneasily. " Ah! if I had only known sooner—if he had but spoken out in time."

Great smarting drops swam in her dark eyes, burning them like liquid fire. An icy chill constricted her heart.

Why did she feel like this at the mere sight of his name in print, linked with that of another woman? What meant that dull pain? Was it jealousy? Before her marriage she fancied the fight was over, and that she had conquered. Instead of thinking of Philip her thoughts now ought to be for the good and honourable man who loved her so truly and unselfishly. Ah! she was very wicked—very wicked. It was as well that the seas would divide them, that henceforth they were not likely to cross each other's path. She had made so sure of his coming back again after he proposed, and had he done so, in spite of every tie, she knew what her answer would have been. She never could have said him " No " a second time. Even now she could hardly realise that he had actually run his head into the matrimonial noose. It all seemed like a bad dream, and every morning she expected to awake from it, and every night went to bed sorrowing because it was no dream but a reality. Once or twice before her marriage she had been on the point of writing him, but the fear of a rebuff deterred her. She did not want to fall between two stools. Up to the last moment she felt like a criminal expecting his reprieve. She refused to believe that he would let her marry anyone else, but now her wedding-day was over and also his. A solid barrier reared itself between them, and it was too late for explanations. He belonged to another woman. She could have wept with rage, envy, and mortification. Henceforth her life appeared a dismal failure. Nothing could redeem the past. For there on her finger shone the wedding-ring, new and bright, and she was no longer Blanche Sylvester but Blanche Vansittart. She and Philip had played too long with edged tools. They had ended by cutting themselves.

Nevertheless, she was whitewashed according to her wish. The friends who had been inclined to show her the cold shoulder were now unanimous in their gush and their affection. One might have fancied that dear Mrs. Grundy had never cast the slightest shadow over her fair name or ever applied that damning epithet " fast." The most virtuous lady of her acquaintance, who had dropped her for over a year, now insisted on her making her house her home previous to Colonel Vansittart's departure for India. After this it was impossible to deny that even in the most bitter cup there are a few sweet drops of compensation. Yet Blanche was ill at ease. In face of all the hospitality and kindness shown to the newly-married couple she could not help asking herself how long the whitening process to which she had been subjected would last. Already in her heart of hearts she doubted its durability, and realised that the pronunciation of certain conventional words which converted her into a wife, bound to love, honour, and obey, could not alter her nature. Her proud, irregulated spirit resented any master, no matter how gentle or loving. When she looked forward to the future a shudder of despair ran through her frame. Although she had only been married a week she already saw clouds on the horizon, which threatened to extend and increase. The Colonel was so good, and he expected her to be so good also. It was difficult not to shock him, and yet, on the other hand, if she considered every word it made her feel hypocritical and uncomfortable. They were not at their ease together. He grew pompous, she dull. She had hoped things would improve after matrimony, instead of which they had gone from bad to worse. His very presence in the room irritated her. Sometimes she could hardly bring herself to be civil to him. And the terrible part of it all was she had not a fault to find with him. He was such a kind, devoted creature. But she could not help it, his devotion bored her intensely. Every time he left her alone— and, good Heavens ! how seldom that was—she experienced a sense of relief. And this was marriage. Should she be able to endure it through all the long, long years to come ?   Would she have strength to act her part to the bitter end, sit opposite to him day after day, month after month, and never let him guess the stormy feelings in her heart ? Could she set her face to one fixed pattern and never for an instant lift the mask ? That was what most good wives did. She had seen it often, and admired the heroic acting which bore slights with apparent equanimity, insults with every outward seeming of indifference—acting so clever, so finished, that only the closest observer could detect the real, tortured nature of the woman, quivering at every stab. Yes, they were heroines ; but for herself she did not possess the qualities which render endurance a virtue. She would rather break than bend, defy than bear.

She and Philip would have spent their lives in wrangling royally. The Colonel never wrangled. He only remonstrated with a pained, puzzled look in his mild eyes. It drove her regularly mad, for it always made her feel that she was in the wrong.

As she read about the wedding at Beechlands a fair face rose to her mind, handsome as a god's, in spite of its shifty expression and insincere smile. Her husband could not understand why she was so quiet and depressed, and took so little interest in their preparations for departure. He hovered round her uneasily, and at length inquired, in a tone of tender anxiety, if his bride were not well.

"Oh ! yes," she answered shortly. "I'm perfectly well. There's nothing whatever the matter with me."

" I thought you seemed dull, my darling, and out of sorts."

" Do I ? " and she laughed a bitter laugh. " It is extremely kind of you to interest yourself so much in the state of my health. The truth is, I am not yet accustomed to the dignity and honour of being 'married and done for.' One feels rather like a bird with his wings clipped at first."

" Blanche, dearest, it grieves me to hear you talk in this way."

" Why ! what have I said now ? I'm always saying something wrong apparently."

" Am I indeed such a tyrant that you think of me as if I were your gaoler."

" Every husband is, more or less, to the woman he marries."

" That is a sentiment with which I cannot agree. Where true affection exists there can be no question of mastery on the one side or of slavery on the other. Do you honestly accuse me of being too masterful."

" Oh ! no you're very pleasant, and all that sort of thing, but——"

" But what, Blanche ? If I have erred it has not been intentionally."

She shrugged her shoulders with an impatient gesture.

" As we have got to live together all our lives I wish you would understand one thing, Weldon. It will save such a lot of trouble if you can remember it from the beginning."

" Well ! " he said, quiet and pale. " What is it ? "

" Don't, for goodness' sake, demand an explanation of every word I may happen to utter. In the first place, I decline to give it, and, in the second, it's irritating beyond conception. If you think I am not lively or cheerful, instead of asking questions, take it for granted that I happen to be in a silent mood, and don't wish to go through a strict cross-examination as to why I feel disinclined to chatter like a parrot. Everybody is dull at times, and it is too much to expect an unfortunate woman always to play the clown for man's edification."

" But, Blanche dear, if you are feeling dull it is for me to try and enliven you."

" It's no use trying when you won't succeed. In future if

you see me with one of these fits on the greatest service you can
do me is to leave me alone."

It was an ungracious speech, uttered in a moment of irritation.
Colonel Vansittart looked at his wife and sighed.

"You are a strange woman," he said. "I feel that I don't
understand you, or you me. Although we are married, we stand
apart. There are times when I almost think that you hate me.
If this is so, Blanche—if any portion of your present unhappiness is owing to me, don't be afraid to tell the truth. I love you
too well, dear, to render your life miserable. Girls occasionally
make mistakes. If you feel that you have made one, and cannot live happily with me, I—I," and his voice trembled a little,
"will go to India alone."

In an instant she saw what her position would be if she were
without a strong hand to guide and support her. A great fear
seized her—a horror of being left to battle helplessly with her
evil impulses. Moreover his kindness and generosity appealed
to all that was best in her complex nature. She laughed hysterically.

"Why, Weldon!" she said, speaking in a tone of artificial
mirth, "what an old goose you are to be sure, to take my
foolish speeches so seriously. Anyone can see that you have
not been much accustomed to womankind." And she laid her
hand on his arm.

He thrilled at her touch. This man who had gone through half
a dozen wars without turning a hair was completely subjugated.

"Blanche!" he cried, passionately, catching her in his arms
and straining her to him, "I do love you so. No, don't re-
pulse me," as she tried to free herself. "I am a great clumsy
fellow, I know; dull when I ought to be gay, and gay when I
ought to be dull. But my affection is genuine, and if only you
were not so cold and hard, you could make what you chose of
me——"

"You are good enough as you are," she interrupted, with real
emotion.

"Oh! my darling, my darling," he continued, growing eloquent from sheer force of feeling. "We are husband and wife,
and ought to be very dear to each other. God is witness how
dear you are to me, but I sadly fear the love is all on my side.
Can't you—won't you try to care for me a little bit?" In his
agitation he loosed his hold, and began striding vehemently up
and down the room.

All of a sudden she burst into a passion of tears, and flung
herself face downwards on the sofa. In an instant he was kneeling by her side, horrified at the effect of his words.

"Blanche!" he cried, "what have I done? Oh! tell me,
wha

She tried to speak, but sobs prevented her.

"I am a stupid brute," he went on, "and have hurt your feelings. I had no business to be so rough, or to take you unawares. Darling, you must tell me of my faults, and I will endeavour to correct them all. There is nothing I would not do for your sake." And laying his big hand on her head, he gently smoothed away the hair from her brow.

The sound of his manly, tender voice, the touch of his strong fingers, filled her with a sense of abasement. She caught his hand and kissed it. The warm blood rushed to his honest face.

"It—it is not y—you whom I dislike, but—myself," she faltered, contritely.

A look of rapture illumined his countenance.

"Can it be that I have made a mistake? Is it possible that I am not so indifferent to you as I supposed? Oh! Blanche, then indeed should I be a happy man."

"You are too good for me, Weldon. I knew it from the first, and ought never to have married you. If your life is broken and marred, I shall be the cause of it." And again she hid her face among the cushions.

He raised her gently in his arms, as a mother might raise a little child.

"My beloved," he said, "your nerves are unstrung, else you never could say so foolish a thing. What next, I wonder! My life broken—my life marred, and through you! I don't think you quite realise yet my devotion, or how proud I am of my beautiful wife. If she would only love me a little, at this moment I could die happy, feeling I had nothing left to wish for."

She turned her tear-stained face away. She could not stand the gaze of those kind brown eyes. They were as a reproach.

"I—I—will try," she said, unsteadily, unconscious of the confession conveyed in her speech.

He kissed her quietly on the forehead. All his passion had fled, forced back like a wave from the shore, for he knew that his fears were confirmed, and that he held no place in her heart. But he was a brave man, and did not despair.

"I must be content to wait for the fulfilment of my happiness," he said, soberly. "Please God, it will come some day."

So saying, he left the room, with an instinctive feeling that she desired to be alone, and did not as yet derive any solace from his society. The knowledge caused exquisite pain, but he registered an inward vow that if kindness, patience, and forbearance could win a woman, he would win her. He was not a man to cry out when he was hurt, and make a great fuss without attempting any remedy. In his quiet way he preferred to act rather than talk.

Although she did not know it, Blanche was fortunate in one respect. She could hardly have fallen into better hands.

CHAPTER XVII.

GOING TO THE MEET.

BLIGH and Philip went to Paris for their honeymoon, intending to stay away a fortnight or three weeks. But Sir Philip, like a good many of his compatriots, hated being abroad, and felt strange and uncomfortable out of his own country. He spoke French with considerable difficulty, and with an execrable accent. Nevertheless, he displayed extreme resentment whenever he failed to make himself understood, and dubbed the natives a set of stupid fools.

Life at an hotel, even when you had retained the best "suite" of rooms in it, was very different, from being at Beechlands. He missed the luxuries of home, his shooting, horses and servants; his cosy smoking-room and particular arm-chair.

Bligh began by taking him to the Louvre, Notre Dame, etc., but she soon discovered that he exhibited no interest in picture galleries, and detested sight-seeing when unconnected with horses and dogs. He frankly admitted that he saw nothing to admire in a lot of fusty old canvases, or in a dingy cathedral. After the first day or two he declined to go beyond the boulevards and the Palais Royal, where he spent his time principally looking at the tobacconists' shops, and criticising the various meerschaum pipes designed by French genius. There were only two things in Paris of which Sir Philip condescended to express unqualified approval—namely, the cooking and the theatres. He and Bligh visited by turns the various restaurants, and where they should dine was always the most important question of the day. Unfortunately Bligh's gastronomic taste was by no means highly developed. Of late years it had not received much cultivation, and she preferred simple fare to costly side dishes composed of unseasonable delicacies. Sir Philip expressed himself greatly disappointed by her want of appreciation.

"I never saw such a person in my life," he grumbled. "It's like throwing pearls before swine. A good dinner is regularly wasted upon you. As for the wine, it does not matter what I order, you always stick to that cold, nasty water."

They did not agree any better in their tastes as regarded the theatres. Bligh loved going to the opera above everything, whereas her husband hated music, and cared only for ballets and burlesques. Even in such trifling matters as eating and acting, it was surprising how few points they had in common. What she thought odious, he termed " prime "; what she considered vulgar, he pronounced first-rate. The one liked simplicity, the other delighted in parade and ostentation ; the one never lost an opportunity of acquiring knowledge, the other was profoundly satisfied with the small stock already possessed. In fact, there was no real congeniality between them. Their natures were too unlike to fuse into a harmonious whole.

Thus ten days passed away, and every morning Sir Philip racked his brains for an excuse to cut the honeymoon short, and return to his native land. For a while he said nothing, being afraid of hurting Bligh's feelings, but at last he could stand it no longer, and in a fit of desperation remarked to his bride—" I say, Bligh, don't you find Paris rather slow, because, if so, it strikes me we might be thinking of going home."

She jumped at the notion. She had striven hard not to let him see how much she longed to put an end to their state of dual solitude—for, after all, that was what this wedding trip of theirs amounted to ; and it was an agreeable surprise to find that his wish coincided with her own.

" By all means," she responded readily. " I am quite willing to go whenever you are."

He was delighted at her accepting his proposition in such good part, and advancing no objections.

" People are fools to come abroad for their honeymoon, when they are so very much more comfortable in their own country and their own homes," he observed. " To my mind, the only time when Paris is really enjoyable is during the *Grand Prix*. Then it's pleasant enough, running over for a couple of days, and hobnobbing with all one's friends ; but now there is absolutely nothing to see and nothing to do."

Bligh's thoughts reverted to the treasures in the Louvre, which he had refused even to glance at ; but she made no answer, having already learnt the wisdom of the maxim, that if speech is silver, silence is golden. The discreet wife holds her tongue when she does not agree, and thus wards off many a quarrel.

" Do you think you could pack up and be off to-morrow ? " he inquired, finding she did not reply.

" Oh ! yes, Philip, easily. I have not much luggage ; indeed, I am inclined to believe you have the most of the two." Then a happy thought struck her, and she added, " Isn't the cub hunting season in full swing just now ? It seems such a pity for you to miss more of it than we can help."

" By Jove ! " he exclaimed. " What a sensible little thing you are ! Yes, of course it's a pity. There are all the horses at the present moment eating their heads off. This very morning I had a letter from Masterton, saying that they were having first-rate sport. Last Monday it appears the hounds got on to the line of an old dog fox before it was possible to stop them, and ran as hard as they could split from Caryl's Clump to Gossington Gorse. An eight mile point as the crow flies. Awfully good, wasn't it ? "

" Yes, very, I should think," answered Bligh, who, where sporting matters were concerned, was somewhat of an ignoramus.

" Let me see," continued Sir Philip, in high good-humour at the prospect of making his appearance in the hunting field a whole week sooner than he had anticipated. " This is Thursday. If we were to start the first thing to-morrow morning, we could travel on from London by the evening train, and providing we arrived at Victoria pretty punctually, reach Beechlands somewhere about half-past ten o'clock. Would it tire you too much to go straight through ? "

" Not a bit," she responded, her eyes shining with delight at the prospect of so soon being with her mother again. " We had much better not break the journey, and then you can get out hunting on Saturday."

" The same thing struck me, and as we seem both to have had enough of foreign parts, I'll go and telegraph to the old lady at once."

For the rest of the day Sir Philip was in great spirits, and showed his glee by ordering an extra sumptuous dinner, on the ground that it was their last one. He called for champagne, and drank freely of the sparkling beverage, to Bligh's inward regret, for she had already had occasion to notice that half a dozen glasses of wine were sufficient to render him exceedingly talka-tive and argumentative. However, the evening passed off without any serious *contre-temps*, and on the following afternoon they had the gratification of once more finding themselves on English soil. Certainly it was pleasant coming home to receive such a welcome. The two dear old ladies could not make enough of them, and fussed and purred over their respective darlings as if they had been away for ten years instead of ten days. Their loving faces were wreathed in smiles and beautified by affection. And they appeared so happy together that it quite did Bligh's heart good to see them. There was so much to say on either side, so many experiences to exchange, that the night was far advanced before the travellers were allowed to retire to rest. But joy does not tire, and Bligh felt no fatigue.

Sir Philip had sent for his stud groom shortly after arriving, and had arranged to ride two of his best hunters on the morrow, when the hounds met within five miles of Beechlands. Bligh expressed a strong wish to go to the meet, and in spite of its being fixed for nine o'clock, Lady Verschoyle volunteered to drive with her daughter-in-law. Sir Philip was pleased at the interest his wife showed in his favourite pursuit, and promised to buy her a nice quiet hack, and teach her to ride, so that after a while she might accompany him out hunting. As for Mrs. Burton, she elected to remain at home. Although much better, she scarcely felt equal to the exertion of rising earlier than usual.

But those who possessed health and strength were well repaid the next morning for losing an additional hour of bed. The day broke clear and fine, with just a touch of sharpness in the air suggestive of autumn. The trees in the park showed very bright and yellow as the sunshine played upon their changing foliage and invested it with those gorgeous tints which herald decay. Every now and then a leaf, dead, withered, and twisted into a fantastic shape, fluttered from its stalk to the ground, where it lay a tiny golden mass on the emerald grass. The birds chirped and plumed their feathers, as if they refused to believe that the summer had departed, and winter frosts were near at hand. Sir Philip's large-eyed Alderneys cropped the fresh herbage, whisking their long tails against their sleek russet sides. Outside the park the hedgerows were adorned as if fairy hands had been at work during the night. They were literally hung with gossamer nets, all sloping in the same direction, the work of numberless busy spiders. Great drops of dew sparkled like electric lights in their shining meshes, illuminating the shrunken form of some bloodless captive.

"How beautiful and fresh the country is!" Bligh exclaimed, as they drove along in a comfortable victoria, drawn by a pair of well-matched carriage horses. "On such a morning as this one feels inclined to bow down and worship at the shrine of Nature. Look at the effect of those cloud-shadows gliding along the field, and how they swallow up the light, only to let it reappear in their train with redoubled glory. Philip was right— Paris is not to be compared to this, and I am more glad than I can tell to be at home again."

Lady Verschoyle smiled pleasantly. Bligh was a young woman after her own heart, who did not care for towns and shop windows.

"I think Philip is glad also!" she said. "How happy and handsome he looked as he cantered away from the front door on his hack. I may be mistaken, but I always consider that he never appears to so much advantage as on horseback. Of course, to-day he was in ordinary clothes, but you should see him in his red coat."

"I can quite imagine it is very becoming," rejoined Bligh, amused by, yet respecting the mother's pride. "Is Philip a hard rider? He talks as if he were."

"A good many of them do that, but I believe Philip goes uncommonly well. I don't know much about it myself, but so I am told. He can't bear to be beaten by other people. It's quite funny sometimes to listen to these sporting folk, when two or three of them get together. You would fancy that to jump a hedge first, and in front of your neighbours, is the proudest distinction in the world. It seems to me there is a good deal of rivalry and jealousy amongst their ranks, and whenever Philip hunts, I am always in a fidget for fear of some accident happening."

"Has he ever had a bad fall?" asked Bligh.

"No. Curiously enough, up till now he has escaped with no worse injury than a few bruises and contusions. But I live in constant dread of some serious mishap, and if he happens to be late I go through a perfect martyrdom of anxiety, imagining all the different evils that may have befallen him. The wife of a hunting man must often have a miserable time of it. For your sake, Bligh, I hope you are not nervous."

"No, I don't think I am; but I have not yet been tested, and my immunity from fear may arise from ignorance. It seems to me though, that to anyone who really knows how to ride, hunting must be glorious work. I can imagine nothing more exciting than being on a good horse, and feeling that you and he between you are prepared to face every obstacle without looking for any help from outside."

"It's all very well as long as people go scot free," rejoined Lady Verschoyle. "But I should fancy that when they broke an arm or leg, or were crippled for life, as is sometimes the case, the question would certainly arise, is the game worth the candle? If you ever do take to hunting, my dear Bligh, which, with such a sporting husband, seems not at all improbable, I hope you will ride mildly."

"I'm not likely to ride in any other way," said Bligh, reassuringly. "One has to begin young in order to be a good horsewoman, and I have never had the chance."

"I don't the least object to ladies going to the meets, and even hacking about the roads," said the dowager, "but I certainly think women ought not to hunt like men, although I am quite aware a great many do so nowadays. In my youth, girls who hunted were considered almost unsexed."

Bligh laughed.

"Dear Lady Verschoyle, you need have no fear about my turning into an Amazon. The first thing I must learn is to stick on, and I don't mind confessing to you, that that feat alone appears to me far from easy."

They were now close to the rendezvous, and passed several mounted grooms leading their master's hunters out to covert. Great strapping animals the horses looked, with plenty of blood and bone, and all the muscle which good oats and condition could give them. At this early period of the season they were very fresh, and started like two-year-olds when they heard wheels behind them grinding over the stone-darned roads. Shortly afterwards the victoria pulled up before an old grey manor house, which belonged to a flourishing yeoman, whose fathers and forefathers had lived in it for centuries. The owner stood at the threshold of his oaken door, which was thrown open to all comers. Hale and vigorous, with a rosy, good-tempered face set in a frame of snow-white hair, he looked as fine a specimen of the real, old-fashioned sportsman to be met with in the United Kingdom. Mr. Hetherington was one of the most noted figures of the Masterton Hunt. High and low respected him equally. Although considerably past his seventieth year, he still rode nearly as hard as in his younger days, and very few there were who in a good long hunting run could beat the gallant old man on his gallant old mare. The pair between them jumped many an ugly-looking obstacle from which younger men thought it no shame to turn away, in all the brave array of scarlet coats and pipe-clayed leathers.

CHAPTER XVIII.

A MORNING'S CUB HUNTING.

WHEN Bligh and Lady Verschoyle arrived the hounds were already congregated on a grass plot in front of the house. Mounted on a powerful brown horse the huntsman stood in their midst, occasionally tossing a bit of biscuit to the young entry. Their elder brethren waved their slender sterns sagaciously, and looked about with an intelligent air, which seemed to say, " We know quiet well what is expected of us later on. We may, therefore, take things easy whilst we can." The whips close by cracked their thongs, and exchanged a few words now and again with the foot people when they pressed too closely round the central group. It was a pretty sight to unaccustomed eyes, and the brightness of the sun, the blueness of the sky and freshness of the day enhanced its attractions.

One by one the *habitués* of the hunt rode up, and exchanged cordial greetings. Scarcely a day went by now without some noted Nimrod putting in an appearance. Sir Philip's arrival was the signal for a regular series of congratulations. Among his own set of fast, well-to-do young men he was popular enough. They enjoyed his good dinners, excellent wine, and capital shooting. Having so much to bestow he was worth cultivating, and they cultivated him accordingly, especially the needy, and that class of destitute gentlemen who may be broadly designated as social parasites. The latter found it very convenient to have the run of a place like Beechlands, and encouraged all the foibles of its master by way of keeping on intimate terms with him. But the other and more influential members of the hunt had, to use a man's expression, never quite "tumbled" to Sir Philip. They all liked the mother, but they did not like the son. They thought him conceited, self-sufficient, and deficient in brains. Whenever they tried to talk to him seriously he seemed to have next to nothing to say, and, if the truth must be told, they put him down as an ass.

However, now he was married they hoped he would turn over a new leaf, and display a little more interest in politics and county matters. His station demanded that he should take some small part in the latter, though hitherto he had entirely neglected his local duties. But all this might be changed, and there was no reason why he should not make a fresh start and become a sensible and useful member of society. So on the present occasion Sir Philip's foes welcomed him with more cordiality than usual, the feeling among them being that as a married man bygones were bygones, and it was their business to encourage him in leading a more settled and domestic life. Everybody experienced a certain curiosity to see what sort of a woman his wife was, and he soon had a small crowd round him begging for the honour of an introduction to the new Lady Verschoyle. The very biggest man in the county—no less a personage than the Marquis of Midlandshire—who until to-day had seldom honoured Sir Philip with more than a stately nod, unbent so far as to express a condescending hope that sometime or other, when they had a meet at Midland Castle, the bride and bridegroom would come over for the night. Certainly the invitation was vague. "Sometime or other" conveyed a tantalising indefiniteness to the mind, which might mean anything or nothing, but the wish had been expressed before a goodly number of listeners, and it pleased Sir Philip—to whom the portals of Midland Castle had hitherto been closed—not a little. With a vast amount of ceremony he introduced the Marquis to Bligh. Unfortunately she did not catch his name, and smiled and nodded just as if he were an ordinary person instead of being a member of the Cabinet and the future Prime Minister of England.   She merely saw in him a tall, somewhat pompous-looking, middle-aged gentleman, and did not feel a bit impressed, except by the extreme shabbiness of his scarlet coat, the tails of which were of a faded purple.

"Poor old man," she thought to herself "perhaps he can't afford a new one.   But he might have it dyed.   It would certainly not look so bad."

They chatted away about the weather and the hounds, Bligh's artless remarks concerning the latter calling a smile to the great man's face.   The conversation did not last more than a couple of minutes, and was entirely commonplace in character; nevertheless, when the Marquis moved away he was pleased to observe to his intimate friend and neighbour, Lord Gossington, of Gossington, that the bride seemed a nice, unaffected little thing, and he only hoped she would succeed in licking that young cub of a husband of hers into shape.   "Though, mind you," he added, "I don't envy her the task.   He's a fool and doesn't know it."

On the whole the verdict pronounced upon Bligh was favourable, if not exactly enthusiastic.   The men dubbed her plain, but pleasant; whilst, as for the women, they were not jealous of her looks, and so pardoned her the position which, in some mysterious and unaccountable fashion, she had managed to achieve. Of course, they pitied Sir Philip.   A wealthy eligible seldom goes to the altar without exciting profound compassion among his female acquaintances, who are unanimous in declaring that he has been "taken in."   And, if the bride be pretty and stylish, they are still more firmly convinced of her designing and artful nature, and experience yet greater difficulty in overcoming their prejudices.

Before long the master gave the word of advance, and a move was made to a covert hard by, known by the name of Blackthorn Holt.   By this time the field included a fair number of people, and as the procession jogged along late arrivals kept joining it from various quarters.   Our heroine's victoria took up its station on the crest of a commanding hill, from whence the occupants obtained an extensive view of the surrounding country.

No time was lost in putting the hounds into covert, and for a space there was silence, broken only by the pattering of feet and the cracking of dry twigs.   Then, all at once, a whimper rang out on the still air, followed by another, and yet another, until at last the whole pack contributed towards an eager chorus of sound.   One could distinguish the deep notes of the veterans, in contradistinction to the high, yelping tones of the puppies. Bligh's attention was riveted on the covert.   Presently she saw a small red object steal out of it, and come gliding swiftly through the long grass towards the—   She strained her eyes to make sure they did not deceive her, and, grasping Lady Verschoyle's arm, said—

"Oh! look, look, it is a fox I do believe. Can you see him? How extraordinary that nobody attempts to go after him."

It took Bligh several minutes to understand that the principal object of cub hunting is to scatter the young foxes and teach them the needful lesson that if they wish to retain their lives they must trust rather to their own fleet limbs than to a snug shelter, apt on occasions to swarm with enemies. Two—three—cubs made their escape unmolested, after much clamouring, and a good deal of patient hunting on the part of the elder hounds, who set the youngsters a most meritorious example of steadiness and perseverance. But the covert was very thick, and several of the juveniles grew weary of a task which required more effort than they had yet been in the habit of exercising. They crept out and gazed wistfully around them, with an air which said, almost as clearly as words :—"This is uncommonly slow work. Let's do something else." They were like young children, and had yet to learn the lesson that idleness was not tolerated among their ranks. On every occasion when they were caught dawdling the whip galloped up, and laying roundly about him with the thong of his hunting crop rated the culprits severely. Two or three vigorous flicks soon sent them yelping back into the covert again, though some refused to hunt in spite of punishment, and lay down feebly amongst the undergrowth.

Just when things were getting slack a loud cry from the foot people proclaimed that yet a fourth fox had faced the open. Countless view holloas rent the air. It was as if every tongue had been suddenly let loose. The huntsman came riding down the centre ride of the covert in hot haste. He knew that this was the last of the litter, and he blew his horn with right lusty lungs. Out leapt the old hounds in response, followed by a certain number of the young division. The field had been growing tired of inaction and of the disagreeable task of trying to induce mad-fresh horses to stand still and not buck or kick. Glad of a gallop they rushed impetuously forward in pursuit of the fox, until a loud and indignant " Hounds, gentlemen, hounds," from the master reminded them that with the best will in the world they could not hunt by the unassisted aid of their own fine horsemanship and love of jumping.

Five minutes' delay, and then hounds settled fairly to the line of the fox. There was a good scent, as so often proves the case early in the season, when the leaves still linger on the hedgerows and appear to retain the delicate aroma of Master Pug. Everywhere the ditches were choked up with nettles and coarse grass. They were things to be looked at and carefully avoided in their present condition. But what are dangers to the gallant spirits of a hunt—those brave leaders who care little whether they bite the dust or not so long as they get to the other side? Nettles and grass can't stop such as these. They would jump a house if it presented itself. And for the more timid procrastination achieves wonders. A single horse sprawling up to his middle in a blind ditch makes a hole in it that gladdens the anxiously pulsing heart and renders the way clear for the majority. Difficulties diminish in the most marvellous manner if people only bide their time. This rule, however, applies to the regular season. In the cub hunting days the fields are limited, and those who intend to jump must be prepared to fall, whilst those who don't had better gallop straight off for the ever-friendly gate.

In spite of Reynard being only a baby he proved a remarkably sturdy one, and although he shaped his course in a circle he ran the ring at a real good pace, which soon told upon the condition of his pursuers. From the top of the hill where stood their carriage Bligh and Lady Verschoyle could see the whole of the hunt stretched out before them like a panorama. First came the hounds, glancing over the green sward in a silver streak, their speckled sides gleaming bright in the sunshine. Half a field behind rode the huntsman, leaning forward in his saddle as he watched every movement of the leaders. He was closely followed by some dozen gentlemen and hard-riding farmers, conspicuous among them being old Mr. Hetherington. In the rear of this gallant group laboured an attenuated string of horsemen and women, who dotted the green fields for nearly half a mile.

Bligh's face was flushed with excitement. She, too, began to feel something of the enthusiasm of the chase.

" I believe I should like hunting if I could do it," she said. " After all, say what one likes about the folly of riding helter-skelter after a little, smelling fox, there must be a good deal in a sport which brings so many and such different classes of people together. Until to-day I never understood what the charm was, but now I can thoroughly realise it. Oh! look, look, they are coming our way." And in her eagerness she stood up so as to obtain a better view of the animated scene.

In effect the fox, finding himself somewhat sharply pursued, made a bend and headed straight back for the covert in which he had been born and bred. To achieve this object he was forced to creep through a large hedge that ran parallel with the road. The two ladies caught sight of his draggled brush, now almost trailing along the ground.

" Poor thing !" exclaimed Lady Verschoyle. " I hope they won't catch him. He looks tired, and my sympathies are always with the oppressed. How awful his sensations must be at this moment! I think there is nothing so cruel as hunting an animal to its death." About five minutes afterwards up came the hounds, their bristles standing, their eyes gleaming ferociously. The air rang with murderous canine music as they raced towards the hedge. It was stiff and full of foliage, and checked their impetuous onslaught for a few moments. But they were not to be deterred, and soon wriggled a way through the thorns. And now the huntsman charged the fence on his good brown horse. There happened to be an extra wide ditch on the far side, and a nasty dip in the ground on taking off, which rendered it anything but a nice place. Neither rider nor steed, however, hesitated for a single instant. Where hounds went there went they. The noble animal cocked his ears, gave his head a resolute lunge forward, and hey! presto! they were over. Nothing could have been neater.

All of a sudden Bligh held her breath, for she perceived that the next man was Sir Philip. Lady Verschoyle shuddered and turned away her head.

"Tell me when it's over," she said to her daughter-in-law. "I can't bear to look on. I know he'll meet with his death some of these days. You'll think me very silly, but I cannot help myself."

Poor dear old lady! On the present occasion she need have had no fears. Sir Philip's horse jumped the fence most beautifully, and that in spite of an ill-judged job in the mouth from his rider just as he was in the act of taking off. He cleared the whole thing with a splendid stag-like bound, and never touched a twig. Bligh began to think that jumping must be quite easy work, but she was destined almost immediately to be undeceived. Sir Philip's successor, scorning a lead, chose a place a little to the right. But his animal stopped in his stride, as if he had half a mind to refuse when he saw how formidable was the obstacle. A vigorous dig of the spurs conquered his indecision; he had lost impetus, however, and landed with both hind legs well in the ditch. He tried to recover himself, failed in the attempt, and with a snort and a groan rolled on to his side. Fortunately the rider was not hurt, and never letting go of the reins was soon up and away again, none the worse, for the accident. To Bligh's indignation directly he regained the saddle he commenced to belabour his steed.

"Oh! what a shame," she cried. "Who is that man? He is a regular monster. I wish I could hit him as he is hitting his poor horse."

"His name is Captain Dashwood, and he is a great friend of Philip's," answered her companion.

"Oh! I am sorry for that. I don't like him one bit. What

a horrid temper he must have to vent his ill-humour upon an unfortunate animal. If you noticed, the man was quite as undecided as the quadruped. Philip and the huntsman rode their hunters at the fence resolutely, and as if they meant to get over, but Captain Dashwood went at it in a very half-hearted manner."

Five minutes later and the entire field were assembled at the covert side, debating the important question whether Reynard should be ruthlessly dug out from the drain in which he had taken refuge, or left to his own devices. Hounds and huntsman were eager for blood, but the master did not choose to run the risk of chopping a fox in one of his best coverts. He therefore put his veto on the spade business. Pug, having well stretched his legs and tested his lungs, was reluctantly relinquished. During the proceedings above narrated, a good deal of time had been spent, and consequently the morning was now well advanced. The sun's rays shone with increasing warmth, and sucked up the moisture lingering on grass and leaf.

Mr. Masterton decided to move on without delay to the next draw. It was some way off, and necessitated a jog of three or four miles. The direction being entirely away from Beechlands, Sir Philip rode up to his wife and mother, and recommended them to go home. He was in excellent spirits, and the exercise had lent expression and animation to his face.

" I'm glad you've seen such a lot," he said to Bligh. " Some days one sees nothing in a carriage, but if the run had been made to order you could not possibly have had a better."

CHAPTER XIX.

TWO " GOOD FELLOWS."

JACK RICKERBY and Captain Dashwood hunted in couples. They occupied a comfortable little lodging in Beechington, in which small country town they had put up for several consecutive seasons. They were both poor, both fond of the best of everything, especially when they could indulge in it at somebody else's expense. This propensity, combined with a love of billiards, card-playing, horse-racing, and wine, often rendered it necessary for them to supplement their income by the exercise of their wits. These had the reputation of being very sharp, and although nobody knew exactly how the two gentlemen subsisted, they managed to keep the wolf from the door somehow. There were a good many queer stories afloat as to the financial shifts to which they sometimes had recourse, but as the couple were always pleasant and insinuating, rode nice horses, and would invariably part with them at a price, most of the members of the hunting field discreetly shut their ears to tales told at their neighbours' expense. Of course a few victims existed, who abused Jack Rickerby and Captain Dashwood roundly. These had generally purchased animals which had been seen going well to hounds, but which, when they changed stables, turned out to be screws. It so happened that Sir Philip Verschoyle had never yet gone in for any horse-dealing transactions with the pair, consequently he voted them capital fellows, and displayed a great liking for their society.

Certainly he must either have been very ungrateful or else very much more observant than he was had he not done so, for nothing could exceed the amiability of Mr. Rickerby and Captain Dashwood whenever they chanced to meet. During their numerous visits to Beechlands they praised his cook, his wine, his horses, and last, but not least, himself. Some people like to be surrounded by flatterers ; others are repelled by coarse, inartistic, and often insincere eulogy. Sir Philip belonged to the former class. He did not care to associate with men above him in intellect and position. Perhaps they made him feel uncomfortable. However that may be, he showed a decided partiality for his inferiors. He liked sycophants whom he could patronise, be as rude to as he chose, and then clap on the back when his good-humour was restored, whilst they cringed and curried favour as if he were a little deity. No doubt this sort of society is not beneficial to a rich young man, with more money than brains ; but there are many who prefer it to any other, simply because, to use a vulgar expression, they feel " cock of the walk." Thanks to flattery, obsequiousness, and complaisance, Jack Rickerby and Captain Dashwood had contrived to establish a considerable intimacy between themselves and the owner of Beechlands. His marriage had been rather a blow, but on putting their sage heads together they arrived at the conclusion that their cue was to try and save their friend as much as possible from falling under petticoat government.

" If his wife once gets the upper hand we shall be turned out, that's very certain," remarked the astute Captain Dashwood to Mr. Rickerby one evening shortly before Sir Philip's return from Paris, when they were talking matters over and facing the winter prospects with a frankness which they never exhibited except when quite alone and summing up their resources. " If we lose Beechlands that will mean at least two extra dinners a week to pay for, let alone the wine."

" Never fear," responded Mr. Rickerby, who was of a

bolder and more sanguine nature than his friend. "Verschoyle's too fond of lapping up the liquor. He may pretend to be very goody-goody just for a bit at first. They always do, these married men : but you mark my words, with that little failing of his he'll soon break out."

"I never saw such a fellow," observed Captain Dashwood contemptuously. "The slightest thing goes to his head. He gets regularly tight, whilst you and I don't turn a hair."

Jack Rickerby smiled. He was a tall, ungainly, loosely-jointed man of about thirty-five, with a thin face, sharp nose, bright, sunken eyes, and a wide, clean-shaven mouth. The principal peculiarity of his countenance consisted in a long, flexible upper lip, as pliable as a piece of gutta-percha. It lent him in turns a facetious, sinister, and benevolent expression. Those who knew him best asserted that when he assumed his benignant air he was most to be feared. A well-known wag once said of him that he looked like a man who had been put together in a hurry, and half a dozen sheets of paper could not possibly convey a more graphic description of his personal appearance. Nature had evidently been pressed for time when she fashioned him and had not paused to round off the corners as she turned him out on to the wide world positively bristling with angles.

Captain Dashwood, on the other hand, was a suave, round, well-nourished personage, dapper and small, who spoke in a subdued, unctuous way, as if he were fearful of giving offence. Occasionally, however, when he forgot his part—which, to do him justice, was very seldom—he would let fall a vinegary note, so different from his usual sugary accents that one could not help asking oneself of what was the real man composed—sugar or vinegar? Then one watched and waited for the mask to fall, and ended by conceiving a grudging admiration for an individual who could play the hypocrite with such consummate skill that nine out of ten ordinary observers never suspected his true character, unless under very exceptional circumstances.

"It would take a good deal for either you or me to get screwed," said Mr. Rickerby, in answer to his friend's remark. "We can stow away as much liquor as most men without being any the worse for it. But Verschoyle's really no better than a child. It's an act of kindness to put him through his noviate, else he'll be so awfully laughed at when once he succeeds in freeing himself from his mamma's apron strings and goes out into the world."

"He was just beginning to kick over the traces when he went and got married," rejoined Captain Dashwood resentfully. "Now it's a toss up whether he develops into a man or a mouse. These spoilt darlings of widowed mothers are generally muffs.

However, we shall soon see which way the wind blows. Verschoyle's a very useful acquaintance, and I should be sorry if anything happened to interfere with our friendship."

"In that case," said Jack Rickerby, with a sneer, which he took no pains to hide, "I should advise you not to attempt to sell him old Corkscrew. It's running too great a risk. Even if you did manage to get two hundred for the horse it would scarcely pay us in the long run."

Captain Dashwood looked at his friend admiringly.

"You're a 'cute fellow, Jack. What I like about you is that you have such a power of looking ahead. Most people only see a thing from one particular point of view, but you take in every aspect. So you think Beechlands, even under the new regime, is worth more than two hundred pounds to us. Well, well, perhaps you are right. Anyhow, I'll do nothing in a hurry. Corkcrew's tendon won't be well before this side of Christmas. So we'll procrastinate, and form our opinion of the bride before we decide upon any plan of campaign."

After this conversation it may be inferred that the friends were extremely pleased when they received Sir Philip's invitation to dine and sleep at Beechlands. They both agreed that, coming immediately on his return home, it augured exceedingly well for the future. His wife's society was, evidently, not all-sufficient, and, like so many newly-made Benedicts, he turned with relief to the bachelor friends associated in his thoughts with jollity and merriment.

So when evening came Mr. Rickerby and Captain Dashwood muffled themselves up well in comforters and ulsters, tucked a thick fur rug round their knees, and drove over to their destination in a high-wheeled dog-cart, drawn by broken-down hunter they were desirous of selling as a harness horse, and whose praises they sang just a little too loudly to be genuine. The friends, when together, were not given to garrulity as a rule.

A terse sentence dropped here and there generally sufficed as a means of interchanging thought. On the present occasion they maintained complete silence until they were clear of the town. Then Captain Dashwood broke it by saying—

"Jack, the brute's infernally lame."

"He is so," came the response.

"Confound it. I had Jim Pouncer coming over to see the wretched animal to-morrow. He wanted something warranted not to run away for his wife to drive. I think we could warrant this one, eh? Now I suppose I shall have to telegraph the first thing in the morning and put him off, worse luck."

As they had started late, and rapid progression with "the best harness horse in the kingdom" was not possible, they kept their host and hostess waiting over half an hour for dinner. Having left off a long way from home Sir Philip had not got back from hunting till past four o'clock. Declining to spoil his appetite by a heavy meal on returning he happened to be more than commonly hungry. It was, therefore, only natural that he should grumble pretty loudly at his friends' unpunctuality and consider himself very much aggrieved by their non-appearance.

" I never saw anything like these chaps," he observed irritably. "They get later and later, and seem to fancy they can just walk in when they choose, without any consideration for your dinner or your cook. What do you say, Bligh ? I vote we don't wait any longer."

"I think it would serve them right to begin," she responded. "Perhaps they may have forgotten the day, or met with some accident."

" At all events I'll ring. If they turn up it will teach them better manners for another time," and Sir Philip gave the bell a violent pull, his patience being quite exhausted. Scarcely had he done so when the sound of a horse's hoofs was heard coming up the drive, and shortly afterwards the two delinquents appeared.

" Not late, we hope," they said, airily, shaking hands with Bligh as calmly as if they had arrived to the minute. " We took it for granted that half-past seven generally means eight, and so——"

" Not in the hunting season," interrupted Sir Philip, severely. "I should have thought that two old stagers like you would have known that by now. We had just given you up, and were on the point of going in to dinner when you arrived."

"Very sorry, old man," said Captain Dashwood, apologetically, as he gave his arm to Bligh. " Fact was, I indulged in forty winks after coming in from hunting, and mistook the time." It was easier to romance than to reveal stable secrets.

" Well, well, come along. Let's go into the dining-room. I, for one, am ravenous." Sir Philip's manner was not particularly genial, so as soon as they were seated at table, the diplomatic Captain Dashwood endeavoured to restor him to good humour.

" What was that you were riding to day ? " he inquired, as a preliminary, knowing that even if a man escapes the temptation of talking about himself, he very seldom can resist discoursing about his horses. " Is he a new purchase ? I don't remember ever having seen him before."

" He is a horse I bought some six weeks ago," answered Sir Philip, who, having swallowed a few mouthfuls of soup, already felt more amiably inclined, and smiled forgivingly at his guests.

" I've never been on him before to-day."

"He's a very good-looking one," observed Mr. Rickerby, deliberately turning his back upon the Dowager Lady Verschoyle, whom he secretly dubbed "a silly old woman." "Where did you pick him up?"

"He came from Toynbee, who furnished him with a most tremendous character, and is Irish bred, by Solon out of Emerald Isle. He won a hunters' race at Punchestown last spring, beating The Rogue and Jane Shore, who have run very respectably since. According to Toynbee, the horse is good enough to go for the Grand National."

"I knew he could travel," said Captain Dashwood, in his suavest tone, "by the way you passed us all to-day in that first little spin. I thought I was on a fast one, but you went by me like a flash of lightning. He gallops nice and low, and steals over the ground at a good pace, when he looks to be only cantering. What's his age?"

"Five off," answered Sir Philip, who, thanks to this judicious praise of his nag, was now in the most amiable mood. "With any luck, he ought to make me a nice hunter by another year."

"He will, indeed," said Jack Rickerby, emphatically. "If I weren't a poor devil, and had the money, I would offer you three hundred for him on the spot."

Sir Philip blinked his eyelids in a gratified manner. People always like being able to say, "I refused any amount of money for that horse." Quite independently of the animal's worth, it flatters their pride.

"Thanks, but I don't mean parting," he said, a fact of which Mr. Rickerby was perfectly well aware. "These Irish quads are always poor in condition when they first come over. They all want a year's good oats put inside them."

"He looks to me like an animal who will improve very much," said Captain Dashwood. "He has a big frame which wants furnishing. Have you any more new ones in the stable? We must look round to-morrow."

"Yes, altogether I have about half a dozen. The hard going at the end of last season played the bear with most of my old favourites. There's Beeswing, for instance. I'm keeping her on, but my private belief is she'll never come out again."

"Dear, dear. What a sad pity! She was a brilliant mare that."

"Yes, she and Guardsman were the two best I ever had."

"What became of Guardsman?" inquired Mr. Rickerby.

"He went the way of all flesh, poor old fellow. Do you remember that rippling run we had last March from Hillside Spinneys. Just before we got to Lotsford village, he pecked, on landing over a nasty drop, and nearly cut the back sinew of his off fore in two. As luck would have it, Higgins happened to be paying a visit in the village at the time of the accident, and he sewed the place up at once. For a few days it seemed to be going on all right. The horse fed, and barring being very lame, did not appear much the worse ; but from some cause or other, symptoms of blood-poisoning set in, and eventually we were forced to destroy him. Poor old Guardsman ! he carried me four seasons, and only once gave me a fall, which is saying a great deal."

" You won't replace him in a hurry," said Captain Dashwood. " A better horse never looked through a bridle. I recollect the day when he jumped Blackthorn Brook, and you pounded all the field."

A gratified smile passed over Sir Philip's face.

" Ah ! that was a tidy jump," he said, striving to conceal his satisfaction.

" It was an extraordinary one, my dear fellow, and I don't believe there is another man in the whole hunt who would have ridden at such a yawning gulf. Just out of curiosity I went the next day and measured it. From bank to bank spanned exactly twenty-four feet, and, judging by the hoofmarks, Guardsman must have taken off and landed with at least a foot to spare on either side."

" You'll never get another to equal him," said Jack Rickerby, emptying his glass in a hurry, as he perceived the butler coming round with the champagne.

" No, I don't suppose I shall," responded Sir Philip, " though when we get used to each other, I am in hopes that this new one may turn out almost as good. He jumped two or three places with me to-day in rare form, and flew them like a real Midlandshire hunter. I confess that once or twice my heart was in my mouth, for the country rides awfully blind still."

" It always does at this time of the year," said Captain Dashwood. " Those infernal nettles regular choke up the ditches. For my part, I never half enjoy hunting until after Christmas. At the commencement of the season one's horses are so abominably fresh, one's nerves are weak just in proportion as the fencing is dangerous. The hedges won't be right till we get a sharp frost, or, better still, a good fall of snow to clear away the long grass."

" There seemed a very fair scent to-day," said Sir Philip. " Hounds ran well both in the morning and the afternoon."

" Yes, at first starting I thought we were in for a real good thing, but these cubs can't keep the ball a-rolling. They're too fat, and soon knuckle under. Still the one we ran to-day will make a toughish customer when he is two or three months older, and he fairly deserved his brush."

"How are we off for foxes on this side of the county?" asked Sir Philip. "Last year they got rather scarce towards the end."

"That was because Dysack is such a desperate fellow at catching them," said Jack Rickerby. "In old Blunt's time it was quite an event if we ever killed. But nowadays things are very much changed, and Masterton told me this morning that they had already accounted for two-and-twenty brace."

"Some people say that the more foxes you kill, the more you have," said Sir Philip, "though I confess I never could quite understand on what principle. By-the-bye, where was old Tim Baldwin to-day? I did not see him out. Isn't he hunting this year?"

"Oh! yes, but he is over in Ireland fishing. Mrs. Baldwin expects him home every day. I suppose you know he has taken a regular kink on Home Rule."

"I did hear something of the sort. But, as you are aware, I never trouble myself much about people's politics."

"I wish everybody were as sensible," remarked Captain Dashwood, who never lost an opportunity of flattering his host adroitly. "You know what cronies Baldwin and Lord Midlandshire used to be. At the present moment, owing to this Irish craze of the squire's, they are scarcely on speaking terms. It's 'Morning, Baldwin,' and ' Morning, my lord,' and that's all."

"Give me fox-hunting," said Sir Philip, "and I am quite content to let my neighbours quarrel about the management of Ireland."

"I agree with you. The chief duty of man in this world is to enjoy himself, and the whole art of living happily is summed up in the one word, amusement."

"That is not a very exalted sentiment, Captain Dashwood," observed Bligh, who so far had been a listener to the conversation.

He turned round upon her with a bland smile. The light from the hanging lamp struck full upon his bald forehead and made it shine, which added to the extreme amiability of his appearance. There was something about it which seemed to say, "You are quite an insignificant personage, but I want you to think me a very nice sort of man. It will be to your interest to regard me as a friend."

"My dear lady," he exclaimed, "I don't pretend to any exalted sentiments. In my experience people who do are nearly always exceedingly uncomfortable. They go about the world trying to impress you with a sense of superiority. If you frankly confess that you are not a superior person, that you have no longings, or cravings after unattainable things, you may not perhaps pose as a hero, but you have a much better time of it."

Bligh laughed in spite of herself, though she did not approve of her companion's sentiments.

" Don't you care to do good, or to live for other people beside yourself ? " she demanded.

" Doing good and living for other people are two entirely exploded ideas."

" In what way ? "

" Shall I prove it to you ?   In olden days, when the country was thinly populated, no doubt it conferred a benefit upon humanity at large to protect and rear the species.   Now the case is entirely different.   If one wanted to help one's neighbours, practically the only plan would be for half the world to commit suicide for the sake of the other.   But even if you were so amiably inclined as to put yourself out of the way in order to oblige somebody else, you would still be open to the charge of selfishness.   Folks do good because they like it, and because they derive pleasure from their own virtue.   Philanthropy is therefore quite as egotistical as fox hunting."

" What a horribly material argument," exclaimed Bligh, indignantly.

" Ponder over it well, and you will perceive that it is not without truth."

" I would rather not believe such things, Captain Dashwood."

" Very well, then, only don't look down upon me because, having studied the art of living for a good many more years than you can possibly have done, I state openly that the wise man is he who enjoys himself."

" What nonsense you're talking, Bligh," called out Sir Philip, who happened to overhear something of the conversation. " Dashwood's quite right.   We're put into the world to make the best of it, and everyone for himself is a sensible motto to steer one's course by.   Who was the lady out to-day on the chestnut horse with the hogged mane?   I saw you speaking to her, Jack," he added, addressing Mr. Rickerby.

After this open snub in public, Bligh relapsed into silence. In fact, she soon discovered the uselessness of trying to converse on any other subject except sport.   Somehow or other, the conversation invariably worked round to it again.

" She is a widow, Benson by name, who hails from Sketchley," responded Mr. Rickerby, with an attempt not to look conscious.

" A widow is she !   Any tin ? "

" Report says about three thousand a year."

"Ha, ha, my boy, and so you're going in for her, are you? Does the lady respond?"

"Come, shut up, Verschoyle, none of your chaff," said the gallant Jack, grinning from ear to ear, for it had already occurred to him that he might do worse than convert Mrs. Benson into Mrs. Rickerby, always provided report spoke truth.

"What do you think of this champagne, Dashwood?" asked Sir Philip, appealing to the captain, who, like most military men, set up for being a good judge of wine. "It's some new stuff which I got down the other day from Sipper and Swallow. They wrote recommending it very highly, and so I ordered a couple of dozen on trial."

Captain Dashwood raised his glass aloft, eyed its contents, then smelt, and finally tasted them, as if he had not already accounted for the best part of a bottle.

"It's not bad," he said, smacking his lips, and screwing his face up critically. "But, since you ask my candid opinion, it's just a trifle too sweet to suit my taste. I prefer a dryer wine, and one not quite so gassy."

"I agree with you," said Sir Philip, who cared far more for quantity than quality. "I don't consider it good enough to lay in a stock of."

"If it is not an impertinent question, may I ask what the figure is?"

"I really forget, but somewhere between eighty and eighty-five shillings a dozen, I believe."

"It ought to be better than it is at that price," said Captain Dashwood, decidedly. "Now, if you would go to my wine merchant, Hickory, in the Strand, I feel sure he would supply you with something very much better at a cheaper rate. Hickory is not a fashionable tradesman, but no one has more excellent stuff. If you will favour him with an order, and use my name as a recommendation, I am sure you will not regret it."

"Thanks, old man. I'll write to-morrow, and tell him to send me down a few specimen bottles."

For one instant Captain Dashwood's and Jack Rickerby's glances met. They owed Mr. Hickory a pretty heavy bill, which he had lately sent in with troublesome regularity. It occurred to them both that in return for introducing a good customer, they were entitled to some reprieve, if not a five per cent. commission.

During the rest of dinner the gentlemen continued to discourse on horses, hunting, wine, and women. It was hopeless trying to start any other topic, and the three ladies sat silent in their seats. Occasionally Lady Verschoyle cast an inquiring glance at Bligh, as if seeking to ascertain the impression made upon her daughter-in-law. The truth was, they were a very incongruous lot, of which fact Bligh soon became aware. At first she had felt amused by the dissertations on sport that took place between Sir Philip and his friends. It was a novel experience to her, and she listened to what they had to say with considerable interest. But when they went over the same old ground everlastingly, and never by any chance introduced any variety into their conversation, unless it were a slight flavouring of personal gossip, she ended by finding it extremely monotonous, and not only monotonous, but witless and unimproving. As for the two dear old ladies in their black silk gowns and white lace caps, they had nothing in common with such men as Mr. Rickerby and Captain Dashwood, who treated them almost as if they had been nonentities. Indeed Bligh felt quite angry at their exerting themselves so little to be polite. She had always been accustomed to see old people regarded with courtesy and deference, and her sense of the fitness of things was outraged by the manner which her husband's friends chose to assume towards his mother, not to mention hers.

As soon as she decently could she effected an escape from the dining-room. A feeling of constraint was fast stealing upon her, which she was unable to attribute altogether to her not being accustomed to society. There was a coarseness and freedom about these men which she resented. Their crafty flattery had not escaped her notice, and after making their acquaintance she quite realised that they were not desirable friends for Sir Philip, and deliberately encouraged his faults, seeking to turn them to their own benefit. Her powers of observation were great, and the instinct which caused her to take immediate likes or dislikes to people seldom proved wrong.

She was going into the drawing-room, when Lady Verschoyle said, with one of those sorrowful smiles that lent such an interest to her thin face—

" We can sit in the boudoir, Bligh, if you prefer it, for we shall see no more of our guests to-night."

Bligh made a gesture of relief.

" Shall we really get rid of them so easily. Do you mean to say they won't appear again ? I am glad."

" You don't like them, then ? "

" No, how could one ? They don't seem to have an idea in the world beyond horses and dogs. Are you sure they won't show up any more ? "

" Quite sure. As soon as they are relieved of our presence they settle down to long cigars, and then retire to the billiard-room, where they stay until the small hours of the morning.''

" Talking of dear old mares and ripping runs ? " queried Bligh, mischievously.

" Yes, I suppose so," answered Lady Verschoyle, with a sigh.

" I wonder what Philip sees in such men as Captain Dashwood and Mr. Rickerby. Did you hear what the first-named gentleman said to me, when, in all innocence, I asked him what he thought of Bismarck's great speech to the Reichstag ? He replied that he never read the newspapers, giving as his reason that he did not think it ' good enough.' The remark made a deep impression upon me, and I could not help asking myself, what sort of a mind can such a person possess. There must be something radically wrong about its composition."

" It always vexes me when Philip asks these men to the house," said Lady Verschoyle. " Their influence is decidedly deteriorating."

Bligh held her peace. It seemed wiser to keep silent than to put her thoughts into words. For there was an indescribable tone about the establishment which she could not help secretly resenting. A change in it was highly desirable, yet she clearly perceived the difficulties of attempting any reformation, unless the mood of the master altered and he backed up her efforts. Although she neither wanted nor expected much attention to be paid to her individually, she realised that as hostess some little consideration was due to her, and to her female friends. She did not consider it good manners for men to come to the house, eat, drink, and smoke, without giving themselves the trouble to wish good-night to the ladies. It was tantamount to saying, " We tolerate your presence during dinner, but we are very glad to get rid of you as soon as possible. In fact, you are bores, and we infinitely prefer our own society." These subtle shades of conduct were hard to define, but she felt vaguely aware of their existence, and in her opinion they constituted the difference between a thorough gentleman and one in name only. Humble as had been their home, both at Elmsley and during her father's lifetime, she had been accustomed to finer manners than those of Captain Dashwood and Mr. Rickerby, and certainly to superior conversation. Music, art, literature, were all subjects on which it was pleasant to discourse, and which offered an immense variety. She feared that this atmosphere of fox-hunting, and of fox-hunting only, could not fail to become oppressive in process of time. It neither stimulated the faculties nor appealed to the intellect. Such were her first impressions. But she reserved her judgment, not deeming it fair to form a fixed opinion from the experiences of a single evening. What she was quite sure of, however, was that she both disliked and distrusted her husband's friends.

By-and-bye loud voices were heard in the hall, a whiff of tobacco mounted to the cosy boudoir where the three ladies were sitting, and then the billiard-room door slammed. Lady Verschoyle was right. Bligh saw no more of her guests that evening.

But when she came down to breakfast the next morning her eyes were red, as if she had been weeping, and her face wore a look of settled melancholy. Sir Philip complained of a bad headache, refused to drink any tea, but called for soda water in its place, and appeared irritable and depressed by turns. Captain Dashwood and Mr. Rickerby, on the contrary, were exceedingly jovial, and, if possible, even **fuller** of horsey talk than on the previous evening. Bligh was civil to them, but very cold, and persistently refused to laugh at their jokes, which possessed a decided flavour of coarseness not at all to her mind. Once or twice she purposely changed the subject, but her attempts in this direction were not very successful. Lady Verschoyle glanced anxiously at her son and daughter-in-law. When an opportunity presented itself, she whispered a question into the latter's ear. Bligh turned as red as a peony, and the moisture sprang to her eyes. She brushed her hand across them.

" Don't ask me," she said, in a distressed tone. " It is better for you not to know the state he was in last night."

No wonder she looked pale, for upon her mind the fearful truth had dawned that she had married a drunkard. Henceforth all her energies must be directed to the task of keeping the terrible fact from her mother. Having done what she had done, Mrs. Burton must never guess at her unhappiness.

CHAPTER XX.

LEARNING TO RIDE.

As the days went by Bligh realised more and more forcibly that she would be called upon to pay a heavy price for the distinguished honour of wearing the name of Lady Verschoyle, for she saw that Sir Philip's wife was at Sir Philip's mercy. It was impossible to reason with him, and her hopes of being able to influence his actions soon faded away. His weakness, vanity, and obstinacy were so great that they offered a perpetual barrier to any scheme of reformation.

To a sensitive, finely-fibred woman no torture equals that of living in close contact with a man made of coarser and commoner clay than herself—a man whose ideas are material, whose standard of morality shocks her best and purest sentiments, and whose conversation, instead of appealing to the higher side of human nature, stirs up its muddiest depths. Just imagine it.

There she is, chained to him, not only by custom and conventionality, but also by the law, which renders escape shameful, and places the weak entirely within the power of the strong. The husband can say what he likes, and behave as he likes. He can fill his house with people who are positively disagreeable to the wife, who render her life a misery, and slight and insult her to her face. Or he can go away and leave her, and only return when he chooses. He can wound her in a thousand different ways, and yet Mrs. Grundy smiles on him leniently. He is masculine, and, therefore, not blameable. He may neglect, and even desert, his partner, and, if she be a good woman, the sole course open to her is to bear all bravely and silently. It is useless complaining of her lot ; besides, she knows by experience that her own sex are ever ready to condemn her conduct. Their sympathies invariably side with the man ; for, however great a brute he may be, it is a peculiarity of every woman to think that she can manage every other woman's husband. Even if they do not agree remarkably well with their own spouse it does not lessen the conviction that they could live in peace and harmony with somebody else's.

It is always " Ah ! poor, dear Mrs. Jones. She makes such a mistake. If she were only to humour him a little more, and shut her eyes to his trifling peccadilloes, instead of going on nag, nag, nag, they would hit it off as well again. But she hasn't any tact, not an atom, and just rubs him up the wrong way. Now if I were in her shoes, I would—etc., etc."

Bligh had seen enough of the world to be aware that the female portion of it invariably suffers, and need not look for compassion. To do her justice she did not want commiseration. She had married Sir Philip with her eyes open, and was quite conscious of having committed a wrong in accepting him. Of two evils—becoming his wife or letting her mother die—she had deliberately chosen what seemed to her the lesser. And now, just because things were not going smoothly, pride, if nothing else, prevented her from making any complaint. She felt that she fully deserved a penalty, and was prepared to bear it courageously, if not happily. But reason with herself as she might she could not control or conquer the physical repugnance with which her husband inspired her. When he came up to bed noisy and excited, ready to quarrel at the merest word ; when his breath smelt of brandy and tobacco, his eyes shone like an animal's; and he reeled about the room, grasping at the furniture for support, she shrank away from him. At such times an unutterable loathing and sense of degradation turned her heart cold, and constricted it as with an iron band. She tried to remember that they were bound to one another, and it was wicked to feel like this; but the instinct of disgust, mingled with contempt, was too strong to be overcome. If she could have respected him then the love would have followed. Her life had been so sad that the least kindness touched her to the quick; but she was not a woman capable of bestowing her affections where her esteem was wanting, and already the castles in the air which she had built of domestic happiness were crumbled to the ground. She foresaw that she might keep her husband's house in order, manage his affairs, save him trouble, and prove useful to him in a variety of ways; but for herself the future must henceforth be dark and dreary. Yet not on that account would she fail to do her duty, or shirk the responsibilities of her position. Whatever were Bligh's faults she started with brave intentions and an earnest desire to act rightly. Owing to Sir Philip's peculiar temperament the situation was by no means easy. The slightest word of remonstrance was sufficient to arouse his wrath. He had such an inordinate opinion of his own dignity and importance that anything that reflected upon them in the very smallest degree rendered him captious and irritable.

To speak out openly about his companions would have been fatal. Bligh perceived this, and therefore advised cautious measures whenever Lady Verschoyle urged her to free the house once for all of men like Captain Dashwood and Mr. Rickerby. But the young head was clearer than the old, and counselled patience rather than bringing on a state of open warfare. Without, therefore, expressing disapproval of her husband's companions Bligh sought gently and tactfully to wean him from them. When alone of an evening, and Sir Philip had no excuse for sitting long over his wine, she tried to teach him chess, whist, and various games, hoping that in course of time he might take an interest in such harmless recreations, and find his home pleasanter than any other place. In short, she devoted herself to him so thoroughly that Lady Verschoyle, who guessed her motives, often looked at her daughter-in-law with sentiments of gratitude and admiration. She began to feel a kind of reverence for Bligh, and insensibly leant upon the younger woman's stronger nature, realising that if it were possible to save Philip from the evil courses into which he had fallen surely she would do so.

Bligh did her best, both for her own sake and that of all the household, and yet she failed. Weary and disheartened she was forced to admit the fact. Things would seem to be going on fairly well for two or three weeks, then, all at once, Sir Philip swore he could stand the dulness of being cooped up with a lot of women nó longer, and, sallying forth into the hunting field, brought back with him a choice selection of its rowdiest members. Beechlands was converted into a sort of superior pothouse, where the gentlemen disported themselves quite at their ease and regardless of the feminine element. Bligh soon grew to hate and fear these jovial gatherings, but she was powerless to prevent them. Sir Philip was like a cross-grained horse, who takes the bit between his teeth at the slightest touch of the curb. He would neither be directed nor controlled. Never was the folly, or rather the culpability, of parents in giving in to the whims of a spoilt only son more apparent than in his case. Argument and reason were wasted upon him. He had no common-sense, and cared but for the amusement of the hour.

Bligh made another attempt. Lady Verschoyle and Mrs. Burton were both old, and it was perhaps natural his wishing for younger society. So she suggested giving a series of dinner parties to a number of the neighbours who had called upon her. But Sir Philip flew into a passion at the first hint of such a thing, and vowed he would not allow her to ask a soul or be pestered by a set of old bores whom he did not care twopence about. It was useless Bligh's representing that it was one's duty to be socially victimised every now and again. He remained obdurate. Entertaining on a large scale thus became impossible. They got into the way, however, of always having two or three men dropping in to dinner; unfortunately, very few were such as the mistress of the establishment cared to receive. Their presence added greatly to her difficulties, for on these occasions the gentlemen lingered long at table, and severe demands were made upon the cellar.

As for the ladies whom Sir Philip honoured with his invitations they were nearly all fast. Whenever he said to his wife, "Oh! by the way, I've asked a charming woman to come and stay with us for a few days," she knew invariably what to expect. "The charming woman," painted and powdered, wore very smart gowns, and appeared in the evening clad in the most trifling of bodices. She swore when put out, and habitually interlarded her conversation with slang expressions. She was noisy, selfish, and inconsiderate; favoured the gentlemen to a great many attentions and her hostess to very few, and spent the major portion of her time in the smoking-room, where she consumed cigarettes and an astonishing amount of brandy and soda. No doubt it showed a lamentable want of taste on Bligh's part, but she did not find the society of these "charming women" very congenial. They struck her as being deficient in ladylike feeling, and she pitied them for possessing no real interests. Unless perpetually amused time hung terribly heavily on their hands, whilst their chief idea of entertainment apparently consisted in running after the men, whose society they courted in a manner which made Bligh often blush for shame. Such conduct was altogether opposed to her notions of delicacy, and according to her opinion, showed a lamentable want of self-respect. Sir Philip's female friends never read, worked, or settled down to any profitable occupation. They had no resources in themselves, and spent the whole day chattering about dress, parties, theatres, and mutual acquaintances, who, if they happened to be feminine, were generally picked to pieces with the charity and good-humour for which the sex are proverbial.

Frequently Bligh felt so disgusted by the talk that she escaped from the room in order to breathe a purer atmosphere, and one less permeated with gossip and malice. She herself rarely took part in these discussions. To begin with, they were distasteful, and, secondly, she knew very few of the people who came under review.

Another thing which astonished her was the familiarity permitted by these ladies. They threw themselves about in attitudes, stuck out their feet, and had not the smallest objection to being patted and pawed like lap-dogs. In fact, they seemed rather to enjoy it than otherwise. The whole style was indescribably offensive to Bligh. It testified to an utter absence of good taste and breeding. Nothing pained her so much as to find what a liking her husband displayed for such fast society, or to see him led away by men and women who had a distinctly deteriorating effect upon his character. Instead of leading him to revere what was good and noble they scoffed at any elevation of thought, and dragged him down into the mire. Bligh believed that it was not well for men to lose their respect for women, and think them all selfish, frivolous, and ready to sell themselves to the highest bidder. Vainly she strove to maintain contrary opinions, and to prove that right and wrong were not mere names. Sir Philip only grew abusive and vented his indignation in public. In order to avoid scenes before strangers she constantly sat at the head of the table and held her tongue, whilst every womanly feeling within her was being shamed and outraged. It required a great deal of self-control, and she had a difficult part to play, for as hostess she could not well reprove people or exhibit her displeasure too plainly in her own house. She was forced by circumstances to keep up a certain show of civility, even when, if free to consult her individual inclinations, she would frequently have shown her guests to the door.

Every day the struggle to keep the peace grew harder, and necessitated more determined effort. If she had loved Philip she must have been jealous of him, for his conduct would have stabbed the heart of any wife. Over and over again she thanked God on her knees that she was spared this crowning source of misery; as it was, she oscillated between a continual state of smothered rebellion and contempt. To live thus was unnatural, and not calculated to improve the temper. She felt she should grow very hard and bitter if forced to exist year after year cultivating an outward calm and suffering all the while from a consuming inward fire. For her nature was impetuous and sensitive to a degree. Not a single unkind remark or sneer but what went quivering into the depths of her innermost being, there to leave a wound which festered, even although she very seldom allowed lookers-on to see how much it hurt her in reality.

Meanwhile, there was one healthy, wholesome pleasure in which she could indulge, and which often served as a means of escape from the " charming women " so much patronised by Sir Philip.

He had bought her a hack, a delightfully docile animal, who never cocked his ears, whisked his tail, or did anything alarming. At first Bligh mounted her new steed in fear and trembling; but King Arthur proved to be so remarkably quiet and well behaved that after she had been out a few times she began to feel positively courageous.

On the first occasion of her getting on a horse her husband accompanied her; but the ride was productive of sundry disagreeable little passages between the married couple which Bligh, for one, felt no anxiety to repeat. Knowing how to ride himself, Sir Philip was under the impression that his wife ought to learn immediately, and because she did not appear thoroughly at home in the saddle he attributed her ill-ease entirely to stupidity.

" Sit firm," he said, " and keep your shoulders well back. You'll never make a horsewoman if you don't."

" I can't, Philip,' she answered piteously, trying hard to obey his instructions. " I would if I could; but it's so difficult.

" Pshaw! There's no difficulty about riding in reality. But you're so awkward. I don't think I ever saw anyone so clumsy."

After this encouraging remark Bligh made heroic efforts to sit upright, and gripped the pommels hard with her knees; but the smallest movement of the horse reminded her of the insecurity of her position, and she longed to clutch hold of King Arthur's silky mane as a means of steadying herself. But her husband's eye was on her, and she did not dare. The expression of his face made her most painfully alive to her own shortcomings. Now, if there was one thing Sir Philip hated more than another it was going slowly. He liked the excitement and emulation of the chase, but he was not really fond of horses, and had little patience for a quiet ride. Consequently they had no sooner emerged from the Park gates than he said, " This is deadly stupid work. We are regularly crawling along. Let's hurry up a bit." Whereupon he gave his horse a touch of the heel and set off at a sharp trot, leaving his companion to follow as best she might. Although gentle as a lamb King Arthur had a high spirit, and did not appreciate being left behind in this unceremonious fashion. He pricked his slender ears, and at once imitated the example of the leader, blowing the fresh air through his nostrils in token of pleasure.

Now trotting may appear a very easy movement to those accustomed to being in the saddle, but it is astonishing what difficulties it presents to an inexperienced person. The motion of the animal possesses a strangely upsetting effect, whilst the reins have a horrible knack of getting jumbled together, until it becomes almost impossible to distinguish the curb from the snaffle. Either the rider seizes hold of the bridle convulsively as a means of steadying herself, or else she loses all guidance over the steed, who, if light-mouthed, is very apt to go in an exactly opposite direction to that intended by the unfortunate novice on his back. When King Arthur quickened his pace Bligh bumped and bumped and bumped in the rear of her lord, until she was within an ace of bumping off altogether. Her breath grew shorter and shorter, her face redder and redder, and her back hair shakier and shakier. She felt as if everything about her were coming to pieces, and looked upon some horrible catastrophe as inevitable unless Sir Philip immediately brought his steed to a standstill. The sensation was too exciting to be pleasant. In this emergency she lost what little control over King Arthur she already possessed, and allowed him to go straight at a stone heap by the side of the road. He swerved so as to avoid it, and gave a half jump, totally unexpected by his rider, whom he reduced to extremities. The sudden jerk caused Bligh to lose her equilibrium, and sent her on to King Arthur's tail. She tottered there for the space of two or three seconds, and then, by some marvel, regained her seat ; but in the struggle her hat flew off, and down tumbled her pretty brown hair in a regular cascade over her shoulders.

It was very long and very soft, and no doubt if it had belonged to anyone save his own wife Sir Philip would have admired it; but at this unlucky moment an acquaintance of the baronet's passed by, who, with a smile of amusement, raised his hat and drove rapidly on.

"Oh! stop, Philip, stop," gasped Bligh, as soon as she was in a position to make herself heard. "I shall tumble off if you don't. You go so dreadfully fast."

———

CHAPTER XXI.

THE HEIGHT OF HUMILIATION.

SIR PHILIP turned short round, and his face wore an ugly scowl, which quite deprived it of its usual good looks.

"I'm going home," he said sharply. "Job himself couldn't put up with it any longer."

"Going home?" echoed Bligh, in a tone of innocent amazement. "Why! we have only just started."

"I know; but I can't stand this sort of thing. And if you take my advice you'll come too."

"But, Philip——" she began.

He interrupted her rudely.

"The long and short of it is, if you want to make a fool of yourself you had much better do it in private, and not give an exhibition on the public roads. I felt hot all over when Douglas Jackson drove by just now and saw you looking like a lunatic. For goodness' sake, next time you attempt to go for a ride get a hat that will keep on somehow, and do your hair up tight. Nothing proclaims the beginner so much as a dishevelled head. Bear that fact in mind." So saying he cantered off home, leaving the poor little woman, who felt like a culprit, to her own devices.

After this inauspicious commencement Bligh did not ride again for a whole week. Her pride had been cruelly wounded by Sir Philip's remarks, although she was aware of the folly of allowing them to make so deep an impression.

"He can't expect me to stick on all at once," she thought, resentfully. "It was very cruel of him to speak as he did, and considering I had never been on a horse's back before I do think he might have had a little more patience. When one is quite conscious of looking a guy already it's adding insult to injury to tell one so to one's face. I don't care if Mr. Jackson did laugh. He was perfectly welcome to if he chose."

But Bligh's reason soon came to her aid and cured the mental soreness from which she suffered for a few days. In spite of her catastrophe she had thoroughly enjoyed the exercise of riding, and was determined to learn how to sit a horse respectably. So the next time she went out she told her husband nothing about it, but took for companion an old groom named Robinson, who was in the habit of driving Lady Verschoyle, and who had been in the family for many years. Bligh was not one of those stiff, stuck-up people given to regarding servants as inferiors, possessing none of the same feelings as themselves. She chatted away to Robinson, and in return the old man took a great fancy to his young mistress, and protected her with a fatherly care, which little by little restored her confidence.

Instead of laughing at her faults, as Sir Philip had done, and weighting her with an odious sense of discouragement, he respectfully pointed out her mistakes, at the same time showing how they should be corrected. Always quick at picking up things, and assisted by an innate love of horseflesh, before long she improved wonderfully. Then she confided to Robinson that the ambition of her life was to go out hunting, and jump—yes, actually jump—the fences as she had seen other people doing.

"Because you know," she added, a trifle plaintively, "I want to astonish Sir Philip. He thought I never could ride."

"You'll ride fast enough, my lady," responded Robinson, with a smile of encouragement. "You've got the pluck, which is more than can be said of arf the field, and, what's more, you're fond of 'osses, and knows how to get on with 'em. There's a wonderful lot of character about 'osses if folk only knew it. Everyone's different, and very often they're a deal more sensibler than the gents on their back."

Bligh was delighted to find that Robinson did not offer any objection to her proposition, and, on the contrary, fully entered into it. He promised to accompany her on a broken-down hunter, who was now coming round, and required long, slow exercise, and declared proudly that his pupil was quite competent to make a successful *début* in the hunting field.

"There's a-many as comes out, my lady, who can't ride any better than you," he averred, in his customary consolatory manner. "You may take my word for that. But, Lord! it's wonderful how soon they improves. That there Mrs. Benson, for instance. I've 'eard say when she first come to these parts, as 'ow she warn't anything like the 'osswoman she is now. Practice makes perfect, and you've got on wonderful."

These observations were distinctly pleasing to Bligh's vanity, and possibly they caused her to estimate her equestrian powers more highly than might otherwise have been the case. The result of Robinson's eulogy was that one fine morning early in December, when the hounds happened to meet within three miles of Beechlands, she and her trusty attendant stole off together, starting a good half hour before Sir Philip, who generally rode out to covert at a hard gallop, and in a desperate hurry. They were so early, indeed, that they arrived before the hounds, and Bligh was able to select a nice quiet corner, where she could hide herself away from the public view, and thus escape the ignominy of being peremptorily ordered home by her lord and master. The ride to the meet had warmed her up, and, to use a sporting expression, she felt " full of go."

King Arthur behaved admirably. Although he pawed the ground with delight at sight of the hounds, to which he was evidently accustomed, he indulged in no disconcerting vagaries, and stood fairly still. His temper was so perfect, that even when a vicious, long-tailed thoroughbred lashed out at him, and missed his sleek quarter by about half an inch, he scarcely took any notice of the affront, but continued to gaze lovingly at the speckled pack. As for Bligh, she looked quite pretty. Her trim little figure was set off to advantage by a neat, well-fitting habit, cut away in front to show a checked horse-cloth waistcoat. She had taken great pains with her get-up, and her tie and hat were irreproachable. The unruly hair was plaited in light coils at the back of her head, and secured by the best part of a packet of hairpins. She had the further satisfaction of knowing that her attire was perfectly neat and correct, since her habit had been manufactured by one of the first London tailors, no less a person than Mr. Scott, of South Molton-street. Altogether Bligh felt on much better terms with herself than usual. The exercise had brought a soft bloom to her cheeks, not often seen there, especially of late, and her luminous eyes, which at all times were bright and full of intelligence, shone to-day with an additional light. The air, the life, the movement, added to the congeniality of the pale wintry sun, all combined to render her happy. Somehow her troubles always seemed to assume a lighter hue after a good canter. Possessing a concentrated, and not very gregarious nature, she felt quite contented jogging about the country lanes. King Arthur was company enough. She much preferred him to the ordinary run of human beings, and it frequently struck her how infinitely nicer he was than men belonging to the Dashwood-Rickerby type. To-day she was secretly elated at the thought of her husband's surprise, when he should perceive her gaily jumping the fences with hounds, as if she had been accustomed to pursuing the fox all her life. She pictured to herself her revenge for his slighting observations. For she was determined to perform prodigies of valour just to prove to him that in spite of his prognostications she had learnt how to ride.

So when the pack moved off, and the attendant cavalcade was in motion, Bligh followed in its footsteps. The first draw was close at hand, whereat she rejoiced, for she found the slow jogging along the road excessively fatiguing. It was so very much easier to trot fast than to go at an amble which just prevented you from rising in your stirrups, and almost broke your back. By the end of five minutes she became quite hot and breathless, and reluctantly acknowledged to herself that she hardly felt up to a regular day's hunting yet. Going for a quiet ride of a couple of hours was very different work. However, she managed to reach the covert at the tail of the procession, and just in the nick of time, since before the hounds were put in, a vociferous cry arose from the foot people, and one of their number informed the huntsman that a fine bob-tailed fox had made good his escape, not deigning to wait for the arrival of the enemy. Without a moment's hesitation, Dysack clapped on the pack. For a second or two the leaders put their noses to the ground, and their white-sterns were to be seen feathering busily; then they flung themselves forward on the fresh hot scent, whilst the many-noted music of their tongues filled the air. Like a thunderbolt let loose, the field galloped off in pursuit. Bligh caught the general contagion, and began to feel the enthusiasm of the chase stealing into her veins. She would rather have died than have been left behind. Forward! Forward! Man and beast were animated by the same spirit. As King Arthur bounded over the springy turf all the small fears experienced by his mistress on the way to the meet vanished. She no longer thought of the disasters that might happen, if her horse trod on a loose stone, shied at a roving pig, or stumbled into a drain. These and countless other dangers disappeared, whilst through her veins the blood coursed warmly and merrily. Life was not all dark. It had its bright moments, and a good run on a good hunter put pessimism to shame.

Old Robinson knew the country well, and steering for the gates, he piloted her capitally. He seemed to enjoy himself quite as much as his companion, and incited her to fresh effort by his laudatory remarks.

"Capital, my lady. Firstrare, he sang out, as side by side they flew a little grip in the field, which King Arthur swung over in his stride. "You're on a regular water jumper. Give him 'is 'ead, and he'll carry you like a bird. He only wants to be let alone."

Bligh's face literally glowed with pleasure. She understood now what people felt when they went hunting. Never had she experienced such glorious excitement. White it lasted it altered the whole character of life, and lifted one quite out of the ordinary commonplace routine of every-day existence. They might have been galloping about ten minutes, and things could not have gone better, when all at once an unexpected event took place. Without any apparent cause, the hounds suddenly threw up their heads, baffled by the mysteries of scent, which neither they nor their masters have yet succeeded in fathoming. The hard riders had the good luck to be in the same field with them, having gallantly ridden over a line of stiff fences so as to achieve this proud position; but the gate division were not equally fortunate, for, unless they retraced their footsteps, or went a long way round, they found themselves compelled to jump. The fence which divided them from the main body of the pack was not much higher than a hurdle, but it happened to be extremely stiff, and had some remarkably strong growers running through it. It was impossible to force a gap, and although by no means a formidable obstacle, it presented decidedly more difficulty than the habitual shirkers were in the habit of overcoming.

But on the present occasion they were fairly caught in a trap, and very few of them had enough nerve to expose their cowardice; for every man in the hunt with any pretensions to riding to hounds was on the other side, looking on with smiles of amusement, and enjoying the fun of watching his less courageous brethren driven into a corner. Even the greatest "funkstick" felt that in this conjunction there was nothing for it but to jump. So, after a brief hesitation, the boldest amongst the gapsters hardened their hearts, and went at the fence. Unfortunately for those who came after, they did not succeed in making a hole, and only added to the miseries of the comrades whom they had quitted. For, charmed beyond measure with their own achievement, they immediately drew rein, and turning round, waited maliciously to see their more timid companions follow suit. Whilst this was going on, Bligh suddenly caught sight of Sir Philip, and their glances met.

"What!" he exclaimed, in astonishment. "You! Pray, how did you get here?"

Now was Bligh's moment of triumph, to which she had looked forward with the eagerness of a child.

"I rode," she said, proudly, "all the way from Beechlands. Would you like to see me jump?"

Before he could reply she gave her horse his head, and let him go at the fence. King Arthur was far from artistically ridden, but she remembered Robinson's instructions not to tug at his mouth, and did not interfere with it. The good little beast, checked for an instant, arched his back, and bucked over with the cleverness of an experienced hunter, no novice at the game.

Alas! alas! Why was not poor Bligh equally proficient? The momentary stoppage, followed by the jerk, proved her undoing.

There! before her husband, the huntsman, and the whole of the hunt, she literally flew out of the saddle. There was nothing to excuse the somersault, no mistake, no peck on landing. As she bumped with frightful force upon the ground, she was cruelly conscious of this humiliating fact. Pride in her case had indeed had a fall. How angry Philip would be! This thought flashed across her brain as she shot through the air. She pitched heavily on to her right shoulder, having lost her balance on the off side, and lay on the wet grass, feeling partially stunned.

And then she saw four shining hoofs and a brown body, surmounted by a handsome but angry face, and heard an irritable voice say quite out loud before everybody, " For goodness' sake, Bligh, go straight home and don't disgrace yourself and me in this ridiculous fashion. We shall never hear the last of it. You will be the laughing-stock of the whole of the field for some months to come. It was madness your attempting to hunt."

Two great tears rolled down Bligh's cheeks. Do what she would, she could not prevent them from overflowing.

"Oh! Philip," she said piteously, "don't scold. Things are bad enough to bear as it is."

" You have nobody but yourself to blame for your misfortunes."

" I know, but that does not make them any better."

" Why the dickens don't you get up? " he said, roughly, not offering to dismount.

" I—I think," she answered, somewhat tremulously, "that I am a—little—hurt."

All at once a gentleman jumped off his horse, and lifted Bligh from the ground. It was Lord Midlandshire, who had overheard the above conversation.

" My dear Lady Verschoyle," he said in a loud, clear voice, casting an indignant glance at Sir Philip, "you must not think anything of this little mishap. I assure you that a voluntary is quite a common affair. There is scarcely a man in the hunting field who does not cut one occasionally, and no beginner need be ashamed of tumbling off at starting. Jumping is not as easy as it looks, but you have plenty of pluck, which is the main thing, and need not feel disheartened." The words were distinctly spoken, so that all those within earshot might hear them. Any inclination to titter ceased, for Lord Midlandshire was the greatest man in the county, and people took their cue from him. If he had laughed, they would have laughed also, but when they found that he saw nothing ludicrous in the occurrence, they didn't either. Sheep are easily led, especially human ones.

If his lordship's speech was kind, his manner was still more so. Bligh looked at him gratefully, wondering why a stranger should display so much greater consideration than her own husband, and take such pains to soothe her wounded susceptibilities.

"You are very kind," she said, in a subdued tone. " I do not deserve kindness after being so stupid, but one appreciates it more when one is in trouble than at any other time. I shall never ride again after this hideous exhibition of incapacity."

"Oh! nonsense, you must not talk like that. Tumbling off is a little annoying just at the moment, but people soon forget all about it. However, I think you have had rather a shake for to-day, and if I may presume to advise, I should recommend your driving back to Beechlands."

"I don't think I can, we have no trap out."

"I have one posted in the village where we met. It can take you home, and return for me later on in the day."

Bligh thankfully accepted Lord Midlandshire's offer. She was far too much ashamed of what had happened to complain of her sensations. But she felt very sick and faint, and she could not help thinking there was something the matter with her right shoulder. When she tried to raise it, it seemed curiously numb and dead. She hated making a fuss, however, and kept silent regarding her sufferings, being aware, as Sir Philip had said, that she had brought them entirely upon herself. She glanced at her husband, as if seeking his assent to the proposed plan. For several minutes the hounds had been busy feathering down the hedgerow, but now a couple stole out in advance of their companions, and began careering over the field.

"By all means, accept such a good offer," said Sir Philip, who was anxious to be off again. "Are you tolerably right now, Bligh?"

"Yes," she answered, " don't let me keep you any longer."

"I would stay if I could be of the least use, but I never did understand the art of mounting a lady, and Robinson is much better at it than I. You'll have to ride back as far as the village. By Jove! the hounds have hit off the line. Good-bye for the present. I shall lose my start if I stay any longer." And glad to escape, he galloped away, whilst Lord Midlandshire looked after his retreating form disapprovingly, and muttered—"These poor little women!   They have a baddish time of it when they are wedded to sport, and their husbands become converted into so many human hounds."   He stayed and held King Arthur by the bridle, whilst Robinson lifted Bligh into the saddle, and then shook hands at parting.   She could have cried with the pain, but she said nothing until once more alone with the kind old groom.   He was alarmed by the whiteness of her face.

"Are you ill, my lady?" he inquired, anxiously.

"I didn't like to tell anybody before," she answered, "but I'm almost certain that I have broken a bone.   If there is a doctor in the village, I will ask him to have a look at it, and—and—Robinson, would you mind going slowly.   I don't feel as if I could stand much jogging.   It seems to go through one."

They proceeded at a leisurely pace, and when they reached the village were fortunate enough to find the doctor just returned from his morning rounds.   He requested Bligh to enter his parlour, and quickly proceeded to ascertain the extent of her injuries.   They did not take long to discover, for he pronounced immediately that there was a slight fracture of the right clavicle, in addition to several severe bruises and contusions. He lost no time in setting and strapping up the injured member. Bligh bore the process heroically, though once or twice the room spun round and round, and she felt on the point of fainting. The doctor, however, insisted on her drinking off a glass of brandy, and the unaccustomed stimulant kept her up.

"You will have to keep quiet for three weeks or a month, Lady Verschoyle," he said, when all was over, "and if I were you, I should go to bed directly I got home, for apart from the breakage, you are suffering from a very considerable shake to the system.   By staying in bed for a day or two, you will recover far more quickly than if you attempt to go about as usual.   Rest is the great thing in these cases."

When Sir Philip returned, about five o'clock in the afternoon, he was astonished to learn what had happened, and perhaps he felt a little remorseful on reviewing his own conduct.   At any rate, he went straight to his wife's room, before divesting himself of his leathers, and said not unkindly—

"Hulloa!   Bligh, this is a bad business.   I had not the faintest idea when I rode off that you had broken a bone."

"I suspected it," she answered, "but after my miserable performance, I did not like to make a fuss."

"Are you in much pain?"

"No, only a little.   It will teach me to stick on better another time."

"If I had known of this I should not have accepted an invitation to go out to dinner," he observed.

"Where are you going, Philip?"

"Only to Captain Dashwood's and Jack Rickerby's. They asked me to-day out hunting. Jackson's staying with them, and they wanted to get up a round game."

Her husband's softened manner gave her a hope. Now was her opportunity. She distrusted these round games. They invariably represented a goodly sum out of pocket.

"Philip," she said, "I do not like those men. They are always trying to better themselves at your expense. There is no occasion to quarrel, but don't you think you might be a little less intimate with them than you are? The last time you went, you lost a couple of hundred."

He shook off the hand which she had laid on his sleeve.

"Bah!" he said. "Women are all alike. They always hate their husband's friends, and try to close the door upon them." And although his conscience smote him a little, he went out to dinner after all, just as if his wife had not been laid up in bed with a broken collar bone.

CHAPTER XXII.

A DIFFICULT CONFESSION.

BLIGH did not recover from her disaster as quickly as might have been expected. The bone, it is true, soon knit, and only occasioned temporary inconvenience, but the effects of the fall made themselves felt for a long time. They caused great weakness and physical prostration, and her medical attendant strongly advised her not attempting to ride again at present.

Consequently King Arthur was consigned to the stables, where his mistress went to visit him daily, and fed him with lumps of sugar. She was reluctantly forced to abandon her dreams of hunting for that season, at any rate, and to content herself with hearing the sport talked about instead, which, however; was not quite the same thing. It wearied and tantalised by turns.

In spite of every endeavour on Bligh's part to influence her husband for his good, he seemed to be slipping further and further beyond her reach. They hardly ever sat down to dinner alone, and their wedded life was deprived of all domesticity. She rarely knew beforehand who was coming, but had orders always to provide for half a dozen. The house was never free from male visitors, and there is no doubt that had she been a flirting young woman by nature, the society with which Sir Philip chose to surround his wife would have proved a source of very considerable temptation.

But, as the reader has probably gathered ere now, Bligh did not belong to the modern school of married ladies so fashionable in the nineteenth century, and she resolutely set her face against all fast or risky conversation. After a while the guests came to understand that naughty stories were not appreciated by their hostess, and never elicited a laugh. They were unanimous in voting her a bit prim and " slow," but the more gentlemanly among their numbers had the grace to reserve their choicest and most sparkling anecdotes until she had quitted the dining-room. Under such circumstances a sense of constraint was well-nigh inevitable, and Bligh was generally as glad to retire as they were to see her depart. Then the bottles passed around more briskly, and tongues wagged merrily, whilst glasses were filled, only to be emptied immediately. None but Sir Philip and his butler knew the immense amount of liquor consumed on these festive occasion. Since the young baronet's majority terrible inroads had been made on the late Sir Thomas's cellar. The bins intended to last for generations were many of them three-quarters empty.

It was with growing pain that Bligh noticed how her husband's complexion gradually parted with its freshness and fairness. The red encroached on the white until it invaded ears and throat, and the contour of his face lost its delicacy of outline. Every day served to alter his appearance for the worse. He no longer carried himself as erect as a couple of months ago. His eyes, formerly cold and clear, were fading now to a duller tint, and his spirits alternated between fits of boisterous mirth and of unnatural depression. Once or twice, when she had occasion to go into his smoking-room after breakfast. she had been horrified to find a decanter containing brandy standing on the table, and when he went hunting he invariably took two flasks filled with the same strong beverage. The smallest remonstrance roused his temper. An uneasy desire to assert the mastery he possessed over his wife rendered him peculiarly irritable to advice. A word from Bligh set him in a fury. She soon discovered this regrettable fact, and gave up any direct appeal to his better feelings. Sorrowfully she admitted that she was fairly nonplussed. This man's character, with its weakness, selfishness, want of sympathy, and morbid craving for power over creatures whom he knew he could bully with impunity, baffled her completely. She did not know how to take it—how to deal with it ; for whether she spoke out, or whether she didn't, she always appeared in the wrong. One thing alone was certain　Whenever she tried to guide him, no matter how gently, he resembled a pig going to market, and resented the attempt. Once or twice it occurred to her to seek assistance from the servants, but when it came to the point her wifely delicacy shrank from taking them into her confidence. A hint to the butler to dilute his master's drink, and to fill up his glass as seldom as possible, might have been productive of good results, but she could not bring herself to make such an open confession of his weakness.

Therefore, during the early part of the winter, she watched and waited, hoping some improvement would take place, and endeavouring to think as leniently as she could of her husband's faults. No one knew save herself how the iron was daily, hourly entering her soul. She kept her troubles secret, and hid them from the two old ladies to the best of her ability. But it was a terrible disappointment to find that she could neither love nor respect the man with whom she had linked her lot. No amount of material comfort made up for it, and the knowledge was all the harder to bear, because since her marriage she realised that for years past a great and silent craving for affection had been slowly springing up within her breast. It only required some fitting object on which to vent itself. When it dawned upon her that for the second time she had made an unfortunate choice, a nameless fear took possession of her, and she trembled to contemplate the future. She had hoped that this yearning for tenderness was dead, crushed back long ago into the shadowy past. When she married Sir Philip, and the desire for congenial companionship, for a happy home and fond husband, grew stronger and stronger in proportion as its likelihood of attainment faded into the background, she distrusted her power to maintain a life-long neutrality of sentiment. Nature called out, " Give, oh! give me something to love."

Bligh was no fool. She had seen in real life, and also gathered from books that a reserve force of unsatisfied feeling forms a frightfully dangerous element in the constitution of a woman. A tiny spark often suffices to fan the smouldering fire into a glowing furnace. Sometimes when her husband's friends arrived she would say to herself, "What a mercy it is that I don't care for any of them. Pray God, I may never get fond of any man again. They make one so unhappy, and, after all, they are not worth the state of unrest which they create. My life with Philip is not easy, but as long as matters stay as they are, I can bear it. Nevertheless, if ever he or I were to fall in love, it would be converted into a hell upon earth."

She knew and saw the danger, but a woman who is happily married does not reason in this introspective manner, and it was a bad thing for Bligh that the instinct of self-preservation possessed by every living creature should have put such thoughts into her head. She would have been better without them. Analysis in matrimony generally signifies discontent.

Luckily, Sir Philip's friends came and went, and were as utterly indifferent to the mistress of the household as if they had been so many pawns on a chess-board.

She continued in this mood until one day, shortly after Christmas, when Sir Philip received a letter, the handwriting of which she happened to see, and which gave her a kind of shock. For it conjured up vivid memories of long ago. She could feel the colour rushing to her cheek in a burning wave, whose intensity filled her with guilty shame.

" Bother ! " exclaimed Sir Philip, peevishly, as he perused the contents of the letter. " This is a most confounded nuisance."

" What's the matter ? " she asked, almost inaudibly.

" I wrote to a friend some time ago, asking him to come and stay a few days, and offering to mount him. My horses then were all fresh and well. Unfortunately he could not get away, and he now writes proposing a visit. The awkward part of it is, I'm infernally short of nags just at present, for I lamed three last week, and three more are coughing badly, and are not fit to hunt. I wish people would come when they're invited, or else not at all."

" Could you not manage to hire something for your friend ? " she suggested pacificatorily, for Sir Philip's tone was far from amiable.

" Yes, I see no other way out of the difficulty. I must write and tell him he will have to content himself with a hireling, for he proposes arriving on Thursday."

" Who is he, Philip ? " she demanded, with an uncomfortable fluttering in the region of her heart.

" I thought I had told you. He's a fellow called Cameron, in the Guards. I met him up in Scotland about a year ago, when I was staying with some people called Mackintosh, and we rather palled. He is the eldest son of a crotchety Scotch peer, who, from what I gathered, keeps his heir uncommonly tight. I don't know whether it is true, but Cameron has the reputation of being always on the look-out for an heiress. He flirted tremendously with an American girl named Waller whilst we were at the Mackintoshes' Everybody thought he was going to propose, but it seems he ascertained just in the nick of time that her fortune had been very much overrated, and so he beat a retreat, leaving the fair one to cry her eyes out. Why ! " continued Sir Philip, abruptly, staring hard at his wife, " what the deuce is wrong with you ? You look as white as a sheet."

"No—nothing," she articulated faintly. "I don't feel very well, that's all."

"Then you had better lie down for a bit, whilst I go round the stables, and find out how the various cripples are progressing. Horses are cursed plagues. There always seems something amiss just when you want them most. Anybody visiting here might fancy I had more hunters than I knew what to do with, and yet when it comes to the point, one is literally not in a position to mount a friend. Cameron is a deuced hard man, I believe, and I should have liked to have given him a decent crock, but it can't be helped, and he must just take his chance." So saying, Sir Philip walked out of the room.

When he had gone Bligh heaved a sigh of relief. For ten years she had never set eyes upon Duncan, and she was paralysed to find that the mere sound of his name and the thought of seeing him again should create such a revolution within her being. Could it be that the old love was not dead as she believed, but simply slumbering? A sudden dread seized her. If she was unable to answer for herself, would it not be better to avoid the risk of meeting him, and of their sleeping under the same roof? She had never thought it necessary to communicate to Sir Philip the details of her unhappy engagement. It was hurtful to her woman's pride to confess that she had been cruelly jilted in her youth, and as he had not alluded to the subject, she had abstained from volunteering confidences which might or might not be well received. But now she regretted her reticence. It placed her in an awkward position, and an inward voice urged her strongly not to let another day pass without making a full confession.

When Sir Philip first imparted the news of Duncan's coming, her presence of mind had fairly deserted her, but reflection soon pointed out that the right and proper course was to tell her husband everything that had happened. Having arrived at this resolution, she waited until she heard him re-enter the house, and followed him into his study. Early as was the hour, an odour of spirits and tobacco pervaded it, and an empty soda water glass stood on the mantel-piece. The atmosphere was offensive to a delicate woman's nostrils and consequently she did not often grace this sanctum with her presence. To-day, however, she had a purpose, and met Sir Philip's gaze of irritable inquiry steadily.

"What do you want?" he said. "I have no end of letters to write, and am particularly busy this morning."

"I will not detain you long," she began, nervously, "but you said a little while ago that this Mr. Cameron's coming was inconve——"

"He is Captain Cameron," interrupted the baronet, showing signs of impatience.

"Captain Cameron then. What I was going to say was, since so many of your horses are on the sick list, don't you think you could manage to put him off? I," and she changed colour, "should be very glad if you would."

Sir Philip stared at her in amazement.

"*You* would be very glad, Bligh! Why, what earthly difference can it make to you?"

She cast down her eyes, and said in a constrained voice—

"I—I would rather not meet him, please, Philip, if it is all the same to you."

"And why not, pray? Isn't the company I associate with good enough for your fastidious little ladyship."

"It is not that, though I honestly confess to not liking some of your friends."

"What is it then? For any sake give up beating about the bush. Why can't you get to the point?"

"I ought to have told you before. I blame myself for not having done so, but—but," and her tone became tremulous, "once, long ago, Captain Cameron and I were engaged to be married. I have not seen him since, and it might be better that I never should."

Sir Philip burst into a hoarse laugh.

"Oh! that old story. Of course I knew it. Everybody did at the time, but I really fail to see what it has got to do with the matter."

"Philip," she said, speaking with evident effort, "I have not told you all. I—I was very fond of Captain Cameron. It was he who gave me up, not I him. I think—I hope I have forgotten the past, but I would rather not run the risk of reviving it. Don't you understand?"

"Well, no, I can't say that I do. People who mix in society are continually rubbing up against their old flames. They have so many that they quite enjoy exchanging tender reminiscences with former loves. It's all the fashion nowadays."

Bligh looked away. The muscles of her lips were twitching.

"I had only one love," she said, quietly, "and on that account perhaps I thought more of it than if I had had half a dozen. If Duncan had not jilted me, we should have been old married people by now." There was a touch of regret in her voice, which roused Sir Philip's indignation.

"Deuce take it all!" he exclaimed. "Do you mean to say you are fond of the fellow still?"

She drew herself up with a proud little gesture, and her clear eyes looked straight into his.

"If you trusted me, Philip, you would not ask such a question. At the present moment I cannot honestly say what my feeling for Duncan Cameron is. I have no wish ever to see him again. As regards your honor, you may rest assured. It is absolutely safe in my hands."

Her words made him feel ashamed of the suspicions which he had begun to entertain.

"Yes, yes, I know that. Whatever your faults may be, Bligh, you're as straight a little woman as ever stepped. In fact, you are too cold to have much feeling."

She smiled. Would she have been cold had she married a man whom she loved and honoured?

"In spite of my being an icicle, Philip, I still beg you to put Captain Cameron off. Surely you can make some excuse now that you know all the circumstances of the case. It will be distinctly disagreeable to me to find myself in the same house with him."

"I can't put him off. You should have spoken sooner. I've just sent a telegram, telling Cameron we shall expect him on Thursday, and one of the stablemen has ridden over to Warlaby's to engage a couple of screws for Friday and Saturday. If you don't care for the fellow, his presence can't affect you much one way or the other, whilst if you continue to make a fuss, I shall believe that you do."

CHAPTER XXIII.

MEETING AN OLD LOVE.

BLIGH was struck by the force of this reasoning.

"It's playing with edged tools," she said, "but perhaps you are right, Philip. Let Captain Cameron come then, only remember that it was you and not I who wished for his society. The responsibility is shifted from my shoulders to yours."

"Oh! bother, don't let us discuss the matter any more. I'm sick to death of all this sentimental rubbish. Cameron's a good chap, even if he did throw you over, and I can't afford to quarrel with all my friends on your account."

"That is a most unfair accusation," retorted Bligh, spiritedly. "No one ever comes to this house except on your invitation, and I always make a point of being civil, whatever my private feelings may be." And so saying she marched out of the room, realising how vain it was to court her husband's sympathy, since he invariably threw her back upon herself. It seemed strange that any grown-up individual should be so utterly unfamiliar

with the workings of the female heart as Philip. Why did such
men marry? They interested themselves in their horses and
their dogs, their runs and their sport, and yet apparently it never
occurred to them that the woman with whom they lived was
worth study. She might be ignored with impunity, and treated
like a stock or a stone. Her most sacred feelings were scoffed
at, and termed nonsensical rubbish. Bligh felt how hard it is
to make confidences when they meet with ridicule and coldness.
But her conscience whispered that she had acted rightly, and it
did not reproach her.

When the day came for Captain Cameron's arrival she was
seized by an overpowering nervousness. She could hardly sit
still for five minutes, and would have given a small fortune to
escape the impending ordeal. Naturally, the more she thought
about it the greater it seemed. Her mother and Lady Verschoyle went out driving as usual, but she declined to accompany
them, pleading a bad headache as an excuse. The fact was she
was afraid of betraying herself. Sir Philip had gone hunting,
and although he promised to come home early in order to
receive his guest, she was aware that this promise could not be
depended upon. If he got into a good run he would think no
more of Duncan Cameron than of the man in the moon. Unfortunately, the expected visitor had left the time of his arrival
somewhat doubtful. He had written to say that, having business in town, he would find his own way from the station, and
not trouble Sir Philip to send. Bligh felt he might walk in at
any moment, and the uncertainty added to her disquietude.

It was a dreary, depressing afternoon. The clouds lay low
and heavy, and a white mist rose from the cold surface of the
earth, and crept round the big trees in the park, until they
looked like so many gigantic ghosts stretching weird arms aloft.
Everything was grey, and moist, and formless. The fog robbed
the surrounding landscape of its clear outlines, rendering them
blurred and indistinct. Bligh looked out and shivered; then,
turning away from the window, stirred the fire into a bright
flame. It lit up the walls of her cosy boudoir, and gave an air
of cheerfulness, in striking contrast to the prospect presented
out of doors. She realised that in spite of many drawbacks she
had still much cause for thankfulness, and, sitting down in an
arm-chair, began to soliloquise.

"Why am I not more content?" ran her thoughts. "What
is it that I want? Many women in my place would feel quite
at rest. They would not hanker after anything beyond riches
and rank, fine diamonds to wear, and plenty of material comfort. I have these, and yet they don't satisfy me. I was
happier when I was a poor, ill-paid music-teacher, forced to

trudge out at all hours and seasons. At least, I was my own mistress then. I had not bartered away my independence. Heigh ho! How different married life might be if one had a nice, kind husband! How different one would be oneself! Men are very foolish. They make a great mistake in their treatment of us, for every woman born with decent instincts is to be won by kindness. If Philip had only gone the right way to work he might have made me love him; but now," and she sighed heavily, "I fear it is too late."

Thus thinking she fell into a reverie, from which she was awakened by the opening of the door. In an instant she sprang to her feet, and stood with every nerve quivering, whilst the man-servant ushered in Captain Cameron. For one short second the room seemed to spin round and round, and then, summoning all her courage to her aid, she advanced to meet him. Oh! what a sudden relief she experienced. Was this Duncan—this stout, middle-aged-looking man, with a corpulent figure, a red face, and no hair on the top of his head? Why! he was not her Duncan at all. If she had met him in the street she should not have known him. Her fears vanished. She was ready to laugh at them, for by some strange metamorphosis of the feminine nature all at once she felt quite at her ease, and the situation, to which she had looked forward with such dread, was completely divested of embarrassment. It was a miracle, for one glance sufficed to assure her that henceforth there could be no danger in his presence. The charm was broken, his power over her gone. Never again could he inspire sentiments of affection in her breast. She knew now for certain that the old love was not merely buried, but dead, and the knowledge brought a great gladness. The burden had dropped, and she was a free woman at last, since the image at whose shrine she had worshipped so long stood revealed an idol of clay.

"How do you do, Captain Cameron?" she said, as composedly as if they were in the habit of meeting every day. "You have come rather earlier than we expected."

He started back at the sound of her voice.

"Bligh!" he exclaimed. "Bligh Burton! Is it possible?"

"But certainly. Why not?"

"I never dreamt I should meet you here, Bligh."

"You mean that you would not have come had you known the pleasure in store? Well, perhaps you would have been right."

"If I am not welcome I can return."

"It is hardly worth while for you to give yourself so much trouble."

"And what have you been doing all these years, Bligh?"

" Will you kindly call me by my proper name," she said, with dignity.

He glanced at her left hand, and perceived the wedding-ring.

" I do not even know it."

" I may have been Bligh Burton to you once, Captain Cameron ; but now I am Lady Verschoyle."

" What ! Sir Philip's wife ? "

" Yes. Do you mean to say that you did not know Philip was married ? "

" I had not the least idea who the lady was. I have been abroad for the last four months, studying the battlefields of Europe, and have only just returned. Pardon my ignorance." Then his surprise overcame his politeness, and he added : " Just fancy your being Lady Verschoyle. By Jove ! you have done well for yourself."

She coloured at this remark, the freedom of which she resented. Was there anything so extraordinary in her having made a good marriage that he should consider himself entitled to make such an observation ? It piqued her not a little.

" That is a matter of opinion, Captain Cameron, and one scarcely necessary for you to discuss in my presence. Your surprise is extremely flattering to my *amour propre*, but I should prefer its being expressed behind my back rather than to my face."

This retort decidedly disconcerted him. Whenever he recalled his love passages with Bligh he always thought of them as an affair out of which he had issued wisely, if not exactly creditably. But as Lady Verschoyle she figured as a very different personage in his estimation.

" Just fancy my being ignorant of your marriage, and actually coming to stay with you as your guest ! " he exclaimed. " Does not it seem odd ? "   Then he looked at her critically, and added : " You have not changed much, Bli—I mean Lady Verschoyle ; in fact, if anything, you have improved."

" Thanks," she answered sarcastically. " Your praise is extremely gratifying. I fancy, however, that my present position has a good deal to do with the improvement which you profess to say has taken place in my appearance."

" At any rate, matrimony has taught you the use of your tongue. You used to be more amiable in the olden days when I was cramming with your father. What jolly days those were ! Have you completely forgotten them ? "

She gave a little, provoking laugh, which had the effect of exasperating him intensely.

" Under my husband's roof," she observed, cuttingly, " it is scarcely good taste for you to discuss old times ; besides, they do not linger so pleasantly in my memory that I should care to dwell upon them. With your permission, Captain Cameron, we will dismiss the past, and confine ourselves exclusively to the present."

He reddened consciously, feeling the justice of her remark, and also its severity.

" It was not my fault," he muttered, in rather a hang-dog way. " I would have come back when I promised had my father allowed me to do so. He was at the bottom of the whole business. I dared not offend him, and, as you know, he was against us from the first. The governor's an awfully obstinate old chap, and when he takes an idea into his head persuasion is thrown away."

" Please don't make any apologies. To begin with, they come rather late in the day; and, secondly, the matter is one of no importance whatever. I have consoled myself, as you see, and managed to exist, in spite of the paternal obstinacy which you are filial enough to deplore. Let us talk of something else—the weather, for instance. That is an unfailing topic, and absolutely safe, even if a trifle dull." And taking up a hand-screen she shielded her face from the fire, in a manner which effectually prevented him from reading its expression. She showed him so clearly that she declined to continue the conversation unless under different conditions that he was forced to take refuge in the first commonplace he could think of.

Had he found her still Bligh Burton, occupying a six-roomed cottage, clad in shabby, ill-fitting clothes, which betrayed her poverty, and living amongst humble surroundings, the chances are he would have met his old love with absolute indifference. But when he saw her at the head of a magnificent establishment, invested with all the pomp and appanage conferred by wealth, his estimation of the woman whom he had scorned rose in a remarkable degree. He felt piqued by her coldness and irony. When he contrasted them with the clinging tenderness of former days he suddenly experienced an overpowering desire to break down the barrier of her frigid self-possession. He could not believe it to be real. His vanity suggested that it was merely assumed as a means of defence, and he refused to credit that her love was all gone. He wondered what had become of it; but it never occurred to him to wonder what had become of his own. He made an inward vow to find out before the end of his visit what were the real feelings of his hostess. Thus thinking he moved his chair, until Bligh once more came within focus. She resented his insinuating glances, for directly she became conscious of them she rose from her seat and rang the bell.

" I expect you would like to see your room," she said. " My mother and Lady Verschoyle will be in from their drive very shortly, and then we will have tea—that is to say, if you ever condescend to drink so mild a beverage. Thompson," she went on, addressing the butler, who appeared in answer to her summons, " show Captain Cameron upstairs, and see that he has everything he requires."

Duncan had not the slightest desire to make a move, and, in fact, would much have preferred staying where he was ; but as his wishes were apparently opposed to those of the lady of the house there was nothing for it but to obey, which he did with a bad grace. He was conscious of not appearing to advantage, and in such circumstances a man seldom feels at his ease.

When he had gone Bligh laughed out loud. She was afraid he might hear, but she could not restrain her mirth.

" How foolish of me to mind meeting him," she said to herself. " If it had only happened years ago what a lot of misery I should have been spared. I should have given up idealising him for one thing. How fat he has grown, and how red and ugly ! And yet I remember I used to think him so good-looking, and so clever. To-day he gives me the impression of being abominably dull. One or other of us must have altered strangely. I wonder which it is. Well ! no matter. I am infinitely obliged to him for restoring me my liberty. Thank goodness ! there is not a man in the whole world now who can cause my heart to beat a stroke faster than its wont. Delightful state of things ! May it last for ever."

Bligh's mood was curiously defiant ; neither did it alter throughout the evening. She treated Captain Cameron with cold, but excruciating politeness, every now and then letting fall some sarcastic little remark, which clearly proved to him that although he was absolutely indifferent to her she had not forgotten or forgiven the offence of which he had been guilty. He knew that beneath her surface-civility she judged him inexorably. During dinner Sir Philip could hear them from his end of the table sparring at each other, like a couple of accomplished fencers.

" I thought you two were old friends," he called out jovially, secretly admiring his wife, and enjoying the Captain's discomfiture.

" So we were," rejoined that gentleman. " At least I was vain enough to think so ; but her ladyship appears to hold a contrary opinion, and to ignore the fact of our friendship."

" Am I the only person who possesses the convenient faculty of ignoring facts ? " she retorted maliciously. " I fancy it was you who taught me so useful an accomplishment in the first instance, Captain Cameron."

Sir Philip laughed.

" Bravo, Bligh ! " he exclaimed. " You had him there. You'd better give up, Cameron," he went on, turning to his guest. " My wife is as good a hand at repartee as anyone I know. You won't get the best of her in a hurry."

" Since when have you developed this charming talent ? " Duncan inquired in a low voice of Bligh. " You used not to be famous for a sharp tongue. Has it grown incisive since your marriage ? Most women's do."

" Is that your experience, Captain Cameron ? If so I congratulate you. You were wise to eschew matrimony, and can derive a salutary lesson from watching the effects of your own handiwork. Women are what men make them. I am no exception to the rule."

He bit his lip to hide his annoyance. No matter what he said she always had an answer ready. How different she was from the little loving Bligh whom he had kissed and re-kissed under the weeping willow in Captain Burton's garden ten years previously. Yet man-like, he infinitely preferred the woman who scoffed at him to the woman who blindly worshipped him. Lady Verschoyle at eight-and-twenty, with two powdered footmen standing behind her chair, dressed in an exquisite Parisian tea-gown, sitting at the bottom of a table laden with costly silver and choice hothouse flowers, appeared to him a very much more important and lovable person than the eighteen-year old Bligh Burton, with nothing to recommend her but a trusting heart and a sweet, childish nature. He conceived for the former a distinct respect and admiration, whilst to the latter for many years past he had seldom given more than a passing thought. Where is the man capable of disinterested affection ?

Society, as composed in fashionable circles, ruins true love. Men simply hunger after the loaves and fishes. What a woman is hardly counts. What she has got is the question. Does she belong to a smart set ? Has she a fine house to ask us to ? Does she give good entertainments, shall I meet the right sort, and will it reflect credit upon me to be seen dancing attendance in her train ? If so I can afford to lose my heart : otherwise it is not worth while.

These are the considerations paramount and the language of the day. Truly the latter evinces much refined and beautiful sentiment, and does honour to the nineteenth century. Chivalry and manhood are magnificently represented.

Captain Cameron, of the Guards, thought Lady Verschoyle of Beechlands worth cultivating. He declined, therefore, to participate in the pleasures of the billiard-room, and throughout the evening exerted himself to be agreeable. He accompanied the ladies to their sitting-room, and sang sentimental songs at

Bligh, in which the words last and past, heart and dart, pain again, ever sever, played a conspicuous part. She listened to them composedly, and with a little mocking smile curling the corners of her mouth. Did he think she was eighteen once more, to be impressed by such transparent artifices ?

When the music came to an end she rose to retire to rest, and gave him her hand with the utmost unconcern.

" Cruel ! " he whispered, as he pressed it warmly. " Are you made of stone ? "

She snatched it away. " Yes," she said, looking him full in the face ; " to you."

His eyes drooped before the withering contempt expressed by her glance.

CHAPTER XXIV

THE BIGGEST COUNTRY IN ENGLAND.

THE Honourable Duncan Cameron possessed one trait in common with a good many of his sex. He was pre-eminently selfish, and in every relation of life invariably consulted his own wishes before those of any other person. Egotism is by no means rare, either among men or women ; but he had a larger share than most people, and as a rule did not take much trouble to hide the fact. The eldest son of a peer, no matter how poor he may be, is alway run after by London mammas, and our friend Duncan had been a good bit spoilt since the days when he declined to study mathematics under Captain Burton. But whatever were his faults physical cowardice could not be numbered among them. He had earned the reputation of being one of the hardest and most brilliant riders to hounds in the United Kingdom, and although the hunting field had not been very frequently graced by his presence latterly the prestige attached to his name still clung to it. Generally he sold his horses at the end of every season, and they fetched fabulous prices ; but a shocking bad Derby, followed by a disastrous Ascot, had deprived him of his available stock of ready money, and reduced the unfortunate plunger to the deplorable necessity of taking a trip abroad in order to avoid the importunity of clamorous creditors.

It was for the above reason that, when he was enabled to return to his native land, his stables stood empty, and did not contain a single decent hunter. At this juncture he recalled Sir Philip's invitation, which had arrived when he was inspecting the fortifications at Metz, and determined to run down to Midlandshire for a few days. Knowing his host to be a rich man,

with a large stud of valuable horses, he calculated on his mounting him, and it proved a considerable disappointment when he
learnt that he must put up with a couple of screws, hired out
regularly at two guineas a day. It was the more annoying because by nature he was extremely jealous, and heartily despised
those of his comrades who did not cut out the work. No matter
how well or how straight they rode he thought nothing whatever
of their performances unless they went absolutely first. To do
him justice, he always showed the way himself whenever he got
the chance. His pleasure, therefore, was very naturally damped
when Sir Philip informed him with well-feigned regret that instead of making his appearance on a brilliant performer he must
be content to fall back upon a hireling. Of course he declared
it did not signify in the least, though inwardly he abused his
friend for not making other provisions, which he felt persuaded
he could quite well have done had he chosen.

Duncan's ruling passion was hunting, and he always enjoyed
being on horseback. Consequently, he came down to breakfast
on the following morning with a smiling face, only a shade less
red than his coat, which had seen much service, and was white
at the seams, purple at the tails. He further wore a bird's-eye
waistcoat, a white stock wound round his neck, which served
as collar and tie in one, and a pair of old leathers. Altogether
his attire was sporting, if not exactly in the height of fashion ;
but a man with his reputation could afford to dispense with ac-
cessories which, had he not already won his spurs in the hunting field, would no doubt have been deemed indispensable. A
well-known pioneer across country may be forgiven if he is not
just as smartly turned out as some novice anxious to make a
good impression by the faultlessness of his equipment. Duncan's
"get up" was workmanlike, but certainly not becoming, as Bligh
remarked to herself during breakfast. Perhaps it was that she
looked at him with different eyes from those of ten years ago.
Anyhow, she no longer thought him either handsome or fascinating, but quite the reverse.

"It ought to be a hunting morning," observed Sir Philip to
his guest. "The glass has gone up tremendously since last
night, and there is a sharp, crisp feeling in the air, which
promises well after yesterday's fog."

"An old sportsman once told me that hounds always run
hard before a frost," rejoined Captain Cameron, "and my experience certainly goes to prove the theory. I was staying at
Melton two years ago, and just before the cold weather set in
we had a brilliant week. It was the finest eight days' sport I
ever witnessed, and directly afterwards it froze like the devil,
and for two whole months hunting was stopped altogether."

" Well!   I hope we may show you some fun to-day," said Sir Philip, "and that your nag will carry you satisfactorily.   I only wish I could have given you a mount, but I have had a regular run of bad luck lately, and nearly half my gees are on the sick list.   The open weather has been responsible for several cripples, added to which a kind of influenza epidemic has broken out among the horses this year, which has committed great havoc. Three of my best hunters are down with it at the present moment, and there is hardly a stable in the county that has escaped."

" Don't mind about me, my dear fellow," responded Duncan, with every appearance of outward cordiality. " No doubt I shall get along all right.   By-the-bye, what about my quad ?   Is he coming here or going to the meet ? "

" I gave orders for him to be led out to Bloxington with my first horse, and, if agreeable to you, we will drive together in the dogcart.   Bloxington is almost the farthest meet we have, and is a deuce of a way off."

" How far do you call it, Verschoyle ? "

" The best part of fifteen miles from here, and the road's none to good either."

" I had a day near Bloxington once, when I was staying in the neighbourhood with some friends," observed Duncan. " If I remember rightly, it's a terrific country, is it not ? "

" The biggest in England, bar none.   Every fence is a downright mantrap.   There is hardly a horse in creation who can cross Bloxington Vale without coming to grief.   It was there that poor young Grigson fractured his skull last season, and was killed, and yet no man rode better cattle."

Captain Cameron turned to Bligh with a smile.

" This is encouraging intelligence for me on my hireling. Will you ask your husband to choose some less gruesome subject, else I shan't have an atom of nerve left ? "

" Report says that your nerves are made of iron," she answered. " I don't think Philip can shake them."

" They have remained fairly good up till now, but nerve is a thing one never can feel certain of.   It is here to-day and gone to-morrow.   Let us hope, however, after this alarming account of the terrors of Bloxington Vale, that fate has had the kindness to provide me with a screw that can jump."

" I think Fate would be kinder if she provided you with one that couldn't," rejoined Bligh.

" And then when I came home you would be the first to laugh at me for showing the white feather."

" You mustn't aspire to lead the field to-day, old man," put in Sir Philip. " Curb your ardour for once, and be content to remain with the ruck.   If all goes well, by Monday I shall be able to give you a mount. Until then, take my advice and let discretion be the better part of valour."

With these words the gentlemen rose from the breakfast table, and were soon searching for gloves, crops, and cigar-cases, previous to starting. Their final preparations took so long that they kept the trap waiting at the door for over ten minutes. At last they seated themselves in the dogcart, and were carefully tucked in by two stalwart footmen, who placed a fur rug and a waterproof apron over their knees. Then Sir Philip whipped up his American trotter and drove off at a great pace, by way of atoning for lost time. Neither he nor Captain Cameron were men possessing a wide range of conversation, or an extensive stock of ideas apart from sport; so they confined themselves almost exclusively to this interesting topic. But after the first two or three miles they apparently wore it threadbare, and were reduced to long cigars and silence, broken only by an occasional spasmodic remark. To tell the truth they were both dull dogs, though they did not know it, and each voted the other stupid in his innermost heart. The drive was long and cold, and they were glad when it came to an end, and they reached their destination before hounds had moved off. Sir Philip's groom rode up immediately, leading Captain Cameron's hunter. Duncan cast his eye over him dissatisfiedly. Certainly he was a sorry steed to look at, and appeared quite incapable of bearing fourteen stone to the front. First inspection revealed a weedy thoroughbred, light chestnut in colour, with a long back and tail, lean angular quarters, curly hocks, and a pair of forelegs which stood very much over, and were covered with wind-galls and blemishes. He was an animal of nice quality, but one who had evidently seen life and also his best days. The poor, half-fed, overworked beast shivered as the keen morning air caused his dull coat to stare. And yet, in spite of hard riding and ill usage, he loved the hounds, and pricked his ears as he glanced at them in a way which seemed to say, "Yes, yes. You and I are old friends. We know each other well, only don't be too hard upon me to-day, for I am hungry and tired, and no longer as young as I was once."

"Humph!" exclaimed Captain Cameron, discontentedly, addressing the groom. "He's not much to look at. Do you know anything about him by any chance?"

"No, Capting; nothing," answered the man, touching his hat respectfully; "but they told me at the stables as 'ow he was a wonderful good old 'oss once he warmed up, and he knows pretty nigh every fence in the county."

"Knows them a long sight too well, poor old beggar, I should think," rejoined Duncan, putting his foot in the stirrup and mounting without further delay.

His steed submitted to this operation with the utmost docility, and apparently asked for nothing better than to stand still until the last possible moment. His troubles, however, were about to begin, and a spur prick in the side caused him to hobble stiffly off to where the hounds were congregated. As already stated, Captain Cameron was a well-known man in the hunting field, and although he had only hunted a few times with the Midlandshire hounds he was hailed on the present occasion by a number of acquaintances. Five minutes devoted to " coffee housing " passed very pleasantly, for it is always agreeable to the feelings to be warmly greeted by people, even when one knows next to nothing about them. Then a move was made, and an outlying spinney applied to, in consequence of some intelligence furnished by a farmer to the huntsman. Often such information leads to poor results ; but to-day there was no doubt about its correctness, for before the rearmost horseman had reached the spinney a fox was set on foot. Unfortunately, the pedestrians headed him, and being baulked in his original intention of flight he turned tail and made off for Bloxington covert, which lay on the opposite side of the road. Having successfully gained this point of vantage he changed his tactics, and showed no disposition to quit it.

" Yoick on to him, my beauties ! Yoick on to him ! " sang out Dysack, in his ringing, tenor voice. But although the hounds hunted most meritoriously, now throwing their tongues with confidence until the deep notes boomed like bells upon the air, anon subsiding into plaintive whimpers of defeat, followed by discouraged silence, Reynard baffled all endeavours for very nearly an hour. It proved a weary interval, which rapidly degenerated into mute despondency.

Human and canine foes were alike giving up hope, when all at once a shrill cry caused every pulse to beat. Was it a railway whistle ? No, for another and another following in quick succession proclaimed the welcome fact that pug had at last seen fit to break covert, and had set his mask for the open. Out streamed the hounds in hot pursuit, and quicker almost than it takes to tell they settled ravenously to the line.

And now both men and horses were called upon to do the very best they knew, for by some instinct of perversity this crafty fox headed straight for Bloxington Vale, disdaining the comparatively easy country which lay on his left. Just at first all went well, for he had the civility to run parallel with a road, and everyone took advantage of the macadam, not a few devoutly hoping that there might be no occasion to leave it. But their inward prayers were doomed to receive an unfavourable response, for very shortly the fox took a sharp bend to the right, with the result of interposing a thick bullfinch guarded by a double ditch between himself and his pursuers.   It was in a direct line, and could not well be avoided.

Quick as lightning half a dozen men shot out from the ranks and bored a hole through it.   Duncan was one of them.   Although on an untried animal, not exactly calculated to inspire confidence, he did not hesitate for a moment.   Promptitude and decision are indispensable qualities for the pioneers of a hunt. He was prepared for a refusal, especially as the fence was a big one to start with, but the chestnut surprised him very agreeably. The experienced animal did not attempt to fly the bullfinch as a younger horse might have done, but, stopping short, popped over the first ditch, and then proceeded to push his head through the thorny screen.   It was not an easy operation, but by force of perseverance he managed it, and also to wriggle his body adroitly through the aperture thus formed.   After this there remained no great difficulty about stilkering down the far ditch and scrambling up its side, with no worse memento of the achievement than a few scratches.   The only objection to which the process was open was that it took time ; but as Duncan's neighbours on either hand narrowly escaped a fall he felt that he had decided cause for satisfaction.

"Bravo ! old fellow," he said, bringing his crop down on the chestnut's neck as a mark of approval.   " You did that uncommonly clever. ' Slow and sure ' is your motto apparently.   Come, let's see if you can gallop."   And, standing up in his stirrups, he gave him a shake of the bridle hand, and tried hard to wrest the lead from a long, thin stranger in " mufti," riding a powerful blood horse.

The chestnut was a descendant of the famous Blair Athole, and a cast-off from a racing stable.   He had experienced various vicissitudes, but even at the mature age of seventeen he still retained a fair turn of speed when warmed up and his stiffness worked off.   The frosty air had dried the ground, and the light going suited him.   Moreover, the hounds, though running fast, were not travelling at racing pace.   The fences were too big and too frequent not to stop them a bit.

Certainly Bloxington Vale deserved its reputation of being the stiffest country in England.   Every ditch was a regular yawner, and the hedges were quickset, planted on banks which added to their size, and adorned by binders that meant a turn-over if at all rudely touched.   And yet it was wonderful how well the horses jumped them as long as they were fresh.   True, the couple of dozen now with hounds represented the pick of

some three or four hundred, for only the very boldest riders had
turned off the road once it became clear that Reynard had
chosen the dreaded Vale for his route.

Duncan's old chestnut really did wonders.   He scrambled and
doubled in the most marvellous way, and although once or
twice he pitched on his head, being a well-proportioned animal,
with good shoulders, on each occasion he managed to recover
himself.   But he had not been accustomed to the post of honour
of absolute first, and after a few minutes the effort of maintaining this proud position told severely on his strength.   Duncan
began to feel him flagging, and had he been as wise as he was
courageous would have taken a pull ; but this was precisely
where his horsemanship became open to criticism.   He would
let a horse die under him rather than yield his place, and
often pushed gallantry to the very verge of brutality.   His
detractors declared that he was an unmerciful butcher, and they
would much rather see him ride his own horses than theirs, and
although jealousy may to a certain extent have influenced their
judgments they contained a strong element of truth.   The delight of swinging over a country that wanted a lot of doing rendered him less prudent even than usual, and he disregarded two
fair warnings given him by the chestnut.   To make matters worse,
every fence seemed bigger and stiffer than its predecessor.
The ditches increased, both in depth and size, and to prevent
monotony they were varied by an occasional oxer.   There were
a great many empty saddles to be seen now, and Duncan
recognised Sir Philip's magnificent grey careering about with a
loose rein.

"Hulloa !" he said to himself. "Hireling versus Hunter.
That is a joke ! Fancy a ten pound screw standing up when
four hundred guineas worth bites the dust ! Hurrah, for old
Stick-in-the-Mud !"   And he gave his steed a friendly job with
the heel.   Grief now became more and more plentiful, for this
particular fox appeared endowed with the special faculty of
picking out the very strongest part of the whole of Bloxington
Vale.

"Hold up, old man," called out Duncan, as the gallant but
exhausted chestnut crashed headlong into a thick hedge and
narrowly escaping a somersault, rose from Mother Earth with
two mud-stained knees and a dirty forehead ; "you must jump
a bit cleaner than that if you want to keep on your legs."

The poor old horse's sides were straining against the girths,
his flanks heaved, the dock of his tail jerked in a truly pitiful
fashion.   Anyone might have told that he was about done for ;
but Duncan had no mercy.   His blood was up.   He set his jaw

like a bulldog, and would have charged a house if needs were, utterly regardless of his animal's condition.

To give him his due he had gone right gallantly and well up to this point ; but humanity now demanded that he should retire from the foremost rank. But such an idea never once presented itself. Only last winter two of his best hunters had dropped dead beneath him, owing to over-riding, entailing a severe pecuniary loss, since he calculated that the pair would fetch at least five hundred guineas at his sale. It was a frenzy which he could not help. After dinner he might preach the folly of pushing a beating horse to the bitter end ; but when on one and he held a good place in a good run, he could no more pull up than he could convert a delicate living creature, capable of acute feeling, into a mere galloping and jumping machine.

Besides to-day he was paying three guineas—or, if he wasn't, somebody else was for him—and he meant to have his money's worth—a very common form of reasoning among sportsmen professing to be fond of horseflesh.

So he dug his spurs deeper into the chestnut's sobbing sides, and forced him along at top speed. Thank goodness ! At last a nice, easy little fence loomed ahead, and on the other side the hounds appeared checking for a moment. It looked as if it might be jumped anywhere, and Duncan was therefore surprised to see Dysack, who rode abreast of him, draw rein suddenly.

"What is it ? " he shouted. " Wire ? "

" No, sir," came the reply. " Bloxington Brook."

" Oh ! is that all ? I'll have a shy at it at any rate."

" You'd better not, sir. There's a ford within a hundred yards, and it's a beastly place to jump." So saying Dysack, who knew the country, galloped off for a gate on the right. As he did so the hounds once more took up the scent and flung themselves forward. Duncan saw that if he jumped the brook he should gain a clear lead over the now reduced field. His thirst for glory rendered him impervious to prudential considerations. Here was a chance of fame and distinction. It might cost a fall, but what mattered that ? He had had so many in his time, and always escaped without any serious injury.

So he took hold of the chestnut's head and crammed him straight at the fence. The old horse was done to a turn, and no longer capable of putting on the requisite pace. When he saw the yawning cavern ahead he checked in his stride, and would have refused, but the resolute man on his back rendered this impossible. At the last moment he made a desperate effort, just succeeded in reaching the opposite bank with his forelegs, and fell heavily back into the muddy stream, crushing his rider beneath him. The water parted, gurgled greedily over horse and man, then hid them both from vision.

A few moments later the chestnut struggled wildly to his legs and wandered up the brook, where, joining the other horses, he floundered through the ford and stood stock-still, a lank, miserable, dripping object, scored all over with scratches and spur marks. It seemed an age before Duncan's head, minus its hat, emerged from the turbid stream, and those who saw it were at once impressed by the whiteness of his face and the look of suffering that it wore. He tried to clamber up the bank, but apparently was unable to move except by hopping on one foot.

"Come and help me, some of you fellows, there's good chaps," he called out, in accents of distress. "The brute rolled upon me when I was down, and I'm a bit knocked out of time. Ugh! how cold the water is!" And he shivered dismally.

This appeal met with generous response, as is nearly always the case when an accident of any gravity happens.

Before long Duncan was drawn to shore by two stout pairs of arms, and carefully laid on the grass.

"Where are you hurt?" inquired his rescuers, bending over him.

"I—I—have broken my right leg," he answered faintly.

"Dear, dear! You don't say so. That's a bad business."

"Will someone go—for—a—doctor. I can't walk a—yard, and must have a trap to t—take me—back to Beechlands."

The words came with difficulty, for he was chilled to the bone and suffered considerable pain. He felt very sick and queer, and was thankful to take a pull at the flask promptly presented to him.

"Don't bother about me," he said presently. "Go on with the hounds. I'm better now, and if you see Sir Philip Verschoyle don't say anything to alarm him. It's no good spoiling his day's sport."

Thus adjured the majority rode off in pursuit of the pack, but a couple of good Samaritans remained with the injured man, and did not leave him until his limb had been temporarily put into splints by the nearest doctor, who at once took charge of the patient and superintended his removal in a fly chartered for the purpose. The broken leg was propped up by cushions, and kept straight by means of hunting crops, and when everything was in readiness they started for Beechlands. Duncan was a strong man, but once or twice he nearly fainted during the homeward journey. Apart from the breakage his leg was terribly bruised and contused, and every jolt of the old-fashioned carriage as it rattled over the stony road caused a dull, yet intense, pain. Three or four times on the way his companion administered brandy, and the stimulant alone prevented him from losing consciousness. That drive remained for ever branded on his memory. It was about the first experience he had had of sharp physical suffering, and very unpleasant he found it. When they at last drove up to the front door he was as white as a sheet, and his face no longer retained any of its usual rubicund tints.

Bligh had caught sight of a carriage coming up the drive, and obtained a peep of a red coat within. After her own mishap she was always afraid of some accident happening. Consequently, before the bell was rung she rushed out, crying, "What is the matter? Has anything very dreadful taken place?"

"Nothing," answered Duncan, trying to speak in his ordinary tone. "I've had rather a nasty spill and broken my leg; that's all."

"All!" she exclaimed. "Oh! poor you, I'm so sorry."

"He smiled. Her compassion had a distinctly pleasing effect upon his nervous system.

"I shan't mind," he said, in a significant undertone, "if it is the means of making you kinder to me than you were last night."

"I didn't mean to be unkind," she responded, rather guiltily.

"Didn't you? A different impression was conveyed to my mind." Then, in a louder key: "I am afraid I shall prove an awful bore. An invalid laid up in somebody else's house is always a most infernal nuisance; but you see how I am situated. For a few days at any rate I cannot help claiming your hospitality. I suppose, doctor," he went on, turning to his companion, "I could hardly get to London in my present state?"

"No; certainly not!" answered that gentleman, decidedly. "It would be madness to think of such a thing."

"You perceive that I do not willingly inflict my society upon you, Lady Verschoyle," said Duncan, a trifle mischievously. "If I could have spared you this ordeal rest assured I would have done so."

"What do you take us for, Captain Cameron?" she answered hotly. "You talk as if Sir Philip and I were the most hard-hearted people in the world——"

"I think you are," he whispered.

"Of course you will stay here," she went on, unheeding the interruption. "This unfortunate accident has occurred whilst you were on a visit to my husband, and he would be the first to insist on your being nursed in his house. Besides, with all due respect for your reluctance to place yourself under an obligation, where else can you go ? "

This demand being quite unanswerable, Duncan allowed himself to be carried upstairs and put to bed without any further protest, leaving Bligh to reproach herself for the severity of her conduct on the previous day.

" I think I was a little too hard on him last night," she mused. " It is better to let bygones be bygones, as Philip said. Even if I had married him he would not have suited me. I see that quite clearly now, though I thought differently at the time. Perhaps everything has turned out for the best. One never knows and it was not quite nice of me to vent my spite so openly. Besides, now that I don't care the very least for him I can afford to be more generous. If he had been brought back dead I should certainly have felt a little remorseful for my conduct. Even when people have injured one it is always more comfortable to make friends."

Having arrived at this decision about an hour afterwards she stole into the invalid's room. Here she proposed so many devices which added greatly to his comfort that Duncan, shaken by his fall, and in a softer mood than usual, felt quite touched. He watched her moving gently to and fro with a sense of peace and security. After all many worse things might fall to a man's lot than to be laid up with a broken bone and nursed by a nice woman. He realised this, and, yielding to a sudden impulse, when she passed by the bed he caught hold of her dress and raised it to his lips.

" Bligh ! " he exclaimed, " what a fool I have been, to be sure. Even if you can forgive me I shall never forgive myself."

She drew her gown away from his grasp, and looked down at him with clear, untroubled eyes, which made him feel the uselessness of trying to regain what he had lost.

" Hush ! " she said, quietly. " You do not know what you are saying, and if you want me to continue to nurse you, you must not talk like that. You are ill and in pain. My wish is to lessen your suffering as much as possible, but it is superfluous to introduce any sentiment into so ordinary a matter."

He sighed.

" I suppose you think me an awful beast, Lady Verschoyle— no, hang it all ! I must call you Bligh."

" If you do I shan't answer. As for your being a beast I admit to having thought you one at first ; but now that I have seen more of the world I think you acted in accordance with the customary constancy and honour of your admirable sex."

"How bitter you are, and how unforgiving! Do you believe all men to be bad then?"

"I really can't say. 'All' is a comprehensive word. I hope—I trust—that there are a few good ones about."

"Such a declaration implies that you have never met them."

She shrugged her shoulders. The retort was irresistible.

"I have met you, Captain Cameron. Surely my experience is sufficient."

"No," he said, with a flush of vexation. "That is precisely where women go wrong, and take such a narrow, illiberal view of men. You judge a whole class from a single unfortunate experience. If a woman hasn't a good husband, lover, or father she hates all men indiscriminately. You are too sweeping in your condemnations."

"Pardon me, but do you say this because you labour under an uneasy conviction that I do not worship yourself in particular, Captain Cameron?"

"I say it because I would give worlds to regain your esteem. Will nothing induce you to forego the enmity which you feel for me?"

"You make a mistake. If my feelings are not those of ardent admiration they fall very short of enmity. But why pursue this conversation? In the present state of affairs it can do no good. I shall be much better employed going downstairs and showing cook how to make you some strong beef tea after true invalid fashion." This proof of her housewifery capacity touched Duncan to the quick. He looked after her retreating form, and once more murmured: "What a fool I have been." He was a bit down on his luck, and for the time being fully persuaded himself into the belief that he meant what he said.

CHAPTER XXV

AN UNMERITED INSULT.

WHEN a man is laid up in bed, and is tended by a woman with any pretensions to amiability or good looks, one result is inevitable. He falls in love with her, or else fancies that he does; which comes pretty much to the same thing.

After Bligh had frankly told Duncan that he must not talk sentiment, under penalty of losing her services, she thought no more about the matter, and took it for granted he would have the common-sense to adhere to her restrictions. In his present condition she was undoubtedly useful to him ; and such being the case, she held the whip hand, and he was likely to transgress. She had seen the inherent selfishness of his character and summed it up pretty correctly, since, perhaps no eyes see quite so clearly as those of disillusioned love.

For a time her anticipations were verified and all went well. Sir Philip hunted regularly five or six days a week, coming home tired, and often cross, for even in the hunting field things did not always go exactly to his mind, and sometimes he made wrong turns, or the horses misbehaved and failed to carry him to his satisfaction. He saw very little of the ladies, preferring to shut himself up with such friends as Dashwood and Rickerby, in whose society he could indulge in his accustomed pleasures, free from feminine restraint.

To tell the truth, he was glad to get away from Bligh. Her watchful eye during dinner irritated him almost to a maddening point ; and to avoid incurring her grave, disapproving glance, which filled him with a sense of conscious guilt, and made him feel ill at ease, he adopted new tactics and began to have recourse to cunning. When she was in the room he would often pretend to drink nothing, just so as to throw her off her guard. Unfortunately, he always made up for his abstention later on.

Between husband and wife a kind of strange armed neutrality prevailed. Although no serious breach of the peace had hitherto taken place, each was conscious that a mere trifle might suffice to bring about a quarrel ; and Captain Cameron's presence in the house did not tend to lessen the friction.

A woman who has once truly loved a man generally retains a soft corner in her heart for him somewhere, in spite of her former misdemeanours. Bligh proved no exception to the rule. When Duncan Cameron was forced to lie day after day on a bed of pain, and his face brightened at her approach, and he showed in a variety of ways how agreeably her presence relieved the wearisome monotony of continuous inaction, the last remnants of her wrath faded away. She felt so certain of herself that she did not hesitate to spend more of her time in his society than would have been the case had the smallest spark of sentiment still lingered in her heart. The first interview over, she realised that he no longer caused any emotion, and she rejoiced to find that he was nothing to her now but a strong young man struck down by suffering, who aroused her womanly compassion, but appealed to no warmer sentiment.

Sure of her own integrity, she nursed him with such kindness and attention that there was perhaps some excuse for his imagining the old love had taken a fresh lease of life, and was once more beginning to put forth shoots capable of bearing fruit. It never occurred to him that it was a very poor return for Sir Philip's hospitality to try and deliberately win the affections of his wife; or, if it did happen to flit across his mind, he dismissed the thought summarily as an unpleasant one, and therefore not to be dwelt upon. Neither did it strike him that if he gained the object which he had in view Bligh's happiness must certainly suffer, and her moral peace in all probability be destroyed.

He was ill in bed, and unable to fall back upon a better diversion than trying to flirt; but after a while he was surprised to find that the amusement was growing serious, and no longer to be regarded as a pastime. He gradually made the discovery that he looked forward with intense eagerness to his hostess's visits, and invented innumerable excuses to prolong them. When he went to sleep he heard the sound of her soothing voice in his ears, and her quiet, graceful movements were impressed upon his memory. No one could shift his pillows, smooth the sheets or raise him in bed like Bligh. Her smile was sweeter, her touch softer, her experience of sick-rooms greater than anybody else's. And so he became exacting, and craved for her presence.

The women whom he had been in the habit of meeting in London society, at country houses, balls, and races, had not tended to raise his opinion of the fair sex. He thought of the majority of his female friends as painted, dressed-up creatures, artificial to their fingers' ends, bent solely on flirtation, admiration and personal advancement—personal advancement meaning to achieve the acquaintance of Royalty, get invited to Marlborough House, secure an inclosure ticket at Ascot, and so on. He recalled his *liaisons*, and the disgust which they had invariably ended by inspiring.

And now he seemed transplanted to a different atmosphere, where the air was clearer and purer; and he realised at length the influence which a good woman exercises over even an indifferent man. Every day he found something fresh to admire in Bligh, until at last he cursed his folly for having wilfully thrown away a pearl of such price.

"I should have been a very different man if I had married her," he mused, when reviewing his past life, and making dismal mental additions of his debts. "She would have kept me from playing the fool, and been fond of me into the bargain. Now I suppose my end will be some society harpy, who will take me for my title and I her for her money. Well! it serves me right. If I hadn't listened to the governor's advice, I shouldn't be the miserable, dissatisfied fellow I am."

After the lapse of ten years it was easy enough for Duncan

to reason in this way, and throw the blame of everything that had happened on his father. To make a long story short, he fell in love with Bligh over again, and this time his passion, if selfish, contained many more genuine elements than the boyish infatuation of his youth, which, in spite of present regrets, had left no very permanent impression.

Had Bligh Verschoyle led the life of a large proportion of fashionable women, doubtless she would not have remained long in ignorance of her quondam lover's sentiments ; but her innocence shielded her. She inspired him with a certain awe which prevented him from speaking out all that was in his thoughts ; and for herself she believed that Duncan quite understood the position, and if her manner showed more friendliness than on his arrival, it was not the result of any greater affection on her part, but purely on account of his accident.

So several weeks went by, and although her husband neglected and left her almost entirely to her own desires she did not complain, and was too busy to be rendered unhappy by the circumstance. As a matter of fact, she felt freer and more at ease when he asserted himself. People, especially those who are bound together, act and react on each other in many curious ways. Philip had a disturbing effect upon her. She was conscious of appearing at her worst in his presence. She could not shine before him. He reduced her to a quite insignificant, rather frightened woman, who constantly dreaded an outbreak, and was too nervous to be natural. If people went away and called her "a stupid little thing," she was thoroughly aware that she often deserved the appellation. He robbed her of her individuality, and, like a snail, she retreated into her shell, and remained there, only peeping out on rare occasions, when she happened to meet with a congenial companion. But her intellect starved, and, like a drooping plant, thirsted for sustenance ; putting on timid feelers in search of it, and then retiring when repulsed.

Matters stood thus, when about the middle of February, a sharp frost set in which completely stopped hunting. Sir Philip grumbled and growled, abused the English climate from morning till night, and displayed a huge self-compassion, but there was nothing for it but to stay at home. Now an idle man possessing few resources and accustomed to a great deal of active outdoor exercise is a pitiable object when deprived of his ordinary amusements. He has nothing to fall back on but pipes and French novels, and with all their charms these cannot quite make out the day. Therefore he goes about the house poking his nose into all sorts of things which don't concern him. The next step is natural. Having no fixed occupation, he takes to finding fault. It is an outlet for his ill-humour, and acts as a safety valve.

Sir Philip had not been at home three days before he came to the conclusion that his wife spent an unaccountable portion of her time in Captain Cameron's room, and although he thought nothing of leaving her from half-past nine until five or or six every day in the week but Sunday during the hunting season, he felt desperately aggrieved at her remaining ten minutes with his guest. He took to wondering what they said to each other when they were alone, and why Bligh deemed it necessary to inquire so often after the invalid. Little as he cared for her in reality, his jealousy caught fire. He recalled the confession she had made to him before the visitor's arrival, and blamed himself for having-treated it so lightly. A crowd of ungenerous suspicions surged up into his brain, and daily grew stronger. Had he but communicated them to Bligh in a straightforward fashion, he would very soon have ascertained how little cause he had for anxiety; but there is a certain order of mind which prefers circuitous and underhand methods to open dealing, and his was one of them.

Then there came a change in the weather, the frost gave, and hunting was resumed. Unfortunately, the very first day that Sir Philip went out, he returned in an extremely bad humor. Everything had gone wrong, as now and again proves the case. He had arrived late at the meet, his horse had been odiously fresh, refused the second fence, and subsequently put him down, owing to which disaster he had lost the run of the season, and never again got on terms with the hounds. The greater part of the day was spent in pounding along the roads in pursuit. Giving up the chase as a bad job, he at length turned his horse's head towards home, when the miserable brute, without any apparent cause, suddenly fell lame. Disgusted with his slow rate of progression, the rider left the poor cripple at a public-house, where, after refreshing his inner man, he hired a gig to convey him back to Beechlands. Such a chapter of accidents will appeal to the sympathy of every sportsman.

Bligh and Lady Verschoyle were sitting in the great hall, Mrs. Burton having gone upstairs a few minutes previously. They heard the front door slam, and then Sir Philip came in, looking very cold and cross, and with a muddy coat. He flung himself down in an armchair before the fire, and stretched his legs to the warmth.

"You are back later than usual," said Bligh, stirring the huge wooden logs into a bright flame. "We were beginning to get quite anxious about you, and you have had a fall I see. I hope you are not hurt."

"No, only a bit shaken. I shall feel all right when I have changed and had my dinner."

"What were you riding?"

"Coldstream. He's a nasty, shifty brute, and I shall get rid of him as soon as I can find a purchaser."

"I thought you liked him, Philip."

"I used to, but he has got confoundedly cunning in his old age, and he has taken to running into the ditches in a most unpleasant fashion. Sometimes I wonder if his eyes are all right, for he jumps a big place so much better than a smaller one."

"He can't be a very safe animal," she observed, "and I should certainly part with him if I were you. Have you had a good day?"

"The hounds have, but personally I've had an infernally bad one." Whereupon he proceeded to narrate in detail the series of misfortunes which had befallen him, waxing eloquent as he recounted Coldstream's various misdeeds. Bligh knew by the thickness of his utterance that he had warmed himself against the cold on the homeward way. She was getting very much on the alert, and experience was fast teaching her to recognise the slightest symptoms of inebriety.

Sir Philip had not finished his recital, when one of the footmen appeared, and going up to Bligh, said, " Captain Cameron's compliments, my lady, and would you be so kind as to step up to his room for a few minutes, if not inconvenient and you can spare the time."

Sir Philip pricked his ears. Dissatisfied with the day's sport, and in that condition which can best be described as " a little fuddled," he was just in the mood to seek a quarrel.

"Damn his impertinence ! " he exclaimed, angrily, as soon as the man had withdrawn. " Does the confounded fellow think that you are at his beck and call, to be ordered about just as if you were his wife and not mine ? I call it infernal cheek, and if I were you, Bligh, I'd give him to understand as much."

"Sick people are apt to be a little exacting in their demands," she answered, soothingly. "It's best to take no notice, and when a person has been laid up in bed as many weeks as Captain Cameron has one must make allowances."

"Oh ! yes, of course. I quite understand that it is easy enough for you to make allowances. Do you suppose I haven't noticed what's going on ?"

"I don't know what you mean, Philip. Nothing is going on that I am aware of."

"It's all very fine for you to deny it, but I know differently. I'm not exactly a jackass, though you pay me the compliment of thinking me one ; and I've remarked how uncommonly fond you are of sneaking upstairs on all occasions to sit with your old lover. No doubt you find it highly agreeable having him in the house, and carrying on together under my very nose, but let me tell you this: I'm not going to stand it any longer."

He had risen from his seat, and his face was flushed with anger.

Bligh looked at him sternly, and with a certain irrepressible loathing.

"Are you drunk or dreaming?"

"Neither," he shouted in reply, "but I happen to have a pair of eyes in my head, which no doubt, is inconvenient. Deny, if you can, that you spend all your time in that man's room, under pretence of nursing him. It's not decent. The very servants will talk of your goings on."

She started to her feet, and there was a dangerous light in her eyes which he did not care to confront.

"Philip," she said, in a voice deep with concentrated passion, "how dare you use such language to me. The only possible excuse is that you are not sober."

"That's right. Try to make me out a drunkard. It's so nice and so wifely."

"Drunk or sober, your words are shameful; for you know, as surely as there is a God above, that what you say is false, and that Captain Cameron is no more to me than any other guest who might have met with an accident in your house. When I first heard of his coming here, I own that I was afraid, and therefore I went to you, and begged you to make some excuse for putting his visit off. Although I plainly stated the circumstances, and attempted no concealment, you refused to accede to my wish, and upon this I declined to assume any responsibility in the matter——"

"Ha, ha!" he interrupted. "You admit to having felt afraid."

"At that time—yes. I was not certain what my feelings would be, and for this reason I ask you to spare me what I fancied might prove an ordeal. But from the very instant I set eyes on Captain Cameron, and saw, as a grown-up woman, him as a grown-up man, my fears vanished. The first glance sufficed to show me that they were without foundation, and I was thankful, oh! so thankful. Do you think," she went on proudly, "that if I had not been absolutely sure of myself I should have been idiotic enough to court temptation? Listen to reason, Philip, and believe me once for all when I tell you that you have no cause to be jealous of Duncan Cameron. He and I are as far apart as if we had never met, and in order to prove the truth of what I say, I intend going straight to him this very moment, and begging him, as a personal favour, to leave the house to-morro morning. There! will that satisfy you?" And she marched out of the room, with her head held high, not waiting for an answer. It took a good deal to move her out of her ordinary calm, but for once she was thoroughly roused, and acted from the impulse of the moment.

CHAPTER XXVI.

"DON'T BE TOO HARD UPON ME."

THE Dowager Lady Verschoyle. who had listened to the above conversation with infinite distress, looked up from her work.

"Oh! Philip," she said, "you should not have spoken like that. It was an insult to Bligh to bring such an accusation against her, and no wonder she resents your conduct. It is unpardonable."

"How was I to know there was nothing in their flirtation?" he said, sullenly, feeling he had gone too far.

"You ought to have known. Nobody ought to have known better than yourself the purity of your wife's character. How can anyone doubt it? To the best of my belief, she has not an evil thought in her."

"It's all very fine to talk, but Cameron was her lover some years ago, and she has always had a sneaking liking for him ever since. She confessed as much to me herself."

"That is quite possible, but to assume that he is her lover now is downright wicked. I heard the whole story of Bligh's engagement from Mrs. Fortescue. If there had been any occasion to warn you, I should have done so; for from the day of Captain Cameron's arrival I have watched Bligh narrowly. I fancied there might be some danger in throwing them together. But he had not been here four-and-twenty hours before I became ashamed of my fears. Bligh showed me they were utterly without foundation, and if she has devoted herself to the patient it was only in the capacity of nurse. She is so kind and charitable that she cannot bear to see suffering without seeking to relieve it, and you—her husband—to attack her as you did was simply outrageous."

Lady Verschoyle did not often speak out so plainly, but the cause of justice overcame her customary timidity. In any unpleasantness Sir Philip had got into the way of always counting upon his mother to side with him. That she did not do so on the present occasion provoked him not a little, and added to the uneasy conviction of having made a mistake which he already entertained.

"It seems that whatever I say or do, I am always in the wrong," he said sulkily.

"You are in this instance, Philip. I only wish to goodness that I could contradict you. Unfortunately, I can't."

"Bligh has perfectly infatuated you, mother. You used always to take my part at one time, now you never do."

"My poor boy. Whose fault is that? I cannot be blind to the very cavalier fashion in which you treat your wife."

"Has she been telling tales? By God! I would throttle her if I thought she had."

"Bligh is the last person in the world to cause mischief between mother and son, but I should have no eyes if I did not see that you fail to make her happy, and are often in a condition which can only lower her wifely respect."

"Oh! hang it all, don't begin to preach. Life is short, and one may as well make the most of it."

"I quite agree with you, but is it making the most of it to besot one's senses and estrange the affections of all those nearest and dearest to you? I do not often allude to the subject—it is much too painful. Nevertheless that is what you are doing. How can you expect a woman like Bligh to be fond of a man who insults her openly whenever his brain does not happen to be in a clear condition? This is not the first time, Philip, that you have been rude to your wife in public."

He made a gesture of impatience.

"Bligh! Bligh! Why should she be everything, and I nothing? I believe you care more for her little finger nowadays than you do for my whole body put together."

"I love her very much," said Lady Verschoyle, gravely. "I don't think anyone who knew her intimately could help doing so. She is thoroughly sterling and genuine ; and I neither can nor will sit by and see you treat her with injustice."

"Oh! all right," he answered, rudely. "Say it's me. When two or three cackling women get together, and enter into a conspiracy in a man's house, the poor unfortunate devil hasn't a chance."

"You are angry, Philip, and therefore talk foolishly. No one has entered into a conspiracy against you, least of all I—your mother, who, however you may behave, cannot cease from loving you better than anything on this earth. At the same time, I preceive your faults, and as a by-stander, conceive it to be my duty to tell you that in speaking to Bligh as you did this afternoon, you are not only making a grievous error, but also doing yourself an immense amount of harm."

"I really fail to see it. I am master. and can act as I choose."

"That is a fatal tone to adopt in dealing with a woman, especially one possessing Bligh's high spirit. There is only one course open to you."

"And pray what might that be !" he inquired, lending a grudging attention to his mother's words.

"Seek Bligh out immediately, and beg her pardon. Tell her you were annoyed by the events of the day, tired and out of sorts, and feel thoroughly sorry for your conduct."

He laughed shortly.

"I'm blowed if I will. I'm not going to eat humble pie to any woman, let alone my wife. No, no, mother, you're a simple creature without any experience of the world, but you may take my word for it, that once a man begins playing at that game, he can't call his soul his own. You know the old proverb, 'A woman, a dog, and a walnut tree, the more you beat them the better they be.' It won't hurt Bligh to have her pride taken down a peg or two, for she has begun rather to give herself airs of late." And so saying, he swung out of the hall, and marched straight upstairs to his dressing-room.

Lady Verschoyle dropped her knitting, and clasped her hands together in despair. She had hoped to have made a more sensible impression upon him than this. She had known that he was weak, foolish, obstinate ; but she had never thought until now that he was bad. Yet she could not reconcile his treatment of Bligh to her conscience. She felt it to be a terrible thing for a mother to side against her only son ; nevertheless her sympathies were all with her daughter-in-law. The attack was not only a foul one, but it had been made in a brutal manner, and before a third person. She recalled her own happy married life, and in her heart she pitied the wife who for months past had borne so many affronts with patience and dignity.

"What will be the end of it, if he goes on as he is doing," she muttered. "Ah ! good God, what will be the end of it."

Meantime, without giving herself time to cool, Bligh proceeded to the invalid's chamber, and put her threat into execution. She paused on the threshold of Captain Cameron's door, and tapped briskly.

"Is it my good genius ? " he called out from within. "If so, pray enter."

She advanced into the centre of the room, where he was reclining on a sofa, with a couple of crutches beside him.

"Good evening," he said. "It was kind of you to answer my summons so soon ; but I wanted to see you."

"The wish was mutual, Captain Cameron. I have come to ask a favour."

Some hitherto unfamiliar reflection in the tone of her voice made him look up in surprise.

"A favour! I am only too delighted to hear that it lies in my power to accede to any wish of yours. May I ask what it is?"

"I am afraid you will think it very strange—very inhospitable, and the worst is I can't explain my reasons; but—but," and she flushed crimson, "for some days past you have been talking of leaving us. Do you think you could manage to go to-morrow?" She put the final question abruptly, and turned her head away from the light. He could see a red glow, however, suffuse her throat and ears; and although he was astonished at the suddenness of the demand, he could make a pretty fair guess at the causes which had prompted it.

"This is a most strange coincidence," he said. "I took the liberty of sending for you, because I wished to say good-bye without disturbing your rest to-morrow morning. I must be off at an early hour, and Robson is coming up after dinner to pack my things. Read this." And he placed a telegram in Bligh's hands. "I received it about ten minutes ago, and intended taking your advice. What you have just said, however, decides me to choose duty before pleasure, and leave at once."

Bligh read the following message :—" Come immediately. Father seriously ill. Doctor fears worst."

"My mother has sent it," said Duncan. "I must go by the first train in the morning."

"But are you fit to undertake the journey?" she inquired, with a sudden sense of relief, which politeness urged her to conceal.

"There is no help for it, besides, I have been here long enough. You will be glad to get rid of me."

She could not contradict him truthfully, so made no reply.

"I know it," he resumed, after a brief pause, "and ought to have gone before, only I could not tear myself away. Poor old governor! I am sorry he is ill, but if he had died this day ten years ago, I should be very much better off than I am."

"For shame!" she cried, indignantly. "What a horrible thing to say!"

"It is true though, nevertheless. I don't suppose you care two straws, but, personally, I never can forgive him for having been the means of separating me from you."

"Your regrets come too late," she answered, coldly, "and therefore it can do no good to allude to them."

"No one knows that better than myself, but since I have been here, and had leisure for reflection, I realise more vividly than I ever did before all I have lost."

"You have gained plenty of assurance, Captain Cameron, to make up for your losses."

He bit his lip with vexation, and then, with a sudden access of passion, said—

"You are always laughing at me, and trying to put me off, but, before I go, I will have my say." His voice changed, and he added, "Oh! Bligh, what harm can there be in my telling you that there is no one in the whole world to compare with you. The thought of leaving cuts me like a knife, for I have grown so accustomed to your presence that I feel as if I could not exist without it. I don't ask much. I only ask you to say a few kind words to me at parting, and promise we shall meet again before long. Am I too bold in thinking that you have seen and guessed my love?" And, stretching out his arms, he sought to draw her to him.

She retreated, her face white with anger. Was this the reward for her kindness—this, coupled with her husband's cruel words? Oh! Life was very hard and difficult, when actions of the commonest charity were liable to be misjudged, and placed a defenceless woman at the mercy of bad men's passions.

"Captain Cameron," she said, in tones of ringing scorn, "I have not deserved this at your hands. My conscience does not accuse me of having encouraged you in any way. Why do you seek to lower my self-respect, as well as your own?"

"You loved me once, Bligh," he faltered in return.

"Yes, I loved you once, but it does not follow that I should love you now. When I was a girl my adoration was so insane that my happiness lay at your mercy. You might have been true to me had you chosen, but you did not choose, and it is cowardly and mean to blame your father now for an act which he could not have opposed had you remained firm. The fault lay in yourself. You found playing at love an agreeable pastime, and possessed the advantage of a convenient memory which soon enabled you to forget. When you began to tire of me, then your Highness remembered that I was an uncommonly bad match for a gentleman in your position——"

"By Jove!" he interrupted, hotly, "you are wrong there. I may have been a brute, but I wasn't such a big brute as all that."

"I beg to differ. At any rate, I could only judge you by your acts, and they were noble. It is not exactly nice, or a pleasant experience, for a girl to be thrown over when she has committed no fault, and the poor wretch happens to have lost her heart, but you jilted me carelessly, cruelly. The best years

of my life were ruined—the years," and her voice became tremulous, in spite of every effort to steady it, "when I ought to have
been happy, and which you rendered dark and dreary. The
suffering I then went through has left its mark upon me. I
have never felt the same since, and only really recovered when
you came here. Then, thank Heaven! the scales fell from my
eyes, and I was cured. I saw that the Duncan of my thoughts
was an ideal personage, totally different from the actual one."

"Changed outwardly, but not inwardly," he interposed. "He
loved you throughout, and will love you always."

Her lip curled.

"Have the goodness to listen. What happened next? After
an immense time, during which I might have starved for all you
knew or cared, fate once more made our paths cross, and you
found me elevated to a fine position, very unlike the one in
which you had left me. It suddenly occurred to you that I was
no longer a nobody, but a somebody. Consequently I rose in
your estimation, not on account of what I was, but of what I
had got. You thought Lady Verschoyle worth knowing, although poor little Bligh Burton was not; and now, because you
happen to have no better occupation, you fancy yourself in love.
Love! indeed." And the corners of her mouth were drawn
down with supreme contempt. "You, and men like you, are
not capable of a real passion. You do not even know its
meaning, else your actions never could be so full of profanation."

"Upon my word, Bligh, you misjudge me."

"No, I don't. I tell you to your face that I despise the
counterfeit passion which you degrade by the name of love, and
for you to dare to talk of it in my presence—a married woman
living under the protection of her husband's roof, whilst you are
eating the bread of a man whom you pretend to shake by the
hand and call your friend, shows that you are devoid of the
commonest instincts of a gentleman."

"People are not always so highly moral nowadays," he murmured, writhing under the sting of her sarcasm. The remark
only served to incense her still more.

"What do you take me for, pray, that you have the impertinence to make such an observation? Are you yourself so bad
that you jump to the conclusion all women are equally wicked?
Don't you believe in such things as honour, and chastity, and
purity? Morals forsooth! It seems to me that your standard
of morality must be strangely low, when you can reconcile it to
your conscience to come to a friend's house, and deliberately
make love to a friend's wife. Oh! for shame, for shame." Her
whole form was dignified by a superb indignation. Never had

he loved her so well, or felt his own inferiority so keenly. He gave up the contest. Her words were too full of stinging truth not to take effect on a nature self-indulgent rather than corrupt.

" Don't be too hard upon me," he faltered, piteously.

" Hard upon you! Have I said anything that you can deny? How could you imagine for one moment that any honest woman would feel flattered by such attentions as yours?" And she brought her flashing eyes to bear upon him.

" I—I don't attempt to defend myself," he said, unsteadily.

" No, because you can't. Your conduct has been mean and despicable throughout. As for me, you have done me an infinity of harm."

" For any sake, don't say that, Bligh. I'm miserable enough as it is, and I'm sure I did not intend to."

" May I ask what you did intend then? "

" I don't quite know. I was mad."

" I suppose even you could hardly flatter yourself that it would be a desirable thing for me to reciprocate your so-called affection? "

" I tell you I didn't think."

" I should imagine you did not often have recourse to so troublesome a process. It might seriously affect your brain; but it appears to me that your ethical perceptions are very gravely impaired. Do all young men about town suffer in the same way? "

" How merciless you good women are!" he exclaimed, goaded into retort by her cutting words. "You live in such a rarified atmosphere that you appear to have no sympathy with the faults and frailties of mankind at large. And the worst of it is, you are always—or nearly always—so horribly in the right. But am I as entirely to blame as you make out? Is there not just a little something to be said on my side? We have seen a great deal of each other lately, Bligh, and although I now perceive my error, was it altogether so unnatural my imagining that you took some pleasure in my society? Ask yourself the question honestly, and then perhaps you may admit that the mistake I made had some justification."

" Justification, no. Cause, perhaps yes," she answered, promptly. " It is possible that I thought more of myself than of you."

" And so, unwillingly, you placed me in the way of temptation, and it did not occur to you that I might succumb."

She thought for a moment, then she said—

" Matters never struck me in that light until two or three days ago, when you said something foolish which made me feel uncomfortable. I gave up coming to your room so often, but I suppose it was too late.   Still, you might have had the decency to hold your tongue."

"Well!" he said, desperately, "I'm going now, and shan't be able to do you any more mischief, for I don't suppose we shall see each other again for ages.   There is one request, however, which I should like to make before saying good-bye."

"Tell me what it is," she responded, a trifle uneasily.

"I want you to forgive me, and recall the cruel things which you have said."

"Most of them were true."

"I know, but I cannot bear them from your lips.   Bligh, Bligh, let us part friends."

She had been very angry with him, but the high tide of her wrath was stemmed.   She knew that she might not have treated his offence with quite such fierce contempt had it not been for the wound inflicted by her husband on her pride.   For a few seconds she made no sign, then she put out her hand and said quietly—

"Very well.   I forgive.   Let it be as you will.   I am not so perfect myself that I should presume to judge others."

He raised her little hand to his lips and kissed it with a restraint and a reverence new to his nature.

"God bless you, Bligh.   I am not a good man.   I never was, and never could be worthy of you, but you have taught me a lesson, and if the day should ever come when you stand in need of a friend—a friend, mind you, not a lover, count upon me."

"Thank you, Duncan," she said, "I will.   Some of these days you must marry a nice, honest girl and be happy.   When that event takes place, write me a line, and I will come to your wedding."

He shook his head and sighed.   Frightened by the sight of a suspicious moisture in his eyes, she stole into the passage, leaving him to his meditations.

That night Sir Philip came to bed early, and in an unusually sober state.   He looked at his wife rather sheepishly, and fidgeted about the room, as if he had something on his mind. She took no notice of several attempts to engage her attention, seeing which, after a while, he approached the bedside, and in a shame-faced kind of way said, hurriedly—

"I say, Bligh, don't sulk, there's a good girl."

"I'm not sulking," she answered, composedly.

"Oh! that's all right.   I thought you were.   By-the-way, I'm sorry for what I said this evening.   I had had an unlucky day, and was a good bit put out, but, of course, I did not mean it."

"I am glad to hear that, but another time I should make quite sure of my suspicions before stating them."

He was relieved to find that she took the affair so quietly, and felt on excellent terms with himself after his handsome apology, which had cost a considerable effort.

He did not know that a man can never unjustly suspect his wife without falling immeasurably in her esteem and rearing a barrier between them not lightly to be bridged over. He thought the offence was wiped out when he deigned to say carelessly, "I'm sorry." But men are mistaken. Those caba-listic words do not always heel the wound inflicted.

CHAPTER XXVII.

THE RESPECTABLE FIRM OF DASHWOOD AND RICKERBY.

AFTER Captain Cameron's departure things went on much as usual at Beechlands. Sir Philip hunted and amused himself, leading an existence devoid of ambition or of high purpose, Bligh was a little more silent and reticent than before their dis-agreement, but she deferred to his wishes with punctilious politeness. She had come to the conclusion that in order to render life bearable she must not expect anything from him, but depend entirely on her own resources. If less happy she gradually became more self-supporting. Fortunately, about this period she found an occupation which diverted her thoughts from domestic trouble, gave an interest to her spare moments, and proved thoroughly congenial. The only drawback was that it necessitated being conducted in secret. As regarded the matter in hand she had a horror of failure and ridicule. Perhaps she was unduly sensitive ; but until success was assured she felt as if she could not take even her mother into her confidence.

For a part of each day she shut herself up in her own room, and when she issued therefrom it was generally with an absorbed and preoccupied air, which gradually wore off when she mixed with the family circle.

Sir Philip saw nothing. He was much away from home, and never troubled himself to inquire how his wife spent her time during his absence. The Dowager Lady Verschoyle was more observant. She attributed Bligh's prolonged disappearances, however, to indisposition, the cause of which was natural, and therefore did not comment upon them.

As for Mrs. Burton, ever since her daughter's marriage she

had been unable to shake off invalid ways, and this in spite of the improvement which for a month or two after the operation had been visible in her health. To her Bligh was the same as ever—always loving, always cheerful, and devoted. In her presence Bligh's brow never wore a cloud. The newly-made wife acted content to perfection. And if Mrs. Burton was to a certain extent deceived by the apparent serenity of her daughter's demeanour her blindness was in great measure excusable, for, poor woman! she had a burden of her own to hide. Since Christmas a pain, first slight, but day by day growing more and more acute, had taken possession of her; until now it proved an almost inseparable companion. She did not speak of it to Bligh, for she was determined not to frighten her. Any alarm might prove injurious to her in her present condition. Consequently, Mrs. Burton maintained an heroic silence as to her sufferings, and surely she was to be forgiven if they blunted her perceptions somewhat and deprived them of their accustomed clearness. With it all she knew more than Bligh fancied. A mother is hard to deceive, especially where her daughter's happiness is concerned; and often a lump would rise in her throat when she looked at Bligh's persistently cheerful countenance and then caught sight of it when she was off her guard. The contrast was too great not to tell tales. But Mrs. Burton was a woman of tact, and perhaps realised that man and wife must fight their own battles.

March set in dry and dusty, with bitter winds, and pale cold sunshine devoid of warmth, and the hunting season wore rapidly to an end. The ploughs were white, the grass turning to emerald green, and the fields were dotted with white-fleeced, shaky-legged lambs, whose tremulous tones filled the air with plaintive cries. A large proportion of the Midlandshire sportsmen were greatly excited by the prospect of a red-coat race, to be run for at the end of the month. It was an innovation in their part of the country, and being the first of its kind, gave rise to a good deal of discussion and also of friendly emulation. Lord Midlandshire had started the idea, and he generously offered a silver cup, value one hundred guineas, as a prize to the winner. It was an elegant trophy, representing a hunted fox showing his teeth to the enemy, manufactured by a well-known Bond-street firm. All the hard-riding men were anxious to win it, and no one more so than Sir Philip.

Unluckily he had used up all his best horses, and the one he would have elected to ride was suffering from a bad sprain of the shoulder muscles, which rendered him so lame he could hardly put his foot to the ground, and meant nothing short of six months' rest. The hunters that remained upright did not happen to possess any particular speed. Now Sir Philip opined that in a race of this sort a fast horse was a *sine qua non.* No doubt there were plenty to be got for money, but the difficulty was to light upon the right animal and one in condition. The time was short, and left little over a fortnight for preparation.

Yet by hook or by crook he was determined to win the race. Ever since Bligh's disaster in the hunting field he had entertained an uneasy conviction that the Marquis of Midlandshire looked upon him coldly, and this seemed an excellent opportunity to win back his esteem and teach him what a mistake he made in underrating Sir Philip Verschoyle, Bart.

" I wish to goodness I could pick up a horse who can gallop as well as jump," he said one night to Captain Dashwood, when they were sitting over their wine. " I'd give a monkey for him to-morrow."

The captain looked a little thoughtful, but merely replied, " Ah ! my dear fellow, they're not so easy to find."

On the following morning, however, he said to Mr. Rickerby, who for the last week had appeared in unusually low spirits, " Jack, I saw you engaged on the pleasing task yesterday afternoon of making up our accounts. How do we stand ? "

" Deuced badly," came the disconsolate reply. " I don't remember our having been in such a corner. We dropped a lot over that brute Circassian at Sandown, and again the other day at Manchester, when Tom Tit fell over the last fence exactly when he had the race in hand. It was crushing luck. We began the season fairly well, but of late we have not succeeded in turning an honest penny even at cards." And he tossed away the end of his cigar with a despairing gesture.

" H'm ! " said Captain Dashwood, reflectively. " I was afraid the exchequer could not be in a very flourishing condition."

" Flourishing ! It's just about as bad as bad can be. Unless we can manage to scrape a couple of hundred or so together in the next ten days it looks very much as if the respectable firm of Dashwood and Rickerby would burst up. At the present moment we literally haven't got enough money to pay the butcher and baker, and if we can't stop the tongues of these wretched tradespeople it means the very devil. They are beginning to clamour as it is. See, there is a nice little bill for forage which came in this morning, and how the dickens we're to settle it Heaven only knows." And so saying he threw across the table a blue ruled document of portentous length.

Captain Dashwood took it up and ran his eye over the items.

" The old story," he said, smothering a sigh. " To bill delivered £81 7s. 1od. Twenty quarters of oats at thirty-one and sixpence; bran, linseed, carrots, beans, and all the rest of it. One can't keep horses for nothing; but I protest against having my temper upset by being forced to enter into these disagreeable details."

"Unfortunately," observed Mr. Rickerby, grimly, "the time comes when it is impossible to escape from them. That time is rapidly approaching us both—you, as well as me."

"Pooh! nonsense, my dear fellow: you take too gloomy a view of the situation."

"Perhaps you would also if you had been pulled up by Field in the public street this morning as I was. The man actually had the impertinence to say that if I did not settle this account within a week he should bring a summons against us."

"And if he does it won't be the first by a good many with which we have been served. Nevertheless, I admit to the thing being a bit awkward. We can't afford to lose our credit; in fact, it's pretty nearly all we've got to go upon. What does the total amount come to?"

"One hundred and eighty-six pounds odd," answered Mr. Rickerby dismally.

"Give the brute something on account. We can't possibly part with so much of the ready in a lump, even if we had it."

"I can't," responded Jack, whose usually sanguine nature appeared conquered by the force of circumstances. "Last night's loo just about cleared me out. I haven't even a fiver to go on with."

"That's the worst of cards. One has to pay up. I O U's may be a convenience, but they don't tide over the difficulty for any length of time. Well! old man, matters being as they are it strikes me if we want to get away from here without a rumpus we must do what we have done before."

"And what might that be?" inquired Rickerby more hopefully, for his faith in his companion was unbounded.

"Why, fall back on our wits to be sure. For my part I see a way out of the dilemma already."

"By Jove! Dashwood," exclaimed the other admiringly. "What a wonderful fellow you are."

Captain Dashwood smiled.

"I don't know about that," he said, with gentle deprecation. "It don't follow that I am a genius because a large proportion of mankind happen to be fools."

"We will call it a fortunate circumstance," rejoined Rickerby, in a very much more cheerful tone than he had hitherto adopted.

"Call it what you like. As long as the fact remains it makes no difference."

"May I ask if you have any particular fool in your eye, though the question is superfluous."

"Yes.   I have spotted him for a long time."

"Is he Sir Philip Verschoyle ? "

The captain nodded his head.

" Your assumption does credit to your perspicuity."

" Forgive me, Dashwood ; but isn't the game just a little too dangerous ? "

" My dear Jack.   When one stands in need of eggs one must kill the goose, even if he be golden.   Every now and then occasions arise in life when one is bound to run risks.   You and I find ourselves placed in this unpleasant predicament.   If we each had five thousand a year no doubt we should be as honest as our neighbours.   Fate has treated us unkindly, and so instead of living comfortably on incomes amassed by our forefathers we are obliged to live on our brains.   It's hard lines on two respectable men, who only require a certain amount of coin to be models of virtue.   But there are a good many others in the same boat, and when all is said and done we're better off than the folks who have neither money nor brains.   If you can suggest a safer victim do so."

" What is your plan ? " said Jack Rickerby, abruptly.   " It's on good moralising."

" My plan is simply this.   I propose to sell Corkscrew to our young friend for five hundred guineas."

" Five hundred guineas !   Ridiculous.   No man in his senses would give such a sum for him."

" That remains to be seen."

" But, Dashwood, Verschoyle knows the old horse by sight."

" I'm not so sure of that.   Corkscrew has done very little hunting this winter, and we only bought him at the end of last season. He is by no means so well-known as you imagine."

" But even then," objected Rickerby.

"Unless some mutual friend interferes I have no fear of Sir Philip.   He goes in for being a hard man to hounds, and all that sort of thing ; but as for being a judge of a horse he hardly knows one from another.   Why, when he goes into his stable he does not even recognise his own quads unless the groom is by and tells him their names."

"That's true," remarked Jack, struck by the force of his friend's argument.

"Now," resumed Captain Dashwood, emphatically, " I happen to know that Verschoyle is dying to win this red-coat race, and don't mind what he gives for an animal faster than his neighbours."

"But Corkscrew hasn't any pretensions to being a racer."

"I never said he had, but that's neither here nor there. If we can once make Verschoyle believe him to be a speedier horse than he is in reality and get five hundred guineas put into our pockets it's sufficient for our purpose."

"Quite sufficient; but for the life of me I can't see how it is to be done."

"You're a capital chap, Jack; but you're deficient in invention. Just listen for a minute or two, and I'll tell you what I propose. At the present moment Corkscrew is fit and well. It has taken the best part of the winter to get that tendon of his right, and, of course, it may spring again directly he is put into work; but we must run our chance of that. Having been out so seldom this year he is not like a well-known animal, and there we possess a great advantage. I confess that had it been otherwise my plan might not have been feasible. But as it is, there really ought not to be much difficulty in the matter."

"Go on," said Jack Rickerby. "You have excited my curiosity."

"To-morrow, then, I propose to ride Corkscrew with hounds. The old horse is a good stayer, and when fresh gallops very fairly fast. If we have a run I shall husband his resources and so manage as to catch Verschoyle's eye at the finish, when, provided all goes well, he will see him going like great guns. Unless I much mistake my man if once I can succeed in passing him the thing's done. There, don't you understand?"

"Yes; but there is one contingency which you seem to ignore and yet it might easily upset everything."

"Name it."

"Supposing Sir Philip were to recognise Corkscrew."

A smile of peculiar cunning passed over Captain Dashwood's face."

"I don't think he will. To begin with, he is far too taken up with his own performances out hunting to bestow much attention on his neighbours' cattle unless they are brought directly under his notice; and, secondly, it is my intention to go to the stables and give orders for the old horse's mane to be hogged and his tail docked. That will go a long way towards altering his appearance, and should the morning prove fine I'll paint a nice bold star on his forehead and give him a couple of white heels. If the baronet has doubts I need only point to them to show that it is a case of mistaken identity."

"Ha, ha!" laughed Jack. "Not half a bad idea; but it wants to be artistically carried out."

"Never fear," responded his companion confidently. "I back myself to do the job as neatly as a regular painter in oils. By-the-bye, we must be prepared with a name and a pedigree. What shall they be? Something Irish generally takes best."

" How do you like Patrick the First, by Solon, out of Mavourneen?" said Jack, glibly. " Will that do?"

"First rate. Couldn't be better. You have a perfect talent for nomenclature. Just write it down on a piece of paper, there's a good chap. My memory is so bad that I'm certain to make some mistake if you don't."

Mr. Rickerby did as desired, and handed the ready-made pedigree to his partner.

" Thanks, that's all right; and now I'll go and lay in the materials for my little decorations. I may find it necessary to invest in a tin of Aspinall's enamel. It comes nearer to the gloss of a horse's coat than ordinary paint. By the way, do you happen to have such a thing as a bob about you?"

Jack felt dubiously in his pockets. They were distressingly empty; but after a protracted search he succeeded in producing the requisite coin, which, however, he parted from with singular reluctance.

"Put it out at interest," he said, in a melancholy tone; "for there are not many more where that came from."

" All right, old man. You seem uncommonly down on your luck; but leave everything to me, and I guarantee that we shall soon be in clover again. These east winds have affected your liver and made you feel depressed. Look at me, I'm as cheerful as possible."

"Yes," answered Jack Rickerby, with a mirthless laugh. "You always are when you are contemplating some fresh roguery."

" My dear friend, your frankness is more to be admired than your civility. There is a brutal candour about that speech which I fail to appreciate."

" I can't help it, Dashwood. You may accuse me of growing squeamish, but I don't altogether approve of this business. We have always drawn the line hitherto at our friends, and if Verschoyle is a drunken sot we've helped him to buzz a good many bottles of wine and eaten a great many dinners at his expense."

" Jack, you're nerve is affected. You've only begun to talk in this childish manner since the widow Benson appeared on the scenes. If you are in love I forgive you. Fellows always turn maudlin when under the influence of Cupid; but in that case why the devil can't you propose and have done with it?"

" I have proposed, and I have done with it," said Jack, in a woe-begone voice, which seemed to proceed from his boots.

"Oh! I understand. You're going to get married. That accounts for your low spirits. You have my warmest sympathy."

" Nothing of the sort. She refused me. Said one husband was enough to disgust any woman with connubial bliss."

" Ah ! the widow Benson is a female of sense and experience. Jack, my dear boy, I congratulate you."

" What on ? "

" Why ! on your escape, of course. Nature never intended you for a benedict. You'd be miserable as a married man."

" I'm not so sure of that, Dashwood. I'm getting tired of this sort of life."

" You'd soon get tired of the other."

" I don't know. When a man is over five and thirty he begins to appreciate ease and security."

" And a precious lot of either you'd get with a hunting wife nearly as old as yourself. You did not care for her, of course ? "

Jack tried to look sentimental, but failed signally in the attempt.

" I—I don't know. I rather think that I did."

" Oh ! come, that won't go down." And Captain Dashwood burst into a hearty laugh.

His friend could not resist the contagion of his merriment.

" I daresay I shall recover," he said. " I don't pretend to say that it was a ' grande passion.' I liked the little woman——"

" But you liked her money better. A man of your figure and fashion, however, ought not to throw himself away. The widow has only a life interest in three thousand a year. If she were to die before you you'd be left without a penny."

" H'm ! " said Jack, reflectively, stroking his chin, " I never thought of that."

" What on earth were you about ? When a man takes such a desperate step as to propose he should think of everything. You're not exactly cut out for a husband, Jack. Still, I don't mean to say but what some of these days you might not extend the firm of Rickerby and take me in as a sleeping partner. Marriage is a bargain like any other, and my opinion is that if you were put up to auction in the matrimonial market to-morrow a fellow with your looks and appearance ought to go for more than three thousand." So saying Captain Dashwood withdrew to the stables, where he spent a busy afternoon superintending the process designed to transform Corkscrew from a forty pound screw into a five hundred guinea steeplechaser.

CHAPTER XXVIII.

CORKSCREW, ALIAS PATRICK THE FIRST.

THE conspirators were in luck. If they had designed the following morning to order it could not have proved more propitious for the execution of their scheme. After a fortnight's drought a copious rain fell during the night, which rendered the turf springy and elastic, and did away with the dryness that for the last ten days had played such havoc with horses' forelegs and feet. The day moreover was dull, and a thick white mist rendered it difficult to see more than a couple of fields ahead. Captain Dashwood chuckled when he rose from his couch and looked out of the window.

The first glance at the garden hedge impregnated with moisture, and the wet pavement beyond, showed him that the principal danger which he had all along feared was now considerably lessened. In the present welcome softened state of the ground Corkscrew's tendon stood a much better chance, and was not nearly so likely to give way.

At breakfast he expressed his satisfaction to Mr. Rickerby, who, after a good night's rest, took a much more hopeful view of the situation, and no longer made any allusion to his scruples.

His spirits were still further raised when he entered the stable yard, and perceived Corkscrew being led from his box to the stone block, where Captain Dashwood, arrayed in all the glories of red coat and leathers, was preparing to mount.

"By Jove!" whispered Jack in his ear. "What an extraordinary change! I never saw an animal so transformed. I declare that even I should scarcely have known him. You have put pounds on to his value."

"I told you so," answered the other, triumphantly. "Admit who was right. The old beggar looks well, don't he?"

"Better than I could have believed. Hogging his mane is a vast improvement, and he always was a rare made 'un."

Corkscrew fully merited the encomium; for he was as nice a topped horse as one could wish to see anywhere. He stood a trifle over sixteen hands high, was almost pure thoroughbred, though up to a lot of weight; and had a lean head, full eye, well-opened nostrils, clean neck, and grand shoulders. A connoisseur might perhaps have said that he was a little light behind the saddle, but the width of his hips and the strength of his great muscular hocks atoned for this defect; which moreover was scarcely apparent after the long rest in which he had lately been indulged. All he wanted really was a pair of new forelegs. Unfortunately, in spite of his ingenuity, Captain Dashwood could not supply these. He had, however, done the best he could in the circumstances, and applied a couple of charges plastered with tow; and over them he had so neatly sewn blue flannel bandages that they detracted very little from the old horse's appearance.

Altogether, as Corkscrew stood there, whisking his tail and arching his neck, he looked an uncommonly sporting animal, and the model of a fourteen stone Midlandshire hunter. A finer, freer fencer was never foaled, and had he only been sound, the price his owner intended asking, though high, would not have been excessive as good horses go. But tendons and age are two things not easily cured, and they reduce the value of the best steeds to a mere nothing.

Jack continued to gaze at Corkscrew with fascinated admiration. He noticed that his forehead bore a white star, and that his hind heels were adorned by a snowy rim just above the coronet, which set them off to advantage.

"By George!" he exclaimed, as soon as the village was fairly left behind, "I have never seen anything so natural in my life. Those heels are a masterpiece. Will they run?" And he winked jocularly at his companion.

"No," answered Captain Dashwood, complacently, "I think not. I stood them in a bucket of water for an hour, and the colour did not wash off in the least. It was bath enamel that I used, and," he added, with a little dry laugh, "I hope it will last until we go into summer quarters."

"How ever did you manage to make such a good job?" asked Rickerby.

"Patience, my dear boy. Patience and perseverance. They're responsible for nearly all the successes of life. A clumsy workman might have done the trick in ten minutes; whereas it took me the best part of the afternoon, for I did not attempt to paint more than half a dozen hairs at a time. Hence the result. Steady, old boy, steady, don't display your ingratitude by upsetting me into the mud," he concluded, as Corkscrew executed a series of bucks, and broke into a canter.

"The old beggar's fit to jump out of his skin," observed Mr. Rickerby, crossing to the other side of the road.

"It's not to be wondered at, considering he has never had a man on his back since the beginning of November. I don't exactly look forward to a pleasant ride; but, as personal comfort should always give way to business, I am prepared to make a martyr of myself for the next three or four hours."

They were now joined by a friendly farmer, with whom they jogged leisurely out to the meet, which, as good luck would have it, happened to be close at hand. Consequently, wh˙˙˙ they arrived, Corkscrew had lost none of the freshness which temporarily lent him such a look of youth and ardour. He pawed the ground, sniffed the foggy air impatiently through his nostrils, and might easily have been taken for five, instead of fifteen. His rider was thoroughly alive to the fact that the more he stood still the worse his forelegs were likely to appear to advantage; so he kept him steadily moving about. Besides, on this particular day, he had no desire to encounter too many of his acquaintances, and therefore slunk out of their way. Some of them, he knew, had sharper eyes than Sir Philip, and also better memories; and he did not care to run any unnecessary risks.

Just before the hounds were about to move off the baronet rode up. Whilst he was changing from his hack to his hunter, Captain Dashwood walked Corkscrew quietly to and fro, apparently with no purpose beyond soothing the nerves of his mettlesome steed; but, in reality, so as to catch Sir Philip's eye. In this he was presently successful.

A sparrow flew out of a hedge hard by, and Corkscrew, from pure light-heartedness, gave a whinny and a bound, which attracted his attention, especially as his own horse followed suit, before he was fairly seated in the saddle. A brutal hit on the head, with the butt-end of his hunting crop, quickly reduced him to order. Sir Philip's hunters served him through fear rather than love.

"Hulloa! Dashwood," he exclaimed. "You're on a lively one for once! Something young and new?"

Now there are rogues and rogues. Burglars are as thick as blackberries, but a real good clever rogue who deceives you so pleasantly and plausibly that you can hardly believe in his knavery when discovered, commands respect in spite of his vices. Captain Dashwood belonged to this latter category. Instead, therefore, of answering in the affirmative, and launching out into a voluble panegyric of his mount, like an old and wily diplomatist he bided his time, and affected to resist temptation. On grounds of self-interest, if from no higher motive, he disapproved of telling gratuitous stories; although he had not the slightest objection to fibs when circumstances appeared to warrant their use. His principle might be summed up thus—"Be honest as long as you can, and there is anything to be gained by your honesty; and when you lie, lie like an artist, and take every human precaution against being found out. The original sin is nothing in comparison with discovery. In fact, original sin has no meaning, except that conferred on it by social laws."

So in reply to Sir Philip's interrogation he merely said—

" He is a horse that I have had for some little time, but as he happens to be rather a more valuable animal than most of my gees, and has not done much hunting lately, I daresay you don't remember him. The fact is," lowering his voice confidentially, " I'm keeping him for our red-coat race."

" Oh ! indeed ! " said Sir Philip, picking up his ears at this. " I did not know you intended starting for it. Has your animal any chance ? "

The captain smiled knowingly.

" I flatter myself that he has an excellent chance, else I should not have specially reserved him all this time."

" You're deuced lucky," said Sir Philip, discontentedly. " Much luckier than I am. With eighteen horses in the stable, I haven't one that can gallop."

" How about Prince Charming ? "

" He's laid up with a sprained shoulder, and can scarcely hobble round his box."

" The Swallow then ? She can go a good pace."

" Lame too. I've had to throw her up, she was so bad. In short, I've literally nothing to enter for the race."

" H'm ! that's unfortunate with such a stud as yours."

" I would buy, if I could find a horse to suit me," said Sir Philip.

" There ought to be plenty going at the end of the season,'' rejoined Captain Dashwood.

" Not of the class I want. What do you call that nag ot yours ? "

" Patrick the First, by Solon, out of Mavourneen," replied the captain, glibly. " He has some good blood in his veins, and is a rare beggar to gallop and stay. I have never got to the bottom of him yet, though I've tried pretty hard once or twice."

Sir Philip looked covetously at Corkscrew, who, with ears pricked and neck bent, was prancing about by his side.

" Do you want to sell him by any chance ? " he asked, trying to appear indifferent."

" Well, no, to tell the truth, I don't," answered the old horse's astute owner—"any way not at present. I don't mind taking you into my confidence, and if I'm not very much mistaken in his form he's bound to win the red-coat race ; added to which I mean to race him in the spring, and hope with any luck to get back what I gave and a tidy lump into the bargain."

" You did not pick him up for nothing, Dashwood ? "

"No," responded the captain, with an involuntary twitch of the facial muscles ; "not exactly."

With these words he rode off, conscious that the train was laid, and he had thoroughly aroused Sir Philip's envy.

The hounds now commenced the business of the day, and the very first covert they drew produced a fox. He ran a fast ring, which lasted the best part of five-and-thirty minutes. Nothing could have suited Captain Dashwood better ; for whilst the foremost sportsmen rode on the outside of the circle, he took care to choose the inner. Thus, whilst their horses were racing, his was only going at half speed ; and what with knowing the country, making short cuts, and keeping a good deal in the company of the second horsemen, he managed to take very little out of him, and yet never lost sight of the pack. He was waiting for his opportunity. Presently it came, as he felt sure it would, if only he bided his time, and was not too precipitate. He was cantering down a road when by a stroke of good fortune the hunted fox crawled across it right in front of him. His brush was draggled, his limbs stiff, and it was easy to see that he could not stand up much longer before the inveterate foes who were chasing him to his death. The captain could now afford to be bold, and gave a loud view hulloa. Two or three minutes later the hounds dashed past him, with bristles up, and murder gleaming from their eyes. The huntsman, accompanied by the hard-riding division, was a couple of hundred yards behind. Now it so chanced that those on the outside of the ring had not only been forced to gallop very fast, but had also encountered an unusual amount of plough, which, after the night's rain, had ridden extremely holding. The severity of the pace told upon the horses, and most of them were hanging out signals of distress. Clouds of steam rose from their heated sides, for the fog rendered the atmosphere very close, and the day was still and windless.

Captain Dashwood waited until he recognised Sir Philip's good bay hunter labouring along in Dysack's train, then he turned Corkscrew sharp round, and jumped him over the fence out of the road, thus obtaining a clear lead of all the field. The old horse, as already stated, was a brilliant performer, and he flew it like a bird. A slight drop on landing sent a thrill of dismay through his rider's frame. For a moment he pulled him back into a trot. Had the tendon sprung ? No, thank goodness. Forward, forward now! That shock and stagger had been but the effect of a too active imagination,

Corkscrew's ears were gladdened by an inspiriting hound-music, which made him forget every ailment, and intoxicated him with delight. Overjoyed to find that at last he was going to be indulged in the pleasures of a gallop, he snatched eagerly at his bit. Before him lay a couple of hundred acre fields, smooth as a billiard table, elastic as a spring-board ; and beyond, showing dark through the vaporous fog, loomed the covert from which puss had been forced to beat a retreat earlier in the forenoon. Now all the poor "thief of the world" asked was to regain its snug shelter, for he was pushed to extremities.

Until this moment Corkscrew had been so carefully nursed that he was almost as fresh as when he came out of the stable. A gamer horse never looked through a bridle, and lowering his well-bred head, he extended himself with a will, and to those in the rear, literally seemed to fly over the grass. Sir Philip, who imagined that his friend had ridden the run fair and square could not take his eye off Corkscrew's quarters. Vainly he spurred the flagging bay, and sought to lessen the distance between them. In spite of every effort, he did not succeed in gaining a yard on the leader, and jealousy flared up like a flame in his breast. What was the good of having forty thousand a year if men with twopence halfpenny were to beat you ? The thing was ridiculous.

A blackthorn fence divided the two fields. It had a good take-off, and a fair-sized ditch on the far side. A five-barred gate stood open within thirty yards of the direct line of pursuit, so that there really was no occasion to jump unless one wished. But the gallant captain might have been a schoolboy home for his Christmas holidays, judging from the way he disdained it. What had he to do with gates when he was mounted on a crack steeplechaser, and conscious of an intending purchaser in the rear? Over he flew in grand style, whilst Sir Philip floundered through on his beaten horse, and muttered curiously, " By Jove ! what a clipper that is of Dashwood's. I wonder how the deuce so good a horse ever came into his possession."

" Tally-ho ! Tally-ho !" suddenly resounded on every side, and just when the poor, weary quarry was within a few yards of the covert, the leading hound ran into him and bowled him over. All were agreed that, although not a straight-necked customer, he had given them a capital gallop. One after another the horsemen straggled in, their faces flushed with pleasure and excitement. The warm blood glowed in their veins, causing them to feel on good terms with themselves, and with all mankind. Sir Philip alone was out of humour, and a prey to secret irritability. He answered his comrades' remarks curtly, and appeared disinclined for general conversation. After a few minutes he dismounted from the bay, who, since the morning, had fallen considerably in his esteem, and went and stood apart, gnawing sulkily at the end of his moustache. Meanwhile, Captain Dashwood was perfectly aware that the baronet was eyeing Corkscrew with covetous approval ; but he appeared to take no notice of his admiring glances. At last Sir Philip could keep silence no longer.

"That's a wonderful good horse of yours, Dashwood," he said, presently.

"The best I ever had, or am likely to have," responded the captain, patting Corkscrew's neck with much apparent effusion. "The worst of it is, an animal like this quite spoils one for riding inferior cattle. It was a fastish thing, and had the fox only run straight, it would have been an A1 gallop."

"Most of the horses look as if they had had about enough," said Sir Philip.

"Yes, your nag is all in a lather. I don't understand it, for mine has hardly turned a hair, and was as gay at the end as at the beginning."

"Mine is a soft brute," answered Sir Philip, "although I never quite discovered how soft until to-day. He could not gallop a yard towards the finish, and scarcely rose a couple of feet at the last fence. I thought he would have tumbled head over heels. The honours of the chase are yours, Dashwood. You regularly spread-eagled the field. Not one of us could catch the brown, and how he jumps !"

"Yes," said Captain Dashwood, with a complacent smile. "He knows his business ; and if he don't win me Lord Midlandshire's silver cup, I shall be very much surprised. Anyway I mean to have a good try for it, especially as I know of nothing going that I need fear."

This last remark determined Sir Philip ; and he made up his mind not to let money stick in the way.

"Look here, old man," he said, without further preamble. "It's no good my beating about the bush. You said just now that you would not part with the horse, but you and I know each other too well to stand on ceremony. I suppose it's a question of price, eh ?"

The captain's countenance assumed a grave expression, becoming to the importance of the occasion.

"I won't deny that in a general way your supposition is correct, my dear Verschoyle ; but to be perfectly honest, I think so highly of Patrick the First that it is my firm conviction I shall make more money by keeping than by selling him."

"If it is not an impertinent question, how much do you expect to make ?"

"Ah ! there you place me in a difficulty. I can only say that if the horse were valued by my expectations he would fetch a very high figure. Whether they will be realised is a different affair; hence the impossibility of replying to your query."

He said this with an air of such exquisite candour that Sir Philip was more than ever resolved to become the proprietor of so valuable an animal.

" I don't often take a violent fancy to a horse," he said, "but I have to yours, and am prepared to give a good price for him."

" I feel extremely flattered," said Captain Dashwood, pretending to draw back, as the other grew keener and keener. "And if I wished to sell we might perhaps come to terms."

" Won't you name the figure ? " urged Sir Philip.

" Really, my dear Verschoyle, you put me in a singular position. To be plain, I don't want to part with the horse."

" Come, come," said the baronet, impatiently. " Shall we say three—four—five hundred guineas. There are a good many expenses connected with racing, and even if you do win a steeple-chase or two, it is not all profit, not that I need remind an old hand like you of the fact."

Captain Dashwood had hard work to conceal his delight at having brought matters to so satisfactory a climax; but he managed to look pensively at Patrick the First's shaky forelegs, and murmured—" Five hundred guineas is a handsome sum certainly. I won't deny that, but——" stopping short.

" But what ? " inquired Sir Philip.

" The fact is," said the captain in his softest and suavest tones. " I entertain a great regard for you, Verschoyle ; and wouldn't for the world that anything should happen which might put a stop to our friendship."

Sir Philip laughed.

" Ha, ha ! I understand. You mean that your friends have not always been satisfied with their purchases. I have heard rumours to that effect."

" I mean nothing of the sort," retorted Captain Dashwood, in a somewhat sharper key. " But what I do mean is this : Horses—even the best of them—are delicate and uncertain creatures, and although in my own mind I have little doubt as to Patrick the First being able to win our red-coat race, In either could nor would guarantee it."

" No, no, of course not, my dear fellow. I'm not such a fool as to imagine that you would. If I buy the horse I am prepared to run all risks."

" Then, too," resumed the captain, with an inscrutable smile, " one must always take accidents into consideration. A horse may break down whilst training, or he may not be fit the day of the race, or he may run well in private and not in public; in short, a thousand disappointments may occur for which it is impossible to hold the seller responsible. Under these circumstances, and liking you personally and valuing your friendship as much as I do, I think—yes," and he enunciated his words very distinctly, "I really think I should prefer not to sell you the horse."

This decision was totally unexpected, and proved a masterpiece of diplomacy. If anything had been wanting to confirm Sir Philip's decision, the apparent reluctance on Captain Dashwood's part clinched the business. For him not to jump at an offer of five hundred guineas proved that Patrick the First was an animal of no common merit. Sir Philip, therefore, became increasingly urgent, as his friend sought to dissuade him from the purchase. He ended by carrying his folly to such a height that he declared a trial was unnecessary, as after what he had seen of the horse's performance, he was perfectly satisfied, and did not even care to throw a leg over him. "I have seen quite enough," he declared, "and am willing to take your word for everything else. All I want is to win the red-coat race."

To make a long story short, the captain ended by reluctantly yielding to the pressure put upon him by his friend, and allowed his scruples to be overruled.

"'Pon my word, Verschoyle," he said, when the bargain was virtually concluded, "I wouldn't have parted with the horse to anyone but you; and even now I half repent the transaction. However, as the deed is done, and Patrick the First is no longer my property, I may as well take him straight home, and avoid running any risks by keeping him out hunting."

"All right," said Sir Philip, in a satisfied tone. "Sorry to spoil your day, old fellow; but perhaps it might be as well. I'll send the cheque over to-morrow morning, and the man who takes it can bring the horse back."

A vision of general stiffness and a bowed foreleg rose before Captain Dashwood's eyes.

"If you don't mind," he said, "I think we had better let it be until Monday. Patrick is rather excitable, and not having seen hounds for some little time, it is just possible that he may not feel quite as usual. I should not recommend a change of stable for a day or two, but please yourself. It shall be just as you like."

"There's no particular hurry," answered Sir Philip. "Monday will do nicely."

"And, by-the-bye," said Captain Dashwood, airily, "if I were you, I shouldn't go in for giving him too much of a preparation. He is a very peculiar horse—not delicate, but peculiar, and my experience is that the less he is bustled about the better he goes. Give him two or three hours' walking exercise a day on soft ground, and he'll carry you like a bird in the race.

He's so eager that he frets himself to death once one begins to gallop him."

" Thanks for the hint," answered Sir Philip. " I shall certainly act upon it. I am aware that a certain proportion of hunters run better untrained than trained, and I suppose he is of the number. By-the-way, don't you think he is uncommonly like an old screw you used to ride at the beginning of the season? I forget his name."

" Oh! Ah! yes, perhaps he is. You notice the resemblance, do you? Oddly enough, several of my friends have remarked upon it also. But Patrick shows a great deal more quality, and in every respect is a far finer shaped animal. And now I'd better be off before he catches cold. Good-morning, Verschoyle, good-morning." So saying the gallant captain beat a retreat, well satisfied with his forenoon's work, and deeming it unwise to prolong the conversation.

The watchful Jack intercepted him before he had gone very far.

" Well!" he said, interrogatively, " have you managed it?"

" Yes," answered his friend and ally, " with the greatest ease in the world." Then he shrugged his shoulders lightly, and added, " I'm taking my steeplechaser—or rather Verschoyle's—back to his stable, and only hope the poor old beggar may be sound enough to go over to Beechlands on Monday."

" Well done! Is the money all right?"

" Yes. I am to receive the cheque to-morrow. One word, Jack. If Verschoyle should happen to cross-question you this afternoon, remember I only sold Corkscrew as a favour, and weakly yielded to pressure. Do you twig?"

" Rather," responded Mr. Rickerby, grinning from ear to ear. " You are a sharp 'un."

" Wouldn't answer to be otherwise, and in an affair of this sort one is bound to leave open a line of retreat, in case of any disaster happening. As it is, I flatter myself, I hold my gentleman tight."

" You are admirable, Dashwood. Scarcely a day passes without some fresh proof of your talent. Ta ta, old chap. When one makes five hundred guineas at a stroke, one can afford to lose half a day's hunting."

" Right you are," said the captain. Whereupon he set the old horse's head in the direction of home, and rode Corkscrew back very gingerly and slowly, taking care to keep him as much as possible on the sides of the roads. This precaution was the more necessary, because his mount went decidedly feeling whenever he was forced to go over a patch of stones. Although not precisely lame, Corkscrew's action was what sportsmen term

" dotty." Twice he nearly tumbled on his nose, and his rider had every cause to congratulate himself on having achieved so clever a sale.

" I never could have done it if Verschoyle had not been such a flat," he mused, as he left the hounds behind. " He regularly rushed at the bait directly that it was brought before his nose. I always thought him a fool, but I never realised the depth of his folly until to-day. Fancy giving five hundred guineas for an animal not worth fifty, and on whose back one had never even sat. What idiots some people are to be sure ! "

His thoughts evidently were pleasant, for his face kept breaking out into smiles all the way home."

" The beauty of the thing is," he soliloquised, " I hold him safe ; for if he turns round later on and tries to slang me, all I have got to say is that I never wished to part with the horse, and only did so because he left me no peace. Yes," and he slapped his hand on his thigh in token of self-approval, " I think I managed the business just about as neatly as it was possible. Jack, dear boy," thinking of his companion's depression, " you need never despond so long as James Mincham Dashwood remains at the head of the firm ; for, after all, the next best thing to having money is having brains, and those, thank the Lord ! I possess in abundance."

" Corkscrew's sold," he said, to his groom, as he entered the stable yard a few minutes afterwards. " Give him a bran mash to-night, and let him have an aconite powder on Saturday and Sunday. They'll freshen him up, and make his coat look well, and he has to go over to Beechlands on Monday."

" Yes, capting," said the man, touching his cap. He was a confidential servant, and nothing ever surprised him.

" And hark you, O'Flanaghan," resumed his master, " if Sir Philip Verschoyle's people come wanting to find anything out about the horse, mum's the word. His name is Patrick the First. Don't forget."

" No, capting, I won't forgit."

" When Cork—I mean Patrick the First has stood an hour in his box, let me know how he is, and if he points that near foreleg. You need not take him exercising unless I give orders. It won't do him any harm to let him stand still for a day or two."

" Beg pardon, capting," said O'Flanaghan, " but did I understand yer roightly, when ye said Sir Verschoyle had bought th'ould baste ? "

" Yes, he intends to win the red-coat race with him."

O'Flanaghan's Irish eyes twinkled, and his face showed signs of merriment.

" That's the foinest joke I've heard for a long time," he said.

" Ah ! capting, ye're a rale clever gintleman, ye are. There's not minny as can bate ye, when it comes to a bargain."

" Hold your tongue," answered Captain Dashwood, angrily. " Deuce take the fellow, I believe he's been drinking again. Look here, O'Flanaghan, if you don't keep sober between now and the day of the point to point race, I'll dismiss you. Upon my oath, I will."

The man looked at his employer with a cunning smile.

" Divil a bit, capting dear. I know too much, and ye're the last gintleman in the world to wish ye're stable sacrates made public."

CHAPTER XXIX.

THE RED-COAT RACE.

MARCH belied its usual character, for the end of the month proved as rainy as the beginning was dry. Thanks to the weather and to Captain Dashwood's judicious warning, Corkscrew was enabled to go through a light preparation for the race without breaking down. He did plenty of walking exercise, principally with the weight off his back ; but he had lost so much in condition during his enforced idleness that the time was too short to get him anything like fit. After Sir Philip had had the old horse in his stables some few days he began to feel rather less confident as to the wisdom of his purchase. The fact was, he had left one very important personage out of his calculations— a personage, moreover, who had no notion of being ignored— namely, his stud groom. This worthy functionary seldom condescended to approve of any animal which he had not been directly instrumental in buying. Report averred that the big dealers with whom Sir Philip habitually dealt were accustomed to pay him a ten per cent. commission on all hunters sold, so as to insure his good-will. It may be gathered, therefore, what a very important individual Mr. Tomling was. And when Mr. Tomling discovered that his master had actually dared to buy a horse on his own judgment and without consulting him he suffered from a very natural and excusable indignation. That Corkscrew —or, rather, Patrick the First—should be doomed was a matter of course. Words failed to express the excellent man's disapproval when the new arrival was installed in the Beechlands stables.

" Look at them forelegs," he said to Sir Philip, jerking his thumb contemptuously over his shoulder. " A child in arms might have seen that the suspensory ligaments are not as they should be.   Charges, indeed! I won't deny that they're useful at times ; but one don't begin by buying hunters whose tendons require their support.   They are the end of all things as a rule, the last resource of old favourites too good to shoot.   No wonder Captain Dashwood cautioned you not to give him much of a preparation.   The reason was simple enough.   The horse cannot stand training, and my belief is he'd crack up altogether if he were asked to do a three mile gallop.   As for his age," wrenching open the unfortunate animal's mouth as he spoke, "he'll never see fifteen again, of that I'll take my oath."

"Nonsense, Tomling," responded Sir Philip, crossly.   "I've bought him, and it's no use crabbing him."

"Well, Sir Philip, all I can say is I hope you did not pay a very high price for the horse ; for not to mince matters, he ain't worth thirty pounds—leastways in my opinion, and I should be a pretty good judge of horseflesh by this time.   He's been a nice animal in his day, but that must have been a precious long while ago, and he's nothing better now than a patched up old screw. That's the truth, and I feel all the easier in my mind for having spoken it."

Mr. Tomling was consumed with curiosity to know the exact sum his master had given, but Sir Philip maintained a discreet silence on this head, and refused to satisfy his factotum's desire for information.   The subject was rapidly becoming a painful one, and he did not care to refer to it more than necessary.   A conviction was gradually growing up within him that he had acted foolishly in not giving Patrick the First a good trial before buying him at so high a price and on the spur of the moment. It was too late now, however, to repair the error, and he felt it to be a case of "least said soonest mended," especially as he was bound to make the best of the bargain, no matter how bad it might prove.   So he answered Tomling's remarks very curtly, and gave him to understand that he did not wish the matter discussed.   "When you have to ride the horses, not I, then you may criticise them," he said.   "Meanwhile, have the goodness to hold your tongue, and don't presume to dictate."   With which sarcastic speech he strode out of the stable, leaving Tomling to recover from his indignation as best he might.

At length the day of the race arrived.   It was ushered in **by** a blue April sky, soft breezes, and bright sunshine.

"Lord Midlandshire had been considerably gratified to find how much enthusiasm his scheme had aroused, and he determined to do the thing in style.   Besides, a bye-election was shortly about to take place in the county, and he wished to secure the Conservative votes.   Consequently, he caused two large marquees to be erected on the course, in one of which he **proposed** to entertain all the gentry, and in the other the farmers, graziers, small tenants, grooms, and tradespeople residing within an area of fifteen miles.

The silver cup which he intended presenting to the winner had given rise to so much emulation among the members of the Midlandshire Hunt that there were altogether between thirty and forty entries, and no fewer than eight and twenty horsemen faced the starter on the important day. A committee of picked men had previously been formed to decide upon the course, and, after much consultation, a fine, flat, well-fenced bit of country was selected. A piece of rising ground stood in the centre, from which an excellent view could be obtained by the carriage and foot people. For a wonder, everyone agreed that the site was singularly well chosen. Those on the hill commanded the whole course, which was circular, and about four miles long. All the fences were good hunting ones, such as might be met with any day in a run to hounds, and though some of them were undeniably large they were fair. Every bit of wire had been removed for the occasion, so that the leaders had nothing to fear from the dreaded enemy which so frequently overthrew them in the hunting field.

A vast concourse of people had assembled from all sides to witness the race, of whose popularity there could be no doubt. Amongst them Lord Midlandshire was conspicuous, mounted on a magnificent white horse. He did not, of course, intend to compete, but contented himself with riding from carriage to carriage, chatting to his acquaintances, and superintending the general arrangements.

It was a pretty scene. The blue sky, broken by great, solid white clouds that looked like marble in their dazzling purity; the green fields, verdant with the hue of spring; the bright sunshine gleaming on the scarlet coats of the competitors, until even their brass buttons shone like points of fire; the rounded hill dotted black with vehicles and people, and the wide Midlandshire landscape rolling away to the horizon in emerald billows of grass, all combined to form such a picture as only our native land can produce.

There was a good deal of delay, as is usual on these occasions, amateurs being harder to start than professionals. Most of the riders profited by it to avail themselves of Lord Midlandshire's hospitality, and lay in a stock of "jumping powder." Sir Philip ran up against Captain Dashwood in the tent.

"Hulloa!" he said. "How are you? I see you content yourself with the part of spectator."

"Yes," rejoined the captain, "I was obliged to after selling Patrick the First. Rickerby is going round the course. Not that he has any chance, but just for the fun of the thing. They've made Major Locock's Paragona hot favourite at three to one. It's ridiculous laying such short odds in a race of this sort."

" I am afraid my chance isn't quite so rosy as you made out a fortnight ago," said Sir Philip, discontentedly.

" Oh, indeed ! Isn't it ? I am sorry to hear that. Nothing has happened to the horse, I hope."

" No. He's about as right as he will ever be with those fore-legs. It has not been possible to get him fit, and, to tell the truth, I had no idea when I bought him that he was quite so groggy."

" Hadn't you ? " rejoined Captain Dashwood, drily. " You had every opportunity both of seeing, feeling, and trying his forelegs had you cared to avail yourself of it. You seem to forget that I had not the least desire to sell you the horse, and that you insisted on buying him whether I would or not."

Sir Philip felt there was a good deal of truth in his friend's statement, and therefore thought it wiser to discontinue the discussion.

" Well, well," he said, " what's done can't be undone, and if Patrick only wins it won't so much matter if he does crack up afterwards. But I fear he's too short of condition. It is a mystery to me how he carried you so well with the hounds that day, for they certainly went a great pace, and the plough rode uncommonly heavy. By-the-bye, I've got two or three of the chaps coming to dine to-night. You and Rickerby will join our party, won't you ? It's always fun talking matters over afterwards, and we may as well make an evening of it."

" Thanks ! " said Captain Dashwood, as Sir Philip wedged his way to the door. " We shall be very happy to come."

" Humph ! " he muttered to himself, tossing off a glass of champagne. " Verschoyle is evidently a bit suspicious, and not quite so pleased with his bargain as he was when he made it. However, that's to be expected ; nevertheless, if the old horse does but run decently I shall come out of the affair all right. Ha, ha ! I soon shut the bart. up when he began talking about forelegs. He curled up directly I tackled him. Those talking, bullying fellows always do."

Shortly afterwards a bell rang, and one by one the competitors issued from the saddling paddock, and after a preliminary parade past the carriages were quickly marshalled into line. A brave show the eight and twenty red-coats made as their wearers sat waiting for the flag to fall. The eager horses stamped and sidled, turning their heads uneasily, as if in search of the hounds, and wondering what sort of a hunt was this without the speckled beauties whose sleek bodies they so loved to watch disappearing over the fences. One or two break-aways occurred ; then the signal was given and they were off, sweeping past the hill at a hand gallop and almost abreast. Very soon, however, the serried order of the rank gave way, and it was curious to see how, almost immediately, the men who went first with hounds dropped into their accustomed places and led the field. Five or six shot out, each one taking a line of his own, followed at a respectful distance by a small cluster of adherents.

Sir Philip went to the front at once ; but although his " pluck " was at all times undeniable he lacked judgment. A desperate hard man to ride he did not possess that Heaven-born gift, a good eye to country. The consequence was he took an unnecessary lot out of his horse in the first mile, and jumped some extremely big places, which the more prudent pioneers avoided by selecting easier spots where the fences were weaker. The truth was that Sir Philip had imbibed just enough of Lord Midlandshire's champagne to render him more than usually reckless.

" The idiot ! " murmured Captain Dashwood, who was watching him closely through his field-glass. " He's regularly throwing his chance away. No animal ever foaled could stand such liberties. I always said that Verschoyle was nothing of a horseman, and the fact was never more evident than to-day. By Jove ! " he added, as Corkscrew flew a wide oxer in brilliant style, " how the old horse does jump to be sure ! "

This same oxer proved productive of considerable grief, and caused no less than five scarlet coats to bite the dust and practically withdraw from the contest. Several others had already fallen, so that the numbers were gradually diminishing. A goodly army, however, still stood upright. Meanwhile the pace, although fair, was not severe. Riders appeared actuated by the same desire—namely, to husband their resources until the finish, and not to expend them fruitlessly at the commencement of their journey.

The line, which had hitherto been all grass, was now broken by an extensive ploughed field, whose wet furrows shone in the sunshine. The leaders were then to be seen taking a pull, and the more experienced steadied their horses almost into a trot. Sir Philip, on the contrary, thought this a fine opportunity of stealing a march ; so, instead of following his companions' wise example, he began to forge ahead, seemingly quite regardless of the fact that his horse's weak point was want of condition. Now the plough happened to ride extremely heavy, and by the time poor Patrick had bravely galloped to the end of it his tail became unduly elevated and his head proportionately depressed. An awkward double barred the way into the grass field beyond. It consisted of a small fence mounted on a bank, ornamented

by a blind ditch on either side.   Sir Philip was not quite sure
how to take it.   At first he resolved to try two jumps ; but as
he got nearer he changed his mind, and determined to fly it.
But he did not arrive at this decision soon enough to give
Patrick a fair run, which was the more necessary on account of
the holding nature of the ground.

The consequence was the horse jumped short, pecked heavily
on landing, and only just recovered himself without a fall.

" H'm ! " observed Captain Dashwood, indignantly, as Sir
Philip belaboured the animal's sides.   " You needn't beat him.
It was entirely your own fault.   A worse piece of riding I never
saw in my life, and you don't deserve to win even if poor old
Corkscrew could.   Upon my word, if I weren't so deuced hard
up I should regret ever having sold him to you."

It was clear that being asked to travel at top speed over the
plough had tried Patrick severely.   His nostrils were wide open,
and his dark neck, usually so arched and pliable, was now held
straight, and covered from the withers to the ears with soapsuds.
His very cheeks were white, and great drops of perspiration
rolled down his forehead.   The girths were wet through, and
seemed to encircle his panting body like iron bands.   Under
him his noble heart beat with the strong, quick strokes of a
sledge-hammer ; but although distressed the gallant animal had
no thought of giving in.   At the end of the second mile he
continued to hold his own right well.

But each fence now cost more of an effort, and he dwelt a bit
both on taking off and landing.   Mutely, but surely, he was
beginning to cry out, " I have had enough."   The human brute
on the dumb brute's back heeded not the appeal for mercy.   A
horse's life, a horse's health, what are they in comparison with
the temporary pleasure of the rider ?   Because the one is only
a soulless animal he may go till he drops, whilst the other, who
calls himself a man, subscribes to charities and talk philanthropy, may be as cruel to his steed as he is to his wife, for the
simple reason that they are both within his power.

There was one thing only to be said in Sir Philip's excuse.
What between drink, excitement, and emulation he had almost
entirely lost what generally represented his head.   The sight of
the red-coats stealing up on either side, and little by little
usurping the pride of place, which he realised he could no
longer maintain, drove him distracted.   A kind of frenzy took
possession of him, and rendered him irresponsible.   He was
not master of his actions, and from sheer desperation rode in an
even more break-neck fashion than he had hitherto done.

Everyone knows that to win a race cool judgment and presence of mind are indispensable qualifications.   Sir Philip pos-

sessed neither, and was actuated solely by jealousy and a mad desire for distinction. His was simply brute courage shared in common with the beasts of the field, and if comparisons had been instituted Patrick probably owned quite as large an amount as his rider.

Though his forces were failing him fast he never flinched nor turned his game head, nor sought to save himself by a cowardly refusal. On, on, he plodded, brushing heavily through the thorns now, instead of skipping gaily over them with a satisfied whisk of the tail. As his elasticity departed the concussion produced by jumping grew greater, and he landed with a grunt and a groan.

Alas! his trials were not over, and his rider, in place of acknowledging defeat, took advantage of the horse's finely-tempered nature to goad him to feats beyond his strength.

Brutes are good enough for brutes, and had poor old Corkscrew been one he would have fared better.

Right in front of them a tremendous fence into a road reared its dark line against the sky. By going thirty yards to the right or to the left it was comparatively practicable; the ditch on the far side being less wide and also not so much up-hill. Sir Philip saw his companions diverge, and also perceived that if he kept on his course he should gain ground. This was all he thought about. So he dug the spurs deep into Patrick's dripping sides and charged the fence right in its very thickest part.

The good horse hesitated when he became aware of the formidable nature of the obstacle, which he seemed to realise was more than he could negotiate in his flagging condition. Then his brave spirit upbore him, and he made a huge, convulsive bound, which succeeded in clearing the hedge. But he had not enough steam left to get over the ditch. He caught the bank with his forelegs and floundered right on to his head. He fell, but did not roll, and after a desperate struggle to regain his equilibrium rose from the ground. In doing so, however, he hit the injured tendon hard with the iron of his hind leg, and all of a sudden Sir Philip felt something give way beneath him.

The next moment he found himself seated on a three-legged animal, whose bobbing ears reminded him of nothing so much as a see-saw. The fourth leg was useless. Poor old Corkscrew simply could not put it to the ground. He had broken down hopelessly, and the only favour that remained for him to implore of fate was a bullet. He stood in the road quivering with pain, a truly pitiable object.

The sight of him—so hot, so weary, so scratched with thorns and smeared with blood—would have appealed to the most hard-hearted. Yet in the first anger of his disappointment Sir

Philip knew no compassion, and even now would have forced
the horse on had he been able. But Corkscrew had sped over
the Midlandshire grass for the last time in his gallant career.
Never again would he skim the fences or point his delicate ears.
keeping time to the music of the hounds. With care and nursing he might have lasted for years. His former master had
treated him better than his present one.

Sir Philip dismounted when he discovered the full gravity of
the case, and burst into a volley of oaths.

One after the other he had the mortification of seeing his
companions pop in and out of the road. None of them were so
foolish as to follow in his footsteps and his sentiments can be
better imagined than described. The situation was full of un-
mitigated torture, and as the red-coats disappeared in the distance
he became more than ever a prey to the green-eyed monster.
His chance of winning the coveted cup was completely destroyed,
and in a few minutes from the time of the accident he found
himself left completely alone with a horse who could scarcely
hobble. Bitterly he cursed his luck.

" There go five hundred guineas," he said, looking resentfully
at poor Corkscrew, who, in spite of his suffering, was trying
to snatch a few blades of grass. " I might just as well have
chucked them into the sea."

He was meditating leaving Corkscrew to his fate when a run-
ner appeared, accustomed to run with the Midlandshire hounds,
He knew the man by sight, and gladly hailed his arrival.

" Hulloa ! Bill," he exclaimed. " Do you want a job ? "

" Yes, Sir Philip. I've come all the way from the start as fast
as ever I could," answered the man breathlessly.

" Well ! you've turned up just in the nick of time. I'll give
you five shillings to lead this brute back to Beechlands."

" It 'ull be easier said nor done, I'm afeared, Sir Philip," answered Bill, tugging at Corkscrew's bridle. " He's that lame he
can hardly stand. Come, my boy, come," patting the horse's
neck with a coarse, but kindly, hand.

" The only plan is to keep him moving on," said Sir Philip.
" If he once gets stiff he'll never do the journey. If there were
a man on the course with a gun I'd have him shot at once."

" It's kinder to give him a chance, Sir Philip. He's a good
horse, even if he did break down."

" D—n him," came the answer as the baronet strode off.

Bill looked after him disapprovingly.

" Ah ! " he muttered. " He ain't like some gentlemen, he ain't.
Forty thousand a year, no nor a hundred thousand, wouldn't
ever make him a good sort. And ride ! why he rides like a
lunatic, without a bit of sense."

Sir Philip started off at a rapid walk. He was in two minds whether to show his defeated countenance on the course or go straight home and fly to the brandy bottle for consolation. It so happened that he was undecided which plan to adopt when an incident occurred that determined him in favour of the latter.

CHAPTER XXX.

TOMLING'S REVENGE.

MR. TOMLING's dignity had been terribly wounded, both by his master's conduct and his language. The latter he considered quite inexcusable, for, apart from any question of personal feeling, he indignantly asked himself how he was to maintain his authority over the underlings of the stable when Sir Philip possessed so little sense of the fitness of things as to request him to hold his tongue in their presence. It ruined the prestige on which he set so high a store, and was fatal to all management and order. If henceforth his word were not to be law in the equine department he might as well throw up his situation, perquisites notwithstanding. There were more masters than one, and although he had lived a good many years in Sir Philip's service he had had as much as most people to put up with, and was not bound to him by any ties of affection.

Thus Mr. Tomling reasoned in the first heat of his wrath, and for several hours after the baronet's visit to the stables he was on the point of giving warning. But, like a wise man, he slept on his anger, and morning induced a milder train of thought. He possessed a wife and family, and he felt that it was incumbent on him to consider their welfare, and stifle the voice of pride rather than let them suffer in any way. Tommy, his son and heir, was getting on so nicely at school that it would be a sad pity to withdraw him; Susan, the eldest girl, had just taken her first place with a prosperous farmer and his wife living in the neighbourhood. His house was exceedingly snug; coals and gas cost a lot if people had to pay for them out of their own pocket; and one way or another the post of stud groom brought in between a hundred and fifty and two hundred a year. Would it not be foolish to throw up all these advantages just because an ungrateful master did not value at his full worth an honest servant who would allow no one to rob him but himself?

So on second thoughts Mr. Tomling smothered his indignation, and determined to rise superior to impulse. Impulse was generally foolish in the long run, and he had arrived at an age when he recognised the wisdom of considering a question from all its bearings. Nevertheless, it must not be supposed that he was tamely prepared to pocket the affront received. Quite the contrary. Mr. Tomling had a high spirit of his own, and if motives of expediency induced him to continue to show a smiling front to Sir Philip he never for one instant lost sight of his original intention to be revenged and turn the tables on his master. Now the manner in which the purchase of Corkscrew had been effected puzzled him considerably. He knew more of Captain Dashwood's and Mr. Rickerby's horse-dealing transactions than he chose to divulge, and looked upon any sale in which these gentlemen figured as vendors as calculated to arouse suspicions. In fact, although he had not yet been able to discover what sum Sir Philip paid for the horse he felt absolutely certain in his own mind that his master had been done. He argued that if he (Tomling) could only demonstrate the fact conclusively it would prove a severe blow to the baronet's pride, and also show him the folly of attempting to dabble in horseflesh without the support and advice of his stud groom.

With this praiseworthy object in view the excellent Mr. Tomling favoured Corkscrew with an unusual amount of his attention, and superintended all his goings out and comings in. Before many days had gone by he made an important discovery, which confirmed his suspicions in a remarkable manner. He became aware that the star on the horse's forehead and the white rims that adorned his heels were gradually fading. At first he thought his eyes must be playing him false, and in order to make sure went in search of a magnifying glass which he used occasionally for spying hidden thorns with.

" By jingo ! " he exclaimed, speaking aloud in his excitement, and peering inquisitively at Corkscrew's heels, " they've been doctored just as I thought; and uncommonly cleverly doctored too. I wonder what stuff the rogues have used. Something special I dare say. That Dashwood is up to all the tricks of the trade, and is as good a specimen of a first-class scoundrel as one is likely to meet anywhere. Paint, by George ! " he continued, regaining an upright position and examining his thumb nail, upon which after grasping the animal's heels, a sticky sediment remained. " Aha ! you varmints. I've found you out now. I always knew from the first that there was something not straight about this business, and here is the proof of it."

He gazed solemnly at Corkscrew, as if appealing to him to reveal the mystery, murmuring meanwhile, " Now, why the deuce should Captain Dashwood have taken the trouble to furbish up a poor old screw in this manner ? There's more in it than meets the eye, and I must just think the thing out, and get at the reason.

If he wanted to sell him why couldn't he sell him as he was? Sooner or later he must have known that his imposture was sure to be discovered." Whereupon our friend Tomling fell into a brown study, which lasted nearly half an hour. He was making an unusual call on his mental powers, and thinking hard. That the effort was great could be seen from the puzzled expression of his face and the furrow which traced itself along his thoughtful brow. All at once he spat away a straw which he had unconsciously munched as a means of assisting the process of reflection, and exclaimed vivaciously—

" I have it. That's it, of course. The captain has a brokendown horse in his stable which he is anxious to get rid of. Unfortunately, he has ridden him earlier in the season, and is afraid of his being recognised. So he sets to work with paint brush and scissors, alters his appearance, and turns him into a completely different animal—at least, as far as looks go. Then, when his nag comes fairly sound again, he takes him out into the hunting field, rides him to sell, and passes him on to the first flat he can catch, which flat happens to be Sir Philip. Yes, yes ; the whole thing is as plain as a pikestaff, and I only wonder that I did not see it sooner. Now, what I've got to find out is this : By what name was the horse known formerly, and how much was my governor fool enough to give for him. If I can't stop Sir Philip buying on his own account in future he'll be even a bigger jackass than I think him." With which conclusion Mr. Tomling chuckled and rubbed his hands together in token of mingled satisfaction and superiority.

For the next few days he did not confide his discovery to a living soul. When his wife said, "What's the matter with you, Tomling ?" he only shook his head and looked mysterious, by which conduct he worked the poor woman's curiosity up to an almost uncontrollable pitch. He bustled about the stable yard, wearing an air of importance, and treated his satellites with more "hauteur" and reserve than ever. Everybody should see before long what a very clever sort of man he was, and how there was no taking him in even if they could deceive his master. Meanwhile he kept a furtive glance on Captain Dashwood's groom. He had hitherto looked down contemptuously on this individual as a " drunken swab," wherein he was not far wrong ; but now he began to cultivate his acquaintance, and once or twice dropped in casually of an evening at the Horse and Hound, where O'Flanaghan was frequently to be found towards ten p.m., exchanging witticisms with the barmaid, and refreshing his inner man with a glass of spirits. He had the reputation of being as discreet and reserved as his employer except during one of his drinking bouts, which generally occurred at stated intervals. Then he

poured forth such a number of amazing tales that it was difficult to know how much was truth and how much the result of his
Hibernian imagination. Mr. Tomling by no means despaired
of catching him in a communicative mood, and worming a few of
his stable secrets from him. At first he thought the matter
would have proved comparatively easy; but he soon found out
that O'Flanaghan, for all his seeming joviality and love of a convivial glass, was a wary bird. It required an astonishing number
of convivial glasses to make him unburthen himself. He would
talk on almost any other subject, but directly Mr. Tomling
delicately alluded to the horses under his charge he dexterously
managed to change the conversation. Baulked in his endeavours Tomling resolved to wait until the day of the race, especially
as the barmaid had confidently informed him that O'Flanaghan
was sure to exceed on that occasion. "He's been sober now
for three whole weeks," she said, "and I'm expecting him to
break out every day. He never goes longer than a fortnight
as a rule, and when he's in liquor—really in liquor I mean—
you can just do what you like with him. His tongue runs on
ever so."

When the eventful morning arrived Tomling proceeded comfortably to the racecourse in a one-horse gig, the property of a
friendly publican of his acquaintance, and, as luck would have
it, the first person he set eyes on was O'Flanaghan, superintending the saddling of Mr. Rickerby s horse, a slashing chestnut
with four white stockings and an uneasy eye.

"Good-morning, Mr. O'Flanaghan," he said, in his most con-
ciliatory manner. "We are fortunate in having such a nice,
fine day, and I hope I see you well."

"'Deed thin, Misther Tomling," responded the Irishman
graciously, "I am that; an' I hope yourself is the same."

He was greatly gratified by this public notice from so great a
man as Sir Philip Verschoyle's stud groom.

"Thank you," answered Tomling. "My health's pretty fair,
although I've only just got over a bad cold. Colds have been
unusually prevalent this spring. The east winds touch up
everybody whose chest is at all weak. That's a decentish looking horse of yours. Are you going to win to-day by any chance?"

O'Flanaghan wagged his head mysteriously from side to side.

"There's no telling. We moight if there waren't anither
animal going to run better nor ours, and one as can clane gallop
away from Misther Rickerby's mount."

"Indeed," said Tomling, "and what horse might that be?"

"He's a horse as yer know, me good friend," rejoined O'Flanaghan, with an impudent wink. "A horse called Patrick the
First, by Solon, out of Mavourneen. Bedad! but it was a bad

day for us when the capting went and sold him.   I felt riddy to cry when I heard Pathrick was to change stables."

"Your tears must be curiously near the surface, Mr. O'Flanaghan."

"A warm heart, Misther Tomling, a warm heart.   A mither could not love her child better nor I did that animal.   He was the best as ever I had the charge of, and such a goer!   It was a plisure to see the clane manger of a morning, it was.   Not an oat left behoind.   Thims the sort for work."

"I agree with you ; still, a racehorse requires something more than a ravenous appetite, though undoubtedly it's a good thing in its way.   However, since you thought so highly of Patrick the First I presume you did not let him go for a song, and that your governor got a good price for him ? "

"Price, Misther Tomling !   By the Blessed Virgin and all the Saints, no price could be good enough for Pathrick.   He's worth his weight in gold.   If I was a gintleman I'd write out a cheque for a thousand pounds for him to-morrow, and think meself lucky. Me heart, it was like a lump of lead when I saw him go out of the stable for the last toime.   He was a credit to it, and we may wait miny a year before we come across his loike again.   A Patrick is only foaled once in a centhury."

Tomling did not believe a word of the above panegyric, and therefore listened to it somewhat impatiently.

"How about your treasure's forelegs?" he inquired curtly. "Did they never give you any trouble, because, if so, you're cleverer than I am."

"Throuble, Misther Tomling.   What! throuble with forelegs like thim?   No, niver, niver.   All the toime we had him he niver once went lame."

"And how long did you have him, Mr. O'Flanaghan ?   Perhaps you would oblige me by answering that question."

The cunning O'Flanaghan scratched his head and put on a perplexed expression.   He felt that he had made a slip, and set to work to remedy it.

"'Deed now, but I can't remimber.   There's so miny horses coming and going in our stable that unless I looked in me book I ralely could not tell ye.   It moight have been months, and it moight have been weeks ; but me memory's that bad for the life of me I can't recollect."

"Can't, won't," muttered Tomling, under his breath.   "You're about as clever as they make 'em, you are.   However, you've not done with me yet."

Finding there was nothing to be gained from O'Flanaghan as long as he continued sober, Tomling now changed his tactics. He talked cheerfully for several minutes on indifferent subjects, and then suddenly complained of the cold, and proposed a little stimulant.

"I don't know how you feel, Mr. O'Flanaghan," he said, with a bland smile, as soon as Mr. Rickerby had mounted his horse and disappeared from the saddling paddock; "but I'm uncommonly chilly. The sun is warm, but the wind is keen, and one feels as if one wanted something to resist it. What do you say to a nice hot glass of whisky and water just to keep the cold out? I believe we should both be the better for it."

"And, indade, Misther Tomling, I am sartin ye're right," rejoined O'Flanaghan vivaciously. "'Tis meself as feels the sharp wind creeping through me bones."

"Shall we move on then?"

"I have no objection, no objection whatever. Me constitooshun is delicate, and Docthor McCarthy, of Limerick, he said to me years ago, 'Jim, me boy, if ye iver feel inclined to take a drop stick to the whisky.' And bedad! I've followed his advice from that day to this. There niver was a docthor to understand me constitooshun loike Docthor McCarthy. He's a powerful cliver practitioner, and sets whisky far afore all the pills and medicine stuffs."

Finding his companion willing the wily Tomling repaired to a booth hard by, and plied him with liquor until his little grey eyes twinkled and the strings of his tongue began to get unloosed. But although he now talked in a vague, rambling way he kept his wits sufficiently about him to retain the very information which his friend was so anxious to obtain. Many people might have given up the attempt in despair, but Mr. Tomling was a man of strong tenacity of purpose. He went doggedly to work, and, like a bulldog, never loosed his hold once he had succeeded in closing with his victim. He saw, however, that it would not do to hurry O'Flanaghan. The process of intoxication was well started, but it proved expensive standing treat. He had already disbursed three shillings and sixpence, and having regard to the Irishman's capacity determined to wait until Lord Midlandshire's marquee—for which they had tickets—should be thrown open. The race, too, was now about to come off. The two worthies watched it side by side, and both agreed in condemning Sir Philip's horsemanship.

"Och! the grand ould horse," exclaimed O'Flanaghan every time Corkscrew successfully cleared a fence. "He's just the foinest lepper as iver looked through a bridle. I wish Misther Jack were on his back."

"Sir Philip's making too much use of him," said Tomling, disapprovingly. "If that's the way he is accustomed to ride in the hunting field I don't wonder at his bringing me back so many cripples.

" It's the hands and the jidgment he's wanting in.   Begorrah ! but what's the man after now? " as Sir Philip charged the fence into the road.   " He must have taken lave of his sinses."

" He's down ; no, he's not," cried Tomling, excitedly.   " By Jove! though, it's all over.   He's done for his horse."

" An' no one to blame but himself," said O'Flanaghan, with severity ; " though no doubt he'll try to put it on to Pathrick. Misther Jack is going strong and well.   The money's on all roight, and he means winning if he can."

" He don't always ride honest, eh? "

" That depinds, Misther Tomling ; that depinds entirely on circumstances."

Certainly the surprise was general when the favourite Paragona fell at the last fence, and Mr. Rickerby's Jack o' Lantern, who had been looked upon as a complete outsider, the betting being twenty to one against him, sailed in an easy winner. O'Flanaghan's delight, as can he imagined, knew no bounds, and in the triumph of the congratulations showered upon him he very nearly succeeded in evading Mr. Tomling altogether.

" By George ! " that worthy soliloquised.   " They are a clever lot, and no mistake.   What between getting rid of a worthless animal at a high figure, and securing such long odds, and keeping the winner so dark they must have made a pot of money. Won't Sir Philip be in a wax.   They've done him brown, and no mistake."

The marquee was now quite full, and O'Flanaghan drank so many healths to " Jack o' Lanthern " that before long he experienced considerable difficulty in standing upright, and began to roll about much as if he were at sea.   At this juncture a gracious arm was linked in his, and Tomling's voice said persuasively, " It's very hot in here.   Let's go for a stroll."

Any power of resistance possessed by O'Flanaghan had by this time completely vanished, and he allowed his footsteps to be guided to a quiet spot in the rear of the tent, where there was just room for two people to stand between it and a straggly fence which bordered the road.   Tomling was now pretty sure of his man.

" Do you smoke, Mr. O'Flanaghan ? " he inquired, as a preliminary.

" I do, Misther Tomling."

" Ah ! I thought so.   May I offer you a pinch of tobacco ? "

Nothing loath O'Flanaghan inserted a dirty finger and thumb into the pouch presented him, and proceeded to fill and light his pipe.   It proved a work of time, and once or twice he was forced to reel against his companion for support.

" The atmosphere's oppressive," he said.   " I niver feel dizzy loike this excipt when there's a powerful lot of electricity in the air. I think I shall have to remimber Doethor McCarthy's advice and take a drop more whisky jist to stiddy meself."

"You'd better smoke your pipe first," advised Tomling. "The excitement has been a bit too much for you."

"That's it, Misther Tomling, the excitement. Nothing but the excitement. I'm a sober man nat'rally. I assure you, I'm so—so—sober."

"Yes, yes; I know," interrupted Tomling hastily. "You're a grand fellow. I'm proud to number myself among your friends."

"Frinds! I tell yer, me heart wint out to yer from the first. It's loike a brother I feel towards ye."

"Then we needn't have any secrets."

"Sacrates, Misther Tomling! Me have sacrates which I would not impart to my bist frind! Sorrah a bit of it."

"Well, now, look here. You and I don't want to quarrel, do we? But I'm afraid there'll be a row between the governors."

"A row? Yer don't say so. And what might it be about, pray?"

"I don't suppose Sir Philip will be best pleased at Patrick's breaking down. Between ourselves it was only what I expected."

"And what iveryone moight have expected who knew a horse from a cow," interposed O'Flanaghan, with a drunken leer.

"Precisely; but, unfortunately, my master was under the impression he stood a good chance to win, and now that Patrick the First is done for he may—mind you, I don't say that he will, but it is just possible he may—suspect foul play."

O'Flanaghan burst into a loud laugh. His potations had chased away any remaining sense of discretion.

"Ha, ha! Patrick the First, man, why what are ye talking about? His name it is Corkscrew."

"Oh! indeed. Names are easily changed and pedigrees invented. Solon, I presume, did not have the honour of siring him?"

"Devil a bit of it. The capting picked him up at Aldridge's one wet afternoon, for forty pounds."

"And the captain being a first-rate artist painted his heels and forehead just by way of keeping his hand in, eh?"

"Ye've hit it to a T, me excellent frind," answered O'Flanaghan, holding his sides with merriment. "Bedad! it was as good as a play. Not one of the gintlemen as fancies thimselves so clever knew th' ould horse again. He had been in the stable iver since last November with the tindon of his off-fore clane sprung. Och! the work we had with it, bandages and fomentations no ind.   To my sartin knowledge he wasn't worth a twinty pound note.   Gad ! but we played Sir Verschoyle a splendid thrick.   The capting hasn't his equal in all the counthree. Jack Rickerby's cute, but he ain't to be compared with the ither."

" You mean that he is not quite such a big rogue ? " said Tomling, feeling a growing desire to knock his "bist frind " down.

" Rogue ! " exclaimed O'Flanaghan, enthusiastically.   " I tell yer, Misther Tomling, and ye can take me word for it, that the capting's far and away the grandest, dammedest rogue iver I see in my loife."

" A proud distinction, especially as I should imagine you had seen a good many, and were yourself entitled to a foremost place."

" Do ye think," resumed O'Flanaghan, with a look of reproach, "that I should stick to me master if he wasn't what I tell ye ? "

" No ; I should not dream of offering you so great an insult. Speaking from personal experience I should say you were a pair."

" Right ye are, Misther Tomling.   We're a pair, and may we niver be anything else is the pious wish of Timothy O'Flanaghan. Ha, ha, ha ! " And he began to laugh again in a maudlin way. "We sould Corkscrew in the nick of toime, for the tiller it was getting uncommonly impty, and the wages more and more irregular.   Howiver, now we're sit up on our legs for the nixt month or two."

"I suppose you haven't any idea what price our governor paid yours for the horse ? " said Tomling, with an assumption of indifference.

" 'Dade now !   An' why should ye suppose me so ignorant ? There's moighty little goes on in our place that your humble sarvint don't foind out.   It's no aisy matter to kape a sacrate from him.   An' jist to prove to ye that what I say is thrue the price paid was five hundred guineas, neither more nor less."

" Five hundred guineas ! " exclaimed Tomling, astounded at the magnitude of the sum.   "Are you in earnest ? "

"Would ye accuse me of a falsehood?" said O'Flanaghan, with tipsy solemnity.

" And you actually mean to tell me that Sir Philip gave that price for the horse ? "

" He was so plased with his bargain he sint the cheque over by hand the nixt mornin'   That I know for a fact."

"Well, I'm blowed !   Human folly can go no further.   You've done us once, Mr. O'Flanaghan ; but let me give you a fair warning.   You won't do us again in a hurry ; and this country shall be made too hot for you and that precious master of yours.

Mine ain't up to much. I don't attempt to praise him, but he's a long sight better than yours; and directly I get home I shall take very good care to let him know how he has been swindled."

"Hist!" said O'Flanaghan, rolling his eyes in alarm. "What is that? I heard somebody moving in the road."

"I don't care if you did. Everybody is welcome to hear what I say. I am not ashamed of my words—no, nor of my actions either."

"Oh! Misther Tomling. I've trated ye loike a frind. Shure, an' ye won't betray me, will ye?"

"Betray you, you infernal rascal! If you attempt to open your lips again I'll knock you into a cocked hat. Drunken beasts like you are a disgrace to our profession, and I'm ashamed to call myself stud groom after seeing what unworthy specimens belong to so honourable a calling."

"Hush, man! don't talk so loud. I tell ye there is someone listening."

Impelled by curiosity Tomling stooped and looked through a hole in the hedge. He saw a man sitting by the wayside drawing on a hunting boot, which had evidently blistered his foot.

"By Jove!" he exclaimed, in an altered voice. "It's Sir Philip."

"Yes," shouted the baronet, springing to his feet. "And he has heard every word of what you and this scoundrel have been saying." His face was inflamed with anger; his eyes were wild and bloodshot.

Tomling felt a shock go through his whole frame; then he recollected that his words had been prudent, and could not tell much against him. He had taken his master's part, and, in spite of the temptation, had refrained throughout the conversation from abusing him. Conscious of his own virtue he realised that the moment of triumph for which he had waited so patiently had at length arrived. Therefore, he did not quail beneath Sir Philip's infuriated gaze, but, after a brief hesitation, answered in his suavest, softest tone—

"I knew it was a conspiracy, sir. I knew it all along. But as I had strict orders to hold my tongue I was bound to obey them. If you had not closed my mouth I could have spared you the mortification of breaking down in public."

The baronet glared at him in speechless rage. He realised that Tomling was trying to assert his superiority and endeavouring to humiliate him still more.

With a muttered oath he turned away, and, chartering the first empty fly, ordered the driver to drive him straight back to Beechlands.

Tomling placed his large hands over his round waistcoat, and stroked it complacently.

"Aha!" he murmured, whilst a smile illumined his countenance. " Every dog has his day, and I flatter myself this is mine. If I'm not very much mistaken Sir Philip will be careful how he cheeks me in future. He's got as good as he gave at any rate, and henceforth I shall rest easy. Here! get away. I've done with you." And so saying he administered a push to Mr. O'Flanaghan which sent him flying full length on the grass.

CHAPTER XXXI.

A BACHELOR DINNER PARTY.

SIR PHILIP was in such a towering passion that it did not occur to him for some time to inquire who had won the race.

When he learnt of the flyman that the much coveted prize had fallen to Mr. Rickerby's share his indignation knew no bounds. He felt more than ever convinced that he had been cajoled into giving a ridiculous sum for an absolutely worthless horse, when all the while the confederates had a much better one in the stable with which no doubt from the first they made up their minds to win. He realised the full extent of Captain Dashwood's duplicity, and perceived that he had been nothing more than a tool in his hands, falling like a foolish fly into the net so artfully spread.

Sooner or later the story was sure to get abroad, and he should find himself the laughing-stock of the whole county. He gnashed his teeth at the thought, for he had not yet arrived at an age to bear ridicule philosophically. It was not so much the loss of the money which enraged him as the knavery and deceit from men professing to call themselves his friends, and who had dined repeatedly at his table. Feeling that he could not trust himself to meet them, and that in his present state he was capable of throttling or horse-whipping them, he purposely left the racecourse, intending, before taking any decided action in the matter, to turn it over in his mind. This, under the circumstances, was a prudent resolve.

As soon as Sir Philip reached Beechlands, he retired to his own room, and gave orders not to be disturbed. His temples throbbed, and his blood seemed literally on fire ; but in spite of the confusion of his brain, one thought stood out clear above every other. He would have his revenge. He did not quite know how, when, or where, but, as surely as there was a God above, he would have it. No one should insult him with impunity. In spite of the five hundred guineas put out of his pocket into theirs, by should live to regret the transaction.　There would be no more dinners—no more presents of game for them in the future.　They would soon find out the difference.

Then all of a sudden he remembered that he had invited his foes to dine that very evening.　A dark smile spread slowly over his face as he recalled the fact.　He began to see a way now of punishing them according to their deserts.　Growing calmer at the prospect, he sat down in an arm-chair, and deliberately worked out a scheme of retaliation.　In spite of all that had come and gone, he still held the trump card, if only he could curb his passion strongly enough to play it properly.　If he did but control himself sufficiently to clearly tell the tale of his wrongs before a company of impartial hearers, he felt persuaded that they would be unanimous in condemning the conduct of his former friends. He fancied he could make it precious hot for these gentlemen. It would not suit their book at all to be cut by every respectable acquaintance, and publicly denounced as rogues and swindlers. Their reputation was not so good already that it could afford to bear being blown upon.　Yet this was what he meant to do.　By degrees, as he sat there with bent head and knit brow, he arranged a programme to his satisfaction.　He would not put Captain Dashwood or Mr. Rickerby off; or give them the slightest warning.　On the contrary, he would receive them with ceremonious politeness, and when they least expected mischief hurl the bombshell over their heads.　Taken thus unawares they must needs confess their sins.　The idea pleased him.　There was a refinement of malice about it which soothed his overstrung nerves, and restored him to comparative good-humour.

Arrived at this stage, it occurred to him that he was hungry and had had no luncheon; so he rang the bell, and ordered his valet to bring him something to eat and drink.

" We shall be two-and-twenty to dinner to-night," he said to the man.　" Let the cook know, and when Lady Verschoyle returns say I wish to see her.　She is not aware we have so large a party coming, for I forgot to mention it this morning."

He ate a hearty meal, washed down by liberal draughts of brandy and soda, and after that fell into a heavy sleep, from which he was only awakened by his wife's arrival.

Bligh came in looking unusually happy and animated.　For a few hours she had thrown off the burden of her married life, and given herself over to the enjoyment of the moment.　It was a new experience to her to be made much of, and every woman feels flattered by being noticed and deferred to.　Bligh had had a success.　Ever since her fall Lord Midlandshire had treated her with peculiar kindness, and to-day his attentions had been unremitting.　He viewed the race from her and insisted on giving her his arm to the marquee before all the other ladies. But what was even yet more agreeable, Bligh discovered him to be a man of high culture and intelligence; and the pleasure of conversing with someone whose ideas soared above the jargon of sport, to which she had been forced to listen all the winter, was so great that she felt like a different being. Lord Midlandshire's conversation transplanted her into another world—a world not of mere amusement and frivolous frittering away of opportunities, but one of politics, real work, patriotism, and noble endeavour. She could not help comparing his life with Philip's, and sighing at the want of ambition, energy, and enterprise displayed by so many men of the younger generation. Were the women to blame because they were not satisfied with such husbands, and wanted ones they could really look up to? It was a difficult question, but Bligh thought it accounted for a good deal of the discontent rife among the wives of the nineteenth century. Lord Midlandshire, in talking of the problems of the day, had lightly touched upon that of matrimony, but feeling the delicacy of the subject, she had dexterously changed it. Nevertheless, it set her thinking—and remarks calculated to provoke thought were so rare since she became Lady Verschoyle that they produced a bracing and stimulating effect upon her mind.

For some time she had not missed her husband. When she did she grew uneasy at his prolonged absence, and returned from the racecourse early. Hearing he was at home, she went at once to his room. The wholesome excitement and fresh air had lent her cheeks a colour. A stray lock of soft hair was blown about her face. She looked deserving of Lord Midlandshire's description, "A dear little woman; not exactly pretty, you know, but ever so much better; genuine and intelligent, and awfully nice."

Sir Philip gave a drunken snore, and woke up with a start.

"Oh! you've come back, have you?" he said, stretching himself sleepily.

"Yes. I was afraid something had happened." She had returned, intending to be cheerful and pleasant, but somehow the very sight of him repelled her, and reminded her of the chains which she was bound to wear through life.

Her face grew instantly grave, and lost its bright expression.

"Something did happen," he returned, sulkily. "My cursed horse broke down."

"Yes, so I saw. Poor fellow! I am terribly sorry for him. Is he very badly hurt?"

"He is done for altogether."

"What a sad pity! I don't wonder you are vexed. But why did you go home without letting me know, Philip? I could not imagine what had become of you, and nobody seemed able to tell me. You were not hurt yourself, were you?"

"No, but I was sick to death of the whole business. So would you have been in my shoes."

"I don't understand."

"It is not necessary that you should." Then a sneer disfigured his countenance, and he added, "So our friend Rickerby won after all?"

"Yes," she replied. "He won quite easily at the end: and somehow or other, I don't think people seemed very pleased at his success. There was no cheering or anything of that sort. I don't know if it is true, but I heard that Mr. Rickerby had gained over a thousand pounds."

"The devil he did!"

"When the report reached Lord Midlandshire's ears," she exclaimed, "he was extremely annoyed to find that such heavy betting had been going on, especially as it appears he particularly requested everyone connected with the race not to let it degenerate into a pounds, shillings, and pence affair."

"His lordship might just as well have appealed to the man in the moon as to our friends Dashwood and Rickerby," said Sir Philip, sarcastically. "I don't suppose those two worthies could refrain from betting to save their lives."

Bligh looked at him in surprise. She was struck by the bitterness of her husband's tone.

"Have you quarrelled?" she asked, feeling that it would be an immense relief if he answered in the affirmative.

"No," he replied, "not yet. But they've treated me very scurvily, not to say dishonestly, and I mean to have it out with them."

"Was it about the horse, Philip?"

"For goodness' sake don't bother me with questions. I'm not in a mood to answer them, and I hate an inquisitive woman."

She changed colour, and appeared about to make a warm retort; then her habitual self-control came to her aid, and she said—

"The mere fact of your no longer being so enamoured of your friends is enough for me. I don't want to know any more. Indeed, I am only too thankful to think that your eyes are at last opened to the true character of the men you have chosen to make your boon companions. From the first they have been false friends, and in my opinion have done you an infinity of harm."

" I swear to do them an equal amount before I've done with them," he retorted, threateningly. " Two can play at that game."

Bligh said nothing. She saw he had been drinking as usual, and knew from experience that when in a state of semi-intoxication he was wont to give vent to excessively bellicose sentiments. Drink generally had the effect of rendering him irritable.

" Well ! " she answered, soothingly, " I'm glad to find you all right, and although you did not succeed in winning the race, you are better off than some people. Poor little Dicky Damer not only broke his leg, but also his animal's neck, and he was so much upset about losing the mare that he cried like a child. For my part, I thought his tears did him great credit, though several of the ladies were laughing at them."

" He's a damned little fool at any time," growled Sir Philip. " And a regular outsider into the bargain. Are you going, Bligh ? " as his wife made a movement towards the door.

" Yes. I thought I would take off my hat and jacket, and then sit with mamma for a little, and tell her the news of the day. Do you want me for anything ? "

" It would not much matter if I did. ' Mamma ' always comes before me in this establishment."

Bligh bridled up at these words.

" I do not think you have any right to make such a statement as that. My mother is an invalid, and therefore requires a certain amount of attention, but give me a single instance if you can of my neglecting you for her. On the contrary, I have always taken pains to consider you first."

He could not deny that his home was much more comfortable since Bligh had assumed the management of it. His mother's rule, though kind and gracious, had not been practical. Under his wife's regime the food was better, his favourite dishes were set before him much more frequently than in former days, the servants attended more punctually to their duties, the fires were regularly kept up, the rooms looked cosier, and last, but not least, the bills were considerably less, in spite of there being several extra mouths to feed. As for his creature comforts, they were studied even to the smallest item. He could not find fault with Bligh, and yet he was discontented. No matter how he behaved, he fancied that because she was his wife he had a right to her affections. He vaguely realised that she did not love him, and even when he went reeling up to bed smelling of brandy and using coarse oaths in her presence, he attributed the entire blame to her of the want of sympathy that existed between them. She was cold, heartless, unwifely ; he, in his own estimation, was not only a man, and therefore incapable of wrong when dealing with the weaker sex, but also all that a husband should be.

Nevertheless, her superiority irritated him. For in his heart of hearts, despite the authority which on every trifling occasion he arrogated to himself, and the dominion and tyranny of his conduct, he knew that he was her inferior. No matter how he bullied and blustered, he never could master her spirit. It soared above his as a skylark soars above a barndoor fowl. Between them stretched an immeasurable gulf, which he was unable to outstride, and for some time past an uneasy sense of failure had begun to steal over him. He realised that for all her outward submission and faultless behaviour, he could not control his wife's thoughts, or prevent them from summing him up at his true worth. Little by little a certain fear of Bligh sprang up within him. Although he tried to resist it, it increased daily. He would rather avoid her eye than meet it; and when she was by he felt ashamed to appear at his worst. Strangely enough, too, although he professed a great contempt for her opinions, and lost no opportunity of laughing at them in public, in reality they made a much deeper impression than he chose to admit.

So in answer to her last speech, he said—

"You never seem to understand a joke, Bligh. I was only in fun, of course; nevertheless, it's a little hard upon me sometimes having to live with a parcel of old women. I think even you must admit that."

"Mamma is very ill," she said, and there was something in her look and voice which silenced him effectually.

"By-the-bye," he said, as if a sudden thought had occurred to him, "we are in for a large dinner-party to-night. I invited a good many of the fellows on the course, and did not know until I came to count them up that even without the ladies we should be twenty-two." Then he paused, and added, awkwardly, "I was wondering, Bligh, as you have done a good deal to-day, and we shall be all gentlemen except the home party, whe—whether," hesitating in his speech, "you would not prefer to stop out."

She jumped at the idea.

"Oh! yes," she cried. "Mamma, your mother, and I can dine in the boudoir. We should prefer it. It will be ever so much nicer. I mean," correcting herself for fear of giving offence, "much nicer for you."

"All right, then," he said. "I'll give orders to that effect."

Bligh went upstairs, delighted at the prospect of spending a quiet evening, and quite unsuspicious of her husband's intentions.

"It's better not to frighten her, especially just now," said Sir

Philip to himself, as she closed the door. " Besides women are always infernally in the way when there is a row going on. They will insist on interfering and taking sides."

At a quarter to eight o'clock the baronet stood in the large drawing-room ready to receive his guests. They arrived by ones and twos, and he apologised for Bligh's absence on the plea of indisposition. It so happened that Captain Dashwood and Mr. Rickerby were the last to turn up. Sir Philip went forward, and shook them effusively by the hand with exaggerated cordiality.

"Delighted to see you," he said, in a loud, artificial voice intended for everyone to hear. "This gathering would have been very incomplete without the hero of the day and his talented coadjutor."

Captain Dashwood shot an inquiring glance at him from the corner of his eye. He could not quite make Sir Philip's manner out. It was just a little too civil to be sincere, especially after the afternoon's defeat. He had expected to find his host in a remarkably bad humour ; instead of which, here he was smiling and benevolent, and apparently with temper unruffled. This amiability differed so much from his ordinary mood, when subjected to the hard usages of adversity, that it set Captain Dashwood on his guard. Knowing Sir Philip as well as he did, he had not been in the room two minutes before he felt that his gaiety was not natural, but merely assumed for some unknown purpose, which conscience whispered boded no good.

" Sit tight, and look out for squalls," he contrived to murmur to Jack Rickerby, as the gentlemen trooped into the dining-room.

Once seated at the table, the conversation soon became general, and it remained so until dinner was brought to a conclusion. Then the men servants retired, after first placing a small army of bottles before Sir Philip. The occasion was a festive one, and as the whole party had taken enough to make them merry, the fun threatened to become uproarious. Tongues were wagging with increasing eloquence, when suddenly the host filled himself a bumper of port, and rose from his seat, glass in hand. Although he had drunk freely up till now he had remained unusually silent.

One-and-twenty pairs of hands began drumming on the table, whilst their owners exclaimed—

" That's right, old boy. Make us a speech."

The flush on Sir Philip's face deepened. The more sober of the company noticed his hand trembled so that several drops of wine fell on to the white cloth, and made an ugly stain. Captain Dashwood tried to catch Jack Rickerby's eye. He had an intuitive presentiment of what was coming, and in order to bear the impending storm with all his wits about him had several times declined to have his glass refilled with champagne. In consequence his head was probably clearer than that of anyone else present.

"Gentlemen," began Sir Philip, speaking in a thick, husky voice, which he vainly sought to clear, " I do not propose to detain you long, which must be my excuse for boldly claiming your attention for a few moments. To get straight to the point, there are some things which society will stand, and some which it won't ; and as I don't wish to be guided by personal feeling alone, I have asked you here to-night for the express purpose of consulting you on a most awkward and delicate matter. Now I want you to tell me frankly what you would think of two men, calling themselves your friends, and professing to be gentlemen, who, for their own ends and purposes, painted up a worthless old screw in order to deceive you."

A murmur of indignation ran through the company. Captain Dashwood and Mr. Rickerby changed colour, and tried not to look conscious.

"What would you say," continued Sir Philip, in tones of rising passion, "if these so-called friends—men, mark you, whom you had trusted and consulted—gave the horse a feigned name and pedigree, and sold him as a steeplechaser for the modest sum of five hundred guineas ? And supposing the very first time you rode this valuable animal he broke down hopelessly ; and you overheard the conspirators' groom laughing at the trick of which you had been the victim, how would you be inclined to take the joke ? It seems to me, gentlemen," he went on, with growing excitement, " that the hunting field is an honourable institution, and we should not tolerate rogues and swindlers among its ranks. I do not know whether you agree with me or not ; but, for my part, I consider it a public duty to prevent my comrades from being fleeced as others have been fleeced before them, and to warn everyone against the scoundrels who do not hesitate to rob a friend, and who possess neither morals nor the commonest instincts of honesty. If you wish to learn their names, there they sit." And so saying, he pointed his finger scornfully, first at Mr. Rickerby, and then at Captain Dashwood.

The latter gentleman's thin lips were set in a hard line. His countenance, though pale, was smiling, and he met the charge with a cool audacity which native impudence and undaunted courage had taught him to maintain in moments of imminent peril.

"I fear that our host has had more to drink than is good for him," he said, in a loud aside to his neighbour. "His manners suffer in proportion as his imagination grows riotous."

"How dare you insinuate that I am drunk?" thundered Sir Philip. "You can't get out of it in that way, you blackguard."

Captain Dashwood rose in his turn.

"Gentlemen," he said, "since our entertainer has set the example of appealing to you, I feel that I cannot do better than follow in his footsteps. You have all heard the epithet he has just made use of. In common self-defence, I beg to state that there are always two sides to every question. You have listened to Sir Philip Verschoyle's, perhaps you will now be so good as to listen to mine. Briefly put, the matter lies in a nutshell. I go out hunting, and ride a horse which our friend, whose nature, as we all know, is somewhat jealous, imagines to be faster than his own. Whereupon he breaks the Tenth Commandment, and covets his neighbour's goods. His next step is to beg me to name my own price for the gee. I answer that I have no desire to sell him, or to disturb our friendship by a quarrel. He insists, and offers three, four, five hundred guineas. Well! gentlemen," and the speaker took a comprehensive glance around, as if to ascertain which way public opinion was setting, "I don't attempt to defend myself. I am a poor man, and the temptation was great. Against my better judgment, I yielded to it, after repeatedly advising Sir Philip not to effect the purchase, but he would not listen to a word of remonstrance, so set was he on having the horse. Was it my fault the animal broke down? He was (he spoke in the past tense) as good and honest a hunter as ever I threw a leg across. You all saw in what manner he was ridden to-day. How many of you here present can produce a horse not liable to meet with a similar disaster, if his rider took the liberties with him that Sir Philip took? He never spared him. He forced him along through the heavy plough, and did not ease the poor brute for a second. Horses are made of flesh and blood like ourselves. They are not mere machines ; moreover, their organisation is so delicate that a very slight thing suffices to throw it out of gear. I venture to contend that any animal might have collapsed in the circumstances. Because Sir Philip lost his head, and rode at an impossible fence, I really fail to see why I should be held responsible ; especially when I made a point of declining all responsibility at the time of purchase. Is it fair to blame me because Sir Philip Verschoyle did not win the race? Had he come in first, do you suppose for one moment he would have brought this charge? The answer is No ; and he knows it as well as I do. Gentlemen," concluded Captain Dashwood, satisfied with the impression he had evidently made upon his audience, "the verdict lies with you, and greatly as I regret this unhappy quarrel, I am perfectly prepared to abide by your decision."

His clear, penetrating voice rang through the room. Like an accomplished fencer, he seemed to possess in perfection the art of thrusting at the weak points of his enemy's armour.

Sir Philip felt instinctively that by a few well-chosen words he had adroitly contrived to turn the tables. Instead of humbling his opponent to the very dust. he now saw that he himself stood a good chance of coming second best out of the contest. This conviction rendered him frantic.

"How about the white star and the painted heels," he shouted, quivering with rage.

"Merely your fancy," responded Captain Dashwood, with unblushing effrontery. "People are very apt to imagine all sorts of impossible things when they have had a skin full of liquor. Knock off the drink, my dear fellow, or it will be the ruin of you."

Clever as he was, Captain Dashwood had overshot the mark. If he had not made that speech, he would have fared better. It goaded Sir Philip into a fury.

"You lying hound," he cried ; and so saying, he threw the glass which he held in his hand straight into Captain Dashwood's face. It hit the mark, and in another second that gentleman's highly-glazed shirt front was dyed red with wine and blood which gushed from a deep gash on his forehead.

He pushed back his chair, pale. but no longer smiling.

"By heaven," he said, in a voice choked with passion. "You shall pay for this." And he flew at his adversary's throat.

"Come on," retorted Sir Philip. "I've been itching all the evening to give you the thrashing you deserve."

The two men grappled with each other, and a scene of wild disorder ensued. Some took one side. some the other ; but the general opinion seemed to be that the opponents had better fight it out : although several of the milder spirits vainly strove to part the combatants. All of a sudden Captain Dashwood's foot caught in the table-cloth, he tripped, and fell with stunning force against the fender. A deafening crash of china followed his downfall. Sir Philip stood panting for breath, his fists doubled, and glaring about him with wild, bloodshot eyes. Then he administered a kick to his prostrate foe. Englishmen, as a rule, are lovers of fair play. At this act of unprovoked brutality, cries of "Shame, shame," resounded through the room, and forcible hands were laid on him.

"Let me go," he cried. "I'll kick the craven life out of him."

"Nonsense," said Mr. Stainton Moresly, one of the oldest and most pacific of the party. "The man is hurt. He is stunned, I believe. You don't want to murder him, surely?"

"I don't care a hang if I do!" And the baronet wrenched himself free.

To what extremities he might have proceeded it is impossible to say, for at this juncture an unlooked-for diversion was created. The door opened, and Bligh rushed into the room. One glance at the disordered table, the prostrate man, the broken china, and her husband's threatening attitude sufficed to prove how disgraceful was the scene that had taken place. Living in constant dread of some catastrophe, she knew in an instant that her worst fears were realised, and that Sir Philip had openly exposed his infirmity. Her one thought was to get him away before any further mischief could be inflicted. Without pausing to notice the guests, she walked straight up to him, and laid her hand on his arm. He started at her touch.

"Oh! Philip," she said, trembling, "what is this dreadful quarrel about?"

He stared at her with drunken anger.

"Go away," he said. "What are you doing here? How dare you interfere!"

"We heard the noise," she faltered, "and were so terribly frightened! Your mother has fainted."

"Bah! Women are always fainting. Come, take yourself off. You're in the way."

She looked round imploringly at the strong men, with their red coats and red faces.

"Won't any of you help me to get him quietly away? Surely—surely you must see that he is not well to-night." And she turned towards them with a gesture which struck compassion in the hearts of all present.

"Bligh," cried Sir Philip, angrily. "I order you to leave the room."

"I do not want to stay—I shall never forget the sight I have seen to-night, but," and her voice grew firmer. "I cannot go, and leave you here."

"Don't you hear what I say?"

"Yes, but I will not go alone."

"Damnation! then I'll make you." And, beside himself, he lifted his hand and struck the woman who in two or three months' time would bear him a child a heavy blow on her delicate arm. She tottered and almost fell, but her purpose remained unchanged. He was mad, dangerous, and it was her duty to shield him from himself.

"Gentlemen," she said, "if you are gentlemen, cut this evening's festivities short. Go to your own homes, and out of pity to me and to him," glancing at her husband, "leave us alone. It is the one kindness you can do me. As for you," she went on, addressing Jack Rickerby and Captain Dashwood, the latter of whom had now regained his feet, "your influence over Philip has been uniformly bad. You have played on his worst passions, and have made no effort to lead him in a right direction. I owe you small thanks. You are cruel enemies to me, and if the treatment you have received this evening has not been good, we can cry quits, and wish each other good-bye. Go!" And she pointed towards the door. Her face was perfectly white, but her eyes were ablaze, and made every man in the room feel ashamed of himself. One by one they withdrew silently.

To-morrow, no doubt, the tale would spread throughout the county, and there would be fine gossip; but to-night she held her own royally.

At last husband and wife were by themselves. Sir Philip stood looking sullenly into the fire. The action of striking a woman had sobered him.

Bligh rang the bell without loss of time.

"Take your master to his room," she said to the butler. "He feels indisposed, and wishes to go to bed."

"I never said so——" he began.

"You will be better there."

He dared not meet her eyes after what had happened; and obeyed like a baby. Bligh remained conqueror of the field. But what a victory! It left her too utterly shamed and disgusted even to feel anger. The disgrace crushed her to the ground; for henceforth every one would know that Sir Philip was a drunkard, and had struck his wife. It was not so much of herself she thought as of him; the wreck, the ruin, the wasted life. A profound sadness raised her above mere personal resentment. The pity and misery of it was so great!

As she stole wearily upstairs, her mother-in-law peeped out of her bedroom door.

"Bligh!" she whispered, horrified by the dejected expression of the young wife's face, "what is the matter?"

"They were quarrelling," Bligh answered, in a strained, unnatural voice, "and Philip struck me before everybody."

"My poor girl. How terrible! Can you bear it?"

Bligh looked away towards the room which was her mother's.

"Hush!" she said, "don't pity me. I must."

CHAPTER XXXII.

"TAKE ME WITH YOU."

It was perhaps, a good thing for Bligh in one sense that during the weeks which ensued her mind was prevented from dwelling too exclusively on her own affairs. Mrs. Burton's illness assumed more and more dangerous proportions. The local doctor was wholly unable to relieve the gravity of her symptoms, and, acting with Sir Philip's consent, Bligh called in Mr. Donnington. She had great faith in him, and looked forward anxiously to his visit. A week passed, however, before he was able to obey her summons, and even in that short time Mrs. Burton grew rapidly worse. Alas! when he came he was unable to bestow much comfort. He told Bligh plainly that the terrible malady from which her mother suffered had not only broken out afresh, but also made fearful inroads on her constitution. A further operation was possible; but, considering how little permanent the effects of the last one had proved, he could not conscientiously advise it.

"Mrs. Burton is so weak," he said, "that I fear it would only be putting her to needless pain."

"Are you going to leave her to die then?" cried Bligh, with the tears rolling down her cheeks.

He gave a little gentle cough.

"My dear Lady Verschoyle, don't think that I do not feel for you; but would you have her stay? See how she suffers, and we are powerless to give any real relief."

"I know, I know," sobbed Bligh, fairly breaking down. "It is dreadfully selfish of me. I ought not to consider myself; but life will be so lonely when she is gone."

"Is not death sometimes kinder than life? You would agree with me if you had seen so much suffering as I have."

"I agree with you now, only," and her voice broke suddenly, "it is hard for those who remain. They cannot help feeling the separation. If I could go too I should not mind."

"You are young, and your time has not yet come. If you give way like this I shall regret having spoken out so unreservedly."

She dried her eyes.

"I . . . . th, Mr. Donnington, bad as it is. At least now," and she sighed heavily, "I can make the most of the time that is left us to be together."

"Dear Lady Verschoyle," he said, with an unconscious touch of bitterness in his voice, "think yourself lucky that when your mother dies your mind will remain stored with tender memories, which are a priceless possession, and of which no one can rob you. Children who have never known a mother's love, whose warm little hearts have been repeatedly frozen by some cold and indifferent woman, wholly deficient in maternal sentiment, are the ones to be pitied. They go through the world feeling that they have been defrauded of the affection which was their due and which ought to have been theirs by rights. Nothing ever repays them for the loss."

Bligh held out her hand in silent sympathy. She felt, without more words, that his childhood had not been happy.

After Mr. Donnington left she devoted herself almost entirely to the invalid. If Sir Philip showed signs of jealousy, which he occasionally did, she looked at him with eyes rendered red by weeping, and said in a subdued tone: "It will not last long. Let me be with her whilst I can." And her deep sorrow appealed even to his dull senses. Since the night of the dinner party he had been unusually quiet, and to a great extent kept out of his wife's way. He avoided being alone with her as much as possible, and in a clumsy, shamefaced manner sought to make amends for his conduct. Once or twice he even tried to express his regret for what had happened; but her heart was hard and bitter against him, and the affront was too great and too recent for her to be able to say freely, "I forgive." She tolerated him, and that was all. And he, realising what a barrier his unmanly act had raised up between them, grew sullen and reserved. In short, things were not going well with the married couple. She was falling back more and more upon her own resources, growing concentrated, introspective, and analytical; whilst he, conscious of the wrong done, degenerated from day to day, and flew to the bottle for consolation. It would have required a strong helping hand to save him. His wife had done her best, but he had repulsed and estranged her, and now she was too preoccupied to devote much time or attention to him. So they drifted apart; not swiftly, but gradually and slowly, as is often the case when once an irreparable breach has been made in a woman's dignity and self-respect.

One morning when Bligh entered Mrs. Burton's room, she found the invalid sitting up in bed and reading a letter. She was evidently suffering from some unwonted excitement, for her yellow cheeks were faintly red, as if the unaccustomed blood had warmed them, and in her hollow, sunken eyes there gleamed a feverish light. Bligh saw at once that her condition had undergone a change, and that some emotion outside of the every day experiences was responsible for it.

"What is the matter, mother dear ?" she inquired, advancing to the bedside and sprinkling a few drops of eau-de-Cologne about so as to chase away the fetid odour which filled the room.

"I have had news, Bligh; wonderful news," answered Mrs. Burton. "Read that." And she thrust the letter into her daughter's hand.

Bligh perused its contents. They ran as follows : —

"DEAR MADAM,—By the conditions of the late Miss Mary Frazer's will we have great pleasure in informing you that the sum of four hundred a year is placed at your entire disposal, with absolute power to leave it to your heirs or assignees. Further particulars will follow by the next post. Awaiting instructions, we beg to remain, dear madam,
"Your obedient servants,
"DANBY, FERRERS, DANBY, AND SON,
"Lincoln's Inn Fields."

Bligh returned the letter to its envelope. With a pang of sorrow she realised that as far as her mother was concerned the bequest came too late. It could not restore her to health or alter the existing state of things.

"I suppose this was the Miss Mary Frazer," she said, "of whom I have sometimes heard you speak ?"

"Yes ; she and I used to be great friends. As girls we were at school together, and long ago Mary said laughingly that if she did not marry and died before me she would provide for me in her will. I never thought anything more of the matter. Just about the time when I first met your poor father Mary was engaged to a young man with property in Ireland. His story was a very sad one. I forget if I have ever told it you."

"No," said Bligh; "never."

"A fortnight before the wedding was to have taken place," continued Mrs. Burton, "he found it necessary to make some fresh arrangements with his tenants. Times were troublous and the Land League agitators even in those days had turned all the people's heads. A meeting was held, at which they demanded thirty per cent. reduction. Mary's *fiancé* could not see his way to granting more than fifteen, for the rents were already extremely low. Two nights afterwards, as he was driving out to dinner in an open car, he was shot at from behind a stone wall. The bullet lodged in the unfortunate young man's right temple, and took fatal effect. He threw up his arms, fell from the car, and died without a sigh. As is usual in these cases, nobody had the slightest idea who had done the deed. The murderer appeared endowed with the gift of invisibility, for although both in coming and going to the spot he must have passed through a thickly populated district, not a soul had seen him."

" Shameful ! " said Bligh. " What about poor Mary ? "

" It well-nigh broke her heart when the news was communicated to her. For many months she was overwhelmed with grief, but after a while she recovered sufficiently to think that she ought to do something with her life, and although she could no longer look for personal happiness it was her duty, especially as she had means of her own, to promote that of others. So she went out to Canada with a number of fallen girls whom she had previously trained as maid-servants, established a Home in Quebec for the relief of women and children, and ever since has remained doing good work. We have not met for nearly twenty years, though we corresponded occasionally. Poor Mary ! " and Mrs. Burton put her handkerchief to her eyes. " It grieves me to know that she is dead."

" She was a brave, good woman," said Bligh. " But no doubt she is glad to be at rest. You need not weep for her, mother dear. Women like Miss Frazer, who have lived pure lives and worked for the welfare of their fellow-creatures, do not often fear death."

" It is strange why our western nations should be so afraid of dying, when nearly all eastern races view the approach of death calmly," observed Mrs. Burton, with a dreamy look in her dim eyes. " It seems to point that the imagination is responsible for much of the alarm which we undoubtedly feel. A Chinaman is comparatively callous. And yet the curious part to my mind is we are Christians, and, therefore, presumably possessed of higher knowledge ; whilst they, at least so we are told, are heathens."

" Do you not think," said Bligh, " that this state of things proceeds in great measure from the wide difference existing between the theory and the practice of Christianity ? The former is nearly perfect, but the latter leaves much to be desired. For instance, we are taught theoretically to cultivate faith as against logic. Practically the lives of most intelligent people are ordered by reason, and the higher their intellectual perceptions the more difficult it becomes for them to preserve a state of childlike belief. Again, we are told that it is easier for a rich man to go through the eye of a needle than to enter the kingdom of Heaven. According to this doctrine no devout Christian should aspire to obtain wealth. Yet, looking round one in the world, what does one see? Nothing but a consuming desire for money-making, directly opposed to the teaching of the Gospels. Numbers of Christians are Christians in name only. They are not sincere, and equivocate both with their conscience and their religion. Consequently, when the reaper mows them down with his ' sickle keen ' very few of them are willing to say good-bye to life. They would like to wait a little longer, just so as to correct their errors and make sure of a place in Paradise."

" I doubt whether you take the mere physical element sufficiently into consideration," said Mrs. Burton thoughtfully. " It alone is difficult to overcome, for there is always some material force which chains us to earth as long as breath remains in the body." She paused for a moment, held out her hand, and added: " And then there are those we love. It is terribly painful to be forced to leave them; but still more so when we know that our dear ones are not happy, and dark clouds of sorrow and suffering roll over their beloved heads."

Her words were so full of tender significance that Bligh could not choose but apply the sick woman's speech to herself.

" If you mean me, mother," she said quickly, " I am happy— at least," colouring at the falsehood, " as happy as most people. I have a fine house, horses and carriages, every comfort. What more can I want ? "

Mrs. Burton shook her head.

" My darling, you cannot deceive me. They might be enough for some women, but they are not enough for you. Do you think I have lived under this roof and not seen what goes on? I, who have the loving eyes of a mother? Oh ! Bligh, I do not know if it is right for me to express my concern, but from the bottom of my heart I pity you. What cuts me to the quick is I blame myself for all that has happened. I ought to have guessed the truth and shielded you, instead of basely profiting by your misery."

" Mother, what do you mean ? is your mind wandering ? "

" Often I wish it would ; but, on the contrary, since this last illness I begin to see things clearly and as they are. Your marriage has all along been a great puzzle to me. There was something behind which I did not understand. I never thought you were a girl to marry a man for mere ease and position ; and yet I knew that you could not possibly be fond of Philip when you consented to become his wife. The match was brilliant from a worldly point of view, and I had no grounds for opposing it. Nevertheless, I was not content, and vainly sought a clue to your conduct. My blindness now seems nothing more nor less than crass stupidity ; for, oh ! my child, my child ! " and she held out her wasted arms, " I know, when too late, that you sacrificed yourself for me. To secure me a home you did violence to your best and most womanly instincts, and not a day, not an hour, passes by but what you pay for this loveless marriage with your heart's blood."

"Mother, mother," cried Bligh, wildly, "you are ill and fancy all sorts of things."

" Can you look me in the face and swear that what I say is not true ? No, you can't," she went on, as Bligh's troubled eyes sought the floor. "I was certain you could make no denial."

" It is past and gone. Let us talk of something else," said Bligh, almost inaudibly.

"I have never talked of it before, and I promise never to talk of it again," rejoined Mrs. Burton, with a pathetic quaver in her voice ; " but I shall die easier if you let me unburthen myself just for once. Words fail to express my sense of your devotion ; but, oh ! my darling girl, what cuts me like a knife is the knowledge that after all your self-surrender, all your filial love, the sacrifice has been made in vain. I was doomed from the first. Dearest, we must part. Something tells me I am not long for this earth, and I cannot bear the idea of leaving you friendless and alone in the power of a man who makes your life miserable and who is unworthy of you in every way. Ah ! " and she crushed the letter into a ball, " why did not this money come sooner ? A year ago it would have saved you. You and I could have lived comfortably on four hundred a year, and there would have been no question of a Sir Philip then."

Bligh hid her face in her hands. Every word spoken by that pale invalid went quivering into the depths of her heart. They were too true to be contradicted, and she no longer attempted any denial. Yet she was annoyed with herself for having acted so badly that the secret, which she believed rigidly guarded, had been patent from the first. One more failure ! How they seemed to accumulate, and how utterly incapable she felt of further struggle. She tried to speak, but could not, and for a long time both mother and daughter remained silent, wrapped in painful thought.

At last Mrs. Burton said—

" I am going to send for a lawyer to-day, Bligh, to make my will. Nearly everything comes too late in this world—our knowledge, our experience, our repentance ; still, one never knows what may happen, and in spite of all your riches a little money of your own might be useful to you some day. You were married without settlements, and if—if the time should come when, in spite of your endurance and forbearance, you may have to leave your husband, then there will be enough to fall back upon when I am gone, my darling, and to place you above want."

Bligh burst into passionate tears. Such language made her realise that the end was drawing very near, and her heart felt like a stone at the prospect.

" Do—do—not talk of g—going," she sobbed. " I—I cannot—live—without you."

Mrs. Burton smiled sadly.

" We all think like that at first," she said. " I remember having the same thoughts when your father died; but Time is a wonderful physician. Few people can resist his healing touch. He changes youth to age, love to indifference, sorrow to apathy, if not oblivion. It is the fashion to abuse old Time ; but for my part I consider we mortals owe him an immense debt of gratitude. If it were not for the gradual alteration to which all Nature is subject existence would not be possible. As matters stand at present if one cannot always laugh, neither can one always weep. It is the admixture of joy and grief, pain and ease, growth and decay, which renders life endurable."

" Ah ! mother," cried Bligh, whose tenderer years rebelled against such argument, " what is the use of moralising ? The heart must always conquer philosophy whenever any contest arises between them, and reason will invariably succumb to the affections. When the pinch comes philosophy fails one and reason flies to the winds."

" Age modifies one's views most wonderfully," said Mrs. Burton.

" It will never modify mine," cried Bligh, passionately. " Oh ! mother, take me with you—take me with you. See, I kneel down and pray," suiting the action to the words. " Good God, when she goes have pity, and do not leave me behind."

Mrs. Burton put out her hot hand and placed it lovingly on her daughter's head. The heart within her was big.

" My darling," she said, " you have your appointed work to do. What it is, or how long it may last, I know not ; but this I do know : however hard may be the burden laid upon your shoulders you will bear it bravely, like the true, good woman that you are. Kiss me, Bligh. Kiss me, my own dear child. I stand on the threshold of death, and everything here below seems to grow vague and dark. My power of judgment goes as I perceive the littleness of human strife, of human cares and emotions. Love and hatred are much to the individual full of strength and vitality ; nothing to him who lies on a bed of sickness. Willingly would I help you, but I can't. Everyone must live and suffer for himself. Nevertheless, if there be a Deity, and the great scheme of creation is really the inspiration of a Divine brain, then those who have stood staunch, like loyal soldiers in the fight, may perhaps meet with reward, and earn the privilege of seeing their loved ones again. All the advice I can give you is—be honest, be strong, be true. Leave the rest to God."

She fell back exhausted on her pillow, and this was the last long conversation which Bligh ever held with her mother. From that day the invalid sank rapidly.

In the beginning of June, when the sweet red roses were warmly blushing amidst their green leaves, when the sun shone bright and powerful, and the earth was decked in the lovely garb of early summer, Mrs. Burton passed peacefully and quietly away. During the last fortnight she suffered but little pain, and the end came in sleep.

Bligh bore up until after the funeral, and then she broke down completely. The strain of the last few weeks had been too severe, and she was worn out both bodily and mentally. She could not cry. She seemed sunk in a tearless apathy that numbed her senses and rendered her indifferent to the lapse of time.

Whilst in this condition the pains of maternity came on prematurely, and she was confined of a boy, who only survived his birth a few hours. When the baby was placed by her side, slowly and hardly tears moistened her dry eyes. And the doctor, turning to Sir Philip, said in an undertone : " She is very ill ; but, thank God ! her reason is saved. If another four-and-twenty hours had gone by without any improvement taking place in her condition it would have been my duty to prepare you for the worst. Now, with care and good nursing she may pull through."

Sir Philip was unused to sickness, and the sight of Bligh lying so wan and pale affected him. For several days he showed so much feeling as to quite take his mother by surprise. She was charmed at this evidence of his possessing a heart, and immediately forgave all the past.

" You see," she said, triumphantly to Mrs. Fortescue, " there is more good in Philip than you ever believed."

" Perhaps," replied that lady sceptically. " But how long will it show itself ? If you ask my candid opinion I consider he has treated his wife brutally."

Lady Verschoyle had not asked her friend for her candid opinion ; so she answered spiritedly—

" I hope Bligh's illness may make a change. I verily do believe he is fond of her at bottom."

Mrs. Fortescue's nose went up in the air.

" Humph !" she exclaimed. " A pretty sort of fondness—
the kind of fondness which makes a woman wish she had never
been born."

The mother made no reply. The worst of Mrs. Fortescue's
speeches was that there was always a sting of truth in them.

CHAPTER XXXIII.

A CONFESSION OF FOLLY.

BLIGH seemed quite content to lie in bed day after day, and exhibited no desire or impatience to return to the ordinary routine
of life. The fact was she hailed illness—anything—with relief
which made a break in it.

Nature, too, had been overtaxed, and required rest. For a
while she succeeded in banishing thought, but directly her
bodily weakness began to decrease mental activity returned,
and she forced herself to face the future. Her mother's death
rendered the horizon very dark. On all sides the clouds seemed
to gather, and nowhere could she discern a ray of light. For
years Bligh and the dead woman had been companions to one
another. A perfect sympathy existed between them. They
resembled two equals rather than mother and daughter, so
completely had the elder lady identified herself with the tastes
and aspirations of the younger. A lump rose in Bligh's throat
when she thought that never again should she look into the dear
worn face, or hear the sound of the well-known voice. Every
time she missed them a rush of sorrow flooded her being. At
first she fretted much over the loss of her baby. If he had
lived, life would not have seemed so dreary and empty.

She possessed the maternal instinct in a high degree, and
had always been devoted to children. To have a child of one's
own had ever appeared to her the best gift which God could
bestow on a woman ; but since her marriage her ideas on this
subject had undergone a gradual alteration. She realised that
children were a blessing or a curse, according to the parents
from whom they were descended and the qualities and defects
which they inherited. Also, that it was an awful thing for a
helpless infant to be born into the world weighted from the
very beginning by the vices of a bad father or mother.

Consequently, when the baby died she forced back her tears,
and said to herself—

"It is well. Better far that the poor mite should only be born to die than that he should live to grow up and be a drunkard. I think I should go mad if, in spite of every care and caution, the fatal propensity were, little by little, to develop itself in my son. I could not blame him. I could only pity him, and look on sorrowfully at the cruel results of hereditary transmission. Or the weakness of the father might display itself in another form, and attack my poor boy's brain. He might be half-witted, or even a complete idiot, incapable of conducting his own affairs. There is no knowing in what way the drink would not break out, and every fresh symptom, every resemblance to the parent, no matter how slight, would make my heart bleed. Poor baby! Poor, dear little baby! Had you lived I could not have helped loving you, but things are best as they are. The wife of a drunkard has no right to the joys of motherhood, for it is a sin to perpetuate her husband's infirmity."

A woman only reasons thus when she has received a scientific training, possesses sufficient intelligence to look ahead, and has been made strong by suffering. For however stern an element of truth this sort of philosophy contains, it must always go against the grain where a tender female heart is concerned. Bligh tried hard to believe that everything had been ordained for the best : but the endeavour did not tend in any way to increase her happiness. The voice of Nature refused to be stifled. Meanwhile, she felt strangely listless and weak. Her whole system suffered from a nervous exhaustion which amounted almost to paralysis of the physical forces, and all the doctor's tonics proved powerless to restore her to strength. The mind was even more ill than the body, and certainly harder to cure.

Generally Sir Philip went to town for the London season, and left Beechlands about the middle of May : but owing to the serious illness first of his mother-in-law and then of his wife, he stayed quietly in the country all through June, only running up for Ascot races, Sandown, or some very special entertainment. Time hung heavily on his hands. He had few resources within doors, and as soon as Bligh was well enough to leave her bed he began to get extremely restless and impatient. She perceived this, and at once guessed the cause. His home, without a bird to kill or fox to hunt, had no attractions for him.

"One might just as well be buried alive as stay vegetating here all through the summer," he said one day when they happened to be alone. "Everybody is away, and one never sees a soul to speak to."

"That is the worst of a crack hunting county," she answered. "The society is more or less dependent on sport. If you are dull why don't you go to London? You could easily live at your club, and get stabling for two or three horses to ride or drive. I am getting on nicely now, and it is a pity for you to stay here any longer boring yourself on my account." In making this suggestion she knew that it would chime in with his inclinations, and, personally, she dreaded the formal periodical visits which he paid to the sick room from duty, and duty alone. The mere sound of his boots creaking backwards and forwards, as he paced to and fro, had an irritating effect on her nerves during the trying stage of convalescence, and she was guiltily conscious that she should much prefer his absence to his presence.

Sir Philip's face brightened.

"Are you sure you won't mind my leaving you, Bligh?" he asked, as a matter of form.

She laughed; a hard, little laugh.

"Oh! dear no. It's the greatest mistake in the world for married couples always to be glued to each other from one year's end to the other. A certain amount of change is not only good, but indispensable. The wise woman lets her husband go where he wants, for then he comes home civil and in a decent humour."

"By Jove!" he exclaimed. "It never struck me in that light before; but I believe you are right."

"I am certain I am," she answered, demurely. "You are tired to death of being here and playing the loving, anxious spouse. Why keep up the farce any longer? Mrs. Grundy is quite satisfied with your conduct. You can do no good by remaining, and it only distresses me to think how much I have already interfered with your pleasures."

She spoke with a thinly-veiled sarcasm, which cloaked an undercurrent of bitterness. He, however, failed to detect it. Her words agreed too well with his wishes for him to waste time in seeking after any hidden meaning.

"Certainly, you have my mother and the nurse for company," he said, trying not to show his pleasure too openly; "and in a few days I daresay the doctor will let you go out driving. So that, taking all things into consideration, I really think I might go away for a little bit."

"I think so too," she agreed gravely.

"Well, then, I'll write to the hall porter at my club and ask him if he can get me a room anywhere handy. Now that Ascot is over, town won't be quite so full as it was; but I shall wait until I receive an answer, just to make sure of having comfortable quarters."

The following morning's post, however, brought a letter which materially hastened Sir Philip's departure. He was sitting at breakfast, opposite to his mother, when he received it, and, as he recognised the handwriting, a sudden flush suffused his whole countenance.

" By Jove ! " he exclaimed, examining the envelope. " This is a funny thing ! Here is a letter from Blanche, and without the Indian postmark."

Lady Verschoyle looked up quickly, whilst her heart sank with a presentiment of evil.

" Nonsense, Philip," she said ; " it can't be."

" It is though," he rejoined, breaking open the seal. " Satisfy yourself if you like." And he tossed her the envelope and proceeded to make himself master of its contents. He had scarcely read more than the first few words when his mother, who was watching him narrowly, saw the expression of his face change.

" Well ! " she inquired, nervously, " what is Blanche's news ? "

" You would hardly believe it, but she is in England. She arrived in London last night."

" Oh ! Philip. You don't say so. What can have brought her back ? "

" I haven't the least idea."

" Depend upon it, something has gone wrong between her and Colonel Vansittart. Dear, oh ! dear ! I would not have had this happen for a thousand pounds."

" You don't know that it has happened yet. Blanche does not condescend to enter into details."

" May I see the letter ? "

" Oh ! yes, certainly, if you like. There is nothing in it beyond the bare announcement of her return."

Lady Verschoyle took up the note which her son threw across the table, and read as follows :—

" MY DEAR PHILIP—You will be surprised to hear that I am here again. I reached London this afternoon, and for the present have taken up my abode at 356, Ebury Street—a respectable lodging-house which I used to patronise in the olden days. Come and see me soon, there's a good fellow, and by so doing prove that you no longer bear me any ill-will. My departure from India was rather hurried, else I should have apprised you of it beforehand. Explanations, however, will wait till we meet. With love to the aunt—I remain, dear Philip,

" Your affectionate cousin,

" BLANCHE VANSITTART."

" I feel certain that there is something strange about this business," said Lady Verschoyle, when she came to an end of her niece's letter. "What do you mean to do, Philip? Shall you go and see her?"

"Most decidedly. I had not intended running up to town until Monday; but now I shall pack up and be off this afternoon by the 2.45 train. It's just like Blanche to set us wondering, rather than mention what brings her back in this unexpected fashion."

Lady Verschoyle compressed her lips into a thin line.

"I should not be at all surprised if she were ashamed to tell us the reason," she said, with unusual asperity.

Sir Philip took exception to his mother's tone.

"There you go again, mother," he said. "Really, for a good, blameless Christian woman professing all the virtues, you are about the most uncharitable person I ever met. Every now and then you fairly astonish me by the severity of your judgments. For goodness' sake, whilst I am away don't go filling Bligh's head full with all sorts of ridiculous tales told at poor Blanche's expense."

"Is it likely I should do such a thing, Philip?"

"It strikes me you are quite capable of it, and I don't want Bligh prejudiced against Blanche, for the chances are I shall bring her back here to stay on a visit."

"Would that be advisable?" asked Lady Verschoyle, uneasily.

"Yes, of course; why not? With the exception of yourself, Blanche is the nearest relation I have, and the only one I care twopence about; and if she's in trouble or anything of that sort I shall certainly stand by her. For all we know to the contrary, the poor girl may be ill, and have had to leave India on account of her health."

"Other people's wives go to the hills," observed Lady Verschoyle.

"They may go to the devil for what I care. That is quite apart from the question. As I said before, Blanche is my cousin, and I intend to do the best I can for her, always providing she has got into hot water, which you seem to take for granted, but which I don't for one moment believe."

"Very well. We shall see who is right."

"Nothing is more natural than that Blanche should write to me," he went on with considerable warmth; "and for you to judge her without even hearing what story she has to tell is, to say the least of it, very unkind, mother. Indeed, if that is all the good you get by going twice to church every Sunday of your life you might just as well stay at home, and be a jolly, comfortable sinner like the rest of us. You pious people are awfully disappointing, for when it comes to the test you are not one whit better than your neighbours."

A faint flush rose to Lady Verschoyle's cheek. Rude as was the reproof an inward voice whispered that it was not destitute of truth. Her heart was set against Blanche, and had always been so from the first. The instinct of antipathy which existed between her and her niece was too strong to be conquered ; but she realised with shame that it undoubtedly detracted from her sense of justice. She was by nature an extremely humble woman, ever ready to admit her own faults. So instead of feeling any anger at her son's speech she folded her hands and answered meekly—

" You are right to reprove me, Philip. In future I will endeavour to be more charitable, and place a stricter guard over my tongue. I don't know why, but I am afraid of Blanche, and still more so of her coming here."

" Pshaw! that's absurd. She is married, and so am I. What in the name of Heaven is there to fear ? "

" I can't explain——"

" No, I should think not, nor anyone else either. Let's have no more of this folly, and remember the less you say about Blanche in my absence the better. Not that Bligh is jealous. I will give her that credit; but, still, women are so odd one never quite knows how they may receive their husbands' former flames."

Lady Verschoyle held her peace. She felt that argument was vain, and would not help to improve her daughter-in-law's cause.

On the afternoon of the same day Sir Philip wished his mother and Bligh an affable good-bye, and gave them to understand that his return was uncertain, and departed with a light heart. Bligh had guessed his sentiments exactly. He was sick to death of the humdrum existence which he had been leading during the last few weeks, and he looked forward with the keenness of a schoolboy to once more having what he called " a fling."

Time had softened the resentment which some months previously he had felt against his cousin, and it startled him not a little to find how much he rejoiced at the prospect of seeing her again. If she had really quarrelled with her husband he was quite prepared to take her under his wing. It gratified him to think that his words were being fulfilled, and that directly things went wrong she was only too ready to apply to him. Representing as he did the head of the family, no doubt it was only right and proper for her to seek his aid in the event of any difficulty arising. Nevertheless, his heart beat fast as any lover's when, somewhere about six o'clock, he knocked at the door of the house in Ebury Street and was informed that Mrs. Vansittart was within. In order to guard against a possible disappointment he had taken the precaution to send off a telegram prior to leaving the country. An untidy maid-servant showed him up a dingy staircase, about which there lingered a faint, but offensive, odour of cooking. He drew two or three deep breaths, striving to suppress his excitement, and in another moment was ushered into Blanche's presence.

The room was small and dark, and the blinds were drawn down in order to exclude the sun; but light enough remained for him to see how greatly she had altered from the Blanche of his recollections. Her form had lost its roundness, her cheeks their freshness. There was no longer anything girlish about her; and yet her dark eyes were more luminous than of old, and he fancied that the expression of the thin white face turned eagerly towards him was softened and more womanly.

"Good God!" he exclaimed, involuntarily. "How you have changed! I declare if I had met you in the streets I should hardly have known you."

She gave a mirthless laugh.

"You don't think me improved, evidently. Well!" and she gazed at him critically, "I can return the compliment. Time has not been much kinder to you than to me. What have you done to yourself, Philip?"

"Nothing," he rejoined, not relishing the tone of the conversation. "What should I do?"

"Matrimony does not appear to have agreed with you altogether," she retorted, a trifle maliciously.

"The same remark applies to you. May I ask what has brought you to England, Blanche? Have you been ill?"

"No," she answered, fidgeting with her wedding ring. "Not exactly. The climate did not suit me, and I had a touch of fever once or twice when the weather set in hot. Still, I managed to rub on as well as most people, and I can't honestly say I left India on account of my health. Understand me, I am telling you this in strict confidence. Can I trust you, Philip?"

"My dear Blanche, you know that you can. Who should you trust if not me?"

She shrugged her shoulders with a somewhat unbelieving gesture.

"Being where I am," she said, "I must try the experiment."

"You speak in enigmas. Tell me first of all why you came home."

"Can't you guess?"

"A row?"

She nodded her head.

"Yes. The long and short of it is I was never cut out for matrimony. Domestic life does not suit me. I found it too confining, and wanted more liberty than my estimable colonel was willing to grant."

"You don't mean to say——" began Sir Philip.

She cut him short, whilst the colour mounted to her dark cheek.

"I mean nothing of the sort. If you will only abstain from placing the very worst construction upon my actions, I am prepared to tell you the whole story ; not," she added, cynically, "that it is a very pleasant or edifying one."

"Never mind," seating himself on the sofa by her side. "Let me hear what it is."

She turned towards him, and as her heavy-lidded eyes sought his he no longer saw an unfamiliar Blanche with faded beauty, but the woman who had ever had it in her power to cast a glamour over his senses. He respected Bligh, and was afraid of her. He did not respect his cousin, and felt comfortable and at his ease in her society. This thought occurred to him as the yellow sunlight peeping in through a hole in the blind played spasmodically on Blanche's neatly-coiled hair. It was ever so much jollier being with somebody who did not perpetually want to keep one in order and look as if everything one did was wrong.

"Philip," she began, "you know me better than most people, and are aware of the reasons which induced me to marry my present husband. When we last met I told you that my marriage was neither more nor less than a pure experiment. Well!" and the corners of her mouth drooped rather pathetically, "the experiment has failed, that is all. It is a common enough experience, and I fancy there are a good many other people in the same boat as myself. I don't suppose I am any worse off than my neighbours." So saying she stifled a sigh, and leant her head defiantly back against the cushions.

"Whose fault was it, Blanche ?" he inquired. "Vansittart's or yours ?"

"That is a difficult question to answer. If you ask my candid opinion, I should say neither Our temperaments alone are to blame. Weldon is strict, upright, and honourable to a degree. His nature is calm and judicial. He takes things easily enough up to a certain point, and regards the majority of his fellow-creatures with charitable indifference ; but where any principle is involved he is as firm as a rock, and nothing can modify his ideas of right and wrong. I am just the reverse in every way. I hate a quiet, monotonous life."

" You never were one of the stagnant sort," said Sir Philip.

" No, nor never shall be. I like plenty of bustle, excitement, and amusement, and have always been accustomed to male society. Women at best are but dull companions, and I don't profess to care much for my own sex. Unfortunately, I can no more help flirting than I can help eating or drinking. A man acts upon me like a stimulant. Am I frank ? "

" Perfectly ! " he answered, with an amused smile.

" As I said before," she continued, " it is a pure matter of temperament. To give Weldon his due, he was very long-suffering, and allowed me more liberty than most women. But India is a bad place for feminine morals, and, I regret to say, mine were already impaired before I left home. However, to go on with my story. Having nothing particular to do I set to work to gain the affections of several of the idle officers. It amused me, did them no particular harm, and passed away the time. Out there it is the fashion of every married lady to have a devoted cavalier, who walks with her, rides with her, and dances with her. I had at least half a dozen. They were like lap-dogs running about the house, and, to tell the truth, I cared no more for them than if they had belonged to the canine species. It was all vanity on my part, and wanting to cut the other women out. My good colonel behaved uncommonly well. He did not exactly relish having his home turned into a kind of lounge for a lot of idiotic young men. but I suppose he thought there was safety in numbers. At all events, he said nothing, and. like an obliging husband, calmly accepted the part of cipher and nonentity. I must say I wondered at him sometimes, and wished he would show a little more spirit.

" I should have kicked every man jack of them out of the house," interposed Sir Philip.

Blanche laughed.

" I daresay you would ; but Weldon is not so jealously constituted. Like a fool I did my best to provoke him. I said to myself, ' He hasn't a scrap of feeling, and does not care two straws what I do ! ' So I went on playing with fire, until one fine day I got burnt. One always does in the long run. No woman can meddle with combustible material without ending by being singed, and I was not an exception to the rule."

" What happened. Blanche ? "

" Nothing very tragic. A new regiment arrived at the station, and the major happened to be an awfully nice man. who consoled me for the loss of my old ' pals.' We soon made friends, and before long were almost inseparable. I don't attempt to defend myself. I was not a bit in love with him, but I liked him and—"
she hesitated and blushed, then added abruptly, " we flirted to

a very considerable extent. He was no novice at the game,
neither was I.   On either side we played at sentiment. Things
went on thus until one night at a ball Weldon overheard some
beast of a woman making disagreeable remarks at my expense
and tearing my poor character to shreds. One always has to
thank one's own sex for setting the match to the fire. The consequence was, when we got home the colonel rounded upon me,
and said, in a quiet voice, which somehow I had learnt to dread :
' Blanche, I have borne a good deal. I do not think you can
accuse me of being unreasonably jealous or of curtailing your
liberty of action in a masterful and domineering way ; but, as a
personal favour, I must ask you to drop the acquaintance of
Major FitzAllan.'

" I could feel the colour rising to my cheeks as I answered
indignantly, ' I shall do no such thing.'

" ' It came to my ears to-day,' he said, ' that you are being
spoken of in a manner injurious to the fame of a modest
woman.'

" ' Of what do you accuse me ? ' I asked fiercely.

" He laid his hand on my shoulder and looked at me with sorrowful eyes, which I fancy I can see now." And, putting her
handkerchief to her face, Blanche sat silent for a few seconds,
her thoughts reverting to the past.

" Well ? " said Sir Philip, anxious to hear the sequel to her
narrative.

" ' My poor child,' said Weldon, gently, ' I accuse you of nothing worse than vanity and an undue love of admiration. Don't
imagine for one instant that I am bringing any more serious
charge against you. It is for your own sake, and to shield your
reputation, that I speak.'

" Good God ! how his words cut into my heart. I experienced
a horrible inclination to run away and hide my diminished head.
If only he had given me a good scolding I shouldn't have felt half
such a fool. To save myself from abject defeat I took refuge
in pride. Instead of confessing my innocence, which, thank
Heaven ! I could have done with a clear conscience, I answered
haughtily, ' And do you suppose that I'm going to cut my best
friend for no reason except that you choose to harbour unworthy
suspicions against him ? No, certainly not. If I renounced
Major FitzAllan's acquaintance it would only give them confirmation.'

" ' Can't you see,' he retorted, ' that, whether guilty or unguilty,
from the moment a woman's fair name is attacked it is not merely
wise policy, but also her duty, to set herself right with the world
again.'

" ' Rubbish ! ' I exclaimed, pettishly. ' What do I care about

the world ?   The world in this instance means that horrid Mrs.
O'Hara, who is as jealous of me as she can be, and half a dozen
other old cats of the same description.'

"'Don't run down your own sex, Blanche,' he said. 'Nothing sounds worse, particularly when you happen to be altogether
in the wrong. In the present unfortunate state of affairs the
world means your husband, who is bound to consider your good
name, even if you decline to do so yourself.'

"'What nonsense, Weldon,' I said. 'Please cut your lecture
short.'

"'You may call it nonsense if you like,' he returned ; 'but I
give you distinctly to understand that you must choose between
Major FitzAllan and me.'"

"By Jove!" interrupted Sir Philip, "I think Vansittart was
right."

"Right!" she exclaimed, with a curl of her short upper lip.
"Of course he was. That's the worst of him. He's always
right, and I'm always wrong. Do you suppose I am not aware
of the fact without having it crammed down my throat ?
However, to finish this nice little story of wifely folly and perversity. From that day, just out of pure 'cussedness,' I flirted
worse than ever with Major Fitz.Allan. You mayn't believe me,
Philip, but there was nothing in it more than I am telling you.
The man was good-looking, specious, agreeable, and I found
his society pleasant. There are some women so constituted
that they cannot help doing foolish things, and it is my misfortune to be one of them. We get the name of being worse than
we really are. Not to weary you with too many details, the end
was Weldon and I had a tremendous row. Once more he
begged me to give up Fitz.Allan, and again I refused. Upon
this he declared that if I insisted on pursuing a course incon-
sistent with his honour he should be under the painful necessity of leaving me. I replied that he need not give himself
the trouble, since I was perfectly willing to leave him. Without my husband's knowledge, I packed up a few things,
travelled down to Bombay and," she concluded, casting down
her eyes, "here I am."

"It strikes me you've made a precious mess of it, Blanche,"
said Sir Philip. "What between your flirting and your pride
you've managed to get into the wrong box. May I ask what
steps you propose taking next ? "

"I don't know," she answered dejectedly, for even in her own
ears her story had not sounded well.

"H'm! Are you sure you did not care for this Major Fitz-
Allan ?"

"Care for him !" she echoed, and all at once her voice lost its hard intonation, and grew soft and tremulous. "Don't you understand? How dull you are! It is the colonel whom I love."

"The colonel!" exclaimed Sir Philip, fairly amazed.

"Yes. He is such a man and a gentleman. If you could have seen him when he said he should leave me! He was splendid. I never realised how much I honoured and respected him until that moment. He was so strong, so stern. It was just touch and go whether I threw myself at his feet or came away."

Sir Philip looked at her curiously. Even although he had heard the confession from her own lips he refused to credit it.

"Blanche," he said, "you are a perfect mystery to me."

"I am not surprised at that, for I am a mystery to myself."

"Do you mean seriously to tell me that, loving your husband, you flirted with all these men as an amusement, and nothing more?"

"Yes; it seems incredible, doesn't it? But I believe there are a great many women like me. I don't pretend to say that we are nice, or calculated to make good wives and mothers, but we cannot help ourselves. And when we marry men who are our superiors it simply means purgatory for both, for we are not so bad as to be incapable of appreciating their virtues, and yet we are too frivolous to remain faithful to the highest when we see it. Consequently, we flutter about like butterflies, here, there, and everywhere." Then, suddenly, she stood up, stretched out both her hands like a person groping for the light, and with tears glistening in her eyes, said, "Don't scold me, Philip. I know I am altogether to blame in this matter. Pity me rather, for I've been a fool, and am very, very miserable."

He put his arm round her waist, and kissed her in a friendly, cousinly fashion.

"Nonsense, old girl; you are tired after your journey, and consequently feel down in the dumps. I intend to look after you and cheer you up. We'll see the season out, and then we'll run down to Beechlands, have some jolly rides together, and put a little colour into those pale cheeks of yours."

His confident tone did much to restore Blanche to a more hopeful mood, and she began to take a less gloomy view of the situation.

"Thank you, Philip," she said. "You are very kind. I was afraid you might cut me after my marriage."

He reddened consciously.

"It was a great mistake," he said. "You and I were always meant for each other. However, what's done can't be undone."

"Are you happy?" she asked.

" Me ? Oh ! yes, I suppose so. My wife is a good little thing, only rather too straightlaced. And now I must be off, for I've promised to dine at my club with a man. I'll take tickets for the theatre to-morrow, and we'll go and see the new burlesque at the Gaiety. By the way, if you should happen to meet any of our old friends say you've been ill, and are home on sick leave. It's no use letting all the world know you've squabbled with Vansittart. I shan't even tell my mother. The less said about these sorts of things the better." So saying he kissed her again and departed.

Blanche went to the window and watched him walk down the street.

" Poor Philip !" she said to herself. " He's not to be compared with Weldon ; but I like him very much indeed. I always did ; and it's a great satisfaction to feel that I've got him on my side. I wonder whether he cares for me still, or whether he's only friendly because he has got over the mortification of being refused." Then she smiled, looked coquettishly at her reflection in the glass, and added, " I daresay I shall find out before long."

CHAPTER XXXIV.

MRS. FORTESCUE GIVES HER OPINIONS.

BLANCHE was perfectly correct in her supposition. Little as it may say in favour of our nineteenth century morals, the fact remains undoubted that lively married women, who wear the chains of Hymen lightly, prove extremely attractive to the ordinary run of fashionable men. In every ballroom and at every race meeting one sees them surrounded, whereas some nice, quiet, modest girl sits totally neglected in a corner, sadly making mental observations as to the uselessness of being well behaved in an age when virtue is decidedly at a discount. It is not exactly encouraging for her to look on, and see what a good innings frivolity—not to say vice—has nowadays. Her notions of right and wrong get strangely upset when she mixes in the gay world.

In less than a fortnight after Blanche's return to England, she made the pleasing discovery that Sir Philip was a hundred times more in love with her than he had ever been during the many years when all he had had to do was to speak in order to assure himself of her affection.

Every morning he was to be seen at her side, walking or sitting in Rotten-row.   He sent to Beechlands for horses, mounted her on his wife's special pet, King Arthur, and they rode together most afternoons ; whilst at night they dined at the various cafés, and afterwards went to the theatres.

Blanche enjoyed herself immensely, and sought by perpetual excitement to chase dismal thoughts from her mind.   At first she was rejoiced to find how well she succeeded.   After several month's banishment to India, it was delightful to be in England again, if only to take stock of the fashions.   Her friends (believing her tale of ill health) were all excessively civil, and professed themselves charmed to see her back in her native land.   Being a handsome, striking-looking woman, unencumbered moreover by a better half, she was asked out a good deal, and she thoroughly appreciated the value of having a settled social position. For the last year or two previous to her marriage she had become aware that people were beginning to fight shy of her as a parasitic young woman no longer in her first youth.   Consequently she had been forced continually to make new acquaintances in order to atone for being dropped by the old.   An independent girl's life may appear very smooth and enviable on the surface, but Blanche had reason to know that it is not unconnected with struggle and strife.   The prizes in the matrimonial market are few and far between.   They cannot be gained without trouble. A great many smiles, wiles and smart frocks go to catch a husband.   There is a terrible amount of hard work and expense about the proceeding, and small wonder if the fair pursuers are downhearted.   But when their man-hunting days are over, and a brand-new wedding ring shines on their finger, then, surely, they have a right to rest on their laurels, and enjoy the status which by dint of much labour they have achieved.

The cousins stayed on in London until the season came to an end ; after which they received invitations both for Goodwood and Cowes.   If a man and a woman are always seen in each other's company, people soon drop into the way of asking them out together.   Their friends were so kind that August was far advanced before Philip and Blanche arrived at Beechlands. In the interval neither Bligh nor Lady Verschoyle was kept very accurately informed of the baronet's movements.   The dowager guessed pretty accurately what her son was about, but she was afraid to say anything after his parting injunctions and the reproof which he had seen fit to administer.   As a rule, Sir Philip went to Scotland for the twelfth, but for once his cousin had not been included in the invitation, and he wrote off and excused himself.   The truth was, things had come to such a pass with him that he did not care to go anywhere unless she went too.   They had resumed their former intimate footing, with this difference. Whereas, in olden days he had been cool and she keen ; now, the warmth was all on his side, and she, although flattered and gratified by his attentions, remained heart-whole. To a great extent she treated him as a convenience; and she never scrupled to accept his presents, ride his horses, and profit by his longer purse. Her pride was not of the refined sort, which recoils from receiving benefits, and would rather give than take. Philip was eminently useful to her. She did not mince the matter, or hesitate to benefit by his generosity.

Bligh had heard the story of her husband's attachment to his cousin from Mrs. Fortescue ; but hers was not a jealous nature, and she looked forward to Blanche's coming rather with curiosity than dread. The Dowager Lady Verschoyle, on the other hand, was ill at ease, and tortured by a presentiment of evil, which, do what she would, she could not shake off. All through the summer months she and Bligh had seen a great deal of each other, and every day the elder lady felt more and more attracted by the solid, sterling qualities of her young companion, and conceived a higher admiration for her character. Unconsciously she stood in danger of transferring her affections from her son to her daughter-in-law. She knew how much Bligh had to contend with, and how little domestic happiness blessed her home. Since the baby's birth Bligh had never been strong, and now to her other troubles was added the crowning one of physical ill-health.

Lady Verschoyle tried hard to receive her niece with a show of welcome, but inwardly she wished her a thousand miles away. She endeavoured to stifle her fears, but it soon became evident they were only too well founded ; for the moment Blanche set foot inside Beechlands, Bligh ceased to be the mistress of it. A single day sufficed to show that it was Blanche whose opinion was consulted on every point, Blanche whose word was law in the establishment.

Hitherto Sir Philip, when sober, had always been in the habit of paying his wife some slight deference ; but now he threw aside the mask, and when his cousin was by ignored her presence completely. If Bligh made a remark he did not listen to it. He addressed himself pointedly to Blanche, and had eyes and ears only for her. As for Mrs. Vansittart, without being positively rude, or actually unkind to her hostess, she treated her with ill-disguised disdain. Her manner seemed to say—" You are and always will be a little nobody. Don't expect me to bother much about you. I am Philip's friend, not yours. It was absurd his making you Lady Verschoyle. He liked me best, and regrets having made such a fool of himself. You'd better keep quiet, for the two of us together are too much for you." Meanwhile, Bligh's delicacy was eagerly seized upon by Sir Philip as an excuse for neglecting her. Whenever they were asked to go anywhere, it was always—"Oh! my poor wife is a great invalid at present. She gets knocked up directly, and can't do anything except lie on the sofa, or take a little quiet drive; but if you'll allow me, I'll bring my cousin instead. I think you know Mrs. Vansittart. She often stayed at Beechlands when she was Miss Sylvester."

The consequence of these tactics was "my cousin" stepped into Bligh's shoes, and usurped her place; whilst "my poor wife" stayed meekly at home, only too glad, if the truth must be told, to be left in peace and quiet, yet vaguely resenting the off-hand treatment· of which she was a victim.

Blanche and Sir Philip possessed a good many tastes in common, which still further helped to bring them together. They were both devoted to outdoor amusements, and were never so happy as when scampering about the country on horseback. They liked lounging away their idle hours in the stable, retiring to the saddle-room and smoke cigarettes, and quenching the thirst thus occasioned by numerous potations. The lady took as kindly to the drink as the gentleman, only, fortunately for herself, she happened to have the stronger head. Their conversation suited almost as well as their inclinations, and was interlarded by so many awfully jollys, beastlys, rippings, don't yer knows, and I don't care a hangs, that an uninitiated listener had great difficulty in following their discourse, or in sifting from such a running stream of slang any slight sediment of sense. They both belonged to the fashionable school, which in these days has so many pupils, and which makes the past generation turn up the whites of their eyes with horror.

As the days passed Lady Verschoyle the elder grew more and more uneasy. She could not disguise the fact that Bligh was being abominably treated, and her gentle heart swelled with indignation.

"I can't think how she can stand it," she said one day, when speaking of her daughter-in-law to Mrs. Fortescue. "I'm sure I couldn't sit still, as she does, and hold my tongue were I in her place."

"Bligh is a very superior woman," answered Mrs. Fortescue. "I have the greatest regard for her, but, all the same, I agree with you. She puts up with too much. A time comes when one's self-respect is trampled upon if one does not assert oneself. The difficulty is to know where to draw the line."

"Bligh is marvellously easy-going," responded Lady Verschoyle, "and although most women would be furious at being treated with such scant courtesy, she doesn't seem to care."

"If she doesn't it's a very bad sign. Human nature is human nature, and no wife likes seeing her husband make love to another woman right under her nose. Even if her affections are not deeply involved, it puts her in a false position, and lowers her both in her own estimation and that of the household. Such conduct on the man's part outrages her finest feelings and destroys her ideals respecting chastity and the sanctity of married life. Either she takes a leaf out of his book, and sets up an opposition attraction, just to show she does not care, and can find admirers too, or else she seeks to hide the bitterness at her heart by turning the whole thing into ridicule. I have seen both plans tried, but neither is very successful as far as the poor wife is concerned. In one case she loses caste; in the other she grows hard and cynical, takes pessimistic views of society, and becomes unduly harsh in her judgments of her own sex."

"I fear you are right," said Lady Verschoyle, with a sigh. "Bligh is not a flirty woman. She does not care enough about men to run after them, and, indeed, despises the great majority of aimless, self-indulgent creatures by whom Philip surrounds himself; but no doubt she might harden. I often wonder that she has kept as soft and womanly as she is, when one comes to know her. Nevertheless, her manner with strangers is very reserved, and often she does not do herself justice."

"The society is not congenial," said Mrs. Fortescue, dryly.

"No, I suppose not. I have felt the same thing myself, and then we both take refuge in our shells."

"You should put out your horns, my dear, and fight."

"Perhaps it would be better, but neither Bligh nor I is aggressive; though I confess that sometimes my blood fairly tingles at the affronts showered upon her at her own table. She bears it all so beautifully too."

"Still waters run deep," said Mrs. Fortescue. "No man can insult a woman with impunity. You mark my words, she'll resent Sir Philip's conduct some day; and when she does break out, she'll surprise him."

"Sometimes I think she has no feeling," remarked Lady Verschoyle. "I can't account for her endurance in any other way."

"No feeling!" echoed Mrs. Fortescue. "Bligh got no feeling! She may not care for her husband—indeed, I don't see how she can—but, depend upon it, he does not utter a single rude word, or commit one unkind action, which she does not feel."

"Poor Bligh! I wish I could help her," said Lady Verschoyle, regretfully.

"You can't, my dear. Things are gravitating towards a crisis, as they do periodically in the lives of all of us. A climax is sure to take place before long. Any ordinary onlooker can see that much; but interference would only precipitate it. Besides I have an idea that matters are not altogether as unsatisfactory as you imagine."

"In what way, Anne? I fail to see how they could be much worse."

"Have you watched Blanche narrowly of late?"

"No. I dislike her so much that I keep out of her way as much as possible."

"Well, I have, and in my opinion she is very much changed."

"She looks older, of course, and sallower——"

"I don't mean that," interrupted Mrs. Fortescue. "I mean changed mentally."

"I only wish she were. She seems to me to be much the same as ever," said Lady Verschoyle.

"I admit that she is still fast, and slangy, and flirty. A few months have not sufficed to eradicate the habits of years; nevertheless, my impression is that, although there is yet room for much improvement, she is on the right road. To begin with, I am almost certain that she has got over her unfortunate passion for Philip. He cares for her nowadays, but she doesn't for him —at least not in the same way as formerly."

"Impossible, Anne!"

"No, I think not; and you are so innocent, my dear Lady Verschoyle, that very often you don't see what goes on beneath the surface. I bring an unprejudiced eye to bear on the situation."

"And is this really the result of your observations?"

"Yes. Blanche told me the other day that she had written to her husband, and was anxiously expecting to hear from him, and she said it in a way, and there was a sad look on her face, which made me feel certain that she cared for him."

"I wish she did," said Lady Verschoyle, impatiently. "She'd leave Philip alone then and go respectably back to India."

"Unless I'm very much mistaken that is precisely what she wants to do," responded Mrs. Fortescue.

"But in that case how do you account for her being so extraordinarily thick with Philip?"

"I believe her to be a born coquette, who can't help trying to captivate every man she comes across, and I further believe that she takes a cat-like delight in punishing him for all he made her suffer in the olden days. She is cured of her love, however; of that I am positive."

"Thank God!" exclaimed Lady Verschoyle, fervently.

" Would you advise me to speak to Blanche, and beg her to be a little more courteous in her manner to Bligh ? "

" I am afraid it would do more harm than good. Mrs. Vansittart is the last person in the world either to accept advice or to brook any interference. If I were you, I should just leave things alone for a bit. Either Blanche will return to India, or else she and Sir Philip will fall out. This fervid pitch of friendship can't be maintained, and if matters are as I suspect, something is bound to cool it before long. I have seen a good many of these flirtations between married people in my time, and they nearly all end the same way, if only the parties are given rope enough to hang themselves with. Very few men are capable of constant passion, and Philip certainly does not belong to their number."

" He has liked Blanche for a good many years," said Lady Verschoyle, retrospectively.

" Possibly, but has he given up anything for her sake, or made the slightest sacrifice on her account ? He is much too selfish to get a black mark set against his name for the love of any woman. He may make you and his wife miserable, and trifle with the object of his affections, but he'll never commit himself beyond a certain point. He covets his cousin now, because she happens to be out of his reach ; whilst she, womanlike, enjoys playing at the game of tit for tat."

" Pray Heaven you may be right," said Lady Verschoyle, feeling very much comforted by her friend's assurances. " It seems horrid of me to side against my own son, but Bligh is such an angel I can't help feeling sorry for her, and wishing it were in my power to render her life happier than it is."

Mrs. Fortescue shook her head.

" I fear that having chosen her lot, we none of us can make it brighter. Life is a strange puzzle, and when we poor mortals attempt to put the pieces together, we always get wrong ; but I suppose there is One above who knows how to fit the crooked bits, and smooth away all the inequalities."

CHAPTER XXXV.

THE WORM WILL TURN.

ONCE more the 1st of September came round, and on the afternoon of that day Bligh was sitting alone indoors. Her mother-in-law was pottering about the garden, snipping at every faded blossom with a huge pair of scissors ; whilst Sir Philip and

Blanche had departed almost immediately after breakfast in pursuit of partridges.

It might have been about four o'clock, when suddenly she heard unusual sounds proceeding from the front hall, and almost immediately afterwards old Deborah, who since Bligh's marriage had been converted into her maid, appeared at the door with a very white face.

"What is it?" asked Bligh, looking up inquiringly from her book.

"Oh! my dear lady," gasped Deborah in return, "it's Sir Philip."

"Well! What of him?"

"He's been and gone and shot himself."

"Shot himself!"

"Yes. The gun burst in his hand, and has blown it almost to pieces. Four of the keepers have just brought him home on a stretcher. It's quite awful to see him."

"Where is he?" said Bligh, starting to her feet.

"Down in the hall, and oh! dearie, he looks dreadful bad. His face is that pale I should scarcely have known it was him; for of late Sir Philip has always had a very high, purplish sort of colour."

"Come," said Bligh, "don't let us waste time by talking. The thing is to see what can be done to amend the mischief."

That it was serious she perceived at once : for when she reached the hall she found her husband lying in an almost unconscious state from loss of blood. His left hand dangled helplessly by his side, and every now and then a moan of pain escaped from him. Her first step was to send a man off for the doctor, bidding him come without delay ; the next—to get Sir Philip to bed. This was not accomplished without considerable difficulty : for the slightest movement increased the hemorrhage, and occasioned severe torture. Fortunately, Doctor Goodwyn happened to be at home, and arrived in a very few minutes. Bligh hailed his presence with relief, for her surgical knowledge had not sufficed to avert the bleeding. He inspected the shattered hand, and his face grew grave. After a careful examination, he pronounced that the two first fingers had been so injured by the bursting of the barrel that it was absolutely necessary to amputate them.

"Can't you try some less severe remedy?" said Bligh.

"It is impossible to save those two fingers," answered Doctor Goodwyn. "By all means have another opinion if you think mine requires confirmation ; but the patient is in great agony, and for his sake the sooner the operation is performed the better. His blood does not appear to me to be in a very good state, and unless prompt measures are resorted to, I fear fever and various complications may superver—"

" Would you give my husband chloroform ? " she asked, nervously.

" Yes, most certainly. I should propose returning to the village for my assistant and a nurse, and could have everything ready in half an hour from now, provided you give me permission."

" Really, doctor. I don't know what to say According to you, the loss of the fingers seems inevitable."

" The bones are regularly splintered," said Doctor Goodwyn. " Sir Philip has had a great escape. As it is the whole of his left arm is riddled with shot, and I shall have to probe for the bullets. My fear is that if the operation is delayed beyond a few hours blood-poisoning may set in, and the whole hand would then have to be sacrificed."

" In that case," said Bligh, firmly, " we will not put it off a minute." She bent over her husband, rested her cool palm on his forehead, and added—

" You agree with me, don't you, Philip ? "

He nodded his head faintly, being almost in a state of syncope.

" Brandy," he murmured.

Bligh looked questioningly at Dr. Goodwyn.

" Yes," he said, " you may give him a little, but only a very little—not more than a quarter of a wineglassful." So saying he went off to make the requisite arrangements, leaving Bligh in charge of the sick room. She opened the door, and called for Deborah.

" Has Mrs. Vansittart returned ? " she whispered.

" No, my lady, not yet. The men were saying she went on a beat by herself after lunch, and knew nothing of Sir Philip's accident."

" Tell the servants not to mention it either to her or to Lady Verschoyle until all is over. The quieter the affair is managed the better : and if they were to rush up here, fussing and talking, they would only excite him, and do more harm than good."

While Doctor Goodwyn was away Bligh and Deborah carried out his instructions, and prepared the room. He returned shortly, accompanied by an assistant and a nurse. He looked at Bligh's quivering face, and knowing how ill she had been, was anxious to spare her. So he said in his most professional manner—

" If you will be guided by my advice, Lady Verschoyle, I strongly recommend your not remaining in the room during the operation. It will only try your nerves unnecessarily, and I have all the help I am likely to require."

She looked about her undecidedly.

" Don't you think I ought to stay ? "

"No," he said. "I am quite sure you ought not. To be perfectly frank, you are not in a fit state of health to receive any shock. Your system is already overwrought."

She acknowledged the wisdom of his counsel, and withdrew obediently; glad, indeed, to have medical authority for doing so. She could not endure to see this strong, selfish man suffer. It seemed so opposed to his usual condition, and so unnatural for him to be the one to bear pain, and not herself.

Half an hour passed in anxious expectation. At length the door opened, and Doctor Goodwyn popped in his head.

"All right," he said. "The operation is well over, and we have got Sir Philip back into bed. In another minute or two he will begin to recover from the effects of the chloroform."

"Oh, doctor," she exclaimed, "is his state very bad?"

"No. I am happy to be able to report that I have succeeded in extracting most of the bullets, and, luckily, no vital part has been injured. I think Sir Philip will go on satisfactorily now. All he requires is care and quiet."

"You are sure that there is no danger?"

"Humanly speaking, quite sure. Of course, in these cases there is always some risk from fever and inflammation, but unless things take an unfavourable turn, which I do not for one moment anticipate, I see no cause at present for the slightest alarm."

Bligh advanced on tiptoe to the side of the bed, and looked down with mingled feelings of compassion and mitigated dislike at the still figure, whose stalwart outlines were suggested rather than defined by the woollen blankets. Her heart was soft. She felt that in spite of all that had come and gone, this accident might be the means of bringing them together. She accused herself of having been cold, passive, indifferent. If he would but make advances, she was prepared to receive them in a spirit of friendship. Such were her thoughts as she stood gazing at his strangely pale face, which was only a shade less white than the pillow against which it rested.

Presently the sick man groaned. In his throat the air accumulated, and apparently formed an obstruction. The taste of the chloroform lingered about his mouth, and his nostrils were charged with the smell. He sighed heavily three or four times, as if oppressed by a weight of woe; the tears forced themselves through his closed eyelids, and rolled swiftly down his cheeks. His lips parted, and he gurgled—at first helplessly, afterwards with more conscious effort. Far off, but gradually becoming nearer and more distinct, he heard whispering voices and the shuffling of slippered feet. Then he made a slight movement, and murmured spasmodically—

"I don't love her—I never did. I only married her in a moment of pique—and to spite Blanche. I don't want her to know—but the fact is, I hate her. She hasn't done me any harm—but I hate her. She looks so solemn and glum when I drink—Blanche doesn't mind. She only laughs, and gets tight too. I tell you I wish Bligh were dead for then I'd marry Blanche in spite of Vansittart. It's very hard—very hard being tied to a woman one does not care for, when there is another whom one likes in the same house. The mere sight of Bligh's face has an irritating effect upon me, whereas Blanche is so jolly, you know—so jolly and so different."

These and many other words to a similar effect came pouring forth in a disconnected flow, revealing the most innermost thoughts of the wretched man's mind, stripped bare of all disguise.

Bligh shuddered as she stood there listening. The depth of the hatred, which she had seemingly inspired, dismayed her ; and completely nipped in the bud, the tender growth of wifely sentiment that his misfortune had caused to arise within her bosom. Once again she felt repelled, and thrown back upon herself.

"You see," he went on, waxing more and more garrulous and confidential as his consciousness returned, although not yet accompanied by the power of self-restraint. "I was always spoony on Blanche, and she on me. It was an awful sell her marrying—I never dreamt she would. Now we are both miserable, and all through that little, puritanical, pasty-faced thing, whose very presence drives me wild. I wish to goodness I could get rid of her—I wish she'd die—then Blanche and I might live happily and comfortable—I don't want to be lectured, I tell you. If I'm thirsty, I'm thirsty, and have no notion of some fool of a woman hiding the bottles away the moment my back is turned—That's what my wife does, you know. It isn't fair—is it——?"

"Hush !" interrupted Doctor Goodwyn, severely. "You must not talk in this ridiculous fashion. Nobody's listening, and nobody approves of your sentiments. Come, be a man. You are quite conscious now, and can put a guard over your tongue if you choose. If you don't, I shall give orders for everyone to leave the room." Then he turned to Bligh, and added in an undertone, "Don't take any notice of this rambling nonsense, my dear Lady Verschoyle. Patients are often very queer after taking chloroform. It nearly always has the effect of making them talkative and lightheaded."

Bligh's lip trembled, but she managed to say quietly—"Yes I know."

To herself she murmured with great and exceeding bitterness, "It is not nonsense. Philip only says what is in his heart. Would to God I had never married him ; for if I make his life miserable, so also does he mine."

The doctor's stern remonstrance produced a salutary effect. It checked the sick man's garrulity, and after a time he lay quite still, too conscious now of pain to experience any longer a desire to converse. When the patient had arrived at this stage, Doctor Goodwyn left him, after giving Bligh and the nurse some particular instructions as to a lotion which he wished used.

"Every teaspoonful must be diluted with forty times the same amount of water," he said. "Please remember that. I shall also send round a medicine to be taken every four hours, which I hope may be successful in keeping down the temperature."

"Shall we see you again this evening?" asked Bligh.

"Most certainly. I will look in between nine and ten o'clock." So saying, he went away.

When Doctor Goodwyn had gone Bligh went to the window, and gazed out at the familiar landscape with dull, unseeing eyes. She felt as if a sledge hammer had dealt her a stunning blow which deadened every faculty. In her ears rang those terrible words : "I hate her. I wish she were dead." Every time she glanced at her husband she seemed to hear them anew, and she asked herself if it were possible for them to live together again after this confession, whose genuineness she did not doubt for a single moment. She had suffered much, endured much at his hands, but now she was wounded to the very quick. Her throat felt parched, her eyeballs strained and distended. A haze descended upon her vision, and she clutched at the nearest chair for support.

"Deborah," she said, almost inarticulately, "I—I don't feel well. I think I must l—lie down for a little. This business has upset me."

"And small wonder," whispered Deborah indignantly to the nurse, directly her mistress's back was turned, "for if ever there lived a beast of a man, there he lies. Upon my word, sometimes I feel as if I could murder him."

"Take care," said the nurse, "or he will hear you."

"I don't mind if he does," answered Deborah, defiantly; "and now I'm sure after all this trouble and work, you must be hungry. Hadn't you better go downstairs to the housekeeper's room, and have your tea? I'll stay and look after him"—glancing resentfully at Sir Philip—"whilst you are away."

The invitation was too tempting to be refused.

"I don't mind if I do," answered the excellent Mrs. Collins, readily. "But if the medicine comes in my absence, don't forget to give it to Sir Philip. Dr. Goodwyn made a point of his having it at once, and it would be more than my place is worth to neglect orders."

Old Deborah stuck her nose up in the air.

"Never fear," she answered. "I'll look after the dear invalid. He and I ain't too friendly, but on a special occasion like this, I flatter myself I'm to be trusted as well as most people."

"All right then," said the nurse. "I will go and get my tea while I can. Sir Philip seems quiet and comfortable at present, and inclined to doze. I only made a light dinner to-day, not knowing I should be wanted, and to tell the truth feel quite faint for want of food."

Whereupon Mrs. Collins went downstairs, leaving Deborah in sole charge of the sick-room.

She had not been gone more than a few minutes before a footman tapped at the door, and handed in a couple of bottles, saying they came from Doctor Goodwyn. Deborah took them, and undid their paper wrappings. One bottle was of a dark blue color, with a large poison label on the outside; the other was white, and its contents were to be taken every four hours. And as she stood holding them in her hand, a terrible temptation assailed this worthy woman, who throughout life had flattered herself she was no worse than her neighbours. All at once a devil's voice whispered—"Why not give him the lotion to drink, instead of the medicine? Nobody need be any the wiser. People will only say you made a mistake; and then your beloved mistress will be free. He makes her wretched, and behaves to her like a brute. The greatest kindness you can do her is to rid her of him for ever. The thing is easy! Just a few drops of one mixture instead of another, and if anybody makes a fuss, all you have got to say is that you mistook the bottles in the dark. Courage now, Deborah, courage."

She looked towards the curtained bed, and a smile passed over her wrinkled face. With that little phial grasped in her right hand, she held the power to destroy her greatest enemy. The thought was sweet; and yet she was a Christian woman, who knew most of the New Testament by heart. Carefully and cautiously she uncorked the lotion, and smelt it. The odour tickled her nostrils. It was strong, pungent, penetrating. She took the cork, and lightly brushed her tongue against its damp end. It was as if a red-hot iron had seared it; and with the burning pain produced came a swift reaction. What was this deed she contemplated? Had she gone mad? How could she, who had spent the majority of her days in faithful servitude, deliberately contemplate ending them as a murderess? The idea was too ghastly: and it only showed how wicked she was for it ever to have entered her head. The atmosphere of this great grand house was unholy. and contained no elements of peace or rest. She had hardly known a single day's real happiness since setting foot in it, and she was persuaded her poor mistress had not done so either. To Deborah s excited imagination it now appeared that some demon of evil was pursuing her, and if she would escape from the committal of an awful crime, her only chance lay in flight. Acting on the spur of the moment, she fled precipitately from the room, and almost unconsciously sought Bligh's.

"My dearie," she said, abruptly, "I must go—I must leave you. Don t think me unkind, but I can t trust myself to stay under this roof any longer."

"Why, Deborah!" exclaimed Bligh, in surprise, "what is the matter?"

"Nurse Collins went down to her tea, and I—I said I would take care of Sir Philip : but directly I was left alone with him a frightful notion took possession of my brain. The devil himself must have put it there. I wanted to—to poison him."

"Oh ' Deborah."

"Don't look at me like that, my dearie. I can't bear it : and it's no use scolding me, for I know that I'm a bad, wicked old woman. I hate him for all he makes you suffer, and all of a sudden the thought came to me that if he were out of the road you might be happy. I was within an ace of giving him the wrong medicine, when something held me back. Another time I might not be able to resist the temptation. Don't you understand now why it is necessary for me to go away?"

A strange expression, partly of horror, partly of sympathy, flitted across Bligh s face.

"Deborah," she said, "we will go together. I, too, am a prey to hard and bitter thoughts of which I am afraid. It is no secret to you that my life is unendurable. As long," and her voice trembled, "as long as mamma lived, and there was the smallest hope of reforming him, I tried to put up with it. But now I despair. You heard what he said this afternoon. That is the only result of my seeking to influence him for his good. From the first it was an uphill task : of late it has become an impossible one ; and the worst of it is, every day my shame and my loathing increase, until sometimes I wish the earth would open and swallow me up. I have done my best. God knows how I have sought to crush my own feelings and to live at peace with him. I never looked for much personal happiness," she went on with growing agitation—" I was prepared to be grateful for receiving food and shelter in return for the surrender of my liberty ; but I did not expect both to be affronted and —and hated."

" It is monstrous," said Deborah. " Drink is fast turning him mad. If he goes on as he is doing, he will soon have delirium tremens."

" Whatever the cause," said Bligh, " after to-day I feel that I have no longer any place in this house, and, like you, shall be better out of it. For months past everything that is worst in my nature has been roused, whilst all opportunity of cultivating the good has grown rarer and rarer. One cannot exist amidst debasing and uncongenial surroundings without deteriorating. I am growing morbid and introspective. I know it, yet am powerless to help the gradual growth of unhealthy thought. Nothing is much worse for a woman than to live in a constant state of smothered rebellion. When confidence is checked she either turns sullen, or else hypocritical. One can't go on doing violence to one's feelings for ever. The effort is unnatural, and must tell in course of time. I have suffered, oh !—how I have suffered——"

She was silent for a moment or two, then resumed in a quieter voice—" And so, Deborah, we will go together to some quiet little place, where nobody will know us, and where we shall be removed from the temptations that assail us here. For I am not better than yourself. The same thoughts have passed through my brain as through yours. If Doctor Goodwyn had told me to-day that my husband must die, I should have listened to his fiat without a tear, and with a guilty gladness at my heart."

" My dearie," said poor old Deborah, aghast at the strong emotion she had been the means of conjuring into life, " I ought not to have spoken as I did. Let me go by myself."

" No, no," Bligh answered, with unwonted vehemence. " The idea of going away is not new to me. Do you suppose that when he insulted and struck me before people, I was made of stone? I want nothing from him—neither his wealth, nor his name, nor his position. I will not leave Beechlands a penny richer than when I entered it. I despise him too much to be indebted to him in the smallest degree, and refuse to touch a farthing of his money. You and I, Deborah," and she smiled faintly, " are accustomed to poverty. We do not care for grand houses and luxuries of every description. Poor as we were, we were happier far in our little cottage."

" Yes, indeed," exclaimed Deborah, fervently, her sunken eyes glistening.

" And we will be happy again," continued Bligh, with feverish gaiety. "We will leave slang, and drink, and sport behind us, and shake ourselves free of fast ways, accompanied by loose talk. Ah ! mother, mother," clasping her hands together, " I wonder if you foresaw when you left me that four hundred a year how soon it was going to prove my only source of subsistence."

" Miss Bligh, dear," said Deborah, making use of the old familiar nomenclature, as she frequently did in moments of forgetfulness, " don't do anything in a hurry. I feel as if I were to blame for your decision."

" Have I not already told you that the thought of leaving has been with me a long time? I was vacillating. What Sir Philip said to-day determined me. We are two wretched people. Let one of us at least be happy. If I go he can enjoy himself as he likes with his cousin. Did you not hear him confess how obnoxious my presence was? It was very kind of Doctor Goodwyn to try and soften his pretty speeches, but I happen to know that people never bare their innermost secrets so completely as when they are just recovering from chloroform. The future lies before me like a closed book whose pages I cannot read. If Philip were dangerously ill, and really wanted me, I might return ; but at present I feel as if I must have a change. The very air of this places stifles me."

" But where will you go ? " inquired Deborah.

" I settled that in my own mind long ago," answered Bligh, with rather a conscious flush. " Do you remember our once spending a few days at a far-away village perched up amongst the Welsh hills? We went there one summer when my father was alive."

" What! Glenarfon! where all the iron works and coal pits were ? "

" Yes. It is hidden from the world, and nobody would ever think of looking for us there. To-morrow morning at six o'clock I propose to leave this house, and God only knows whether I shall ever come back to it."

Deborah looked wistfully at her mistress.

" Thank the Lord for one thing," she said. " There is no man in the business. Your worst enemy cannot throw stones at you, or couple your name with that of a lover."

" No," said Bligh, gravely. " I have been spared the crowning misery of an unlawful love. It is the greatest misfortune from which a woman can suffer, and I bless Providence for not having added it to my other trials."

CHAPTER XXXVI.

A LONELY WOMAN.

BLIGH sat up late that evening, writing a letter to her husband.

"My dear Philip," she said, " I am leaving you at a time when the world will probably judge my conduct unfavourably, and consider that I have failed in wifely duty towards you. The reproach is no light one, and yet I am prepared to bear public censure, for I feel that I can no longer remain in this house. When you lay unconscious a few hours ago you stated repeatedly that you loved Blanche Vansittart and hated me, and that I embittered your life. Those were not pleasant words to hear, and no doubt you spoke them under the influence of chloroform. Nevertheless, I know that they were the expression of your innermost thoughts. I stand in your way. Well! rightly or wrongly, I will do so no longer. Unfortunately for us both it is not in my power to untie the fatal knot by which we are bound; but one thing I can do—namely, relieve you of my hateful presence. If you had only told me how obnoxious it was to you we might have come to some arrangement sooner. As it is, I have determined to leave Beechlands and to trouble you no more. Let me disappear from your path as if I had never crossed it. Our marriage was a mistake. Why not honestly admit the fact, and discontinue to be fettered by one another. Henceforth, as far as I am concerned, you are at liberty to return to your old bachelor habits, though I fancy you have already availed yourself of that permission. But understand me. I go more in sorrow than in anger, and should a time ever come when you are in difficulty or I can be of the least real service to you, then I shall remember that the law has made you my husband, and will return. With such a contingency in view I take the precaution of enclosing my solicitor's address. Meanwhile, I feel sure you will agree with me in considering there is nothing to be gained by our corresponding. Hoping that my absence may serve to materially increase your happiness, and that you will soon regain your usual health, believe me to remain——" Here she came to a sudden stop, unable to find a signature which sounded neither too formal nor too affectionate. She failed, however, to get one to her mind, and at last ended by adding hurriedly, " Yours truly, Bligh Verschoyle." She could not put " Yours lovingly " or " Yours devotedly." They sounded positively hypocritical when her heart was so charged with bitterness and pain. The note written, she sealed and addressed it, and then heaved a sigh of relief. Her spirit began to rise at the prospect of escaping from the uncongenial moral bondage which for months past had held it captive. Reviewing her married life it seemed like some oppressive nightmare, from which she was only too thankful to awake, devoutly hoping it might prove a bad dream rather than a reality. She had but one regret, leaving Lady Verschoyle, for she knew that her mother-in-law would miss her even if Sir Philip did not. The lonely old woman would be still more lonely when she was gone. The thought of her pricked Bligh's conscience, and she strove to dismiss her from her mind.

" After all," she argued, " Lady Verschoyle will be no worse off than she was before I came. She managed to exist without me a good many years, and no doubt she will continue to support life in the future."

Nevertheless, this reasoning did not satisfy Bligh, and she obtained very little rest. She felt too excited to sleep, and during the silent watches of the night could not conceal from herself the gravity of the step she proposed taking. And yet she did not repent her decision, and early the next morning she and old Deborah left Beechlands in a hired fly. Their modest luggage was piled on the top, and half an hour later they found themselves seated in the train, which was destined to bear them to Glenarfon. There were several stoppages *en route*, and the afternoon was far advanced before they arrived. Bligh experienced a severe shock of disappointment when, upon issuing from a tunnel just outside the station, she perceived how greatly Glenarfon had increased in size since her last visit, paid some ten years ago. Then it had been a quaint, grey-slated little village, nestling in a narrow valley that ran transversely between two ranges of rounded hills, on which the purple heather bloomed, and the cock grouse cackled to his mate. At that time the iron-works and coal pits were almost disused, and managed on old-fashioned principles, which yielded small results, and still less profit. Now all was changed.

On every side tall funnels belched forth dense columns of black smoke, which, curling upwards, gradually dispersed amid the hazy, overcharged atmosphere. Huge blast furnaces greedily swallowing up the ores with which they were fed, reddened the evening sky and emitted their waste gases. All round the station a town had arisen almost with the rapidity of an American city. Rows of streets greeted the eye. They swarmed with little, dirty, bareheaded children, who rolled recklessly in the black coal-dust that even in dry weather gave the roads an uncleanly appearance. Rough, untidy women lounged about the open doors of their grimy cottages, laughing when some drunken miner came reeling along the unevenly-laid pavement and flung a coarse word at them. The dull roar of the works higher up the valley could be heard above the squalling of babies and the scolding of impatient young mothers. In addition to the furnaces and chimneys, the sky-line was broken by enormous ash-heaps, which resembled bare, grey pyramids. No verdure grew on their naked sides. Not a single green weed or blade of grass redeemed the uniform ugliness of their appearance. Engines whistled, trucks rattled, hammers beat, steel plates clanged, steam hooters hooted, machinery creaked, fires blazed, and water trickled. The scene, even viewed from a distance, was one of unparalleled activity, and to the tired travellers, weary after their day's journey, the noise and confusion appeared insupportable. Instead of the quiet asylum she had pictured it seemed to Bligh that she had come to a regular pandemonium.

She looked about her with a crestfallen expression, which would have been comical had it not also been pathetic.

"What are we to do?" she said to Deborah. "It is always the way in this world. Nothing is ever so nice as one fancies. Since I was here last the place is evidently ruined, and it is useless to expect peace or rest amidst such a din."

"It is too late to go on anywhere else this evening," replied Deborah. "We had better stay here to-night at any rate."

"I suppose we must," said Bligh, with a sigh of resignation.

"I think it would be advisable. You are tired, and consequently dispirited. To-morrow you may feel less despondent. But bear this in mind, dearie. It's all one to me where I am so long as you are happy. You've only got to please yourself."

Bligh shot a grateful glance at her faithful attendant, and, acting on her advice, proceeded to inquire of the station-master if he could recommend a decent hotel.

"They ain't up to much," he said : " leastways, for a lady like you. But if you go to Mr. William Williams, of the Mountain Ash, his good woman will give you a clean bed to lie upon and a tidy supper. You see," he added apologetically, "we don't have many tourists come this way, only gents on business and connected with the works."

"We are not very particular," said Bligh, "and no doubt shall find every comfort at the Mountain Ash. Is it far from here?"

"No; not more than two or three minutes' walk. If you go straight up to the top of the High-street and take the first turn to the right, you cannot fail to see it."

"How about the luggage?" she inquired. "Can we hire a fly?"

"We ain't got no flies here, marm. We're too far from London to have much call for carriages. Mr. Williams he keeps an old omnibus; but you won't want it. My boy will put your things on a barrow and trundle them up to the inn in a trice. He'll be there almost as soon as you."

Satisfied with this arrangement Bligh and Deborah started along the High-street. The afternoon sun poured obliquely down upon it, and generously sought to gild the squalid pawn-broker, tobacco, and refreshment shops, of which it was mainly composed. The latter displayed a queer assortment of miscellaneous comestibles, pork pics, sausages, red herrings, ship biscuits, buns, bull's eyes, green apples, and periwinkles being the articles apparently most in favour. Every household contributed to the gutter its contingent of children. Indeed, the highway resembled a rabbit warren. They rolled in the mud, got under the horses' feet whenever a heavily loaded waggon went by, and appeared ubiquitous. Half-clad, half-starved, left almost completely to their own resources at an age when many of them could hardly toddle, and exposed to dangers which would have driven most mothers out of their minds; they yet seemed to thrive. Scarcely a woman under forty who did not hold a baby in her arms, wrapped up in an old plaid shawl, and looking like a dirty bundle rather than an embryo human being.

Cabbage stumps, broken plates, cast-off shoes, ashes, rusty pails minus a bottom, and refuse of every conceivable description ornamented the roadway. The setting sun's warm rays caused a faint, but offensive, odour to arise, not noticed by the inhabitants, but exceedingly distressing to unaccustomed nostrils. It was a mingled stench of decaying garbage, putrid bones, defective drains, and unwashed humanity. After an unusually hot day the air was charged with this peculiar fragrance, and once or twice Bligh was forced to put her handkerchief to her nose. Feeling more and more disheartened she and Deborah walked on, until they turned down a bye-street, at the end of which a glimpse of rough moorland was to be obtained. They came to a halt before a detached house built of grey stone, and wearing an air of solid prosperity not to be mistaken. Outside the porch grew a stunted ash, bent by the wind, whose blackened leaves were smothered in coal dust like everything else. There was a gap in the buildings on the opposite side of the street. Through it could be seen the ruddy glow of the furnaces and the dark outline of the heather-clad hills. Bligh rang the bell, which was promptly answered by a tall, superior-looking landlady, who, upon hearing her requirements, at once showed her to a couple of rooms, which, if some what scantily furnished, at all events possessed the merits of scrupulous cleanliness.

Until to-day Bligh had never thoroughly realised how little strength she had regained since her illness : but now, what with the early rising, the excitement and emotion consequent upon leaving home, and the long railway journey, she felt quite tired out. So, directly after tea—for not one woman in twenty indulges in the luxury of dinner when left to her own resources— she retired to rest, firmly intending to quit Glenarfon on the following morning and seek some more picturesque spot, where the beauty and calm of Nature might soothe her wounded spirit. But man proposes, and God disposes.

After a long night's sleep she was inclined to take a more cheerful view of the situation. Their rooms were comfortable, the landlady most civil and attentive, and the necessity of setting off again on her travels no longer appeared quite as urgent as on the previous evening.

"I think," she said to Deborah after breakfast, "that we might stay here for one day. It would be interesting to go over the works, and there are several places I should like to revisit. If I remember rightly there was a beautiful park and house belonging to a lunatic lord somewhere close by, where papa, mamma, and I spent a delightful afternoon. I will ask Mrs. Williams about it."

She touched the bell, and the landlady came running up the stairs in hot haste.

"Anything I can do for you, m ?" she inquired breathlessly.

"Yes," said Bligh. "Several years ago I stayed a few days at Glenarfon. It is wonderfully altered since then, and I no longer know my way about. In those days it was nothing but a little country village, now it has grown into quite a large town, with streets and shops, and an increasing population——"

"It's the works as has spoilt the place for visitors." interposed Mrs. Williams. "We don't have a quarter of the strangers we used to have in olden days. The fact is, that ever since poor Lord de Bretton died and his nephew came into the property everything is changed. The present owner's first step was to get a new manager, and, as it so happened, Mr. Vaughan—that's his name—was mad on improvements. Leastways, he calls them improvements, though there are a good few of us who hold a contrary opinion, and don't like seeing our pretty valley given over to miners and machinery."

"The old lord is dead then ?" said Bligh.

"Yes : the poor gentleman had been queer in his head for many years, and obliged to have a keeper, as perhaps you may have heard. Nobody knew exactly how it arose ; but one night a terrible fire broke out at the hall, and he threw himself out of the bedroom window, and was picked up stone dead. His nephew, Mr. Bernard de Bretton, inherited the title and estates."

" Does he live at the Hall ? " inquired Bligh.

" No. We only wish he would. But although he has not the slightest objection to spending the money made by his hard-worked miners he considers himself much too great a man to reside in their midst or to manage his property personally."

" I don't call that right," said Bligh.

" Nor do I ; but the present Lord de Bretton has got the name of being a very gay, fast young man, who cares only for amusements. Why! bless you, marm, it's close upon seven years since he succeeded to his uncle, and, would you believe it, he has only twice set foot inside the Hall, and then but for a couple of days. My husband he goes on ever so about absentee landlords and the obligations of property. He says that the upper classes nowadays live for nothing but pleasure, scoff at the word duty, and then feel very much aggrieved because honest working men refuse to worship them like demi-gods."

" Is Mr. Williams a Radical? " asked Bligh.

" I don't know what he calls himself ; but he is a man who has got a good head on his shoulders and plenty of common sense ; and he don't think it right for fine gentlemen to take all the wealth they can out of a place and then never come near it."

" How many men does Lord de Bretton employ? " inquired Bligh, who was getting interested in the conversation.

" What with the pits, furnaces, and one thing and another, several thousand," answered Mrs. Williams. " The whole valley belongs to him, and they say the rents alone bring in over eight thousand a year, though most of the cottages are in a disgraceful condition, and many of them are hardly fit for human beings to live in."

" It is abominable," exclaimed Bligh, indignantly. " Instead of spending so much money on himself Lord de Bretton ought to be made to repair them. Parliament should pass a law which would effectually prevent such landlords from shirking their responsibilities. Is there much distress among the people? "

" Lately there has been a great deal. The men have nearly all joined the trades' union, which in many instances forces them to strike quite independently of their personal wishes. At the present moment they are standing out for an increase of ten per cent. Mr. Vaughan says he can't afford to give it. The consequence is two-thirds of the colliers have struck work, and, being thrown out of employ, do nothing but quarrel and drink, leaving the poor, unfortunate women and children to starve. It's them I'm sorry for, since they are always the principal sufferers."

" I fear that is ever the case," said Bligh, who listened with
growing attention to Mrs. Williams's remarks. " The weak invariably go to the wall all through life."

" It makes me mad to hear the nonsense that's preached
about foreign missions," went on the good landlady, garrulously.
" Last Sunday as ever is I went to church, and a strange clergyman exchanged duty with ours. The whole of the discourse
was about blacks and heathens. He tried to prove that it was
our duty to subscribe money to send out missionaries to convert
them; but, Lord bless you, marm ! to my thinking it's nothing
but a pack of nonsense. How do we know how our shillings
are spent when we send them off to Jericho? Shillings are
wanted at home, and charity begins there, as the saying very
properly is. For my part I feel sure that if any Christian lady
or gentleman would settle down in this place, and go about
among the people, trying to teach them to behave a little less
like savages, the result would be very much more satisfactory
than worrying some poor, ignorant darkey into adopting all our
ideas and discarding his own. The truth is there's plenty of
work to be done right under folks' eyes if they would but see it."

" I expect you are not far wrong," said Bligh, thoughtfully.
" How long did you say it was since Lord de Bretton's last
visit ? "

" Getting on for three years. He was then going a voyage
round the world."

" And what is Mr. Vaughan, the manager, like ? "

" Oh ! he's a shrewd, sharp man, who thoroughly understands
that his business is to keep the money-grinding machine in good
order for his employer, and supply funds whenever they are
required."

" Is there a Lady de Bretton ? "

" No ; we wish there was," said Mrs. Williams ; " for then
perhaps he'd live part of the year at any rate at the Hall, and see
for himself that there are plenty of other things besides the
works as wants improving. A public reading-room is very badly
needed, also some sort of institute where amusements might be
provided after the day's work is over."

" Do you think," said Bligh, " that I could get someone who
knows Glenarfon well to take me all round, and show me the
schools, the homes of the women, and so on ? "

" Are you going to stay among us by any chance ? " asked
Mrs. Williams.

" Yes," answered Bligh, forming a sudden resolution. " If
by so doing I can employ my time profitably. That is just what
I want, for I am a lonely woman, without any ties, and my father
and mother are both dead. My name is Burton—Mrs. Burton.

I intended to have left to-morrow, but after what you tell me I feel greatly tempted to stay. Even if I can't help the men I can assist the women and children—especially the children— by getting up classes, and teaching the girls how to cook and sew, and giving the boys drawing lessons, reading and arith- metic."

Mrs. Williams put out a rough, but hearty, hand.

" I wish there were more ladies like you in the world," she said. " You may not credit the statement, but quite half the quarrels which arise between our young married couples here are owing to the wife having no knowledge of keeping her home comfortable or how to serve up a tidy dinner to a tired man when he comes back of an evening. He cares mighty little then about ribbons, and fal-lals, and all the rest of it. What he wants is something decent to eat."

" High or low," said Bligh, gravely, " if a woman would find favour in the eyesight of man she must appeal to that sen- sitive seat of affection—his stomach. You are of opinion that cooking classes would succeed ? "

" I am certain of it," said Mrs. Williams. " They are what we want more than anything else."

" All I wish is to be useful and to do what good I can," said Bligh, with a sad smile. " I have nothing else to live for."

" Then," said Mrs. Williams, " Providence must have sent you here. And now, if you will allow me, I will take you to see our clergyman, Mr. Davies. No one knows the needs of the people so well as he, and if you want work he'll soon give you plenty."

" Do you really mean to stay here, Miss Bligh, darling ? " in- quired Deborah, as soon as the worthy landlady had bustled from the room to put on her bonnet and cloak.

" Yes, I think so. I don't mean to say that Glenarfon is an ideal abode, or one which I should have selected had I con- sulted my inclinations alone ; but that is precisely what I desire to avoid. I have suffered lately from the deterioration of character which results from leading a purely selfish and self- indulgent life, and I am anxious to turn over a new leaf. I foresee many difficulties ; but surely it will be a better thing for me in the end to employ myself actively and usefully rather than sit disconsolately at home brooding over the failures of matrimony. If I am not precisely happy that is no reason why I should nurse my sorrow at the expense of others. I don't intend to be guilty of such a mean weakness if I can help it. For a time at any rate we can live here happily and in accordance with our resources. What say you, Deborah ? " and she held out her hand. " Are you willing to try the experiment ? "

Deborah seized it and devoured it with kisses.

"My angel," she said, "all I ask is to be where you are. But I fear you will do too much. You are far from strong yet, and your health should be the first consideration."

Bligh sighed.

"It is so horrid not to do things like other people, and to feel fettered by one's horrible body."

"You are sure to get well in time, honey, if you will but take care of yourself."

"I can't take care of myself, Deborah. Why should I? What for? I am possessed by a feverish energy. Don't you see that unless I am busy and occupied I shan't be able to exist? I find it impossible to drive away thought, to forget the past. All I can look for in the future is to tread the rugged path of duty. Other women are loved and cared for. Henceforth love stands outside my horizon. I must live and die in harness, straining against the instincts which God has seen fit to bestow on my sex.

A lump rose in Deborah's throat. She made no reply, but looked sadly out of the window, where the setting sun was illumining the ragged forms of two little yellow-haired children. Ah! why had the white wings of death enfolded her dear mistress's baby?

CHAPTER XXXVII.

"SUCH IS MAN."

A FORTNIGHT from the date of Bligh's arrival at Glenarfon she was settled in a small, but comfortable, cottage perched half-way up the hillside, and which looked serenely down upon the busy valley. It was situated high enough to be removed from the smoke that spread beneath it like a dense, black pall, whilst heather and tufted grass grew close round its door. Bligh sent to London for some nicknacks, and by the aid of these, a few yards of Indian muslin, Japanese fans and screens, she soon converted the parlour into a very pretty sitting-room, which bore the impress of a refined and cultured woman.

Before long she had not only felt thoroughly at home in her new abode, but also persuaded herself that she was completely happy. As Mrs. Williams had foretold, she did not want for occupation. Her days were fully employed. Aided by Mr. Davies, who entered heartily into her schemes, she instituted a series of classes. Every afternoon was devoted to them, and as the weeks passed they became more and more popular, and she had the satisfaction of feeling that she was really benefiting her fellow-creatures in a practical way. And this conviction brought an inward peace which it was many months since she had experienced. From early morning until late at night she never lacked for employment, and if her strength was frequently somewhat overtaxed her mind gradually recovered its natural, healthy tone. Removed from the atmosphere of Beechlands her ideas righted themselves, like a ship when its ballast is properly adjusted after having got loose. She perceived even more clearly than heretofore that the society of exclusively sporting men, who twaddled away all through dinner about one particular fence, and made some grubby old ditch do duty for the whole of dessert, was not exactly calculated to strengthen a person's brain power or improve the intelligence. And when she recalled the way in which her husband and his fast friends talked of women, and the want of chivalry displayed, and the utter absence of all consideration and reverence for age, she positively shuddered. Many a time had she sat at the head of her own table and heard the points of some fair Amazon summed up precisely as if she had been a yearling filly.

The married men past forty were the worst. They professed to be unable to talk to a woman over twenty-five. After that they declared the bloom was off, and they vastly preferred seventeen. It was quite old enough for them. What they admired was roundness and freshness and rosiness. The sign of a wrinkle, the least symptom of age, and their ardour cooled at once. They were never weary of discussing a girl's face, figure, hair, and complexion; but her mental attributes were entirely beneath their notice. If she were fast, flirty, slangy, and run after by other men, that was perfectly sufficient for these middle-aged Benedicts. A nice, modest woman, no matter how great her qualities and intellectual abilities might be, had not a chance. She was always voted slow, or prudish, or—more damning than either—too long in the tooth! These representative specimens of a fast hunting set were not capable of appreciating chastity or reserve in the opposite sex, and certainly did little by their conduct to encourage such virtues. They went in almost exclusively for looks, though now and again they would condescend to allow themselves to be amused by a comparatively plain woman, provided she possessed the enviable reputation of being " good fun " and was able to tell a naughty story with commendable verve and audacity. Sterling merit they viewed with profound indifference. They only expected that of their wives—the poor, despised drudges who stayed quietly at home, managed the household, did all the hard work, and were invariably held responsible for every tiny mishap. What effect their examples might have upon them, or how they might be affected by the marital neglect and unfaithfulness of their lords, never gave them a thought. It was their place to amuse themselves, the wife's to bear the kicks and abuse, and never complain. That was their notion of matrimony. For the man, pleasure, for the woman, work. For the stronger vessel, license and idleness; for the weaker, struggle and self-control. Oh! short-sighted policy! since it renders the weak strong, and the strong weak.

Bligh had seen this phase of life, and although she dearly loved horses and everything connected with them, she was not so sorry to escape from it when it represented the total extinction of every worthier or higher aim and the entire surrender of ambition. Sport, according to her ideas, was a delightful amusement; but not an absorbing business, to which every other pursuit should be subservient. In Sir Philip's case it had not taken her long to discover that it was made an excuse for neglecting nearly all the duties entailed by his rank and position. It seemed to her that he and his chosen companions were frittering away the talents with which God had originally endowed them, and allowing self-indulgence to swallow up any impulse of energy and enterprise. In the home which she had left she was accustomed to feel oppressed, repulsed, and isolated. It was useless trying to give utterance to her thoughts. They were not congenial. Amongst this rough mining population she had already discovered finer gentlemen and truer friends than during her residence at Beechlands. She did not know as yet where her present life might lead her, but she knew that it was better in every respect than the one she had quitted. Honourable toil brought a sense of substantial repose, which made the pursuit of selfish enjoyment appear a poor, unworthy thing. All Bligh prayed for now was that matters might remain as they were, without any fresh event occurring to disturb the even tenor of her ways.

"I have done with love," she constantly said to herself. "It is such a comfort to outlive one's emotions, and remain absolutely indifferent to the admiration of men. The older one grows the more clearly one sees that it is the bane of a woman's existence, and how much happier she really is once she gives up taking a vital interest in the opposite sex. The truth is she knows no peace until then."

Having been disappointed in her own particular ventures Bligh took refuge in philosophy, and argued herself into the belief that henceforth she was quite incapable of that supreme folly, losing one's heart to a man. And yet Balzac assures us thirty is the most dangerous age of any where a woman's susceptibilities are concerned, for if the romance of youth may have

had taken ; and now, because I sink, you dare to reproach me.
Ah ! Geoffrey, men like you, who take into their keeping a
woman's life, and arrogate to themselves dominion over her
soul, are no better than moral murderers. They little realise
the mischief which they commit. Do you imagine that your
preaching and your conduct produce no effect on a sensitive
young mind ? Can you suppose that the wives whom you
neglect and desert are creatures of stone ? Are you so stupid
as to fancy us devoid of the most ordinary feelings, whilst you
may sin—aye, sin, for that's the word—as you like without
retribution being meted out to you in some form ? Again I
repeat I am but what you have made me. Once upon a time
I was as plastic clay in your hands, and if I stand here to-day
disgraced, fallen, lowered for ever in my own self-esteem, you,
and not I, are to blame."

The book ended in the poor wife, after much temptation and
misery, returning to the faith of her childhood, and resolving to
cling to the essence, even if she were no longer able to accept
the detail, of Christianity.

" After all," she said, in conclusion, " it is the best teaching
that has yet been given to the world. Let people say what
they will, and pick the Testaments to pieces, man in his present
stage of development is far too faultily constituted to be able
to dispense altogether with religion. A few powerfully organ-
ised minds may manage to exist without it, but for the majority
belief is essential. True or untrue, Christ's life is a good
enough example for most of us. Henceforth all my endeavours
shall be humbly to imitate it."

The novel appealed both to the old and to the new school of
thought, and at once brought the author's name into prominence.
Great curiosity was exhibited as to who he or she might be, but
the secret was well kept. Nobody knew it except Messrs. C.
W. Gray and Co., of Bedford Street, Covent Garden, and two
lonely women living in a little cottage amongst the Welsh hills.

Bligh's apprenticeship to her father had borne good fruit.
It had given her a knowledge of composition which, under other
circumstances, she might never have gained. For years past
she had unconsciously been absorbing impressions and assimi-
lating them in her strong, clear mind ; so that when she took
up her pen she had a goodly stock of subject matter to draw
upon. The result of her first attempt was a novel remarkable
for its interest, originality, and power. Naturally she felt
gratified by her success, though its effect was to render her
more anxious to improve and do better in the future. She knew
how difficult it was for a beginner to get a start in the literary
world and how publisher after publisher would return an un-

known author's MSS. unread, with a brief intimation that they thanked Mr. So-and-So for his kind offer, but they were not in a position to entertain it. Her father's struggles and disappointments ere he finally attained the gratification of seeing his name appear in print had to a certain extent let her behind the scenes, and she realised her luck in having been able to set her foot on the first rung of the ladder. If she should ever climb was a question of time and her own ability; but at all events she was fairly floated, and Mr. Gray had already begged permission to bring out her next book, on which she was earnestly engaged. His letters—always models of style and replete with epigram—were now complimentary into the bargain, a sure sign that the new author was worth cultivating.

Wonderful to relate, the reviews were mostly favourable. They contradicted each other as a matter of course. One alluded to the heroine as a very wicked, unprincipled young woman, who deserved all and more than what she got; the next spoke of her in glowing terms, as one of the sweetest and most lovable creations of modern times, and refused to see a flaw in her moral conduct. A slashing critic, who wrote for the " Twopenny Twaddler," bemoaned that what Stonyer Stone evidently meant for wit was only vulgar pomposity; whilst his *confrère*, a gentleman who furnished sparkling articles to the " Weekly Gossiper," described the unknown author as the coming humourist of the day.

As a matter of fact there was not much real instruction to be gained from the reviews. They were either foolishly flattering or else ruthlessly severe. Nine times out of ten the reviewer displayed but a superficial knowledge of his subject, called the characters by their wrong names, and held the author responsible for every printer's error. At this stage of her career Bligh was not so thick-skinned as she afterwards became, and she took the majority of these criticisms very much to heart. Like all novices she began by feeling exceedingly elated whenever she received a favourable clipping from the News Agency to which she subscribed, and proportionately dejected on the receipt of an uncomplimentary one. She very soon saw, however, that a really intelligent review, setting forth the author's faults in a manner by which he might profit, was rare, and that in this respect the country press was decidedly in advance of the metropolitan.

Meanwhile the book went on selling, which was the main thing. Three library editions were sold out in almost as many months; an eminent statesman wrote an article on its theological aspect in the " Nineteenth Century," which materially increased the sale, and the name of Stonyer Stone was in everybody's mouth. Women especially praised " Such is Man." They not only acknowledged its truth, but were delighted at the raps given to the sterner sex. On all sides it was admitted that whether agreeable or the reverse, the author undoubtedly possessed a graphic and forcible way of putting things, which struck home ; and the book, whatever its faults, had the merit of never being dull. From the first page to the last the reader was engrossed, and experienced no inclination to skip.

So, while Bligh worked amongst her women and children, teaching them to cook and to sew, and gradually regained the moral equilibrium which her uncongenial marriage had done so much to destroy, the fame of Stonyer Stone went abroad, until it reached even to the remote Welsh valley, where a quiet little lady, believed to be a widow—one Mrs. Burton by name—had taken up her residence, unknown and unsought after.

Mr. Davies startled her by saying, shortly before Christmas, when they happened to be walking together—

" I must lend you this new book, Mrs. Burton, which everybody is talking of. I had it lent me from the library yesterday by good luck."

" What new book ? " she asked, quite innocently.

" Why, ' Such is Man,' of course. Surely you have heard of it."

She made some inaudible reply. The shock of finding herself famous quite took away her breath. And she had been so ashamed of her handiwork at Beechlands ! So terrified lest anyone should guess how her spare hours were spent !

CHAPTER XXXVIII.

BLIGH SPEAKS HER THOUGHTS.

BLIGH had obtained leave from Mr. Vaughan to wander about Glenarfon Park at any time that she felt inclined. The permission was one which she valued highly, and frequently availed herself of whenever she wanted a pleasant walk without going very far. The Hall was enclosed on three sides by a solid stone wall that effectually shut it out from the works, which, however, were situated close by, at a distance of only a few hundred yards. Peeping through the massive iron gates which guarded the park, and gazing longingly at the cool green grass within, the shadowy trees and noble mansion with its palm-houses and conservatories, many a weary miner trudging home after his day's toil in the dark bowels of the earth, might have been excused for casting wistful glances at Lord de Bretton's property. Amid the dirt, the dust, and griminess for which Glenarfon was conspicuous, it did indeed resemble an oasis in the desert.

And as Bligh noted the want and destitution everywhere apparent without those ponderous barriers. and the beauty and the luxury that reigned within, her spirit rose up in indignation against the wealthy owner of the land.

" He does nothing—absolutely nothing for the people," she said to herself. " It would be so easy for him to open this place—say once a week, on a Sunday afternoon, and let the poor workmen with their wives and children rove about the park, and have a sight of something green. It would do very little harm ; I am persuaded of that : and even if it did, it would not count for much when weighed in the scales against the innocent pleasure conferred. People who have to work by the sweat of their brow require refining influences to prevent them from degenerating into mere beasts of burden. Occasional amusement is not good for, but necessary to their barren. toilsome lives. It keeps them human : but I suppose such ideas as these never enter his lordship's head. From all accounts, he must be an odious, selfish wretch who thinks of nobody but himself. Such men as he are not fit to hold property, and my only wonder is that the lower classes are as good as they are. Were I in their place, I should feel very strongly tempted to overleap Lord de Bretton's stone wall, and enjoy what is on the other side of it."

One bright spring day Bligh was meditating in the above manner. Profiting by the mildness of the weather, she had taken out her palette and colour box, and was busily engaged in sketching a view of the valley. She had chosen a spot not far from the park gates, which had frequently struck her as forming a fitting subject for a picture. In the foreground on a rising knoll stood a group of very old birches. their stems bent by the wind, and stripped of their white bark. On the right rose the square ivy-covered tower of the church. with its slender steeple glistening in the sunshine. Farther off the works and great smoky furnaces were to be seen softened by a becoming distance, and in their rear the outline of the purple hills stood but pure and clear against the blue March sky. For weeks past Bligh had intended making a water-colour from this particular place, but hitherto the weather had been against her putting her purpose into execution.

She soon was busily engaged, and after a couple of hours, steady application had nearly finished her sketch to her satisfaction, when suddenly she was startled by hearing a voice behind her say—"May I be allowed to look?"

She gave a jump of astonishment, not having the least idea that anybody was scrutinising her work. The voice was smooth and pleasant in quality, and evidently belonged to a gentleman. This was her first impression. Then she turned round, and her eyes encountered those of a good-looking young man, whose age might have been somewhere about thirty-one or two. He was tall and fair, with a well-cut aquiline nose, and a remarkably clear complexion which betokened an excellent constitution. The expression of his face was sunny as a child's, and singularly attractive. All this Bligh saw at a glance.

He wore a checked tweed suit, and a cap of the same material. His manner was easy and natural, without being the least intrusive, and she perceived immediately that he had nothing in common with the travelling bagmen and agents, who were in the habit of visiting Glenarfon. The stranger, whoever he might be, was a gentleman, and accustomed to good society. His soft, refined accents betrayed that fact.

So in answer to his request, she said politely, "You are welcome to look if you like, but I am no great artist, and fear my poor sketch is not worth inspection."

He advanced a step nearer, and examined the little water-colour critically, and with the eye of a connoisseur.

"On the contrary," he said, "it is extremely good, and displays a great deal of true artistic perception. Those birches are admirable. One can almost see the wind bending their weather-worn trunks, and your colouring also is capital; but if I might make a suggestion, I would point out that those hills in the background are just a trifle too vivid. They give a flatness to the general effect. Now, in my humble opinion, if you were to tone them down a little you would at once put a great deal of extra distance into the picture. It only wants that to be perfect."

Gratified by the stranger's praise, Bligh at once profited by his hint, and was delighted with the result. He had hit upon the chief defect of the sketch.

"Ah!" she cried. "You must be an artist yourself. No one else would have seen my fault so immediately."

He smiled, and answered carelessly—

"I dabble a little in the fine arts from time to time, but only as an amateur. To be an artist means six or eight hours daily of serious study, and I am afraid I have not enough patience for that. You are very clever to have succeeded in making such a pretty water-colour; for it seems to me this dirty, unpicturesque valley presents but few subjects worthy of the painter's brush."

"I thought like you when I first came here," she answered,

frankly, "and was packing up the very next morning after my arrival; but with all its drawbacks, Glenarfon grows upon one on better acquaintance. There are so many human interests concentrated in the works that in course of time even the perpetual noise seems quite like an old friend. And then it is impossible ever to feel dull in a place of this sort."

"Indeed! You surprise me. I should have thought Glenarfon the dullest hole on earth."

"To my mind, no place can be dull where there is so much to be done," she replied.

"In what way? May I venture to beg you to enlighten my ignorance?" And so saying, he seated himself on a round granite boulder, a few yards from the spot where she had pitched her camp-stool, evidently with the intention of continuing the conversation.

"I mean that there is so much to be done among the people," said Bligh, gravely. "Many of them are little better off than savages, and although they pay high rents for their cottages, you never saw such damp, miserable, tumble-down holes as they are. Fevers are continually breaking out, and the doctor told me only the other day that the great mortality which takes place is almost entirely owing to defective drainage."

"Everybody is mad on drains nowadays," remarked her companion.

"I do not think you would say that if you were to take a five minutes' walk round the town," she returned. "In winter the smells are not so bad, but when the weather is hot they are something awful. Dr. Watkin is very anxious to start a scheme of public sewerage. Unfortunately, the proprietor of Glenarfon, whose real business it is to contribute to everything calculated to improve the condition of his men, takes very little interest in the welfare of the people he employs."

"Are you sure that is the fact?" inquired the stranger, shifting slightly on his seat, as if he found it hard.

"Everybody says so, and certainly my personal experience tends to confirm the statement. Go into the town, the works, or the cottages, and on all sides one hears the same story, 'Lord de Bretton is an absentee landlord. He never comes near the place, and does not care twopence what becomes of it, so long as he continues to draw his rents regularly.' For my part," she went on decidedly, "I think Lord de Bretton must either be a fool, or a very bad man, and in either case I admit to feeling strongly prejudiced against him."

Her interlocutor desisted from sucking the knob of his stick —an occupation which during Bligh's speech apparently afforded him considerable pleasure—and looked up sharply.

"Why do you take such a violent dislike to a person," he asked, " whom, according to your own account, you have never even seen ?"

" For a very simple reason," she said. "It does not fall to everyone's lot to have wide opportunities given them of doing good. Lord de Bretton might do so much—gladden the lives of so many miserable people if he did but choose, and he does nothing—or next to nothing. The money which he draws from Glenarfon he spends elsewhere, and he simply ignores his responsibilities as landlord. Surely wealth has some obligations. The saying, '*Noblesse oblige*,' also holds good in the case of riches. His lordship has a large income without ever having done a thing to earn it. In some countries the mines from which he derives the principal part of his revenue would be regarded as State property. One hears a great deal in these times of unearned increment, and this valley is an exemplification of it. Without its coal and iron, what would the estate be worth? Not five hundred a year, for the land is so rough it is only fit to graze mountain cattle upon."

"That may be, at the same time I fail to see why Lord de Bretton has not a right to do what he likes with his own."

" Is it his own ? Is anything a man's own which he can only keep going by the help of his fellow-creatures? What good would these mines be to his lordship without hired labour? They would lie idle and unprofitable. I maintain that the people who toil have a right to be treated with consideration, and one of the first things is to give them decent, weatherproof houses to live in. Year after year, Lord de Bretton amuses himself by touring round the world, and so on, instead of residing here a portion of the time, as he is in duty bound to do. I would give all I possess to take him to a place called Pit-row, and show him a lot of cottages there. Without exaggeration, they are not fit for human habitation, and yet the unfortunate inmates have to pay a rent of eight shillings a week for these wretched hovels, which are literally very little better than pig-sties. If you ask why they don't apply to their landlord to effect the necessary repairs, the reply is always, 'Oh! he is travelling abroad, and will do nothing.'"

The stranger drew his cap over his eyes. He seemed to find the sun somewhat dazzling.

" You appear to have a great dislike to Lord de Bretton," he observed. "Has it never occurred to you that he may not know all that goes on in his absence ?"

" Then he ought to know," she retorted, with considerable spirit. " I don't consider that any excuse, for it is his business to know. Why should he leave everything to a manager when it is his duty to inquire into

The stranger rose, and for a moment his bright, good-tempered face became overcast.

"Well!" he said, looking uncertainly at her with a pair of well-opened blue eyes. "Perhaps you are right. Anyhow I am much obliged for the interesting information which you have been kind enough to volunteer. Good-morning." So saying, he doffed his cap, showing a close-cut crop of fair hair, and sauntered leisurely away in the direction of the works.

Bligh could not resist an impulse which prompted her to look after his retreating form. The stranger possessed an engaging personality, which, in spite of her indifference to the sex, proved attractive. She felt that she should like to see more of him, and experienced a strong desire to know who he was.

"I wonder who he can be, and what brings him to this part of the world," she mused. "He neither looked like a tourist, nor yet a business man. Somehow or other he had an air about him which gave one the impression he was a personage of importance. One can nearly always tell."

Thus meditating, she finished her sketch, and trotted off home. It was not an every-day occurrence to meet an interesting stranger at Glenarfon; nevertheless, she omitted to mention the circumstance to Deborah; although in her capacity of confidential servant she generally told her every little event that took place during the day. At three o'clock Bligh went to the schoolhouse, where she remained until five, giving practical illustrations of the culinary art to a large number of single and married young women, who had assembled for the purpose. It was not only hot, but also tiring work; and when the lesson came to an end, she put on her hat, opened the door, and stood for a few minutes on the stone steps that led from the classroom to the ground, enjoying the fresh breeze that came sweeping down from the mountains. Just then she perceived two figures coming straight towards her. One belonged to the parish clergyman, Mr. Davies, the other—she recognised it at once—was that of the good-looking stranger who had accosted her earlier in the day. They ascended the steps, evidently with the purpose of addressing her, so she stood still.

"Good afternoon, Mrs. Burton," said Mr. Davies, with a warm shake of the hand. "We have been to your house to pay a formal and respectful call, but were told that, as usual, you were charitably employed. May I introduce Lord de Bretton, who is anxious to make your acquaintance."

The surprise was so great that Bligh took a step backwards, with the result that the door against which she had been leaning, and which was only partially closed, flew open, and she fell bodily to the floor in the most undignified manner. Both gentlemen rushed to her assistance, and raised her to an upright position.

"Are you hurt, Mrs. Burton?" inquired Mr. Davies, anxiously.

"Yes—no, yes," she responded, all red and confused. "I am almost afraid that I have sprained my ankle. It is very stupid, but I can hardly put my right foot to the ground." She tried to hobble a step or two, but the pain was so intense that she was glad to desist from the endeavour.

"Sit down," said Mr. Davies, fetching a chair. "You are not fit to walk, that's quite evident, and if Lord de Bretton will look after you for a few minutes, I'll run round to the vicarage and fetch my pony chaise to convey you home."

"Thank you very much," said Bligh, gratefully.

Hitherto his lordship had not spoken, but when Mr. Davies had departed on his errand, he said, apologetically—

"I feel as if I were in a great measure responsible for this unfortunate accident, Mrs. Burton. I may have been wrong, but it seemed to me that the mention of my name came as a surprise, and startled you considerably."

"I admit to having been rather taken aback," she confessed, "particularly when I remembered our conversation of this morning."

"Why should that disturb you?" he said, with a smile.

"Lord de Bretton, it is useless my trying to soften my words now, or attempting to deny that I spoke my thoughts. I can only say in self-defence that had I possessed the advantage of knowing who you were, I should certainly not have been guilty of the rudeness of giving such frank utterance to them."

"Pray don't distress yourself, Mrs. Burton. It does one good every now and again to hear the truth, even when it is not altogether palatable."

"That may be, but it is scarcely the place of an absolute stranger to inform one of one's faults."

"I don't owe you any malice for informing me of mine."

"Then generosity must be rank amongst your virtues," she rejoined.

"If I possess any," he said, with a laugh. "You did not give me much of a character, certainly. Do you know it was one of the most curious sensations I ever experienced in my life, sitting on that stone listening to the list of my shortcomings. I had no idea it was so formidable before. Your words made quite an impression, and I have been thinking over them ever since."

He spoke so seriously, and yet with such perfect good-humour, that Bligh felt encouraged to say—

"What I told you about the cottages in Pit-row is all quite true. They are in a dreadful condition."

"So I gather. Vaughan ought to have informed me long ago that they needed repairs."

"Since you are here," she said, placing an unconscious emphasis on the "are," "would it not be more satisfactory to see the cottages with your own eyes, instead of trusting to the report of a third person?"

"By Jove! Mrs. Burton, you are right. What do you say? Shall we make a bargain?"

"That depends very much on what it is," she answered, guardedly.

"Will you come with me?"

She hesitated for a moment, then said—"Yes, as soon as my bothersome ankle gets well."

"All right. I shall keep you to your word. Do you know that since my arrival this morning I have been making a tour of the place, and wherever I went I heard nothing but your praises sung. I had a kind of an idea who you were when I committed the rudeness of overlooking your sketch."

"Indeed!" she exclaimed, playfully. "Then you took a mean advantage."

He laughed.

"If I did you can't complain, Mrs. Burton, for you punished me severely."

She reddened consciously. His manner was so winning that in his actual presence it became almost impossible to judge him harshly. It occurred to her that his sins proceeded more from heedlessness and thoughtlessness than from a bad heart.

"I don't exactly know why I should wish to excuse myself to you," he resumed, after a slight pause, "but I do; and there are a few extenuating circumstances which I should like to put before you. To begin with, I was horribly strictly brought up by an old uncle and aunt. They meant well, no doubt, but they rendered my life a burden. My spirits were naturally high. I had an intense love of fun and merriment, yet I was never allowed to mix with any young people of my own age. Their influence was supposed to be contaminating. From morning till night this excellent old couple talked goody-goody talk for my edification. My aunt dragged me to church three times on Sunday, and would have liked me to spend my weekdays toddling round the village dealing out tracts and quarter of a pound packets of tea."

Bligh could not help laughing. The tone in which he recalled his childhood was so infinitely dismal.

"Go on, please," she said. "I gather that you did not take kindl

"An extra narrow, rigid, and religious education very seldom answers with young men," he continued. "It nearly always has the opposite effect, and drives them to commit every sort of deviltry. I know it did with me. I was so bullied and badgered by my fond, but injudicious relatives that, when they both died, and shortly afterwards I came into this property, I resolved to have a real good time of it. I was then twenty-five, and am now thirty-two. Doubtless all that you said this morning about the obligations of property and so on is perfectly true. Once or twice lately the same thoughts have occurred to me, but can't you understand a colt who has been hobbled kicking up his heels a bit when he first regains his liberty?"

"Yes," said Bligh, demurely, "so long as he is a colt."

"Ah! you mean that my coltish days are over, and that I am past the days of sowing my wild oats?"

"Are men ever too old for that process?" she inquired, a trifle maliciously.

"I intended to have a good time," pursued Lord de Bretton, "and I don't mind confessing I have had it; but, latterly, whether it is because I'm getting old, developing a liver, or what not, I have taken quite a serious turn, and have begun to tire of perpetually seeking pleasure. Some few months ago I was in Africa, shooting big game, and I came across an old Scotch missionary. He lived in a mud hut, slept on the floor with a wooden rest for a pillow, and was as poor as Job. He spent his days among a lot of ignorant savages, and for thirty years had never once visited his native land. Looking at his life from an outside point of view, it struck one as being about as lonely and miserable as could well be conceived. And yet that good old Scotchman was the happiest, most cheerful, and contented person I ever came across. I was laid up with fever in his hut for nearly two months, so saw a great deal of him. As I lay day after day, it set me thinking, Mrs. Burton, and I asked myself why is this man who has nothing to make him satisfied so much more so than I. For a long time the problem beat me, but I solved it at last. He was happy because he had succeeded in subduing every selfish instinct, and devoted his days to ministering to his fellow-creatures."

Lord de Bretton glanced tentatively at Bligh, and encouraged by the sympathetic look which encountered his, he continued—

"I am a thoughtless, harum-scarum fellow by nature; but I learnt a good deal from that old Scotchman. It began to dawn upon me that I was perhaps neglecting my duties at home; and when I met you this morning, and heard the impression my conduct had produced on an absolute, and consequently impartial stranger, the idea received strong confirmation. The long and the short of the matter is, Mrs. Burton, I have come here now with the desire to do what is right. The worst of it is," and he changed colour, " I am horribly ignorant. I don't take kindly to schools, and parsons, and that sort of work, and then people impose upon one all round."

" You must not be discouraged by a little imposition," said Bligh. " We most of us have to put up with that occasionally."

" I have no right to ask a favour at your hands, Mrs. Burton, especially as Mr. Davies has already told me how fully occupied your time is, but will you—will you help me ? "

Bligh stretched out her hand impulsively. There is one temptation which a good woman never can resist, namely—that of reforming a wicked but agreeable man. It is her special weakness ; and if she can but convert him, she is ready to forgive him all his sins.

So in response to this appeal she said, " Yes, willingly. Only you must not expect too much from my aid."

" I shall find it more valuable than anyone else's," he responded.

The conversation was here interrupted by the return of Mr. Davies.

" Come, Mrs. Burton," he said. " I will drive you home, and I have taken the liberty of asking Dr. Watkin to call at your house, and bind up the poor ankle."

" That was indeed thoughtful," she returned.

By the help of the two gentlemen, she was put into the pony chaise. Lord de Bretton lifted his hat.

" Good-bye, Mrs. Burton," he said. " I shall look forward to the pleasure of meeting again before long, and reminding you of your promise."

" Well ! " said Mr. Davies to Bligh, directly they were alone. " What do you think of our landlord ? "

" I think," she answered, " that he is a bad landlord, but a charming man. His manners are extremely pleasant."

" Yes, it is impossible to help liking him when one is with him, however much one may disapprove of his actions."

" Lord de Bretton appears anxious to turn over a new leaf," she said, " and in that case it is our duty to help him."

" Just so, Mrs. Burton. I am quite of your opinion. He strikes me as being more thoughtless than bad."

" No one could be really bad with such a face," she said, decidedly.

She was firmly persuaded that to teach this handsome young man to forsake the broad for the narrow path would not prove a difficult task, provided the teacher went the proper way to work.

For herself she feared no danger. She was thoroughly disgusted with men, and consequently love-proof. Henceforth, she fancied she could put her head inside a hornet's nest, and not be stung.

Clever women make mistakes as well as stupid ones ; and in spite of disappointments and disillusions, few are absolutely callous where the opposite sex are concerned. They may resist male influence for months—nay years, then one fine day they awake to find themselves mysteriously attracted by some magnetical affinity, which completely upsets all their preconceived ideas.

CHAPTER XXXIX.

CONFESSIONS OF AN AUTHOR.

ALTHOUGH Bligh's sprain fortunately did not prove very serious, Doctor Watkin declared that it would be necessary for her to keep perfectly quiet for a few days. As good luck would have it, the next morning's post brought plenty of employment, for Mr. Gray wrote saying he was anxious to bring out a cheap edition of " Such is Man" as soon as possible, and sent a large bundle of proofs in case she wished to make any alterations. Several months having elapsed since the writing of the book, Bligh was now conscious of numerous mistakes, and eagerly hailed this opportunity of rectifying them.

So she caused her sofa to be drawn up to the table, and was soon busily engaged. Mr. Gray had recommended some condensation of the work, otherwise the three volumes, when compressed into one, would, he affirmed, form a bulkier book than it was advisable to place on the bookstalls. Bligh was aware that Smith, roughly speaking, represented the entire trade, and realised the wisdom of conforming to this advice. At the same time, she did not altogether like the job, for few ordeals are more harrowing to a young author than being called upon to prune his highly-cherished periods. The outpourings of his fantasy are dear to him. They read so well in print, and he has not yet sufficient experience to have arrived at the puzzling fact that the writer's pet passages are nearly always those least appreciated by the public. They skip his most beautiful descriptions, and only care for what they call the story. In short, it requires a great deal of practice to know what to strike out and what to leave in. It is not always easy to effect a compromise between the author's vanity and the reader's taste.

Bligh was honestly anxious to comply with Mr. Gray's demand ; but whenever she ran a black line through a sentence the action occasioned a pang. "Can you shorten by about a hundred pages without interfering with the plot?" wrote Mr. Gray in his letter. "If so, it would be better in every way."

She had a great respect for his judgment, and did not venture to question it ; but never had she been requested to perform a more disagreeable task or one so repugnant to her feelings. She counted the lines in order to ascertain how many there were on each page, and then put down the number excised on a piece of blotting paper, and added them up at the end of five or six chapters to see if the scoring out progressed fast enough. But it was work that went against the grain, affording an immense amount of anxiety and very little pleasure. In some instances it proved excessively difficult to take up the thread of the story and dexterously rejoin it after it had been snipped asunder. Bligh plodded away patiently at her inevitable task, but before very long she discovered that it was both much quicker and easier to make her corrections in a bound three-volume copy than to handle the long strips of paper sent her by Mr. Gray, which kept dropping to the floor and getting out of order. Meanwhile, her cheeks grew hot and her head confused, owing to going over the familiar sentences so often. Having lost the charm of novelty they ceased to make an agreeable impression.

"What horrible stuff it is," she murmured to herself dissatisfiedly. "I'm sick to death of the trash, and wonder what on earth anybody can see in it."

By-and-bye she would pause and re-read one of her favourite passages, and think, "There's something in it, after all. It's not so very, very bad. The characters and situations are true to life, and strike home. That is the great thing." Whereupon a smile curved the corners of her mouth, and she continued her occupation with renewed energy. Indeed, she was so engrossed by it that she never heard the front door bell ring, nor a manly voice inquire if Mrs. Burton were within. Visitors before luncheon were so rare that it had not occurred to her to pronounce those convenient words "Not at home," without which no man is lord of his own castle. Therefore, when Deborah ceremoniously ushered Lord de Bretton into the room she looked up with a start of confusion, and made a vain endeavour to sweep all the loose papers with which the table was covered into her lap.

"Good-morning, Mrs. Burton," he said, apologetically. "I

was passing by this way and could not resist the temptation of calling to inquire how you were."

"Thanks," answered Bligh, not very cordially, for she was vexed at being surprised in her occupation. "You are extremely kind."

"Meaning to say that I am an impertinent dog to intrude where I am not wanted. But, tell me how is the ankle?"

"Pretty well," she returned, beginning to recover her presence of mind.

"Is it going to be a long job? I am thinking of Pit-row." And he smiled brightly.

"No, I hope not. Doctor Watkin assured me that if I laid up for a few days I should soon regain my walking powers——"

She stopped suddenly, aware that Lord de Bretton was not listening. His eye was fixed on the table.

"Ah!" he exclaimed. "I perceive that you have been lucky enough to get the book which has created such a sensation, and which the libraries seem quite unable to supply. Will you allow me to have a look at it? I am so anxious to read it that I am seriously contemplating an expenditure of twenty-one and six." Before Bligh could reply, he took up the first volume, on which she had been engaged, and began eagerly turning over its pages.

"Why!" he cried indignantly. "What's the meaning of this? Somebody has been playing old Harry with the author's work. There are whole sentences struck out in the most ruthless manner." Then, all at once, as he gazed into Bligh's crimson face, a light illumined his comprehension, and made the whole thing clear.

"By Jove! Mrs. Burton," he ejaculated, "I believe I have discovered the secret which everybody is dying to know."

"What secret?" she mumbled, with a vain effort at maintaining her composure.

"Who Stonyer Stone is. In other words, the writer of that remarkable book, 'Such is Man.'"

She saw that it was useless to dissemble.

"Lord de Bretton," she said, with gentle dignity, "you are a gentleman, and as such I appeal to your sense of honour. Accident has placed you in a position to discover that which I am desirous of keeping from the rest of the world—at any rate, for the present. You will not betray me, will you?"

"Betray you! My dear Mrs. Burton, of course not. You may trust me implicitly. Not a word of this will I breathe to a living soul. Your secret is safe in my hands. But how clever you must be to write such a book! No wonder I felt small when you condescended to lecture me!" And he looked at Bligh with so profound an admiration that she turned redder than ever.

"It is no great accomplishment to have written a silly novel," she said, deprecatingly. "Almost every other woman whom one meets nowadays aspires to be an authoress. Before long we shall have to pay the readers not the authors. That is what things are coming to."

"You may belittle your performance as you like, Mrs. Burton, but you forget that amongst the army of aspiring writers there are comparatively few who succeed. As a rule, novels sink or swim pretty well according to their merits, and the public are excellent judges of what they like and dislike."

"I think there is a good deal in just managing to hit off a popular subject," she said, modestly.

"You can't do that without talent," replied Lord de Bretton. "But tell me how you work. I have always had the greatest curiosity to know how authors manufacture their masterpieces. Do you wait until the inspiration seizes you, and then—no matter what the time or the place—fly to pen and paper?"

Bligh laughed.

"That is the orthodox idea; but, personally, I find there is a good deal of nonsense talked about inspiration. If you were always to wait for its advent you would get through very little real hard work. Perseverance and steady application are truer friends, in my humble opinion, than fitful flashes of genius, which, if not continually cultivated, soon flicker away to nothing at all."

"I daresay you are right," said her companion, thoughtfully.

"I can't speak for others, but I know that I am right in my own particular case. Often and often if I were to give in to the idle instincts which assail me I should remain at a complete standstill. There are days when my disinclination to write is so great that I hail the smallest incident as an excuse to prevent me from sitting down to my desk. I am dull, tired, drowsy, averse to mental labour. But," and she clenched her little hand, "I won't give in. Over and over again, when suffering from such a mood, I have shut myself up in my room, and said, 'Now you shan't come out until you have done so much.' At first I wrote mechanically and with conscious effort; but, gradually, I would warm to the subject, and in the end my will invariably triumphed. In that way many of my best chapters have been written."

"You interest me extremely," said Lord de Bretton. "Pray go on."

"It requires a good deal of resolution," she continued; "but I hate the idea of being conquered by my inclination. However, the reward comes by degrees, for in process of time one acquires a habit of work and of concentrating one's thoughts at will into a given channel. And the habit, once formed, is of infinitely more value than inspiration. Of course, I am speaking merely of my own personal experience."

" Don't you find writing a very amusing occupation ? " he inquired. "It always seems to me that it must be delightful work."

She shrugged her shoulders.

" To that question I can unhesitatingly answer No. People's ideas naturally vary, but I cannot understand anybody whose literary ideal is in the least exalted looking upon writing as a mere amusement. It is interesting, engrossing, absorbing if you like, but amusing—no."

" Indeed ! you surprise me, Mrs. Burton."

" You are subjected to too many difficulties and perplexities," she resumed ; " and the more successful you may be the greater becomes your sense of responsibility towards the public. You feel that they expect something from you, and you have no right to disappoint them. For this reason an author can never relax or take liberties with his reputation—that is to say, if he would maintain it at its highest level. Book-writing is a profession like any other, and entails a vast amount of labour. No one need imagine that it is all easy and fair sailing. Brain work is frightfully exhausting. It tries the whole frame, and unless people are prepared to put their shoulder very resolutely to the wheel they had much better not attempt the toilsome hill of literature. You can't step to the top with a giant's stride except in very rare instances."

" And yet," observed Lord de Bretton, jestingly, "when you get there the sun seems to shine very brightly and warmly."

" Only for a brief period," she responded, in a graver tone. " You can't afford to bask in its rays. Look at me, for example. My first book has been—what the world is good enough to call —a success. In consequence I am filled with apprehension about my second. It is in the nature of things that it should disappoint, owing to the high expectations which, unfortunately for me, have been formed. If the public are kind they forgive you one failure, and suspend their judgment ; but if your third book does nothing to enhance your reputation then you must be prepared to sink gracefully down into the sea of oblivion. It follows, therefore, that an author has always to be on his mettle, or readers who give half-a-crown for a book at a bookstall in almost every instance want their money's worth."

Lord de Bretton gave a smile of amusement.

" You seem to take a very matter-of-fact view of the situation," he remarked.

" I flatter myself that I take a common-sense one," she replied.

"But it appears to me, Mrs. Burton, that you entirely leave fame out of your calculations. Are you not ambitious?"

"Yes, very, in my own particular way; though I see no good in talking about one's aspirations when one can't realise them."

"Haven't you realised yours?"

"Me!" and she stifled a sigh. "No, I should think not. Fame, such as I have achieved, counts for nothing in my eyes. It is not fame, but only a nine days' notoriety. If Stonyer Stone can continue for the next fifteen or twenty years to write a series of good books, then, perhaps, she may feel that she has won her spurs."

"I don't think many authors hold such modest opinions," said Lord de Bretton. "The few whom I have met have always appeared singularly satisfied with their own performances."

"They are much to be envied, and I wish I could imitate them," she said, "for it has ever seemed to me that self-satisfaction must be a most comfortable state. Only I doubt if their standard is high. To me the struggle is intense, since, strive as one may, one never can realise one's ideals."

Lord de Bretton glanced at her admiringly.

"You ought to go very far," he said.

She shook her head.

"No, I do my best, but there is something lacking. A wide gulf exists between talent and genius. Generally speaking, a woman's life is too narrow and confined for her to make a great novelist, in the true sense of the word. She marries or she doesn't marry. She is happy in her domestic circle, or the reverse. As a rule, home constitutes all her world, by which she shapes her ideas. When she writes of love she writes of her individual experiences, and of men the same. Her heroes are either demi-gods or devils. There is no *juste milieu*."

He laughed merrily

"I like hearing you talk, Mrs. Burton. You are so funny."

"Thanks. I am charmed to contribute to your amusement. No woman nowadays can indulge in the luxury of being dull, for the male sex seem to consider that they have a right to be entertained. But allow me to disillusion you. I am not naturally a 'funny' person, and cannot keep up my drollness for any length of time. Do you intend making a long stay here, because if so it will be fatal to my reputation as a clown."

"That depends on how much you find for me to do."

"Then I predict that you will be a fixture at Glenarfon for months."

"Are you prepared to go on being 'funny' for my edification?" he asked jestingly. "I like to be entertained."

"You shall be entertained as you have never been before— with

"I'll try to like it," he said, submissively.

"And in return, Lord de Bretton, I intend some day to ask a favour of you."

"What is it, Mrs. Burton? Needless to say, your request is granted beforehand."

"I want to know if either you or Mr. Vaughan will take me down a coal-pit, for I have the greatest curiosity to see one."

"Most certainly; as soon as ever your ankle is well we will go together. I am almost ashamed to confess—especially to you—that it is years since I last went underground. And now," he added, rising and taking his hat, "I feel that I have intruded long enough on the famous Stonyer Stone's time: but, before I go, may I put a counter request?"

"Certainly," said Bligh.

"Would you—would you be so very good as to lend me a copy of your book, always provided you have one to spare. I wanted to read it awfully before I came here, but since making the author's acquaintance my wish is naturally intensified."

"I have a very good mind not to give it to you," she said, banteringly, "for you will no longer bring an impartial mind to bear upon my poor stuff, but allow your judgment to be influenced by your impressions of the writer." But, in spite of her words, she wrote his name in a fresh copy, and presented it to him with a smile.

"Will you accept this as a peace offering?" she asked.

"Won't I, that's all. The arrows of your contempt still quiver in my heart, Mrs. Burton; but I am determined not to leave Glenarfon until I have earned a place in your good graces."

She laughed and gave him her hand.

"You have done that already," she rejoined, with a rising colour. "But my good graces count for nothing. I want you to gain those of the people, which are infinitely more important."

CHAPTER XL.

IN THE CROFTAGE MINE.

A FORTNIGHT went by, and on some pretext or other Lord de Bretton contrived to see Bligh every day. She did not dare ask herself why the time passed so quickly and pleasantly, or why this particular spring seemed so much brighter than its predecessors. She only knew that she was happy, with a happiness which instinct whispered it was not wise to analyse. Every night she looked forward expectantly to the morning.

A certain recklessness of consequences was beginning to steal over her spirit. She tried hard not to reason, and when disturbing thoughts refused to be banished, she said to herself, " I have had so little pleasure in my life, surely there is no harm in my enjoying myself whilst I can. One of these days he will be going away, and then I shall have nothing left but the old routine of struggle and duty to fall back upon."

Nevertheless at times an uneasy feeling warned her that she was entering on a foolish course ; but she refused to listen to the voice of prudence, and for a whole fortnight succumbed to temptation, and lived in a fool's paradise. She was fully aware that she could not continue to do so, and knew that sooner or later a change must come ; but she did nothing wilfully to precipitate events. As long as Lord de Bretton remained in Glenarfon she could not resist the pleasure of seeing him. Unconsciously, she had learnt to listen for his footstep, to brighten up at the sound of his cheery voice. Things were in this state when one morning he called as usual ; for he had got into the way of popping in about eleven o'clock, either bringing some choice hothouse flowers, or else to see if she would take a walk.

" How do you do, Mrs. Burton," he said. " I have come to-day to escort you down a coal-pit, according to your wish. Vaughan wants me to inspect the Croftage Mine, where we employ between two and three hundred hands, so I remembered my promise to you. He—Vaughan—is unable to accompany us, having an important appointment. but he has arranged for Mr. Llewellyn, the chief underlooker, to meet us at the pit's mouth, and do showman."

Bligh's ankle was now quite well again, so she eagerly hailed the above proposal ; more particularly as she intended to write a colliery chapter in her new book, and was anxious to have the details correct.

" Do you happen to possess such a thing as a short skirt and a pair of goloshes ? " inquired his lordship. " I fancy one gets uncommonly wet and dirty."

" I'll wear my waterproof," she answered. " It's of the orthodox colour—black, and won't easily spoil ; and I'll get Deborah to lend me her goloshes. Then I can defy the mud." So saying, she ran upstairs, and soon appeared sensibly, if not ornamentally, clad for the occasion.

He looked at her smilingly and said, " You'll do fine," and Bligh felt quite gratified by his approval.

A short walk of five minutes brought them to the pit's mouth, where they found Mr. Llewellyn awaiting their arrival.

Before descending he explained that the three seams of the Croftage Mine were worked by one shaft, but that there was

also an upcast shaft for ventilation, with a capstan affording
means of egress.   The workings, moreover, were connected
internally with the Bridget Colliery, about half a mile distant,
so that the men could pass to and fro.

" You must not feel nervous, Mrs. Burton," said Mr. Llewellyn,
with a reassuring smile.   " Some ladies are rather timid when
they go underground for the first time ; but there is really no
cause for alarm.   We flatter ourselves that we are tolerably safe
against accidents.   By-the-bye," he continued, addressing Lord
de Bretton, " the Government Inspector was round the other
day, and I am happy to be able to inform you that he reported
most favourably on the condition of the mine."

" That's right," said Lord de Bretton, jocularly, " for we don't
want to scare Mrs. Burton by an explosion."

The words were lightly spoken, but as they seemed to cast an
imputation on her courage, Bligh interposed spiritedly—

" I beg leave to state that I am by no means so easily frightened as you appear to imagine."

He contented himself with smiling at her in reply.

They now entered the cage, and were let down a distance of
over a hundred and fifty yards.   As the light at the pit's mouth
grew fainter and fainter, until at length only a mere speck could
be seen, and the darkness and gloom momentarily increased,
Bligh confessed to herself that the sensation of being transported
into the bosom of the earth was decidedly awesome.   It produced a feeling of oppression, and cast a weird spell over the
senses which held them in thrall.

" Allow me to assist you, Mrs. Burton," said Mr. Llewellyn,
when the cage came to a standstill.   " It is often difficult for
visitors to see until their eyes get accustomed to the light—or
rather want of light."

Bligh looked around.   She found herself in a large subter-
ranean passage, whose black walls glistened and dripped with
moisture, as the rays of Llewellyn's Davy lamp fell upon them.
Hearing a rumbling noise ahead, she shrank aside, just in time
to make room for a sleek and powerful cart horse drawing a
truck heavily laden with coal.

" What ! " she exclaimed, in astonishment.   " You actually
have horses here ! "

" Yes," laughed Mr. Llewellyn.   " Our stable holds twenty,
and if it held double the number we could employ them easily."

" And they live underground ? "

" Aye, and thrive better than above.   Did you not notice what
a gloss there was on that fellow's coat ? "

" It all seems wonderful to me," she said, with a quick in-
drawing of the breath.   " I had not the least idea what a mine

was like, and I am very glad to see one, if only to be able to realise the life of so many of my fellow-creatures. It must be horrible though to spend the greater part of one's days deprived of the light of the sun."

"The men don't seem to mind," responded Mr. Llewellyn. "They get used to it from their boyhood, and numbers of them declare that they prefer working underground, where they are sheltered from wind and rain, to being on the surface. Custom is everything."

"Yes, I suppose so," she answered, with a shiver. "For my part, I should call it no better than a living death."

They now walked along the main passage four or five hundred yards from the shaft, and Mr. Llewellyn took them into several of the headings to show them how the men worked. If Bligh's compassion had been aroused in favour of the miners before, she pitied them doubly now, when she saw big, stalwart fellows, many of them six feet in height, lying on their backs picking away with laborious strokes at the hard coal by which they were surrounded, some had hewn regular caverns that had to be supported by props of wood, and wherever the roof showed symptoms of giving way, it was upheld by powerful brattices. A number of empty waggons stood close to where the men were at work. Half a dozen lads, from fourteen to sixteen years of age, were engaged in loading them. When full they were conveyed by horses to the shaft, drawn up, emptied on the bank, then sent down to be refilled.

Bligh found her accoutrement stand her in good stead, for the farther they advanced the wetter became the passage. They splashed their way through one black puddle after another, and the moisture dripped in large drops upon their heads.

"I don't think we need go on to the bitter end, Mrs. Burton," said Lord de Bretton, after a while. "When you have seen the upper seam, you have seen the lower ones. They are all pretty much alike; and it's rough walking for a lady. What do you say? Shall we retrace our footsteps?"

"I am perfectly willing," said Bligh, who, every yard she advanced into the mine, suffered more and more from a feeling of oppression. "My curiosity is quite satisfied: and to tell the truth I long to regain the fresh air."

"I am afraid you would never make a miner, Mrs. Burton," said Mr. Llewellyn, jestingly.

"It is a most interesting sight," she said, apologetically. "I would not for worlds have missed coming; at the same time, the mine gives the effect of a prison. Are we far from the pit's mouth?"

"About four hundred and fifty yards," he replied. "I took

you to the new headings on purpose, because just at present we have a great number of men employed there, and also, because I thought his lordship would like to see how we are extending our operations in that direction. The coal in this upper seam is very plentiful and of good quality, suitable for household purposes."

"And how deep is the deepest seam?" she inquired.

"Over five hundred and fifty yards below the surface. We have nearly a hundred hands working there just now."

"Poor things!" she said. "I pity them."

"They are very well sa——" began Mr. Llewellyn, when suddenly his attention was arrested by a putter boy, who, with a white scared face, came running from the interior of the mine as if pursued by a hundred devils.

"Hulloa! my lad," he exclaimed. "What's up?"

The words were scarcely out of his mouth before the entire passage was illumined by a rush of light, and at the same moment the lamps were extinguished. The earth quivered beneath their feet, and a deafening explosion was heard, accompanied by a furious blast of wind which hurled workers and visitors to the ground just as if they had been so many ninepins. Props were demolished, movable timbers flew shivered in all directions, and a number of the waggons were lifted out of their places, and violently upset. One of them fell on the boy who had sought to raise the alarm, and crushed him severely.

Both Bligh and Lord de Bretton were rendered unconscious by the force of the shock. His lordship was the first to recover sensibility. He had not the least idea whether he had lain there for minutes or days. He breathed slowly and with difficulty, fighting against a horrible sense of suffocation. By degrees his mind grew clearer, and he realised that some apalling accident had taken place. Immediately his thoughts reverted to Bligh. She had been standing quite close to him, and could not be far off. Tremblingly, in the darkness, he put out his hand. It rested on the soft plaits of a woman's hair. The contact infused new life into him, and raising himself on one elbow, he strove to pierce the surrounding gloom. And then he dimly saw an awful sight.

Men were lying prostrate in every direction. Some had been killed by the explosion, and lay as they fell in different postures; others, stifled by the deadly gas, had fallen forwards on their faces, and seemed as if asleep; whilst the injured writhed in agony, and uttered piteous cries for help, to which there came no response. Fright added to their sufferings. In many instances it was pitiful to behold how terror robbed them of their faculties. One great, strong, burly fellow was positively delirious with fear, and kept on repeating the letters of the alphabet in schoolboy fashion, shouting them out at the top of his stentorian voice. Altogether it was a scene of surpassing horror.

With mingled awe and dread Lord de Bretton staggered to his feet. There, straight before him, with blackened face and scorched clothes, lay the dead body of Mr. Llewellyn. His eyes were open, his lips parted as if the words he fain would have spoken in life had died suddenly arrested. And then for the first time a sensation of physical anguish seized Lord de Bretton. He stooped down, raised Bligh's prostrate form in his arms, and following the direction taken by the survivors, staggered blindly towards the pit's mouth. The atmosphere was well nigh insupportable. Every minute he expected to be suffocated by the foul and poisonous after-damp which pursued his footsteps. Desperately he groped his way on, stumbling frequently—for the passage was no longer clear. but choked with *débris*. Some of the horses had got loose, and as they rushed madly to and fro, squealing and snorting, a prey to the wildest panic, they served but to intensify the danger of reaching the shaft. The perspiration poured down his brow. Each moment increased the difficulty of respiration. Urgent as was the necessity for speed, he was obliged to rest occasionally and collect his forces, otherwise they would have failed him altogether. There was a strange singing in his ears, and his brain reeled. He looked down at the precious burden which he carried. Bligh's head hung heavy on his right arm. He could see that her face was white and rigid.

And then, suddenly, in spite of the pain and death from which he was seeking to escape, a temptation assailed him on which, almost immediately after he had yielded to it, he looked back with shame.

Here in the dark bosom of the earth, removed from the glaring light of day, he felt that she was his own—his very own. The woman, of whom for days past he had dreamt, who, in his secret heart he worshipped as the best and purest of her sex, lay at his mercy. With a wave of passion inundating his whole being, and conquering even the terrors of the situation, he stooped his head, and kissed her warmly on the lips.

" Bligh," he murmured, " Bligh, whether we are destined to live or die, let me hear you say once that you love me."

Strange ! but the fierce hot kisses revived her to life. She sighed, opened her eyes, and encountered his ardent gaze.

"Where am I ?" she inquired, faintly. "Is anything the matter ?"

" Don't be afraid, darling little woman," he said, "you are with me. I will take care of you now and always."

"What has happened?" she asked, in a strange voice.

"I scarcely know, but there has been a dreadful explosion."
She shuddered.

"Ah! yes, I remember. We were in the mine. I saw a flash of light, and then all was darkness. Where are we now?"

"In the mine still. Bligh, you are brave. If anything goes wrong with us—if—if we can't succeed in effecting our escape, it won't seem so bad dying together—like this—in each other's arms, will it?"

She looked up into his face, and realised the danger; but she was not afraid; on the contrary, she experienced a thrill of joy, believing that their last moments were at hand, and there was no longer any need of concealment. All at once the laws and restraints imposed by men for the sake of society seemed to grow curiously small.

"No," she whispered, laying her head on his breast. "It is much easier to die than to live apart."

"Bligh," he said, straining her to his heart. "Say just once that you love me."

"Bernard, you know that I do, and have done so since the first moment we met."

Their nerves were unhinged by the shock of the explosion, and they were not themselves. They forgot the lesson so hardly learnt of civilisation, and, like the first man and the first woman, spoke out that which was in their hearts. They loved, and with death staring them in the face, it mattered little whether there were obstacles to their love or not. And yet, the confession once made, Bligh's modesty took alarm. A fierce blush dyed cheeks, throat and ears crimson. She was glad of the darkness.

"Let me down," she said, with sudden embarrassment. "I am too heavy for you. You could get on much better without me, and besides—I can walk."

His strength was nearly spent, and he allowed her to slip to the ground, retaining tight hold of her hand. She uttered an exclamation of dismay.

"Oh!" she cried. "The ground is all wet. Don't you feel the water coming rushing in! It's nearly up to my knees already."

In his excitement he had scarcely noticed this new danger by which they were threatened. His mind was fast losing its usual clearness. Just then a couple of miners, wild, pale, and haggard hurried by at topmost speed.

"Make haste," they shouted. "Run for your lives. Some old workings must have given way, and caused a fresh rush of gas and water."

"God help us," murmured Lord de Bretton, hoarsely. "This air is killing me. It is as much as I can do to stand upright."

"Bernard, Bernard," she cried. "Do not give in. Make an effort—the pit's mouth can't be far off." And with incredible strength she dragged him along. The water continued to rise. As they struggled on, they could feel its cold, insidious moisture mounting higher and higher. It was an awful race—a race for life. And yet at this supreme moment the consciousness of being together produced a secret exaltation which rose superior to physical fear. Had death overtaken them thus, with hand clasped in hand, and their hearts full of love, both felt that he would have been deprived of half his terrors.

And now the cold black water gurgled and swirled almost up to their waists ; but nearer and clearer above their heads gleamed the blessed light of heaven. The shaft was close at hand. Around it were collected a crew of panic-stricken men, impatiently waiting for deliverance. The cage was broken by the force of the explosion, and a signal had been sent to the engine-house to repair it without loss of time, whilst those who had managed to effect their escape were eagerly expecting its appearance. A great mound of *débris* had accumulated since the morning at the bottom of the shaft. The men mounted on it, so as to keep out of the water. Some thirty or forty had congregated upon it, and other sarrived by degrees, though their numbers were lamentably few.

Half a dozen pairs of rough, blackened hands were stretched forth to the rescue of Bligh and Lord de Bretton as they neared the mount. If the water did not rise any more they were safe— always provided relief from above was not delayed. When the crisis was past Bligh began to feel deadly faint, and would have fallen had not Lord de Bretton held her up. He, on the contrary, revived on inhaling the purer air which descended the shaft. An anxious half hour followed, when suddenly a hoarse shout was raised by the men. All eyes were strained upward, and slowly the cage was seen to descend, filled by an exploring party. The instant it reached the bottom there was a rush towards it, and a scene of confusion threatened to take place, when Lord de Bretton called out in a ringing voice, "Hulloa! my men, where are your manners ? Let the lady go first, and with her those who are the most seriously injured. Have patience only for a few minutes more, and you will all be safely brought to the bank."

His words produced an immediate effect, appealing as they did to the better instincts of his listeners.

"Aye, aye," shouted a great muscular fellow, who had nothing on but a burnt shirt and a pair of trousers. "His lordship says true. Let the lady and the lads have first turn. They won't keep us waiting long, I'll be bound."

Bligh turned and looked entreatingly at her companion.

"You won't let me go alone?" she said. "You will come too, won't you?"

Lord de Bretton shook his head.

"For my sake," she pleaded, softly.

"Dear," he said, in an undertone, "there are very few requests of yours which I could find it in my heart to refuse, but if I were to seize the first opportunity of safety, and leave the men whom I employ in danger, I should never forgive myself. It is my duty to stay."

"Bernard, this is madness. You can do no good."

"Perhaps not, but I shall try my best to relieve the sufferers. There is that poor boy who was crushed under the waggon. I can't bear the thought of leaving him lying there. He may be dead, but he may also only be wounded."

"How can you reach him with this water?"

"I don't know. I only know that I mean to try. Besides, the water is going down. I have contrived to measure it whilst we have been here, and in the last ten minutes it has sunk an inch."

"Do you actually mean to go back into the mine with the exploring party?" she asked, horror-stricken.

"Such is my intention."

She grasped tight hold of his arm.

"Bernard, Bernard, don't do it. It will be the death of you. Let the others go, but not you—not you. Your life is too precious."

He disengaged himself gently, and looked at her with steady eyes.

"Bligh," he said, in tones of tender reproach, "it is not like you to prevent me from doing my duty. Remember, dear, that love must not make us selfish."

The colour rushed to her face.

"God forgive me," she said, "I think I must have gone mad. You are right. Whatever happens, of course you are right, my good and noble Bernard."

"I shall get through my work quicker and better, Bligh, if I can think of you as being safe. Will you go in the cage to please me?"

"Yes," she said, submissively. "I would do anything in the world to please you."

The cage was hoisted to the top, and in a few seconds she once more breathed the fresh air of heaven. The explosion had occurred somewhere about twelve o'clock in the day, and immediately afterwards a great crowd collected round the pit's mouth. When the cage came to a standstill the agitation was piteous to witness. Every head within range was stretched eagerly forwards, and the gravity of the situation soon became apparent. By two o'clock seventy men had been brought up, of whom thirteen were dead, and a large proportion seriously injured. As the bodies were carried through the crowd to their temporary resting-place, heartrending glances were cast at them. Wives recognised husbands, children fathers who would never speak to them, nor play with them again. And then, above the hum of voices, the patter of feet and the roar of the machinery rose a mournful wail. Those who had been fortunate enough to escape were thankfully welcomed by friends and relatives, who hurried them away to their homes.

A stable close by was converted into a mortuary, and there the dead were laid upon heaps of straw covered with sacking. This proved a great centre of attraction for all those whose relations had been at work in the pit, and round it there gathered a vast concourse of weeping women and silent men. By twos and threes they went in, seeking those whom they dreaded to find. The stable was but ill-lighted for the purpose of identification, and the windows were constantly blocked by anxious faces, striving to penetrate the dark background where the dead men lay. One or two of the men seemed to have been drowned, but the greater number were blackened and scorched, whilst in some instances the force of the blast had literally ripped their clothes to ribbons.

There were no extravagant demonstrations of grief, but the subdued sobbing of the children, the blank dismay depicted on the countenances of the women, and the settled melancholy visible in the men, proclaimed how greatly they felt the calamity.

The first exploring party, headed by Lord de Bretton, had not returned, and considerable anxiety was experienced on their account, particularly when it became evident that a change had taken place in the course of the ventilation. After a period of suspense those above were horrified to observe that the smoke was coming up the pit shaft, and the air going down the ventilating shaft, which was just the reverse of the proper order. This was regarded as a certain indication that one of two things had happened—either another explosion had occurred, or there had been a heavy fall of earth. The liveliest fears were consequently entertained as to the safety of the exploring party.

Again and again the signal to the bottom of the pit was kept running. Things looked terribly grave, when, to the general relief, the ventilation appeared suddenly to be restored. After a brief consultation, it was resolved to send a small band of men down to ascertain the fate of their brave but unfortunate comrades. Four gallant fellows immediately volunteered for this dangerous task. Their names were Aaron Roberts, John Williams, James Jones, and William Thomas. They got into the cage, and were slowly lowered down the pit.

Everybody was now ordered away from the mouth, since a second explosion was momentarily expected. Presently the signal to cease lowering the cage was sounded, quickly followed by the " Draw up."

Even the belief, amounting to almost a certainty, that a rush of poisonous gas and a mass of heavy *débris* might at any minute come up from the pit's mouth, did not induce the people to remain at the safe distance to which they had been removed.

With one impulse they ran to the shaft, and none faster than Bligh, who, refusing to go home, had waited about, a prey to mortal apprehension. She no longer attempted to disguise from herself that she loved Lord de Bretton with her whole heart and soul. It seared her like a red-hot iron that she had ever dared to despise and lecture this man, whose magnificent courage rendered him absolutely godlike in her eyes, and effaced the memory of all shortcomings. From the moment when he went back into the mine in order to succour the men whom he employed she looked upon him with reverence, as a hero at whose shrine she must ever prostrate herself. It seemed impossible to make amends for the contemptuous opinion which she had once so wrongly and foolishly held. No one could talk of England's effeteness, when she produced such splendid specimens of manhood as this. But where was he? Why did he not come? He had done enough, and more than enough to show the noble elements of which he was made. It was time now to desist from labour.

She was the first to reach the cage. Her heart turned to stone, for alas! alas! only the brave four who went down returned.

" Where is Lord de Bretton ? " she asked, wildly. " Have you not found him ? "

" No, marm," answered Aaron Roberts, with the moisture springing to his hollow eyes.

" Oh! but you must. Do you hear what I say? I will go myself. We can't leave him down there—to die."

" We have done our best," said Aaron Roberts, " but when we had gone about a hundred yards, we met such a power of gas that to save our own lives we were obliged to return. Don't think we wouldn't find his lordship if we could."

Bligh made no response. She put out her two hands, clutched

reelingly at the air, and fell heavily to the ground. A merciful unconsciousness once more descended upon her senses.

CHAPTER XLI.

THE JAWS OF DEATH.

WHEN she came to herself she was in bed in her own room, with Deborah anxiously bending over her. Little by little the mist cleared from her brain, and as she recalled all that had taken place an icy chill crept round her heart. Bernard was dead. He had sacrificed his life in the cause of duty. She should never see him again, nor hear the melodious sound of his voice. All at once the world was robbed of the brightness which only a few hours previously had made it seem so fair. A wave of exceeding bitterness swept over her spirit, and she cried aloud,

"Ah! how cruel God is to part us. Why did he not let me die also when I was in the pit."

Deborah thought at first that her mistress was delirious, but when she perceived the misery depicted on her countenance she realised that she was in the presence of one of those terrible griefs which even time can never wholly efface.

" Hush, dearie," she said gently ; " you have had a wonderful escape, and if it has pleased the Almighty to take others and spare you, depend upon it He has done it for His own good purposes."

"How long have I been lying here ? " asked Bligh, impatiently.

"About an hour ; you were carried home by Doctor Watkins's orders.   He sent word that you were to be kept perfectly quiet."

The colour flew to Bligh's pale cheeks.

" Deborah," she said presently, in a constrained voice, " has —any news been heard of—Lord de Bretton ? "

" No ; none."

Bligh laughed hysterically.

" And you fancy that I can lie here quietly when at any moment his dead body may be brought to bank ? I tell you, Deborah," and her eyes glittered feverishly, " I must get up. It is impossible for me to remain doing nothing."

" But, my dearie, the doctor said you were suffering from after-damp and general shock to the system, and his orders were that you should stay in bed."

" What do I care about his orders, or the orders of a hundred doctors. Cart ropes couldn't keep me here. I must and will

go back to the colliery. Oh! Deborah," she exclaimed,
a sudden burst of despair, looking up piteously at her faithful
old nurse, " I daresay it seems odd to you, and I can't explain ;
but you—you don't understand."

An expression of infinite compassion stole over Deborah's
aged face.

" Ah! " she said, wagging her head, " I understand more than
you think for. Do you suppose that I have been blind this
last fortnight ? I always feared something of the kind would
happen sooner or later. You are a young woman, and it was
only in the nature of things."

Bligh turned her face to the wall, and sighed.

" I was so happy," she said, plaintively ; " so happy, and it
is years since I have known what real happiness meant. Of
course I knew it could not last ; but still I thought I might
enjoy it just for a little while. We were bound to part before
long ; but I—I could have borne that as long as he was alive
and well. To have had a letter from him occasionally and to
have seen him once or twice a year would have satisfied me.
I should not have expected m—more."

" My poor dearie," said Deborah, pityingly.

" D—death is so horrible," continued Bligh, with a shudder.
" It takes away all hope. And I have a feeling that I drove
him to his end. If I had not spoken as I did on the occasion
of our first meeting I don't believe he would ever have considered it his duty to go back into the mine. It was my fault
—Deborah, my fault."

" His lordship behaved like a true and honourable gentleman,"
said the old woman ; " and for my part I would rather die,
leaving the memory of a good action behind me than live on
like a selfish pig "—she was thinking of Sir Philip—" as so
many men do."

" That may be true," said Bligh, struggling to her feet ; " but
it is hard for those who stay behind. Oh! Deborah, don't
try and comfort me at present. It's no use. Only just let me
go and seek him." But even as she spoke her head spun round
and she fell back onto the bed.

She burst into tears.

" I can't walk—I can't do anything. This stupid body of
mine simply refuses to answer my will."

" You are ill," said Deborah, " and whether you like it or not
must lie where you are for the present. But I'll tell you what
I'll do, Miss Bligh, darling. If you will be good, and promise
to keep quiet whilst I'm away, I'll put on my bonnet and shawl
and run down to the pit's mouth, so as to bring you back the
very latest news."

"Oh! Deborah, that will indeed be good of you. But don't be long—make haste ; I can't bear the suspense."

The old servant at once departed on her errand, leaving Bligh to a host of sorrowful thoughts. She could not forgive herself for having brought the wrongs of the people of Glenarfon so prominently before Lord de Bretton's notice. If she had left him to manage matters in his own way, and not been so miserably presumptuous as to judge his actions, she felt convinced in her own mind that this catastrophe would never have taken place. Her words had first piqued, then influenced him. And who was she to judge her fellow-creatures—to say you have done wrong here, neglected your duties there ! "What business was it of mine to point out his faults ?" she mused, bitterly. "God knows I had enough of my own to correct without wanting to correct other people's. I am punished as I deserve. Yet what a punishment ! I feel as if I never could hold up my head again. Bernard, Bernard, if only I could see you just once, to abase myself at your feet and ask forgiveness. Alas! though, that can never be." And she sobbed aloud.

A quarter of an hour might have passed, spent in bitter meditation, when Deborah came rushing breathlessly into the room. Her face was radiant, and a single glance showed that she was the bearer of good news.

"Miss Bligh, Miss Bligh," she gasped. "Cheer up. Don't grieve any longer."

Bligh put out her hand, and clutched convulsively at Deborah's skirt.

"Tell me—tell me at once," she said. "Is he safe ?"

"Yes ; not only Lord de Bretton, but also the whole of the first exploring party. It appears they were entombed by a heavy fall of earth, which closed the passage in the Agecroft mine ; but eventually they managed to escape by the Bridget Colliery."

"Praise be to God !" ejaculated Bligh. "Was he hurt, Deborah, or burnt ?"

"I heard some of the men saying that his lordship was unconscious when first brought to the pit's mouth ; but Doctor Watkins was not alarmed about him, and anticipated a speedy recovery. But, oh! dearie, it has been a terrible explosion. Over a hundred men are still missing, and they have had to give up all hope of rescuing them. The whole town is in mourning, and the women are crying their eyes out. Poor things ! There are many of them will lie down widows to-night who only this morning were happy wives. Ah ! it is sad to think of."

"I ought to be very thankful," said Bligh, gravely. "Providence has, indeed, been kind to me."

Deborah pursed up her mouth doubtfully. Now that the crisis was passed she felt by no means sure that Lord de Bretton's continued existence was likely to prove an advantage to her mistress.

" I wonder what will come of it all," she said, in a serious tone of voice. " I don't so much mind for him. A man can always look after himself, but I am afraid that things may go hardly with you."

" I can bear everything now that he is alive." And so saying Bligh turned round peacefully on her side, and, being thoroughly exhausted by all she had gone through, before long fell asleep.

Deborah watched her with the tears stealing down her cheeks.

" Poor darling ! " she soliloquised. " No sooner is she out of one trouble than she is into another ; but I sadly fear that this will prove the sorest trial of any, for a woman never knows the sharpness of pain until her love and her duty come into conflict. I wonder what she will do next. I wonder what on earth she will do next."

Deborah was not destined to remain long in ignorance on this head, for the following morning Bligh startled her by saying—

" I intend to leave Glenarfon to-morrow, and must ask you to stay behind for a few days, just so as to shut up the cottage and pay off anything that we may happen to owe."

" Leaving to-morrow ! " exclaimed Deborah, in astonishment. " Bless my heart alive ! why, where are you going ? "

Bligh put up her hand to her brow with a weary gesture. She had been awake most of the night.

" I don't quite know ; but I am inclined to think home."

" Home ! You do indeed surprise me."

A faint smile caused the corners of Bligh's mouth to droop pathetically.

" I have been thinking a great deal," she said, in a subdued voice. " And the result of my reflections is I can't possibly remain here. The whole thing is wrong—quite wrong. No one can pluck forbidden fruit without paying for it. I ought never to have left Beechlands. It was a deviation from duty, and not many women are fortunate enough to escape the toll when they forsake the straight and narrow path. Sir Philip is my husband. Nothing can undo that fact, and whatever his faults may be I had no right to leave him."

" I don't see that," said Deborah, indignantly. " A woman is not bound to stay with a drunken brute who ill-uses her."

" Two blacks don't make a white. It is better to endure to the uttermost rather than lose one's self-respect and yield to temptation. That is what would happen to me if I stayed on at

Glenarfon. I can't resist Lord de Bretton's influence. I don't say that it is bad in itself, but it is bad for me. In his absence common-sense comes to my aid. I see things as they actually are, not as I wish them to be ; but when he is by I thrill in response to his slightest word, and my thought is only for him. Until recently it never occurred to me that in adopting and living under a false name I was no better than a fraud."

" Lots of people change their names," said Deborah, stoutly. " Besides, it was your own before you married."

" It is not mine now. In proof of what I say look at the result of my duplicity. I have had a fortnight's unalloyed happiness. It will ever linger in the desert of my memory as a bright oasis ; but the time has come to render payment. One always has to pay for everything nice in this world. As long as Lord de Bretton spoke no word of love the situation, if strained, was possible."

" And can't you continue as you were ? " inquired Deborah. " Just good friends, and nothing more."

" No," she responded, tremulously. " To-day in the pit— something happened. We believed that we were dying ; all motive for concealment appeared at an end : and—and we confessed our love. No blame is to be attached to him. The fault, from first to last, has been entirely mine. He never doubted for an instant but what I was a widow and free to wed——"

" I wish to goodness you were," interrupted Deborah.

Bligh strove to conjure up a faint smile.

" Being as I am," she continued, trying to speak steadily, " it is impossible for me ever to meet Lord de Bretton again on the old terms. Since I can no longer consider him a friend and nothing more I dare not stay here. With every good resolution I might succumb, for where he is concerned I know myself to be pitifully weak. I feel that if I go back home to the narrow, cramping, deadening life, it will be safer, although much more wretched. Hemmed in by matrimonial cares, I shall be my own mistress. The horse who stands too long in his stable soon forgets how to work, whereas the one used to harness is forced to face the collar. Deborah ! " she burst out excitedly, " don't look at me with those pitying eyes. Scold me. Say hard, true, horrible things to me. I can bear them—anything—better than your compassion. After all I am not the first woman to whom love has come too late. Others have suffered a similar misfortune."

For sole answer Deborah gathered her up in her arms and sobbed, " My darling—my poor darling : I would give everything I possess in the world if this had never happened, for if you were not happy, at all events your heart was at rest, until Lor

Bligh looked at her faithful attendant with luminous eyes.

"I don't regret it," she said. "Don't think for one moment that I regret it."

All the next day she was occupied in making preparations for her departure. When they were completed she sat down and wrote a farewell letter to Lord de Bretton. "Forgive me," she said. "I have deceived you. My name is not Burton, but Verschoyle, and my husband is still alive. You will understand why I am leaving Glenarfon, and why we must not meet in future. Had it not been for the explosion we might, perhaps, have continued friends. I never meant to let you know how things were with me: but when death seemed so near my heart spoke. You are a man, and will soon forget. I cannot wish you a better wish than that my memory should speedily be effaced from your mind. Until that time arrives I humbly ask forgiveness for any wound I may thoughtlessly have inflicted. To go right out of your life is the best service I can render you. So, good-bye, Bernard, good-bye." Here a great tear, smudged the paper. "May God in Heaven bless and protect you."

"To-morrow, when I am gone," she said later on to Deborah, seeking to force back her tears, "you will give this note to Lord de Bretton. If he asks any questions, and wants to know where I have gone, don't answer. It is impossible for us to meet at present. To do so would only inflict needless pain on us both."

Early the next morning she stole like a thief from Glenarfon, and did not breathe freely until the train put many miles between her and the mountain valley where such a revolution had been effected in her life.

A short distance from Chester she had to change trains, and there was only just time to secure her luggage and jump from one carriage into another. The guard slammed the door, the station-master waved his flag, and the engine puffed noisily out of the station. Then all at once she became aware that the compartment was occupied by another person. She looked towards the slouching figure sitting muffled up in a huge fur coat, whose high collar almost concealed the owner's face, and an exclamation of genuine astonishment burst from her lips,

"Philip "

"Bligh!"

And the next moment husband and wife were shaking hands almost as cordially as if they had parted but yesterday.

"Hulloa!" he said, gazing at her with considerable curiosity. "This is a strange encounter. Oddly enough, I was just thinking of you, and wondering when I should see you again. Where are you going to, if it is not an impertinent question?"

"Did you not get my telegram?" she inquired a trifle unsteadily. " I wired yesterday to say I was coming home."

" No. I have been staying away for some races, and have not been to Beechlands since last month. My mother is there, with some old tabby of a female friend to keep her company. And so your ladyship is actually coming home, eh ? "

Bligh flushed up. There was a certain sarcasm in his tone which did not escape her notice.

" Yes," she said, meekly. " That is to say, provided you have no objection to receiving me."

He laughed a mirthless laugh.

" Plenty of husbands in my place would decline, no doubt : but, fortunately for you, I'm not one to bear malice. I suppose it never struck you, however, when you took yourself off as you did that it was anything but pleasant for me, all the neighbours declaring that my wife had run away ? "

Again the hot blood mounted to her cheeks.

" In cases of this kind," she replied, " I don't know that it much matters what other people say. There is always a certain amount of unpleasantness which must be borne on either side. Perhaps I acted too hastily ; but," and her voice trembled a little, " I—I thought that you did not want me, and th—that I only stood between you—and B—Blanche."

" Look here, Bligh," he said, " we may as well clear this matter up once for all. I don't mind admitting I behaved like a fool. After she was married Blanche cared no more for me than she did for those newspapers lying yonder," pointing to some on the opposite seat. " She simply made use of me and got all she could out of me, whilst I was idiot enough to believe that she was consumed by an ardent flame for Sir Philip Verschoyle, Bart. In reality she was head over ears in love with her own husband, though I found the fact out too late to be of much good. A few days after you left she got a letter from Vansittart, and went posting back to India in a tremendous hurry. Before she went my eyes were thoroughly opened, and I can honestly swear that I am completely cured of my infatuation. There ! will that satisfy you ? "

" Yes, as far as Blanche is concerned. I don't think she behaved well cither to you or to me ; but it is no longer our affair."

" As for hating you, Bligh," he continued, " I ought not to be held responsible for what I may have said when I was ill. Besides, everybody says things now and again which they do not mean. When we were married we neither of us pretended to a very violent affection. We went in for being a sensible matter-of-fact couple. But I can truly declare that if you had nothing else you had my respect."

"A pretty way you took of showing it," was the retort that rose to her lips, but by an effort she refrained from a sharp answer, and said quietly, "How was it, Philip, that you never wrote to me through my solicitor?"

He hung his head.

"To tell the truth, Bligh, I knew I had behaved like a beast. After Blanche went I was laid up with a sharp attack of delirium tremens. The doctor warned me that unless I knocked off the drink he would not answer for my life. I kept sober then—as sober as I could, and when I got better I thought a good deal about you. At first I determined to rout you out; but after a bit I said to myself, 'Why should I bring her back? I only lead the poor thing a devil of a life. She is happier anywhere away from me,' and so—and so," he concluded, unsteadily, staring at the window-pane as if ashamed of his emotion, "I arrived at the conclusion that I would wait patiently until you chose to return of your own accord. For goodness' sake don't make a fuss," he resumed, after a brief pause, perceiving that tears stood in his companion's eyes. "I'm far from strong yet. My nerves are horribly shaken, and they can't stand a scene. I am very glad to see you, Bligh. There, there; that's enough. Don't let us talk any more. It only upsets one." And so saying he pulled his cap down over his face and relapsed into silence.

Bligh stared at him in astonishment, and as she did so a huge compassion crept into her heart. He was terribly altered. His face wore a purple, bloated appearance. The complexion had lost its clear hue of health. His eyes were dim and sunken, and beneath them were swollen bags which added years to his age. The air of smartness and freshness which had formerly distinguished him was gone. His very figure seemed to have altered. It was strangely shrunken, and his clothes hung loosely upon it. She noticed, too, that whenever he raised his poor maimed hand to his moustache it trembled like that of an old man. In short he was a perfect wreck, and in his present state he appealed powerfully to her pity.

"Hulloa!" cried Sir Philip, suddenly. "I wonder what's up. We're passing Crewe without stopping."

Bligh put her head out of the window.

"I think something must have gone wrong," she said. "Or perhaps we are going to shunt back into the station. I see a man on the line waving a red flag with all his might, and there's another one coming running up behind him. What can it mean?"

The words were scarcely out of her mouth when she was thrown down by a fearful shock. The floor of their carriage rose and broke up into splinters, the roof tumbled in, and she fell with stunning force on to the rails. After that she remembered nothing for a time. When she recovered her senses she immediately became conscious of an intolerable weight, which crushed her legs and held them fast as in a vice. With difficulty she managed to raise her head an inch or two, and perceived that she was wedged in amongst a mass of wreckage. Once more there came borne to her ears those terrible cries of suffering humanity which, having once heard, she was destined never to forget. How Inscrutable were the ways of Providence ! Had she only escaped from the perils of the mine to perish miserably in a railway accident ? This second disaster following so quickly upon the first completely unstrung her nerves.

"God is visiting my sins upon me," she thought. "But why does He not kill me straight out, instead of torturing me as a cat tortures a mouse ? " And in her anguish she made a desperate effort to free herself from the heavy beam which was causing such acute physical suffering. Immediately an agonised voice cried out, " For God's sake, keep still. You will be the death of me if you move."

The voice was her husband's. She recognised it at once.

" Philip," she said. " Is that you ? "

" Yes—yes," he moaned. " This cursed beam is upon my chest. If you stir it again as you did just now it will roll over and do for me altogether. I'm regularly caught, like a rat in a trap. Oh, Lord ! oh, Lord ! what infernal pain. Why does not someone come and release me ? " And he screamed aloud.

Bligh's brain had been clouded, but now it suddenly became preternaturally clear. A kind of vengeful delirium seized her. The past rose up like a panorama.

" Ah ! " she said to herself, " I can pay him out for all he has made me suffer. I hold his life in my hands. The pain is excruciating. Why should I be expected to bear it better than he ? I have only to move, and I shall be free—free to marry Bernard. Philip alone stands between us. A man who drinks till he has delirium tremens is better out of the world than in it. He is miserable himself, and makes everybody else miserable."

For a few seconds the temptation was almost irresistible. It assailed her furiously.

" Bligh," groaned Sir Philip, and this time his voice sounded weaker than before, " keep still—it is my on—only chance."

All at once a strong reaction set in. Those piteous, pleading tones moved her to the very depths of her being. She recalled Lord de Bretton's gallant conduct in the mine and the noble example of unselfishness he had set.

" He would hate me," she mused. "if he knew—hate and despise me.　I could never look into his face again, or feel myself fit to touch his hand.　Oh! God, forgive my wicked, wicked thoughts."

She breathed hard.　Every moment the pain was growing more intolerable, and her brow was moist with perspiration.

"Do you hear what I say, Bligh?" gasped Sir Philip.

"Yes," she answered, in a curiously gentle voice.　"Do not be afraid.　I will not move—or consciously harm you in any way.　If one must die it shall be me, and not you."

Fainter and fainter sounded the cries of the wounded in her ears; dimmer and dimmer appeared the outside world.　Were those men's forms hurrying to and fro, bearing ghastly burdens in their arms. or merely black, ghostly shapes?　Was this sudden sense of relief and freedom real.　Did she hear her husband's voice in a dream crying out, "Save me—oh! save me first.　I am suffering the pains of hell."

Or had she fallen asleep during the journey, and her imagination running riot conjured up horrible scenes and situations, in which she, and Philip, and Lord de Bretton were hopelessly mixed?　Was this life, or death, or what?

She no longer knew.　A great darkness descended upon her faculties, and annihilated thought.

CHAPTER XLII.

THE CHAINS ARE SUNDERED.

THE papers were full the next day of the Crewe railway accident.　It seemed that before nearing the station the brakes. from some unknown cause, refused to act, in consequence of which the train ran on past the terminus at a rate of five-and-twenty miles an hour, and dashed into some empty trucks standing ready for shunting.　The first six carriages were completely telescoped.　Nine people were killed on the spot and eighteen seriously injured.

Lord de Bretton, reading an account of the disaster, came upon the following passage :—

"We regret to say that Sir Philip and Lady Verschoyle are included in the list of sufferers.　They were seated in the fourth compartment from the engine, and how they escaped instant destruction is a miracle, as it was completely wrecked.　Sir Philip was badly crushed, and is now lying in a precarious condition at the Angel Hotel, Crewe, it having been found impossible for him to continue his journey to Beechlands.　Lady Verschoyle, who is well known in the literary world under the *nom de plume* of Stonyer Stone, is also suffering from contusions and severe shock to the system, but Doctor Carter, who is in attendance on the gi ted authoress, does not regard her injuries as serious."

The above paragraph was a revelation to Lord de Bretton. He was acquainted with Sir Philip Verschoyle, and could well understand all that his wife would have to put up with. Rightly o: wrongly he now felt that he could not stay quietly at Glenarfon whilst the woman who filled his heart and occupied his thoughts was perhaps in peril of her life. Conscience told him that he had no business to seek her out, but love triumphed over every prudential consideration. If he could but see her for one moment just so as to ascertain that she was well and safe, then he told himself he should rest content. Five minutes spent in her society would satisfy him and quiet the torturing doubts by which he was assailed. Moreover, if Sir Philip were as ill as represented she might be glad of a friend to render assistance, and, if not, well, if not he could but return, after calming his mind as to her state of health.

Thus he argued. So he packed a portmanteau, told his servant he would telegraph if he found he required him, and set off for Crewe. He arrived at his destination in safety, and drove straight to the Angel Hotel.

"Will you give this card to Lady Verschoyle," he said, "and say I particularly wish to see her if she is able to receive visitors."

During the journey he had thought over the best means of gaining an interview with Bligh. At first he decided to withhold his card, and merely send a message to the effect that a friend had called to inquire after her ; but on further reflection he discarded this proceeding as mean and sneaking. He would do nothing underhand, nor take an unfair advantage. If she did not wish to see him he would not force himself upon her, without even giving her the option of refusing. Therefore, he sent up his name, and waited anxiously for the hall porter to reappear. Presently the man came back, looking portentously grave.

"Her ladyship is in great trouble," he said : "but she desires that you will step this way."

Lord de Bretton's heart beat fast.

"She loves me," he said to himself. "She loves me after all. God bless her for this mark of confidence."

He was shown into a darkened sitting-room, with the blinds drawn down, and, imagining it to be unoccupied, he was taking up a position with his back to the mantelpiece, when suddenly he was startled by the sound of a smothered sob. Looking in the direction from whence it came he perceived a small dark figure lying huddled up on a horsehair sofa in one corner of the room.   He forgot that his visit was no longer to Mrs. Burton, but to Lady Verschoyle.

"Bligh!" he exclaimed, "what is the matter?   Why are you crying here, all by yourself?"

She turned a pair of wild eyes upon him.

"Haven't you heard?   Don't you know?"

"No, I know nothing, except the meagre information conveyed by the newspapers.   Oh! my darling, forgive me for coming; but I could not rest when I thought of you in danger."

"It is not me, it is Philip," she said, with a shudder.

"What of him?"

"He is dead."

"Dead!"   And a guilty joy thrilled his heart.

"He died about half an hour ago, in the greatest agony.   His sufferings were awful to witness."

Lord de Bretton knelt down by the side of the sofa and took one of her hands in his.   It was burning hot.   Her cheeks were flushed, and she trembled in every limb.   With a strong effort he controlled the passion rising within his breast.   He did not like her manner.   It was feverish and excitable.   She looked as if a dangerous illness were hovering over her.

"Are you here all alone?" he asked.

"Yes.   I have not even Deborah, and I feel so lonely and miserable."

"Poor, darling little woman!   I wish I could help you."

"You are very kind.   My head feels in a whirl.   I can neither think nor act.   The shock has stunned me, and yet there are ever so many things I ought to do."

"You must let me do them instead," he said, tenderly. "Have I not a right to take the burden off your shoulders?"

She looked at him, and as she looked a great hot blush dyed her face crimson.

"Please don't," she said, in a hoarse whisper.   "I feel so guilty.   It is that which makes me unhappy.   If I had loved him better I should not have reproached myself as I do now."

"You have nothing to reproach yourself with, Bligh, I am sure."

"Ah! but indeed I have.   You don't know how awful it is when a person dies suddenly.   All sorts of little things come back to one.   Ah! if people only realised in time how seldom they regret their kind actions, and what a lifelong sting their unkind ones leave behind."

"Did Sir Philip make you happy?" inquired Lord de Bretton curtly.

"No; but that is another affair.   I forgive all his faults   He was nice to me towards the last—he held my hand in his, and said he was sorry if he had ever made me suffer. I am so glad I was with him. The doctor ordered me to remain in bed, but I could not stay. And now there will be the—the funeral to arrange for, and my mother-in-law to write to, and——" She broke off suddenly, gave an unnatural laugh, and added, " My brain is on fire. I really don't know what I'm about."

" I will telegraph to Deborah to come immediately," he said.

" Ah ! dear old Deborah ; I want her more than anybody at present."

" You don't care to see me ? " he asked, it a tone of involuntary reproach.

" I want to rest," she said, with a little tired sigh. " I am so weary. When I lie down I see a succession of dreadful scenes, one more awful than another. Horrible cries ring in my ears. I am haunted by mangled bodies, and Philip's pain-drawn face rises up before me like a vision. Oh ! kind friend," and her voice broke, " you must be patient with me. I have had a great shock."

" You are ill, Bligh, and ought not to be left alone. Where is the doctor, and why has he not provided you with a suitable attendant ? "

" There is a nurse in there," she said, pointing to an adjoining bedroom, where lay her husband's dead body.

Lord de Bretton tapped at the door, and a respectable person appeared in answer to the summons.

" I am afraid Lady Verschoyle is very unwell," he said. " She looks to me as if she were going to have an attack of brain fever. Can't you persuade her to go to bed whilst I fetch the doctor ? "

" Indeed, sir," replied the nurse, " her ladyship has not any business to be up ; but this trouble seems to have gone to her head, and there's no keeping her quiet. It's the nerves, sir, that's what it is, and small wonder after such a dreadful accident."

" Take every care of Lady Verschoyle till her own maid comes," he said, slipping half a sovereign into the woman's hand.

Then he returned to Bligh, and, putting his hand on her shoulder, said, " I want you, dear, to do just as you are bidden. Don't trouble about anything. I will make all the necessary arrangements and carry out your wishes in every respect."

" Go away," she said, excitedly, staring at him with bright, unseeing eyes. " You come here to tempt me. I love you— but I will never tell you of my love. Day after day, year after year, I shall live and keep my secret to myself. Do you want to know why? Because," and her voice dropped to a whisper, chilling him with the fear that her reason was impaired. "I—am—a—married—woman. My husband was a bad man. He drank, and struck, swore at, and insulted me in every way My blood used to boil. I felt as if I could have murdered him. But what did that matter? I was his wife, his slave, and therefore bound to endure. It was no use my trying to escape, and to live a life of my own. Women always suffer, they always suffer in the end."

"Hush! dearest," he interposed, trying to quiet her. "There are better times in store."

"We are poor fools," she continued, with growing vehemence. "Our affections invariably betray us, and upset all our theories and resolutions. Look at me. I was a coward, and so I ran away. But what was the good? His eyes and his smile pursue me. Do you know what happened just now?" And she touched Lord de Bretton's sleeve confidentially "I heard his voice. That's how it will always be. Why can't I forget him? Even at a time like this, oh! why can't I forget him?"

"Bligh!" he cried, thoroughly frightened by the wildness of her manner. "Don't you recognise me?"

She pushed him from her with delirious force.

"Ah! that voice again. Shame that I should hear it when Philip—poor Philip!—has been dead just half an hour." And she burst into a flood of hysterical tears.

"I think you had better leave her Ladyship to me, sir, and go for the doctor at once," said the nurse, who had stolen into the room unperceived. "Your presence seems to excite her. She is suffering from shock to the nervous system, and requires complete rest and quiet. It looks to me very like brain fever setting in. She has all the symptoms."

Lord de Bretton took up his hat, and, with a parting glance at Bligh, walked sadly out of the room. He realised that the time had not yet come for him to prove of any comfort to her. She would feel more at home in the arms of her faithful old Deborah than in his. He could do nothing but wait, and pray that her mental equilibrium might be restored.

CHAPTER XLIII.

PAID IN HER OWN COIN.

FOR a whole fortnight Bligh lay dangerously ill, and it was just touch-and-go whether she pulled through or not ; but a good doctor and a good nurse restored her to life, and by the end of April she was sufficiently recovered to undertake the journey to Beechlands. Of her husband's last moments, and of all that had immediately succeeded them, she retained but a vague and confused recollection. As she grew stronger, however, she became aware that someone outside the sick room was thoughtfully attending to her wants.

Every morning regularly there came a fresh supply of flowers and choice hothouse fruits. Her curiosity was aroused, and one day she pointed to an exquisite bouquet of white lilies, and said—

"Deborah, where does this come from ? Who supplies me with all these luxuries ? "

"Lord de Bretton," answered the old woman, casting a sidelong glance at her mistress.

A vivid blush suffused Bligh's pale cheeks.

" Is he in Crewe ? " she inquired, after a tolerably long pause.

"Yes."

" Since when has he been here ? I have a kind of an idea that I saw him before my illness ; but the past seems so misty and dreamlike that somehow I can't remember things rightly. I think I must have had the fever on me even before Philip died."

" I am sure of it," said Deborah. " As for his lordship, he has never stirred from Crewe since you were taken ill. He took up his quarters at the Goat—a rival hotel—and calls three times every day to inquire. If ever a gentleman loved a lady truly and well I should say he loved you."

"One never can believe men," said Bligh.

"You will be very foolish if you don't believe him," rejoined Deborah, significantly. " Though, of course, it's no business of mine."

Bligh did not reply to this observation. She shook her head and sighed ; nevertheless, for the rest of the afternoon she lay with a faint smile hovering about the corners of her mouth. It

was clear that Deborah's assertion had not displeased her.
the eve of her departure Lord de Bretton asked permission to
be received. He had secured an invalid carriage, made every
arrangement for the journey, and she felt that in return for all
his kindness he was entitled to her best thanks, if nothing more.
And yet, strange to say, she shrank from meeting him, and with
the incomprehensibility of her female nature had put off doing
so until the last moment. She loved him, but was determined
to fight her love inch by inch, if only to make sure of their passion on either side being genuine.

" It never does to trust to men," she kept saying to herself.
" They think ever so much more of you if you keep them at a
respectful distance. How do I know that Bernard is any better
than the rest of them ? Very likely it is only my fancy. One
leap in the dark is enough. I have no wish to take another."

Thus she argued against the whisperings of her heart and
prided herself on her impenetrability and wisdom. Although
convalescent she was still extremely weak and easily upset ;
therefore, before admitting Lord de Bretton Deborah requested
him not to stay more than five minutes.

" Lady Verschoyle tires very easily," she said, " and as she
has to travel to-morrow I want to keep her fresh."

" Quite right," he responded. " You may trust me not to
overfatigue your mistress."

He and Bligh met quietly, and with a feeling of conscious
restraint. She thanked him for his kind attentions, talked of
the weather, the journey—anything rather than herself, and
managed effectually to keep him at arm's length. In fact if he
had been a complete stranger she could not have treated him
with more scrupulous politeness and conventionality. For days
he had looked forward to this interview, and her reception chilled
his secret hopes. Could it be that she repented of the words
spoken in the Croftage mine ? She looked pale and fagged.
One glance showed that Deborah's warning must be respected,
yet when the five minutes were up they were still talking platitudes. To part like strangers was impossible. His self-control
was not equal to so severe a strain. As he rose from his seat
reluctantly she tendered a little, cold, passive hand, which he
warmly clasped in his. Then he spoke out a small portion of
what was in his mind.

" Bligh," he said, " it seems hard to leave you like this ; but
I can understand and respect your feelings. Why are you so
afraid of me ? Why won't you trust me ?"

" I do trust you," she interrupted.

" No, dear, you don't—at least, not fully. Perhaps you fear
that I shall hurry you, that I don't sufficiently consider what

decency imposes. I don't ask anything at present. I only want you to say when we may meet again. Surely my demand is moderate."

"I can't fix any time yet," she said. "It is better for us to go our different ways."

"No, it is not, Bligh—at least, not for me. Of course you may have changed your mind. If so let me hear the truth. I think I have a right to know how we stand. If you don't care for me say so. I would rather be told the worst at once. For myself I shall love you always."

There was a direct simplicity about this speech which went straight to her heart. But Sir Philip's sudden death had not only created a strong impression, but it had also occasioned a curious reaction in her mode of thought. She no longer made plans for the future. It seemed folly to do so when fate upset them so easily. In answer to Lord de Bretton's appeal, she drew herself up with gentle dignity and said—

"It is not fitting to discuss this matter now. You are my friend, and I shall ever regard you as such. If you like I will write a few lines now and then. There can be no harm in that."

"And are we to part thus?" he asked, striving hard to conceal his disappointment.

"Yes, for the present. Believe me, it is best." Illness had rendered her physically weak, and her emotions were kept ir check by a sense of numbness and weariness. She imagined that this passive state would last forever, not realising that directly she regained strength the acuteness of sensation would return.

He shrugged his shoulders with an angry gesture. It was perhaps natural that he did not understand her mood.

"You are an enigma, Bligh."

"All women are," she responded. "Even to themselves."

"And you will really write and give me leave to see you?" he said eagerly, trying to make the most of the small advantage he had gained.

"I did not say that; but you shall hear from me within a week."

He could wring no further concession from her, and they went their respective ways, both rather sad at heart, though Bligh persuaded herself that she had behaved with the utmost decorum and prudence.

For seven whole days Lord de Bretton went about feeling utterly miserable; but on the eighth his eyes were gladdened by the welcome sight of his lady-love's handwriting. He tore open the envelope. Imagine his consternation when he read the following:—

"My dear Bernard,—

Since returning home I have been seriously thinking over the situation in all its bearings. You say that you love me. Well, I too love you, but am determined not to let my affection spoil your life. Men are capable of a hundred loves. Therefore, when they marry it is incumbent upon them to marry wisely. A wife does not interfere much with their flirtations; but she does interfere with their comfort, unless she be sensibly chosen. Now allow me to put the stern facts before you. You do not realise all my shortcomings, and I scorn to take any unworthy advantage of your proposal. To begin with, I am thirty years old. At that age, according to the men with whom I have associated since my marriage, a woman has long ago ceased to be attractive. In their refined and delicate phraseology 'the bloom is off,' and she is neither worth looking at nor talking to. The unfortunate has to accept the position as best she can. Her youth once gone—an unpardonable fault—no matter what qualities she may possess, she is voted 'no use, and long in the tooth.' Ah! yes, you needn't contradict me, for I know; and, moreover, have enjoyed many opportunities of hearing your own sex discuss the one to which I belong. At thirty a woman is assigned a back seat; a man, on the contrary, is regarded as a mere boy—a kind of jaunty youth who, in his own estimation, remains ever young and fascinating. I ask you to look at matters plainly. When we are both forty you would still be in the prime of manhood, whilst I should have sunk down into an old and sickly female, for I am not strong. That is another of my drawbacks which I wish to bring before your notice. A single woman can afford to indulge in the luxury of ill-health, but it is a crime when she is married, and one that is always being thrown in her face. From an impartial point of view you ought to marry some nice, pretty girl of eighteen or twenty, likely to prove an ornament to your position, not a broken-down middle-aged person like myself, whose ideas have been rendered sober by trouble and sickness. As I said before, I have neither youth nor looks to recommend me, and the majority of men value nothing else in a woman. My best years are gone. I can only look forward in the future to growing plainer and plainer, more and more faded. You are suffering from a temporary infatuation, which will soon pass away. Bernard, I love you. I don't attempt to disguise that fact. But think of my pain if after a few months I discovered that you regretted the step you had taken. You are fond of gaiety and amusement. Take my advice. Go to London for the season. You will see plenty of young and pretty women there, and when you have found one to your mind, and who is calculated to

make you happy, then bring her to see me. I promise to greet you warmly, and shall be much surprised if you do not thank me for having considered your interests rather than my own.
"Ever your attached friend,
"BLIGH VERSCHOYLE."

When Lord de Bretton finished the perusal of the above letter he was beside himself with anger. What did Bligh mean by writing to him in this strain? Did she consider men incapable of constancy or love worthy the name? He seized a pen and a piece of paper, and, acting on the spur of the moment, wrote—

"DEAR LADY VERSCHOYLE,—You are quite right. Many thanks for your disinterested advice. I am off to London in search of the 'pretty girl.' No doubt I shall not have much difficulty in finding her. There are plenty of them about who will take compassion on a 'jaunty youth' like myself of two-and-thirty. Expect to see the turtle dove turn up before long to receive your congratulations. Until then, believe me
" Yours always,
" DE BRETTON."

Bligh sighed when she received this hastily scribbled note. Oddly enough, although the writer expressed his intention of adopting her suggestions, its contents disappointed her. She had no cause for complaint, and yet she was not satisfied. On the contrary, she was intensely dissatisfied.
" Ah!" she mused, despondently. " He is like all the rest of them. He can't stand being put to the test, and, when tried, is found wanting. If he had loved me as I love him it would have been simply impossible for him to go in search of a strange woman just because he is advised. Heigh ho! Men seem to possess an extraordinary capacity for transferring what they call their affections from one object to another. How lucky it was I did not throw myself into his arms. Where should I have been when he tired of me. Oh! dear, what a fool I am to be sure. He is not remarkable either for talent or faithfulness. He is only just his own bright, easy-going self, and yet I love him better than anything else on this earth. I never thought he would have taken my advice." A sad smile played round her mouth, and she added, "After all, it is better so. He will be happier, and it does not matter about me."
This conclusion was most heroic; nevertheless it did not succeed in putting any colour into Bligh's pale cheeks. During the summer months she went about listless and wan, and defied

all Deborah's attempts to discover what had taken place during her last meeting with Lord de Bretton.

"There's something gone wrong," soliloquised the old serving-woman. "She ain't happy, that's quite clear, and hasn't picked up one bit since she came home. I've half a mind to write to Lord de Bretton on the sly and ask him to run down and pay us a visit. I'm sure it would hearten her up. Happy thought! I'll act upon it."

One fine July morning shortly afterwards the post brought a letter which for weeks past Bligh had been secretly expecting and dreading to receive. As she read the contents she uttered an exclamation of dismay. They ran as follows :

"My dearest Bligh,—Adopting your excellent advice I have been spending a very pleasant time in town. It seems to me that there are more pretty girls about this season than usual, and I know you will be glad to hear that I have been paying considerable attention to a young lady of whom I feel tolerably certain you will approve. I am proud to be connected with one of the nicest and prettiest girls in London. She is very honest, very straightforward, perfectly unaffected, and a lady in every sense of the word. When I say that she reminds me of you I need not write more in Miss Dennison's praise. I trust you will give me joy. Looking forward to the pleasure of shortly introducing her to my best friend, believe me,

"Yours ever,

"De Bretton."

Bligh groaned aloud. Her worst fears were realised. Now she knew for certain that he could never have cared for her really.

"Ah!" she cried, indignantly, "this is beyond a joke. He vowed he should love me always, and three months have hardly gone by before I am forgotten. Talk of constancy after that!" And she laughed a mirthless laugh. "It is an outrage. And he actually has the impertinence to say that his bread-and-butter Miss reminds him of me. Fool! fool that I was not to keep him when he fancied himself fond of me. Now I have lost him for ever; but I won't cry—I won't, I won't. He is not worth crying about." But in spite of her resolve she sobbed as if her heart would break.

CHAPTER XLIV.

"SUCH IS WOMAN."

THE forenoon passed away like a bad dream, and Bligh wandered uneasily about the house, seeking relief first in one room, then in another. She could not rest. An inward fever consumed her. She suffered from an imperious need of action ; yet common-sense told her that in the circumstances there was absolutely nothing to be done but to submit to the hard grasp of destiny. There was a dull, gnawing ache at her heart, which, as the day wore on, and she realised more completely the full significance of Lord de Bretton's letter, increased to positive pain. His smallest word and action recurred with fresh force to her memory, and as she recalled his good temper, his bright and sunny disposition, his charming manners, and personal fascination, her regrets grew more and more poignant. She had held the apple of love in her hand, and refused to taste it. Her folly had been inconceivable. She saw this clearly now that it was too late to go back from her words.

Out of doors the sun shone with dazzling brilliancy. The trees, decked in their summer foliage, stood cool and shadowy against a cloudless blue sky, whilst numberless birds chirped amidst their leafy branches. The flower beds were gaudy with scarlet geraniums and yellow calceolarias. The garden was full of bloom and fragrance. Its sweet odours were everywhere wafted into the house through the open windows. A couple of gardeners were engaged in mowing the lawn, and every time the machine required emptying, the sleek pony put his head down and nibbled greedily at the smooth green turf. Bligh gazed at him with envy.

"How happy and contented he looks," she said to herself. "I wish I were an animal—I wish he and I could change places. Surely life must be easier for these dumb beasts than it is for us. I wonder if they suffer tortures through their affections as we do. They seem so placid and satisfied compared with ourselves. It makes one sceptical as to what extent reason and intelligence are acceptable gifts."

She turned away impatiently. Everything looked so sunshiny and bright that it hurt her to see the world's exceeding fairness. The voices of the birds seemed to mock at her grief. There was no commiserations in their cheerful chirrupings ; and the gorgeous sun with its glowing rays shamed her despair. How was she to go on living with this terrible chill turning her heart to stone, and compressing it as in an iron band ? She dared not contemplate the future. The outlook was so dark, so drear.

" It has been my own doing from first to last," she mused, in speechless agony. " Entirely my own doing." But this reflection did not tend to lighten her sorrow. On the contrary, the knowledge that she had only herself to thank for all that had taken place added to it a thousandfold.

She had carried her distrust of men too far. Other women were wise. They made the most of themselves, showed off their good points, and kept their bad ones in the background. They did not consider it necessary to enumerate all their imperfections. If instead of volunteering the information that she was sickly, and unattractive, and thirty, she had given him to understand that she was extremely clever, a most talented authoress, and had all the world at her feet, then he would not have thrown her over so lightly. People estimated you at your own value. It was absurd to run yourself down. Diffidence and self-depreciation were totally out of place when dealing with the masculine creature. Not one man in a hundred was capable of appreciating the reasons which prompted a woman genuinely in love to act as she had done. Naturally enough they judged on the surface. No doubt Bernard thought she was a flirt, and did not care a bit for him. He had not detected the deep, underlying current of sacrifice and tenderness which ran through all her bitter sayings and sarcastic speeches. He had failed to perceive that in great measure they were prompted by an almost morbid yearning for affection, accompanied by an inward dread of being again disappointed, again disillusioned. All too effectually she had disguised her real nature. His powers of observation were not sufficient to discover the hidden motives which had actuated her conduct. And now it was too late for explanasions. She had held the trump card in her hand, and played a wrong one in its place. Thanks to this mistake, she might enjoy the doubtful pleasure of seeing that lucky young woman, Miss Dennison—whom she hated—converted into Lady de Bretton. Some errors of judgment could be retrieved, but others again were fatal. Hers belonged to this latter class.

Altogether, Bligh was thoroughly miserable. Generally, when in trouble, she turned instinctively to Deborah for sympathy ; but to-day her faithful nurse irritated her almost beyond endurance. Deborah must have perceived how wretched and heartbroken she was, and yet the unfeeling old woman did nothing but nod her head and smile. Bligh felt personally insulted by her maid's excessive cheerfulness. She did not understand it, and disdained to inquire its cause. Fortunately. the Dowager Lady Verschoyle happened to be away from home on a visit to a friend. Bligh was thankful for the solitude. Until she could recover partially from the stunning shock inflicted by Lord de Bretton's letter. she asked for nothing so much as to be left alone.

After luncheon she withdrew to her own room. telling Deborah that she had a bad headache. and would not receive any visitors should they happen to call. Thus the afternoon passed slowly and wearily away. In all the subsequent years Bligh never forgot the torture of it. It stamped its impress upon her spirit.

The shadows on the velvety lawn out of doors were beginning to lengthen, and it might have been about five o'clock when a tap came at the door, and Deborah entered. her face radiant with smiles.

" Please, my lady." she announced, with an air of delighted importance, "there's a visitor in the drawing-room waiting to see you."

" A visitor ! " exclaimed Bligh. irritably. " Really. Deborah, this is too tiresome. Did I not tell you to let Marshall know I was not at home this afternoon ? "

Instead of looking contrite, Deborah's countenance assumed a yet more joyous expression.

" Yes. my dearie ;" she said, " but the gentleman would not be denied—it was not Marshall's fault—he said he was sure you would see him."

" See him ! See who ? " asked Bligh. with a sudden presentiment of what was coming.

" Lord de Bretton," answered Deborah. not making the smallest attempt to conceal her satisfaction.

Bligh turned; deadly pale. Her heart gave two or three rapid beats, then seemed to stand quite still. A convulsive twitching attacked her eyelids. whilst showers of little black bubbles descended before her eyes.

A sudden stricture of the throat impeded speech. She tried to speak, but the words died away in inarticulate sound.

" Goodness gracious. my dear Miss Bligh ' " ejaculated Deborah in alarm, " I thought you would have been pleased. Are you ill ? "

" No," said Bligh, struggling hard to regain her composure, " but I—I cannot see him."

" Not see him after he has come all this way—and you such friends ! That would indeed be unkind."

Bligh was about to respond. when the expressions used in her own letter flashed across her mind. "Enjoy yourself. See plenty of young and pretty girls, and when you have found one to your mind, and who is calculated to make you happy, then bring her to see me. I promise to greet you warmly."

After that, was it possible to refuse to receive him, without revealing how matters stood with her? Once more she had brought the situation on herself. Lord de Bretton could only put one construction upon her conduct, if she declined to grant him an interview. The mere thought of being accused of jealousy brought the blood rushing to her cheeks, and caused her to reconsider her previous determination.

"Is—is his lordship alone?" she inquired, faintly.

"Yes, I think so," returned Deborah.

"You are sure th—that there is not a—a lady with him?"

"Positive, for I saw him come in by the front door."

Bligh heaved a sigh of relief. She was spared this crowning ordeal. He had not rendered her task doubly difficult by bringing Miss Dennison. A week hence, perhaps, when her brain assimilated the idea of his marrying and became more accustomed to it, she might be able to offer her congratulations in a sufficiently calm and friendly manner. At present she was too completely overwhelmed by the news to fulfil her promise of cordially welcoming the engaged couple. Nevertheless she realised that after what she had written in black and white, it was impossible for her to send Lord de Bretton away unseen.

She rose from the sofa, and glanced at the glass. Ugh! how plain she looked. Uglier and older than ever. Her eyes were red with weeping, and the anguish of the last few hours had left its mark upon her small, pale face. No wonder he had forgotten her so easily. What charms had she to keep captive a gay and handsome young man? Her appearance no longer mattered, however. His thoughts were full of another. He would have no eyes left for the woman whom he had professed to love so truly three short months ago. Comforting herself with this reflection, she smoothed her hair and went downstairs. Her heart thumped against her ribs like a sledge-hammer.

"Oh! God," she murmured. "Have pity on me, and keep me from betraying myself."

Then she turned the handle of the door, and stood in the presence of Lord de Bretton.

He advanced towards her with a joy-illumined countenance. An additional pang shot through the poor woman's frame.

How handsome and happy he looked! It was evident that love agreed with him.

"Forgive me for taking you unawares in this off-hand fashion," he said, brightly, as the

" I was half expecting you," she, answered, unsteadily. Then by a supreme effort, she added—" So you are going to be married. Allow—me—to—offer—my—congratulations."

He laughed and turned a pair of penetrating eyes on her delicate face.

" Are you glad, Bligh ? "

She felt the blood tingling beneath her skin. Oh ! it was cruel of him to ask such a question.

" Yes," she stammered. " Of course. I—I'm delighted."

All of a sudden, to her unutterable amazement, he caught her in his arms and kissed her.

" No, you're not. You're telling a story, and deserve to be punished accordingly."

" Oh ! but this is monstrous ! " she cried, quivering with indignation, and struggling desperately to regain her freedom. " I wonder how you dare—I wonder how you dare." And her voice rang with scorn and anger.

Again he laughed—this time more merrily than before.

" Are you afraid of Miss Dennison by any chance ? " he asked, mischievously. " Do you think she will be jealous ? If so, allow me to set your mind at ease. She is much too sensible."

" For shame," panted Bligh, in a white rage. " Let me go this minute."

" Not I, Bligh ! Bligh ! you wicked, perverse little woman, you escaped me once, but now that I've got you, I mean to keep you. There shall be no more running away and putting me off with letters in the future."

" Lord de Bretton," she said, bursting into tears. " What have I done to deserve this insult ? "

" Nothing, except your very utmost to wreck our joint happiness."

At his words a delirious joy began to steal through her veins. It is so hard for a woman to resist the man she loves, and after all he might have some explanation to offer.

She clutched one of his big hands in hers.

" Bernard," she said, hoarsely, " I do not know what you mean. For God's sake don't trifle with me, for I "—looking up at him with a glance which told all—" I cannot bear it."

" Do you want to see the pretty girl you were so anxious for me to find ? " he inquired, playfully.

" No, no, I detest her."

" Oh ! you do, do you ? I'm glad to hear that. It was just as well I did not bring her then. Truth to tell, I was doubtful all along of the reception you might accord her."

" I shall die, Bernard, if you go on talking like this. It may be play to you, but I have suffered so terribly." He dropped his bantering tone and became serious.

"Very well then, I will begin from the beginning. When I got that odious, cruel, ridiculous letter of yours, Bligh, it drove me regularly mad. My first impression was that you did not care two straws about me, and I determined to give you back as good as you gave——"

" I am sorry," she interposed, meekly. "Perhaps I ought to have worded it differently."

" Sorry, indeed ! Well you may be. The whole thing was preposterous from first to last. Did you take me for an idiot, to require to be told what you were? I flatter myself I had found all that out already."

" I thought you might do so much better, Bernard, than marry me."

" Yes, you thought. That's precisely where you made the mistake, and did not give me credit for having any mind of my own."

" But Miss Dennison. It all seems so strange. I don't understand," she said, in a bewildered tone.

" The explanation is perfectly simple. The day I received that precious concoction of yours—which, by the way, I mean to keep as a specimen of female folly—my widowed sister, Lady Dennison, wrote to me, asking if I would stay with her in town, as she intended to introduce her only daughter, Violet, but yet felt unequal to going much into the world herself. A male relation of immaculate character is useful on such occasions. I went, and had the pleasure of chaperoning my niece, and taking her about everywhere. She proved a great success, and was voted the belle of the season. Just before I came away young Lord Turfdom proposed to her, and was accepted. I am very fond and very proud of Violet, and want to introduce her to you at the first opportunity. Now to go back to your letter. I read it over so many times that at last its true meaning became revealed, and I arrived at the conclusion that you did not care for me after all——"

" You might have known that long ago if you had had any sense," she interposed.

" Excuse me, it was not so easy. You managed to wrap your meaning up in so many sweeping denunciations of my unfortunate sex that I honestly think it was pardonable stupidity on my part if I mistook your real sentiments. As time went on, however, I grew uneasy at your silence, which I kept hoping and expecting you would break. Then I lost patience, and determined to play a mean trick on you ; so I wrote as if I were about to be married—at least, I knew that was the construction you would place on my communication. Meanwhile Deborah acted the part of a good friend. The other day she sent me a line, saying you seemed moped and out of spirits, and advised me to come to Beechlands and plead my cause in person. So," he concluded, with a fond embrace, "here I am. Now what have you got to say?"

"Deborah did that!" exclaimed Bligh, clenching her little fists. "Deborah wrote and said I was pining away for your sake. Oh! I shall never, never forgive her."

"Are you so sure?"

"Yes, of course, I'm sure. Think of the indignity of being made out to be madly in love with a man, and having to write letters to get him to come. Deborah shall live to repent her interference."

It was all very well for Bligh to give herself airs, but with Bernard's arms holding her tight, with his warm breath stirring her hair, and his eyes looking lovingly in hers, her wrath soon died away. At best it was only feigned. Into her heart there stole an exquisite sense of happiness, and once for all she abandoned the folly of steeling herself against that divine passion called love. The sun shone, the birds twittered, but they no longer produced a feeling of irritability and depression. Her mood was changed. Where darkness had reigned, now all was light. For several minutes she did not speak. Then she said softly—

"You really care for me, Bernard, in spite of my age and everything? I don't want to take you in, remember."

"Yes," he laughed, in reply. "In spite of all the drawbacks which you have insisted on presenting to my notice, I care for you very really and truly. Henceforth the endeavour of my life shall be to prove to you that some men do exist capable of loving a woman because she is tender and honest, pure in mind and brave of spirit, and who value goodness, modesty, and intelligence more than mere outward beauty."

Bligh's arms crept round his neck.

"Ah! Bernard," she murmured, "forgive me for ever having doubted you. I will never do so again."

"Dear little woman," he said, pressing her to his heart, "you are much too good for me. Please God I may make you happy."

She looked at him with her clear eyes. A wonderful light illumined them.

"I have no fear of that. We will both seek our happiness by helping others. That is the best way."

A year after Sir Philip's death they became man and wife, and acted up to their words.

The poor people of Glenarfon bless the day when Lord de Bretton married Bligh Verschoyle, alias Mrs. Burton. Pit-row was pulled down and rebuilt, schools and free libraries were erected, and an era of peace and prosperity descended on the working population of the far-away Welsh valley.

Bligh wrote another book twelve months after the birth of her son and heir. She called it "Such is Woman," and it was even more successful than the famous novel by which she had first earned her literary laurels. Strange to say, the heroine was over thirty, and yet the public liked her, and found her interesting.

THE END.